Deathly Doings in

Dickleborough.

P. M. Langford.

How it all started.

Daphne settled down in a comfy chair by the window of her spacious apartment. From there she could see all the way across Dickleborough to the patchwork of countryside beyond. Sipping a Scotch and soda she opened her laptop; it was always interesting to look through the recent successful matches… and the not so successful.

She gazed out of the window and allowed her mind to drift back to her own disastrous wedding to Wayne. As an only child her parents had been ecstatic when they heard the news of her engagement. Her mother almost phoning the florist on the day her engagement to Wayne Wyatt had been announced.

A marquee had been insisted upon with caterers, local musicians, and even a flock of doves.

The big day had arrived and the sun had shone as the horse drawn carriage pulled by a beautiful dappled grey horse pulled up outside the local church. A joyous and enthusiastic Vicar, who was also a family friend, had swiftly performed an enigmatic ceremony.

The journey back to the marquee on the lawn had been a little more eventful. When a surprised pheasant had flown out of the hedge in front of the horse, which had leapt with fright and taken off at a good gallop. The driver had managed to keep the horse heading the right direction, and after a speedy charge across Father's precious lawn it had eventually come to a stop.

The vicar and guests had hurried along behind, mostly on foot. They too had galloped into the garden and had sought refuge in the marquee with the caterers, they had stayed there until the horse drawn carriage had left.

Daphne had been able to hear her father's noisy laughter above the chatter of well-fed guests, who had been served with copious amounts of wine and champagne. The local band had played Mendelssohn melodies as the drink had continued to flow. Her new husband Wayne had simply smiled and drunk steadily throughout.

Aunt Beatrice had brought her white Pekinese dog with her because; 'Mr Phoo loves a wedding'. After Aunt Beatrice had eaten her fill and had nodded off to sleep; Mr Phoo had taken advantage of this opportunity and had wandered away, eating whatever left overs he could find under the tables, plus a lick or two from an occasional discarded wine glass. Unfortunately Uncle Miles had stepped on him by accident. A furious Mr Phoo had bitten him hard on the ankle. Uncle Miles had leapt into the air screaming, falling over one of the caterers who had fallen into the basket containing the white doves that were to be released later. The terrified doves escaped, flying in all directions, liberally scattering droppings as they frantically searched for a way out of the marquee. The confused and panicking guests had been shouting, falling over the tables and each other. Daphne had been able hear her father's laughter above it all and the band had played jazz as soon as the chaos had begun.

For reasons known only to herself, Aunt Florence had chosen this moment to begin tap dancing energetically on the boarded dance floor, which had been covered in spilt drinks and dove droppings. She had skidded and tapped across the floor with flaying arms, before crashing into a table and landing among the strawberry tarts, legs akimbo. She denies all knowledge of this incident despite the photographic evidence.

Aunt Beatrice had been frantic when she woke up, and a great search had been launched for Mr Phoo, who was nowhere to be seen. He had eventually been discovered, fast asleep and snoring in the basket where the doves had been.

Wayne had been knocked off his seat during the chaos, a tablecloth laying over his head like a shroud, as he sat cross-legged on the floor, still grinning, and swigging out of a champagne bottle. '*I should have had the marriage annulled right then,*' she thought.

Wayne had been clever, smart and wealthy, but a disaster in the bedroom. He'd taken little interest in Daphne from the moment they returned from their uninteresting honeymoon. The relationship had gone speedily down hill, ending in divorce. Uncle Miles had always been more supportive than Father and had given her a sum of money to help her get back on her feet. This she'd used to start up her Two to Tango dating agency. Bless Uncle Miles she thought going back to her laptop.

1
First match.

Timothy smiled at himself in the mirror. Mr Average am I? Well it's high time you changed that old son, there's going to be a new chapter and a new me from this moment. He straightened his very bright tie and left for the bus stop with a spring in his step.

Timothy was about to join his local dating agency called 'Two to Tango' run by Daphne Mortesque, affectionately known as the 'Tigress' by both friends and rivals in the business. He took a breath and steadied his nerves.

A sign on the entrance read '*To Find Romance - Ring and enter.*' He rang the bell and waited. A petite, mousy looking woman opened the door. 'Come in. Do you have an appointment?'

'Yes I do.' He was hoping that maybe this was perhaps *the* Daphne Mortesque. 'I'm a few minutes early I'm afraid. Didn't want to be late, you see.'

'That's fine Mr…?'

'Sorry, it's Timothy Parkes,' he said, with feigned confidence, while fiddling with his tie.

'Please take a seat, Ms Mortesque won't be long,' she pointed him in the direction of some pink uncomfortable looking chairs.

From her station behind the reception desk, she was hoping to catch his attention. One of their more attractive customers, she thought; medium height and build, neat brown hair, nice kind face - shame about the yellow tie.

Timothy was too nervous to notice Jane. He fiddled with the collar of his new shirt, a gift from Mother, who insisted he needed 'brightening up a bit'. Being partially colour blind he had to take her word for this.

An office door of the office swung open as an overly cheery voice boomed; 'There you are then. I look forward to hearing good news after your meeting. He's such a *nice* man you just have to look beyond the hair, dear. There *is* a lovely person inside, I'm sure.'

A young woman with cropped dark hair, wearing lots of make up and a nose stud, came out of the office, looking doubtful. 'Well, I'll meet him, but if I don't like him I won't stay for long. Seems a bit educated for me.' She barely glanced at Timothy as she left.

Daphne Mortesque, a tall attractive woman with a more than ample figure, a mop of red hair and piercing blue eyes, turned her attention to him.

'Timothy Parkes! My dear, do come in. Goodness, what a bright tie … is it new?' she added, standing alarmingly close as he entered the office. 'Err … sort of,' muttered Timothy. All the rehearsed chat and confidence seeping away as he studied this self-confessed worker of match-making miracles.

'Come along, Timmy. Sit down and make yourself comfortable.' As she pulled out a chair for him, he felt her bosom brush across his shoulder, the strong smell of perfume filled his nostrils, making him feel a little uncomfortable in the trouser area!

He sat down quickly and took several deep breaths, trying to maintain his composure. He hoped to create a good impression, and *not* appear like a stammering idiot. Memories of his headmistress at junior school flashed through his mind.

'Now then Timmy,' said Daphne, leaning over her desk. He tried hard not to stare at the mountainous cleavage escaping over the straining top button of her blouse. 'Have you had many lovers?' she whispered seductively.

' I … err … well, there was this lady once, she was very …,' he stammered, surprised by the forthrightness of the question. Daphne leaned further forward, smiling, Timothy was sure the top button of her blouse would pop open at any moment, he tried to ignore it.

'I'll take that as a 'no' then, dear,' she said, the gaze from her sharp eyes making him feel naked. Timothy fidgeted.

Suddenly, she stood up making him jump. 'Don't be nervous Timmy.' She marched across the office, opened a drawer of the filing cabinet and, after a lot of rummaging and murmuring, swung her hip firmly against the drawer, slamming it shut with a clang.

Striding back with two files she looked directly at Timothy. 'Now then, Timmy dear, there are two possibilities here. The first date is always a bit of a test, but I'm sure you will find it interesting and perhaps helpful. Josie McWick is a lovely sensual woman.'

She leaned alarmingly close again, smiling while whispering the last words softly and oh no, the waft of perfume again. He took a deep breath and fidgeted. The leather chair made unfortunate noises when he moved, Daphne didn't appear to notice. 'The second,' she said, suddenly sitting upright again, 'is a nice lady who seems to like cats. Do you like cats Timmy?'

'Well … they're okay, I suppose,' he replied cautiously.

'Well that's marvellous, dear,' she beamed, 'I've read your portfolio and now I've seen you in the flesh, so to speak. Do you have any other ties? Never mind,' she went on before he could respond. 'I'm certain you will get along just fine. Here are the places and times of your meetings. One is at the lady's home … I was sure

8

you wouldn't mind. There we are,' she said, 'you'll find everything you need in here.' Daphne leaned toward him again and he suddenly felt very hot. Not wanting to fidget, and trying hard not to shake or stammer, he rose carefully out of the chair, which announced his departure with a fart. She eyed him hungrily, like a tigress eyeing a meal. He picked up the files and began to back out of the office. 'Well ... thank you,' he managed, 'I'll let your secretary know how I get on. Thank you ...good bye.' Feeling quite uncomfortable, he managed to walk out of the office slowly and calmly.

'Alright?' enquired Jane as he went past, hoping for a smile.

'Fine thanks,' he replied, making a bolt for the door and slamming it shut behind him. *Phew outside at last!* Knowing if he wanted any more dates with ladies he would have to go back into the tigress' lair. A wave of relief swept over him; the first hurdle was over and done with.

Jane Fitzmoore watched him leave. Sighing, she wondered if he'd even noticed her. Daphne had said when she took the job as receptionist-secretary, she might meet her 'knight' if she was very lucky and Timothy was *definitely* 'knight' potential!

Back home Timothy settled down with the two portfolios. The first, Josie Mcwick, was described as: *'5'8', medium curvaceous build, shoulder length dark hair, brown eyes. Smart dress. Ou going, sensitive, thoughtful and giving personality. Own home and car. Works as a receptionist at a small hotel.'* The second, Linda Pickles: *'5'3', collar length mousy brown hair, light blue eyes, sometimes wears glasses, medium slim build, dress tidy. Works part time as a Dental nurse.'*

He knew he had to take the initiative and arrange to meet both. A date with Josie, was made for the following afternoon at her house. As it was only four miles away, he decided to cycle over. You never know she might like to cycle too, he thought hopefully.

The next day the weather was fine, there was a good breeze and the sun was shining, as he set off for date number one. As usual, he'd spent some time agonising over which trousers would go with the shirt that had been another gift from Mother plus the colourful tie. Surely his mother couldn't be wrong on both counts? The bike ride should be pleasant, and since he liked to be prepared for all eventualities, he would have his orange waterproof jacket over the lot.

He lived in the small market town of Dickleborough, surrounded by open countryside, dotted with several small villages and many out lying farms. He cycled through the labyrinth of narrow lanes that to a stranger all looked the same. Cursing when the sun suddenly vanished behind the clouds and it began to rain. A loud clap of thunder, a flash of lightening and the lane became a river.

Timothy struggled on with water pouring down the back of his neck and off his face; it was like cycling in a power shower! As he turned into Duns Lane and started to look for number 14, the rain had eased slightly. There it was! His stomach churned nervously as he got off his bike and walked a little unsteadily up the short path. He took a deep slow breath before ringing the bell. The door opened slightly but no one was there. Cautiously he stepped inside.

'Hello, there,' he called, 'it's Timothy Parkes, I believe you're expecting me.' Feeling pleased with himself he crossed the hall toward the stairs and called again. Looking down he realised with horror that large pools of water had been dripping from his jacket. Another large pool was sinking into the carpet as he stared at the mess.

'Ooh, hello gorgeous,' said a husky female voice from the top of the stairs. Timothy froze, not sure how to react and hardly daring to move, he looked up. At the top of the stairs an attractive middle aged lady of generous proportions was smiling down at him. 'Looks like you could use a shower darling,' she purred.

Unable to reply he could only feel a mixture of terror and fascination.

'I'm Josie,' she said, starting down the stairs.

As she moved, parts of her body, including her large shapely breasts, appeared to be moving independently from the rest of her; the tie of the silk dressing gown slowly unravelling. Timothy was rooted to the spot, a strong heavy scent of perfume wafted down the stairs ahead of her. *Oh no! Not perfume again.* He felt like a thousand spiders were crawling around in his pants and still unable to speak, made a move for the front door.

'Oh darling, don't rush off. A nice hot shower and drink is what you need,' crooned Josie.

As quick as an octopus, she wrapped herself around him, pressing her body against him and backing him into the corner. Gulping for breath and feeling unbearably uncomfortable in every part of his body, Timothy managed to wriggle free. He was too quick for a second assault as he lunged for the door, leaving a soggy trail behind him, not to mention the spurned Josie.

Leaping onto his bike, regardless of the torrential rain, he cycled home at double speed. Briefly waving to a couple of his neighbours standing under the bus shelter. 'Hello Timothy,' they called, as he sped by. He pushed his bike up the path, fell in through his front door as

11

though every demon of hell were after him, and sank slowly to the floor. Once recovered he mopped up the pool of water in the hall, peeled off his wet clothes and ran his own bath with lots of foam. He lay back in the hot water, idly popping the bubbles with a plastic submarine, reflecting on what had just happened. Surely they can't all be like *that*! There must be a woman out there who was kind and gentle, with a sense of fun. Who was pretty, and perhaps would eventually like to live in a cottage in the country, maybe have a few animals? *Surely there must be someone*. He decided there and then not to give up, but to meet as many women as the agency found for him, and if nothing else, it would be interesting if occasionally hazardous.

2
Linda's story.

Linda Pickles had been raised on the edge of Dickleborough, on one of the more classy housing estates. A studious young lady, she had left school with qualifications to attend college, train and qualify as a dental nurse.

She had her own small terraced cottage, which allowed her passion for cats to develop at will. As a member of a cat charity, she had adopted numerous cats herself, and fostered others while they waited for new homes. The house was in a quiet road with little traffic and a reasonably sized back garden, so the cats were happy. Anyone who took an interest in Linda had to like cats too, and this was where her troubles began.

Adrian who she'd met at the Dentist's surgery, had been lovely. He was kind, bright and nice looking, and they'd had several evenings out together. Eventually she'd asked him home, where she'd prepared a meal. She'd slaved all afternoon cleaning up her little house and preparing food: Prawns with avocado, followed by chicken and vegetable stir-fry, and meringue nests filled with fruit and lots of whipped cream. Linda had mentioned she had several cats, but hadn't dared say how many.

Adrian had been visibly shocked at the amount of cats in the house. Half way through the meal his eyes had begun to water. His nose had become blocked, making it difficult to breathe. He sneezed violently causing several cats to rush out of the room. Before being served desert he'd been coughing and sneezing.

'Need air!' he'd gasped, making his way to the front door. Once outside he'd gulped the fresh air into his lungs. Linda had been mortified and had offered to call an ambulance. 'No, no, I'll be alright, just need to be outside,' he'd wheezed. She'd fetched him a soothing drink and they'd sat in her garden for a while, until Adrian had been able to drive himself home.

If that hadn't been enough, she'd walked back into the house to find that several of the cats had found the leftovers. One had been tucking into the cream on top of the nests, one had been sick on the table, while another had stolen a whole nest and taken it onto the sofa. Two more had been fighting over something under the table. 'Oh you guys! I'm never going to find a husband at this rate!' she had cried.

Linda then decided to join a sports club, she booked in for tennis lessons and regular visits to the gym. A popular club, it was well attended but all the men were either engrossed in their sport, with a partner or had a wife and children at home. Undeterred, Linda went along every week and booked herself in for more lessons in different sports, hoping just one day there might be someone. As the months passed, she became very fit and accomplished at both tennis and squash, even making the clubs ladies' team in both.

A friend had suggested she try meeting someone from the personal columns in the local newspaper, saying she knew of a woman who had met her husband that way. Linda decided to give it a go. She bought the paper for several weeks; finally there was an advert that caught her eye. '*Single business man, likes animals, pets and sports, seeks lady for possible relationship in local area.*' His physical description was to her liking too. '5'9'. Slim/medium build, brown hair, thinning slightly, clean shaven. Dress: casual/smart. Non smoker, social drinker.'

After thinking about it for a day and a half Linda made the call. He sounded pleasant and fun on the phone, so they agreed to meet up in the café of her sports club. Linda now knew quite a few people in the club and felt she would be safe meeting there. They arranged to meet that evening. Linda arrived early, having telephoned her friend, Henri, to be on stand by to hear all about it at the end of the evening.

She waited at one end of the bar as arranged. It meant she could get a good look at people walking through the club entrance, easily picking out anyone fitting Martin's description. She didn't notice when a balding fifty year old walked into the bar, but was shocked when he walked up to her and said, ' Are you Linda by any chance?' She was unable to respond for a minute, taken aback by the man in front of her. Not only was he older than he'd led her to believe, but considerably heavier and almost totally bald. 'What can I get you to drink?' he asked, smiling.

'Just some ginger ale, thank you,' she replied, wondering how long to sit with him before making an excuse to leave.

'Nothing a bit stronger?' asked Martin.

'No, that will be fine, I hardly ever drink. I just have to pop to the ladies room, I won't be a tick,' said Linda.

'Okay, I'll be waiting over there,' said Martin, pointing to some chairs and a corner table.

'Fine,' she smiled. Once in the 'ladies room', she pulled out her mobile and rang Henri.

'Hello it's me!'

'How's it going? Is he gorgeous?' asked her friend excitedly.

'NO! He's old, fat and bald! I need an excuse to LEAVE without hurting his feelings!' said Linda, nearly shouting down the phone in panic.

'Why are you so worried about his feelings? He didn't exactly give you a truthful picture of himself in his ad, or on the phone, did he?'

'No, but he seems like a nice man,'

'Then spend an hour or so with him and I'll ring you, so you can make an excuse,' suggested Henri.

'Okay, call me at 9.30. No later!' This agreed, Linda went back to the bar. Aside from not being what she'd hoped or expected he was nice enough, or so she thought. He ordered another ginger ale and another double Scotch for himself. 'Shall we have something to eat?'

Linda suddenly wasn't very hungry. 'We can have something here if you like, they have a nice simple menu.' She'd tried to keep the conversation impersonal and general. Martin *was* charming and polite; Linda began to warm to him. At 9.35, her mobile rang. 'This is your best friend's 9.35 call as ordered!' said a deep, badly disguised voice down the phone.

'I understand, thank you. I'll be there shortly,' she' said, switching her mobile off before any more of Henri's dramatics. ' I'm afraid I'm going to have to go, one of my cats has become unwell.'

'Can I give you a lift somewhere?' he offered.

'No, I don't think so, thank you.' Linda replied.

There was a lot of noise coming from the other side of the bar; obviously it was someone's birthday party with loud music and whooping and shouting from the guests. As they left and approached the double doors leading to the lounge bar, the loud music changed. A scantily dressed woman rushed passed them, all smiles. As she entered the bar she shouted; 'Back up! Steady now,

16

boys!' She squirmed and wriggled in time with the music and began to remove some of her chiffon scarves. Martin started to laugh heartily, eyes sparkling as if he couldn't believe his luck. 'It's a stripper-gram!' he chuckled, licking his lips and moving forward to get a better look. This was Linda's opportunity to exit. Martin was too engrossed in the gyrating, now nearly naked woman to notice her leaving.

Once home she called Henri and told her the story. Her friend shrieked with laughter. 'It could only happen to you love! Perhaps you would be better trying an agency? There's a good one in town, something Tango; you'll have to look it up!'

'Well I'm glad you find it so funny, I'm just thankful to be home. I'll see if I can find the name of that agency and give them a call,' said Linda yawning. She replaced the phone, jotting down the name of the agency she had already heard of.

Linda made the decision that more help was definitely needed, so the following day she plucked up the courage to call Two to Tango.

Having survived the interview and rather direct personal questions from Daphne Mortesque, she stressed that any man she met must like cats, and left with a file on Timothy.

As soon as she was outside Linda called Henri. 'I've done it!' she cried down the phone.

'Done what? Found a hunky man?' replied her friend, enjoying Linda's adventures, perhaps even more than Linda herself.

'Not yet. I've joined that agency, and I'm meeting Timothy tomorrow, in the café on Hope Street,' said Linda, feeling proud of herself.

'Oh my god! Do you know anything about him? Other than his name is Timothy? Perhaps I should be in the café this time and look out for you,' said over helpful Henri.

'No, it's alright, I have a folder here with all his details. Listen, he sounds nice, his name is *Timothy, he works in a book shop, oh, and he likes animals as well*.'

'Wow that will be three dates in less than a month! Pretty good going. I can't wait to hear how this one turns out, it's so exciting!' said Henri.

'Actually it's a bit scary, but I'm going to do it, or I'll be sitting in this house on my own with the cats forever!'

'That would be a really good test!' exclaimed Henri, 'remember what happened with Adrian. If he seems nice, ask him back to your house to meet the cats. *Then* you'll know if he could be a future husband. I will lurk around outside in disguise. I'll give you my opinion on how I think he looks, and hang around across the road, in the pub or - something! If he looks dodgy, call me and I'll come and knock loudly on your door!'

'Oh, I'm not sure about that! I suppose it would be safer, and I need to know if he can get on with all the cats. Okay, I'll call when I have the times all set up, and we'll get organised. By the way, do you have any more nice houseplants? The house looks more homely with some plants around, it's just the cats have destroyed the ones I used to have and I threw the others out after they pooped in the pots. I must get some cake mix too. The house will feel more welcoming with the smell of baking, and it will help to disguise the stink of cats!' said Linda, thinking on her feet.

'Good idea. I'll have a look and bring some more plants over,' said Henri, ' I really hope this will go better than the last date'.

'I couldn't believe it when the cats chose to use the plant pots as a toilet. I had to use three bottles of anti-stink cleaner to get rid of the stench, and it took ages to clear up the soil they had scattered everywhere. It's hardly surprising Adrian left,' she sighed.

'You know, darling it would be so much easier if you didn't have so many cats around,' Henri suggested.

'Well I know, but what can I do? The poor things have no homes, the sanctuary is full and when I see their faces looking at me, I have to help. I can't just abandon them; I'm hoping one day there will be someone nice, who feels as I do about animals.'

So with everything in place, more cakes newly baked, the houseplants replaced, and Henri on standby, Linda organised the meeting with Timothy.

3
Timothy meets Linda and the cats.

Linda lived too far away to cycle so Timothy elected to take the bus. An afternoon appointment in a café, close to her home. Ok, not too much can go wrong in a café.

Dressed in the now usual bright shirt and tie, he walked into the café and looked around. A couple of elderly ladies were the only other people there. He ordered a coffee and sat down at a table near the window, so he could see who was entering the café without looking too obvious. The fake red rose in his lapel kept tipping sideways.

Fifteen minutes early, he sipped his coffee, hoping he appeared calm and cool. Lots of people walked past the café; several looked at him through the window. A lady wearing a long multi coloured knitted coat and an awful huge orange hat, the brim hiding most of her face, stared at him as she walked slowly by.

The ladies in the corner never stopped chattering, and some old 70's music played on the radio. He was sure the lady behind the counter was also giving him shifty looks. He waited.

He watched people go in and out of the shop across the road. The lady in the orange hat walked past again, and it had begun to rain.

He missed the young woman approaching the café, and nearly jumped out of his skin when the door bell gave a loud jingle. A small lady with brown hair, and a fake red rose pinned to her jacket walked in, they smiled sheepishly at one another. Timothy stood up, and moving toward her he hoped like mad that she was the person he'd arranged to meet.

'Hi, I'm Timothy, you must be Linda'? To his relief she nodded and smiled, looking up at him through a thick fringe of wavy hair. 'Please sit down' he went on feeling relieved, 'would you like a coffee or something'?

'Thank you, I'd love a coffee,' she replied, and sat down with a rather fixed smile on her face, glancing nervously out of the window.

After chatting for a while, the tension eased and they were soon pretty relaxed in each other's company. The two older ladies in the corner were obviously eaves dropping. The door jangled and the strange woman in the orange hat walked in out of the rain; and sat at one of the tables nearby, rain water dripped from her coat and hat, creating puddles on the floor.

'Oh Timothy, it's lovely to meet you', said Linda enthusiastically, 'I'd love to introduce you to my family at home.'

Timothy froze, already? This is way too fast! 'Don't you think it's a bit soon for that'?

'Oho no! I mean my feline family,' she giggled, 'they're all at home waiting for me. I'd love you to see them before you go. Please come Timothy. They say cats are good judges of character. I'm sure they will love you!'

Timothy wasn't sure he really wanted to be loved by cats. He *was* pretty sure there would be some disaster or other. 'Well, I think maybe we should leave that for another time Linda, I mean, you and I have only just met and…….'

The woman, wearing the orange hat that was now soaked and drooping, got up and walked over to the counter. She prowled purposefully up and down, pretending to examine the cakes and sandwiches.

Shuffling her feet noisily, she finally ordered, and scraping her chair back she sat down.

'Oh Timothy, *please!* Come on, I have been so looking forward to introducing you to all my cats', Linda pleaded, trying to draw Timothy's attention back from her mad friend.

Henri stirred her drink enthusiastically then proceeded to have a coughing fit.

'Is that lady alright?' asked Timothy.

'I'm sure she won't die!' Linda said, a bit too loudly, giving her friend a look that meant 'buzz off'. Henri stopped coughing, smiled across at Timothy and began eating her cakes. The two ladies in the corner, who had been watching the drama, were silent.

'You know, Linda, I really feel it would be better if we arranged for me to meet your cats another time,' said Timothy gently, alarm bells clanging in his head.

Linda slammed her cup on the table missing the saucer completely, and glancing over at her friend she said, '*But you have to!* Please Timothy, just for a few minutes.'

Timothy found himself agreeing to go. He didn't know much about cats; his aunt had a big tom that used to hiss at him if he went near. He hoped these cats wouldn't do the same. As he got up to pay the bill, the orange hatted woman knocked her cup onto the floor where it shattered.

The waitress rushed from behind the counter with a brush and cloths, giving them all filthy looks.

Linda quickly linked her arm through Timothy's and walked him to the door. The two ladies in the corner were beaming and nodding at them. Henri watched them leave, rushed to the counter and, apologising for the mess and with her hat and knitted coat still dripping rain water on everything, she left the café and followed.

'This is it,' said Linda, outside a small terrace cottage.

Inside there was a smell Timothy vaguely recognised from his aunt's house years ago, rather like a tin of cat food. Several cats came to greet them, mewing and rubbing around their legs and the furniture. 'Oh look, Marvel and Suki like you already,' cried Linda excitedly. Walking ahead she called, 'come along, the sitting room is in here.' Taking his hand she gave him a firm tug pulling him into the room as he was trying not to trip over the two cats. To his amazement there were many more cats in this room, some on the chairs, on the sofa, and perched on the dresser and on the windowsills. He hesitated. 'How many cats do you have?' he asked, hoping he didn't look how he felt.

'Only fourteen now,' said Linda, shoving two off a chair and signalling for Timothy to sit down. Reluctantly, after scrutinising the chair, he sat.

The room was a little on the dark side with old sash windows, net curtains, many large plants and a small fire place, the fire ready to light. The cats all stared at Timothy. Not sure how to react he sat still; Linda went off to make a drink that neither of them really wanted. Thinking he should perhaps try and give a good impression, he began talking to one of the cats nearby.

' Nice puss cat, puss puss puss.' he ventured.

This had more of a reaction than he was expecting. A large ginger and white cat suddenly leapt onto his lap, purring and dribbling. Timothy carefully stroked the animal as it dribbled over his trousers. When Linda came back from the kitchen she exclaimed, 'Oh Timothy how wonderful, Mr Snudge has made friends with you, he can be naughty you know, would you like tea….. Morning tea, Lapsang, Earl Grey, Lady Grey, lemon tea ……..coffee or chocolate'? Linda was beaming at him with that fixed smile of hers.

'I don't think I want another drink,'

'Oh you *must*, just a small cup of something?' Linda persisted.

'Okay, just a small cup of plain tea thanks,' he said, not daring to move. The cat on his lap had begun digging sharp claws into his thighs, and when Linda went out of the room, he tried to persuade the cat to get off. 'Shoo!' he whispered, giving it a gentle shove with his hand. 'Go on, shove off,' he said, more firmly.

'Is everything alright in there,' called Linda from the kitchen.

'Yes... fine,' he lied, as the cat dug its claws in deeper, and began hissing and growling. Linda came in to the sitting room with a tray, and handed him a dainty cup and saucer complete with teaspoon and biscuit. There was nowhere to put it, so he held it in one hand and sat still, hoping the cat would get down. Linda settled in another chair, after pushing a couple more cats onto the floor; they glared at Timothy as if it were all his doing.

He was feeling pretty uncomfortable, with the cat claws jammed into his thighs and cramp starting in his left hand - carefully clutching the dainty cup and saucer full of scalding hot tea. He decided to stroke the big cat on its chest and asked gently,' Do you think that you could lift this cat? *YEOW!!!*' , he yelled, as the cat suddenly sank its teeth straight into the back of his hand. He leapt up as the scalding tea spilled on his other hand; the cup and saucer went in one direction, and the cat in another, making a horrible noise. Blood began pouring from the back of his hand, several other cats fled the room, knocking down ornaments, plants and pictures as they went. 'Oh no,' screamed Linda, sounding just like a cat. ' Let me help you. Oh what a mess, *oh dear, oh dear.*' Her usual fixed smile was more of a grimace thought Timothy, not sure which hand hurt more, the mauled one or the scalded one.

'Come with me,' said Linda, grabbing his sleeve and pulling him toward the kitchen. Too shocked by it all he didn't resist. Tripping over yet another cat, that yowled and spat at him in disgust, Timothy was dragged into the kitchen, where Linda pulled out a drawer-full of bandages, plasters and antiseptics. He wondered if something like this happened often, as she was so prepared.

As soon as he could, he left the little house, Linda, and the cats! And with large bandages on both his hands, his trouser legs embarrassingly dampened with cat spit and tea, he walked quickly to the bus stop in the rain. The woman in the dreadful drooping orange hat stared at him as they passed each other. People getting on and off the bus looked at him sympathetically while he struggled to get money from his pocket with his bandaged hands.

He resolved not to meet anymore cats or ladies with cats, and wondered if this dating lark could get any worse!

Linda was in tears, cleaning up the mess in the sitting room. She knew the knock at the door would be Henri. 'Come in,' she called, tearfully.

'Oh Linda, you're upset. What happened this time? He looked so nice!'

'Mr Snudge bit him!' said Linda tearfully. 'What am I going to do?'

'Come on love, let's sit down and talk it through. I'm sure we can sort something out,' Henri sympathised.

4
Back to the Tigress.

Determined to find the woman of his dreams, Timothy plucked up the courage to face Daphne Mortesque again! On entering the office the girl at reception rushed over, and for a moment he thought she was going to kiss him. Straightening himself up to his full height he smiled politely. ' Oh Timothy, do come in. Can I take your jacket?' she asked politely.

Handing over his jacket he said, 'I'm sorry, I don't know your name'.

'My name's Jane. How did you get on with your dates, any good?' she asked with a sheepish grin.

'Well actually no, they weren't quite what I'd expected. I don't think I will see them again,' he replied.

'Oh that's a shame. What happened to your hands?' Jane looked concerned.

The door to the office burst open and the commanding voice of Daphne Mortesque boomed,

'Who have I next Jane, anyone interesting?'

'Timothy is here.' said Jane, retreating behind reception.

'Timmy dear,' cooed Miss Mortesque, wrapping an arm firmly around him. *Oh that perfume!*

He tried not to pull away too sharply, and walked into the office ahead of her, making sure there was a chair between them. 'Do sit down and tell all Timmy dear,' crooned Miss Mortesque, now behind her desk, and with her blouse straining to bursting point over her bosom as usual. 'Well, to be honest, they really weren't my type, Miss Mortesque, I was hoping for someone a little less complicated,' said Timothy.

'Oh what a shame Timmy,' she purred, ' Josie said you left in a bit of a hurry. Was there a problem?' Her bosom seemed to act independently as she breathed, in front of Timothy, strong wafts of perfume filled his nostrils. Timothy crossed his legs and fidgeted, ignoring the unfortunate noises the chair made every time he moved, he was determined to remain in control of the situation. 'Really not my type,' he said firmly.

Miss Mortesque frowned, 'what about Linda Pickles? More your type perhaps?' Timothy managed to look her in the eye for a moment 'Well not really, you see there was a bit of a problem with the cats,' he glanced down at the bandages on his hands.

'Ah the cats, I see. Don't you like animals Timothy?' she asked, almost sympathetically.

' Yes actually, but there were so *many,* you see,' he replied, trying to look anywhere else but at Daphne's breasts.

'Well Timmy dear, I have a couple more ladies for you to see and I hope you do better this time. Have you got a different shirt and tie?' she asked, suddenly standing up, making Timothy flinch, much to his annoyance. 'Now let me see,' she went on, striding over to her filing cabinet, wrenching open a drawer, rummaging and muttering. 'Aha,' she exclaimed, pulling out two files. She whacked the filing cabinet closed with her customary swing of her hips, and strode back to her chair. She stared at the computer screen and tapped furiously on the keyboard, then staring at Timothy she said, 'I really don't get on much with these confounded machines ! You *will* like one of these ladies Timothy.'

Timothy thought he was getting the measure of Miss Mortesque, meeting her gaze for a moment.

'I hope so Miss Mortesque, I hope so,' he said. Not waiting for further conversation, he picked up the files and began to leave the office.

'Say thank you dear,' she said, in a more sinister tone, without looking up, her fingers furiously tapping the keyboard .

'Thank you, goodbye,' said Timothy.

Feeling more confident than he had the first time he was there, Timothy said, 'Good day Jane,' as he walked Past the reception desk. Unfortunately, when he pulled his jacket off the coat rack, it somehow stuck. He gave a little jerk whereupon the whole rack slowly came away from the wall and fell to the floor, tearing a chunk of material from his jacket. As plaster and dust filled the air and scattered over the office floor, Jane leapt to her feet screeching. 'Oh Timothy! Oh gosh Oh no!'

A booming voice from the office cried, 'What's going on out there?'   As the office door opened, he fled from the building. Enough was enough!

He arrived at the bus stop panting and flustered. Unfortunately, as Dickleborough is such a small town, he thought he recognised some of the people he had seen when catching the bus after his incident with the cats! He kept his head down and hoped they didn't notice the large rip in the back of his jacket.

He arrived home to find a message waiting on his answer phone. The bright chirpy voice of Mother said, 'Timothy! Coming to see you. Will be with you about eleven in the morning. Aunt Maude is having an operation, and I will be visiting her in hospital. It would be handy if I stayed with you a while. You don't mind, do you, dear?'

Timothy's heart sank. *oh no Mother!*   Better tidy up! How was he going to meet his ladies without twenty questions from his dear mother?

Later that evening he relaxed in his favourite chair with the files of the new dates he was to meet. The first, Everelda, was described as; *medium height, slim, vegetarian and loves animals. Enjoys gardening, cycling and reading.* Sounds nice he thought. He wasn't too sure about meeting at her home after the last two experiences, but made arrangements to go anyway. He would make up something to satisfy Mother's curiosity and hope she believed him.

The second was *Fiona… slim with auburn hair, likes cooking and food, cinema, reading and holidays.* He decided to go along and meet her too, perhaps one lunchtime at a local pub. Timothy wasn't going to let anything get in the way of his mission, not even his dear Mother!

Cycling back from work the following lunchtime, he noticed the windows of his house were all open and the sound of the vacuum cleaner was coming from inside. Mother had arrived! He opened the front door calling, 'Have you got the kettle on?'

'I have the kettle on and made your favourite banana and honey sandwiches for lunch. Who bought that jumper, I don't like it!' she commented, as she hugged him tightly.

He was used to his mother's direct manner. 'Where's that nice jumper I knitted for you last time I was here? Do you wear it much? The colours really suit you,' she added.

'Yes Mother,' he sighed, parking his bike under the stairs.

'You still keep that bike indoors, I see. Not done anything about a shed then?' she went on.

'No Mother,' he replied, wondering how he was going to escape her scrutiny. 'How long do you think you'll stay, then?'

'Oh, I thought about a week or so. Maude is quite poorly, you know. Will you be able to come and visit her sometime?' she asked cheerily.

' I expect so,' he sighed. 'I had planned to visit a friend this week, but you'll be alright, won't you Mother? You can come and go as you please, of course,' he waited for the reply.

' Well yes, but *who* is this friend?' she asked, following him into the sitting room, still clutching a bundle of dusters, always nosy about his personal life.

'Oh, just a friend from work.'

His mind was busy plotting how he could leave without Mother realising he was dressed for a date, and the usual barrage of questions. Well, maybe he could tell her about the awful weather forecast? Plenty of waterproofs!

He ate his nursery sandwiches, knowing she meant well, and reflected it would be nice to have the housework taken care of for a while. He gave her a hug before going back to The Bookshop; at least he wouldn't have to cook tonight!

He'd been working at The Bookshop for five years now and knew most of its regular customers pretty well.

The shop resembled a Tardi: a small window on the outside, but with many small rooms, a steep narrow staircase, and three floors on the inside. All the rooms were stuffed to the ceiling with towers of books, along the walls and in the centre, books of all sorts, with just enough lighting to see and read the titles. Some of the larger rooms had reading tables with better lighting for those who wished to use them.

'Afternoon,' called Timothy as he entered the shop.

'Afternoon,' replied a chorus of voices. One was his good friend Derek who was also the owner of the shop.

The other, he was sure, came from Mrs Brown, an older lady and regular customer, who always bought several books at a time.

'Hello Mr Parkes,' said the sweet whispering voice of Mrs Jones, another older lady and also a regular customer.

'Afternoon Mrs Jones,' he replied, ' and what have you brought for us today?'

The ladies always returned the books they had read to be resold in the second hand section of the bookshop. Mrs Jones was bending down below the counter, rummaging in the depths of her bottomless shopping trolley. Eventually she stood up with a groan and dumped a pile of books on the counter. 'Just a few to return today,' she said, 'and I would like to buy these.' She beamed at Timothy as he looked through the pile.

' You wish to buy these?' he asked, looking at the titles. *Vampires in the Basement*; *Death comes back to the Castle* and *Poison, Sweet Medicine*.

'Yes, nothing like a good read at bedtime Timothy,' she whispered. She was standing on tiptoe, her smiling face getting nearer as Timothy moved away and began to tot up the bill.

'That'll be £7.87 please, Mrs Jones,' he said.

The old lady counted out the money to the penny before handing it over. Mrs Brown joined them with her own pile of books and shopping trolley. She also piled them onto the counter, some to return and some to buy. *Bloody Picnic, Dungeons of Terror* and *The Stolen Blood Bank*.

'A little light reading Mrs Brown!' said Timothy smiling.

'Quite a good selection today, keeps me happy for a while.' she said, packing the books away in her trolley. 'Thank you Timothy, see you *very* soon.'

Both ladies were wearing a similar uniform of flowery frocks, light overcoats and flat sandals; they left the shop together, tugging their trolleys behind them.

'Managed to scoot them along today Timothy,' said Derek.

'Yes, thank goodness,' he replied. 'I wanted to confirm the few half days I asked you about this week, Derek'

'No problem. Got anything planned?' asked his boss.

'Not much, just seeing a few friends, and Mother's staying for a week or so.'

' I'll be off now, okay if I leave you to lock up?' said Derek.

'Yes, see you in the morning.' Timothy was used to being on his own in the shop and didn't mind the odd things that sometimes happened. Books coming off the shelves by themselves and odd scraping noises. He decided if it was a ghost, perhaps it just wanted to read. So he left the books he found on the floor on the reading tables at night when he locked up. No one else seemed to notice any odd goings on, and he fancied he was the only one 'the ghost' knew would leave the books out.

5
Everelda and the goat.

The afternoon he was to meet Everelda came and he decided to put his plan into action. Dressed in another knitted jumper and bright tie, he managed to dodge Mother before pulling on his yellow waterproofs. 'Right, I'll be off then.'

'Gracious dear, aren't you going to be a bit warm?'

'Bad weather forecast,' he said firmly. 'Must be off... see you later... not sure what time... bye.' He managed to get himself and his bike out of the door as Mother was saying,

'But what about a meal?'

'I'll be alright today. Thank you!' he called over his shoulder, jumping on the bike.

Everelda lived out of town and he had quite a long ride ahead. The wind had dropped, the sun shone, and Timothy got hotter and hotter. Throwing back the hood and opening the jacket, there was little he could do about the leggings; he was almost steaming as he cycled along.

He turned into a steep narrow lane, eventually finding the cottage at the bottom. As he approached, six dogs came bounding out, barking like mad. He managed to stay upright on his bike but only just, as one of the dogs kept jumping up, barking loudly in his ear. Aiming for the little gate into the cottage garden, he peddled as best he could while being pushed this way and that by the bounding dog. They both somehow squeezed through the gate just as a goat cantered out of the front door straight towards him. Swerving to avoid the goat and bumping over the flowerbed, he lost his balance and fell into a large rosemary bush. The dogs thought this was a great game, and all piled in on top of him barking excitedly.

'Help!' he cried from the depths of the bush. Suddenly the dogs went quiet and backed off. He could hear a woman's voice saying 'Are you alright?'

He clambered out of the bush, pulling away the twigs sticking through the spokes of the wheels. 'OK, I think', he managed. A strong scent of rosemary filled the air. 'Are you Everelda by any chance?' he asked the tall female standing before him.

'I guess you must be Timothy?' she giggled. ' Sorry about the welcome… aren't you hot?'

'I am a bit, but there *is* a reason,' he said. While peeling off his waterproofs he quickly explained. The dogs were happily lying around the garden with the goat grazing peacefully by the gate; Timothy kept a nervous eye on them just the same.

'Ah, so you're sort of in disguise,' grinned Everelda, 'no wonder the dogs were suspicious of you! You must be in need of a cool drink.'

'That would be great,' he replied, following her indoors. The cottage was quite untidy with an aroma of animal but looked clean. He glanced around for any further surprises; suddenly a high voice said. '*Watchya*'! Startled he jumped, then realised that an African Grey parrot was perched on the other side of the room. It began bobbing up and down when he looked at it. 'Don't mind Cyril,' said Everelda, 'he gets a bit bossy sometimes.' Timothy decided to keep his distance, as the bird appeared to be loose, and only sitting on its perch from choice.

The rest of the afternoon was spent pleasantly, sitting on the porch of the cottage sipping nettleade, with all animals peacefully doing their own thing. Timothy began to relax and wondered if he could cope with such a menagerie. He was aware that the goat had wandered over and was affectionately nibbling his shoulder; he gently stroked the animal, relieved when nothing untoward happened!   It was all going quite well and so he found himself agreeing to stay for a meal. The goat gave a gentle tug on his jumper as though encouraging him to stay. It was summer and would be light until after ten, plenty of time to get home before the batteries in his lights ran out.

Timothy remained on the porch while Everelda was busy in the kitchen. All the animals appeared to be watching him, so he dare not move. The goat gave his jumper another affectionate tug and he wondered if perhaps this time he could leave unscathed despite his chaotic arrival.   Suddenly there was a screech as the parrot decided to fly into the porch. Timothy was too afraid to move, and stared at the parrot, willing it to leave him alone. The goat, however, was tugging at his jumper again and somehow it felt reassuring. Through the open doors he could see where Everelda was laying the table for their meal.   'If you'd like to come through?' she called.

'I'll be right with you', replied Timothy, getting up very carefully, hoping not to disturb anything. As he got out of the chair one sleeve of his jumper fell down over his wrist, no longer attached. Not sure what to do, he pulled it off and hung it over the back of the chair. 'Smells good,' he commented, going into the cottage.

' I hope you like home-made vegetable lasagna? What on earth happened to your sleeve?' Everelda looked bemused.

'Oh it came off.'

'*I see,*' she said doubtfully.   Timothy realised he was actually quite hungry and the lasagne did look appetising. Everelda served him with a generous portion. Several glasses of elder flower wine helped to make them feel more relaxed, and they enjoyed chatting for some time after their meal. Timothy had been ignoring the continued tugs on his jumper and wondered if there would be much left to take home!

The light was beginning to fade. Completely relaxed after more elder flower wine, he felt confident and comfortable in the company of Everelda. As he stood up to leave however, what little remained of his jumper fell to the floor.

'Goodness your jumper,' she exclaimed, rushing out after the retreating goat.

Timothy followed, 'It's alright', he said reassuringly, ' I didn't like it much anyway, I've got several more at home.'

'Are you sure?' asked his embarrassed hostess, ' I can knit a new one for you if you'd like?'

'Oh, please don't worry,' pleaded Timothy. 'I really do have several more at home, my mother knits all the time you see. I must be off, as my lights aren't that good, but I've really enjoyed today. Maybe we could do this again sometime?' He was feeling quite pleased with himself.

'I'd like that,' she replied, 'I've really enjoyed it too, and you seem to be quite comfortable with the animals.'

'Yes the animals are fine,' said Timothy, secretly wondering if he would eventually run out of the dreaded jumpers. Pulling on the waterproofs he said, 'thank you so much for the lovely meal and the wine, my treat next time.'

He cycled along the lane waving as he went, watching Everelda waving in the rear view mirror attached to the handlebars. As he rounded the bend he noticed black shape in the corner of the mirror which was moving along the road after him. He cycled faster but the shape was slowly gaining. Then it disappeared. Timothy slowed to catch his breath. Suddenly a dog darted out from behind the hedge and grabbed hold of the bottom of his waterproof trousers with its teeth, shaking its head vigorously and keeping pace at the same time. He shouted and tried to kick the dog away; it wasn't giving in, and gripped more firmly. As the dog pulled harder it became almost impossible to cycle. He slowed and the dog, keeping tight hold of his leggings, began to gallop forward pulling him with it. They went along the road with Timothy's leg sticking out sideways and the dog's jaws clamped firmly on to his trousers. The dog suddenly darted down a small embankment, and he had no choice but to follow as he and the bike were pulled off the road. They all hurtled down the bumpy embankment before crashing at the bottom. Timothy and the bike skidded sideways before finally stopping; the dogs jaws was still gripping his leggings, that were in danger of being pulled off. He desperately held on to the waistband, shouting as loudly as he could. The dog stopped pulling but held on, looking him in the eye and wagging its tail.

'*GO HOME,*' he yelled.

The animal appeared quite hurt by this, and releasing its grip, it moved toward Timothy, still wagging its tail. He shouted again. This time it quickly turned tail and ran for home. He tucked his shredded leggings into his bicycle clips, and pulled the bits of grass and clumps of mud off the bike. Back on the road he checked that everything was in working order. With the lights flickering on and off, he cycled home; despite having been a very pleasant time, he doubted he would be seeing Everelda and the animals again.

6
Another day another date.

The following morning Timothy woke to the smell of frying bacon. That was the upside of his mother staying – the luxury of cooked breakfast. His head felt a bit woozy after the elder flower wine, but apart from that and several new bruises, he felt relatively unscathed and ready for the fray. He wondered if everyone had such traumatic experiences when dating. Despite the recent dramas, he thought he would quite like a life out of town, with animals around, as long as they weren't all cats!

Another date had been arranged for lunchtime and he planned to go straight from work to the pub, where he had arranged to meet Fiona.

'Post is here,' said Mother, putting the envelopes beside his bacon and eggs.

'Thanks, I should be back around six this evening. I'll call if I'm going to be any later,' said Timothy, tucking into his bacon.

'Okay dear. I wonder if you could come over to the hospital when you get back and visit Aunt Maude? She will be so happy when she sees you,' said Mother.

'If I'm not too late I'll come.'

'Make you work long hours in that shop don't they?' she commented

'Sometimes,' he smiled.

Mother appeared quickly out of the kitchen. 'You're looking tidy these days, anyone would think you had a young lady?' she said casually, but with a gleam of hope in her eyes. 'And you're wearing another nice jumper.'

'Got to look tidy for the shop,' said Timothy, cringing as she planted a kiss on his cheek leaving the usual lipstick imprint. As she plucked a handkerchief from her apron and spat on it, Timothy ducked out the door .

He arrived at the shop early, only to find one of his customers waiting outside. 'Morning Mrs Pugh,' he said, unlocking the door.

'And a good morning to you,' said Mrs Pugh, laughing and winking at him as she beetled into the shop. The sprightly seventy-year-old was a regular visitor to the shop, and an avid contributor to the second hand book section.

Once Timothy settled behind the counter, Mrs Pugh re-appeared. She had already unloaded her returns and placed today's selection in front of him. *Demons and Vampires Through Time. Are Your Friends After Your Blood? Murder made Easy.* She handed over her money, and began loading her books into her bottomless trolley.

'Thank you Mrs Pugh, see you next week', said Timothy.

'Have you looked in a mirror lately?' she asked, while squeezing her books into a small bag. 'Not since shaving this morning, Mrs Pugh.'

'Our little secret then,' she replied, winked at him again and left the shop. Puzzled, he collected the returns and began putting them back on the shelves.

It wasn't until he went to the bathroom for a brush up that he understood why Derek had been giving him some odd sideways glances and asked about the morning's customers. Timothy looked in the mirror, he could see orange lipstick still visible on his cheek!

Chuckling to himself, he wiped it off and got ready to leave for his lunch date.

The Old Dog was within walking distance and he looked forward to some of its real ale also called *The Old Dog*.   He went straight to the bar, ordered a pint and settled down to study the menu and waited for Fiona to arrive.   Several ladies came in, some older, some who looked like his mother, some young girls barely old enough to be there.   Then a tall slim lady with auburn hair walked in and Timothy's stomach did a back flip. Could this be Fiona? If it was Fiona, she looked amazing he thought, watching her walk toward him. He was half standing when suddenly it was obvious she wasn't actually looking at him.   Feeling embarrassed, he quickly sat down and smiled at her as she walked by. *She was gorgeous* he thought ruefully, sipping his beer.

Just as he was thinking of ordering another pint, a well-rounded lady with auburn hair walked in, and began looking round.   He thought ungallantly that she resembled a baby elephant and had the sinking feeling she was looking for him. *Uh oh,* he thought, standing up as she approached. She had an attractive smile, displaying a good set of rather prominent teeth.

' You must be Timothy. Is that the menu?' she pointed to the menu on the table.

'Yes…. pleased to meet you,' replied Timothy, handing over the menu as they sat down. The arrangement had been for lunch, so good to his word, Timothy ordered some steak and chips. Fiona pondered for some time, not really saying much, and holding the menu really close to her face as if she were hiding. Perhaps she's really shy, thought Timothy feeling sorry for her.   ' What can I get you to drink?' he asked.

40

Fiona almost jumped when he spoke. 'Oh, I'd love a pint of beer,' she replied, smiling at him over the menu card.

'Fine I'll order for us both,' he said. When he returned with the two pints, Fiona was still studying the menu. 'Have you decided?' he asked.

'Yes, I'll have number six please,' she replied brightly, her dark blue eyes squinting up at him.

He went to the bar, where the young barman was poised with a pen ready.

'I'll have one number nine sirloin steak and chips, and one number six, please.'

The young man looked puzzled, 'One number six and one number nine?' he repeated.

'Yes please,' said Timothy.

'For the two of you at the window table?' the barman asked again.

'Yes that's right,' said Timothy, thinking he was being very thorough. Handing the menu to the barman, he went back to the table. 'Shouldn't be long. What did you order? I didn't look at the menu,' he confessed.

'It said something like a combi with meat and salad and things,' replied Fiona.

'Lovely,' he said puzzled. He'd thought that number six was for *two* people.

Fiona picked up her pint and said, 'Cheers,' before downing a good half of it in one go. 'Hmmm I do love the beer in here,' she commented.

'Yes good isn't it?' said Timothy, sipping his own pint.

Fiona proceeded to tell him all about her previous relationships, how badly they had all turned out and how much she loved the last man in her life with whom she still had contact, and should she tell him to clear off? Should she keep talking to him?

'Dunno,' shrugged Timothy, already bored with the conversation.

Luckily the food turned up. There was barely room on the table for the combi platter, the steak and chips and the extra garlic bread that came with the combi. Fiona immediately picked up her knife and fork and began to eat hungrily, apparently unfazed by the pile of food in front of her. Timothy tucked into his steak and chips, glancing up occasionally to see Fiona still eating like she was starving. Neither spoke.

After finishing his meal he sipped on his beer and noticed Fiona had managed to down yet another pint while eating. ' Would you like coffee or another drink?' he asked politely.

'Ooh, more beer, please!' she replied cheerily, with hardly a breath before continuing to eat.

He bought two more beers and set them down on the table. He could not believe the speed at which Fiona ate; she had almost finished. Wondering how he could escape the situation he ventured, ' I'll get the bill, if you don't mind'.

Fiona stopped chewing for a minute, looked at him and said, 'Oh well, if you like. Lovely food, any more beer?'

He paid the bill, bought Fiona yet another beer and a coffee for himself. He noticed her eyeing the two complimentary mints that came with his coffee. My, this lady *can eat* he thought, and *drink beer*! He tried not to hurry his coffee, but eventually he had to take the bull by the horns, this really wasn't the lady for him. Pleasant enough, but he knew there would be no romance between them. It did go through his mind that maybe she was only interested in free lunches.

'Right then,' he said, as he stood to leave, 'lovely to meet you, Fiona. It has been an experience I won't forget! Hope you get yourself fixed up with someone soon. I must be off back to work.' He put the two mints from his coffee down on the table, next to her glass; she had eaten everything else, she may as well eat those! Before she could respond he turned quickly and walked out of the pub. Well, at least nothing dreadful had happened, he thought, while walking back to work. No cats, no mad dogs, nothing.

As he walked along the pavement among the lunch hour shoppers, he heard a high female voice calling his name: 'Timothy, oh Timothy, you can't leave yet.' It was Fiona. Timothy froze for a second, then pretended he hadn't heard and quickly carried on walking.

There was a screech of breaks and a loud crash behind him. *Now what?*

He turned around to see Fiona had somehow caused a taxi to swerve into the side of an oncoming bus. He was sure the faces in the window of the bus were familiar! Horns blaring and people shouting, cars queuing up and down the street. In the midst of the mayhem, he could see Fiona's round face still smiling. She was waving, and calling his name, apparently unmoved by the chaos. With a huge pang of guilt, he decided the only thing to do was run for it! He turned tail and ran. He wanted to get out of sight and into the shop before she saw where he worked. Running like a frightened rabbit down the street and away, dodging people, prams, and shopping trolleys as he went. The shop door was in front of him, he dove straight in, shot behind the counter, ducked down and hid! He remained sitting on the floor with his head in his hands, keeping out of sight, while getting his breath back.

' Lost something down there?' asked Derek, appearing around the counter with a grin and several books in his hand.

'Hmmm,' was all Timothy could say. Derek continued to serve a customer, then turned his attention to his friend, who had made himself more comfortable and was sitting cross-legged in the corner. 'Spill it,' said Derek, 'Who's after you?'

Remaining on the floor, Timothy decided to confess all, including his last few experiences. At the finish Derek was laughing so much, he was unable to speak and held on to the counter top for support. 'Well, it's alright for you. I never hear you having this trouble with women.' Timothy said, finally deciding to risk standing up.

He told Derek about the dating agency, and explained he was to meet some more women in due course. 'Let me know when your next dates are set. I'll keep a look out for mad women and wild animals' laughed Derek, sympathetically patting Timothy on the shoulder.

7
The hospital visit.

Timothy had never had occasion to visit a hospital. The first thing that hit him was the smell peculiar to hospitals, which he found quite overpowering.

'This way,' said Mother, striding ahead. As they walked along one of the many corridors, a group of medical staff came hurrying Past with something covered in bandages on a trolley. It looked rather like a mummy with tubes and bottles attached to various parts. Timothy's stomach turned over as they all rushed past.

'Oh poor thing,' said Mother, walking on again.

As they walked through the ward he noted how very sick everyone looked, his stomach churned again as the smell seemed to get stronger.

Aunt Maude was looking extremely pale, dark rims around her eyes and a tube coming out of her arm. This close up and personal confrontation was quite a shock for Timothy; he felt dizzy and, taking some deep breaths, he steadied himself. The strong *hospital smell* filled his nose and mouth. He felt even more fuzzy, and was in fact swaying back and forth.

He could hear voices, and a lady he didn't know was in front of him smiling and taking his hand. Suddenly everything began to go grey and he reached out with his hand, aware of falling. There was a distant crashing sound as the trolley beside his aunt's bed tumbled over with him and then everything went blank. Timothy had fainted!

While more nurses rushed to the scene, Mother promptly sat down on Maude's bed in shock, squashing one of her legs, but no one heard Maude moaning through all the fuss being made over her nephew, who was lying on the floor. He had cracked his head when he fell; blood was trickling down the side of his cheek. He began to come round and the smiling face was in front of him again.

'Hello Timothy, can you sit up?' the nurse asked.

He could, with a little effort; he rubbed the side of his face with the back of his hand. Seeing it covered in blood he began to feel woozy again. The nurses spotted this and while one was saying, ' don't look at your hand,' the other was wiping his hand clean. Mother was given a chair, and Maude was feeling the circulation coming back into her leg.

Eventually Timothy was helped to his feet, and one of the nurses suggested 'I think we'd better get a doctor to look at his head, it may need a stitch or two.' Timothy felt sick again.

Mother and Maude had been presented with a calming hot drink, while Timothy was given a wheelchair to take him to A&E. 'Oh it's okay, I think I can walk,' he said quickly, feeling embarrassed.

'I think it's altogether safer if I take you in the chair, we don't want any more accidents,' said one of the nurses sternly. He submitted, and when his head was stitched and bandaged, he walked back to the ward, a nurse in close attendance beside him. He found Mother telling his aunt that she would come again and bring Timothy with her. Maude was vigorously shaking her head and clutching her sister's hand tightly, pleading, 'No, you *don't have to bring him*. Please, he's a busy boy. I'll be better soon.'   No one was really surprised at this emphatic reaction.

As they got on the bus to go home, Timothy kept his head down and pulled his collar up. 'What on earth are you doing that for?' exclaimed Mother, 'you look like a gangster!'

'Just felt a bit of a chill,' lied Timothy, glancing around at the people on the bus, imagining they were the same passengers who witnessed the results of his previous fiascos.

8
Jemima's story.

Jemima had been born into a comfortably off family and 'spoilt rotten'. Badly educated at boarding school, she attended college mainly for social reasons. It was at a summer BBQ she met Giles Dunall and fell for him big time. Giles had an eye for the ladies and was never short on dates, so Jemima had to work hard to catch her man. She made sure she always attended the same events and parties.

Giles was a member of a wealthy family. His parents owned a large house and gardens, with a farm attached. His Father was in Africa, and Giles lived with his elderly Mother in Dark Wood House, where he employed Seth (a grouchy old gardener), to look after the gardens. The attached farm produced eggs from overly intelligent chickens and milk from bad tempered goats. Jemima was sure Giles would inherit the estate one day, unless his brother, who was currently living with in the old family home in Africa with a woman no one talked about, came home!

Jemima eventually caught her man and married him. Giles and Jemima moved into the family house; his mother who allegedly suffered from dementia went into a home shortly afterwards. Jemima kindly helped the family choose the home for her.

A few years later Giles' father died and his brother was allegedly savaged by rogue lions, so Giles inherited the family estate. Giles had never talked about any other children that he spent his early years with in Africa. He thought they were related but as he never saw them again when his Mother brought him back to East Anglia, he never gave them much thought.

Giles and Jemima often held dinner parties, and the family solicitor Clive Coombes was usually included on the guest list. This ensured that the three of them became firm friends.

After a lot of wheedling Jemima convinced her husband to formally change his will, leaving her the house and gardens. She had no interest in the chickens and goats.

They lived convivially together for a number of years, despite a turbulent relationship. They were not the most popular people in the village since Jemima had developed a rather superior attitude toward the locals, believing she was the 'Lady of the manor', even if no one else believed it.

As time went on their relationship deteriorated. Jemima was bored, and as Giles wasn't the exciting husband she'd hoped, for she plotted to take fate into her own hands once again and soon hatched a plan. Unfortunately for Jemima Giles was a healthy man and rarely ill. She needed another angle, and so organised a long weekend away with some friends. She left Giles plenty of food in the fridge, food that he could quickly heat up in the microwave. His favourite fish pie, with lots of 'fools parsley', she hoped, would ensure that when she returned from after her weekend away, she would find her husband conveniently dead.

Her plan worked after a fashion. Returning home she did indeed find him dead. But only a small portion the fish pie had gone, the rest had remained untouched!

Closer inspection revealed that he had been stabbed...but who would stab Giles?

Confused and panicking she decided to get rid of his body, the fish pie, and the blooded bedding. She set to work, and using several black refuse bags, she wrapped his body up like a black pudding. This also made the body slippery and easy to tug off the bed and bumpety-bump down the stairs, headfirst into a wheely bin. She tipped more kitchen rubbish on top of him and put him out with the other refuse sacks awaiting collection. Housework and maintenance were not normally a priority, and the house had deteriorated a lot since she had moved in. Today though the bedroom and stairs were all scrubbed clean using plenty of disinfectant, the bedding she burned on the garden bonfire, removing all evidence. All she had to do now was make sure no wandering dogs or foxes raided the 'rubbish.'.

What she didn't know was all this activity was being observed from the overgrown bushes, by the even older and more grouchy gardener.

The following day the refuse lorry arrived and Jemima watched from an upstairs window as they tipped the sacks into the back of the lorry. One of the men hesitated for a few moments as the machine 'ate' the long parcel of bags, shaking his head as he carried on loading the other sacks. As the lorry drove off along the lane, she waved and sighed, 'Bye- bye Giles, *sooorry.*'

She spent the rest of the day nervously going through her deceased husbands papers and diary, to see if she could figure out who had stabbed him. She was almost miffed at the thought of someone else beating her to it; it wasn't at all what she'd had in mind. All she discovered was that he'd had an appointment with Clive Coombes while she had been away. Now what was that about? Did he keep the appointment?

After what she felt was a respectable few days, she called Clive and explained that she'd come back from her weekend break and Giles was nowhere to be found. She asked him if he had spoken to him or had any contact at all during that weekend; he hadn't.

The next day, Jemima plucked up the courage to walk into her local police station and reported Giles missing. She Explained that he had been at home when she left for her weekend break but no one had seen or heard from him since. The police agreed to 'look into the matter'.

This left Jemima in the large family house with little money to pay the bills, since she hadn't taken this into account and was finding it difficult to manage. She ended up living mostly in the kitchen, which did nothing to improve her humour.

The gardener was pilfering anything worth a penny or two from the garden and house, by way of collecting his wages. He hadn't been paid a penny since Giles went missing. He couldn't make too much fuss as he had had a rather cushy number there for a few years, since he came back from Africa with Mrs Dunall and Jemima. He'd been employed as gardener / body guard, by Giles originally. These days he was getting his pension and hardly did any work to speak of; a little bit of gardening when he felt like it suited the old boy quite well. Nevertheless he watched the 'goings on' from the garden, and often had a sneaky look at the mail, when taking in some logs for 'the bitch'. He had noticed that paintings were disappearing from the walls of the house and guessed that money was tight for Giles.

When Jemima finally dropped in at the solicitors' office, Clive was not his usual easy-going, friendly self. He kept questioning her about her break away, and when she got home, and where her husband could be. 'What exactly did you see when you arrived home? I want every detail. Giles can't just have disappeared, he just can't,' he shouted in quite a threatening manner, while pacing around his office. She was shocked at his behaviour, and too upset to think straight. She wanted closure, and the deeds of the house. And what had happened to all Giles's money and African investments?

Clive stepped right up to her and pushed his face about and inch from her own. 'Where is Giles?' he demanded. Keeping her face close to his she shouted back, 'I DON'T KNOW!!' Well she wasn't really telling a lie, how did she know where the body had ended up.

Unfortunately in that moment she realised her mistake: Without a body no one could legally declare Giles dead, and she could not inherit the estate.

Meanwhile she had to survive somehow. If she were to 'meet' someone else they wouldn't need to know *everything*, would they? They would only need to know that she was waiting for some legality to be sorted out before she inherited. Someone solvent and generous, she thought, but she would also need to keep Clive in the dark.

That afternoon she bought the local paper and called 'Two to Tango'.

(Fools Parsley = is an herb related to Water-Dropwort and Hemlock, and like them it is poisonous, but less so than Hemlock. It is also used to make medicine.)

9
Eluding Jemima.

Timothy's next date was out of town. He decided to
cycle the distance and, hopefully, fool Mother. He still
had stitches in his head, but felt fine. He'd come to the
conclusion that a few stitches weren't really going to
make that much difference anyway! His date was
expecting him in the late afternoon, so with new
batteries in his bicycle lights, he dodged Mother and set
off.

The weather was warm and dry, although dark clouds
loomed on the horizon when he arrived in the village.

There were crooked iron gates at the top of a long drive,
the house was called Dark Wood Manor – he wondered
if this was really his thing. A noisy crow greeted his
arrival.

In its day the house had been magnificent, but sadly it
was now in need of extensive restoration and repair.
The garden was overgrown, and the unchecked growth
of plants and bushes along the drive to the house made
cycling hazardous. The front door was almost obscured
by ivy, and the stone porch floor was covered in a thick
layer of dried leaves and dust. Dark windows and
shabby curtains gave the house a sinister appearance.

Timothy shivered as he leaned his bike against the
trunk of an old yew tree. He approached the front door,
pushing the ivy to one side, and wondered if anyone
actually lived there.

Lifting the heavy knocker he rapped loudly, the noise
echoing as though the house was empty. He waited,
wondering if he should just get back on his bike and go;

he surely didn't want a date with anyone who lived here!

As he turned to leave, the heavy front door creaked, and jerked open. A sickly soft, well spoken voice said, 'Deliveries around the back.' He was confronted by a woman with a large round face, she had a body to match and black hair tied up in a bun. Her dark brown cow-eyes did not reflect the soft tone of her voice. 'I'm Timothy Parkes from the agency, we have a date I believe,' he said, trying to smile, but really thinking he should leave…now!

'Oh. I see,' she said, sounding disappointed, and looking him up and down; 'well, I suppose you had better come in then.' Her voice was deceptively sweet and soft, and gave him the creeps. he wished he could find a polite way of escape!

Thunder rumbled in the distance. 'Actually I think this…..' was as far as he got.

Suddenly her voice changed. 'NO! You come in this way!' she barked, opening the front door wider. Reluctantly he followed.

'I don't know what that agency told you? I'm called Jemima Dunall and you are?' She turned suddenly, looking directly at him, her eyes becoming larger as she stared.

Timothy cleared his throat, 'I'm *Timothy Parkes,* but I really feel……' he managed before she cut in again.

 'Ah, Timothy is it? I suppose you better have some tea as you're here. Follow me,' she commanded. Timothy followed.

The inside of the house was in much the same state as the outside. Once luxurious wallpaper was now faded and dingy; the old curtains were full of dust and moth holes. Furniture was sparse, and there were some family portraits on the walls with cleaner gaps in between where others had once hung. Thick cobwebs were draped in the corners and across the tops of the doors and windows. There was a strong smell of disinfectant. On entering the drawing room, she said, 'Sit here!' pointing to a huge, old, dusty sofa. He walked over as directed and wondered what would happen when he actually sat on it. Thick layers of dust told him that no one had sat on it for some time; gingerly he sat down. 'Stay there, I'll fetch the tea,' said his hostess, leaving him to study his surroundings. .

In one corner there was a grand piano swathed in dustsheets, with a large decorative vase full of dead flowers on top. As he looked around he could hear squawking. 'Uh oh, animals again!' The squawking grew louder. and the thunder rumbled a little closer. Then he could also hear munching and scratching sounds. He rose to his feet and was just looking around when the door flew open, and Jemima marched in with a tray, making Timothy jump. He sat down quickly, startling two mice that shot out of the sofa and scuttled across the floor. Using her foot, Jemima kicked a small table into the middle of the room and set down the tray. The tray contained an old tarnished silver teapot with matching jug and sugar bowl, along with two stained and chipped mugs, and a small plate of biscuits. 'Milk and sugar?' she asked.

'Err, yes please. You know, I really feel…..' tried Timothy again.

Cutting him off while pouring the tea, she commented casually, 'The storm is coming in, so it might not be wise for you to leave tonight and I have a delicious fish pie ready to cook.'

His stomach 'back flipped' with panic, he had no knowledge of what the fish pie may contain but all his instincts were screaming; *get out!* Perhaps he would find an excuse after tea, and effect an escape then! The thunder rumbled overhead.

He politely took the mug of tea she handed to him, but declined the biscuits. Sniffing the tea hoping she wouldn't notice, he tried to smile but she glared back at him. He saw there was an old dead pot plant within reach; hopefully he could wait for her to be distracted, so he could offload the disgusting brew!

A flash of lightning lit the room, and the squawking, that came from the fireplace, grew louder. They both leapt to their feet, just as an enormous amount of soot came down the chimney, billowing out of the inglenook and filling the air. It was followed by an irate crow. They quickly retreated, tripping over each other and the tea table in the process, sending them both sprawling. With her legs waving in the air, Jemima lay on her back screeching.

Timothy jumped to his feet, and a quick look around told him this could be a good time to get out!

The crow was flapping frantically around the room, covering everything in more layers of soot with every desperate beat of its wings.

Jemima continued to screech!

The window, Timothy decided, would be the quickest means of exit. The metal catch was really stiff, he struggled and finally managed to get one of the windows to open, and then leapt across the old stone sill into the garden below, ivy and overgrown bushes making for a soft landing. As he scrambled out of the bushes, the crow flew out of the window with a squawk of triumph, sprinkling more soot from its feathers as it went.

Timothy rubbed his head and realised he was also smothered in soot.

Big drops of rain began to fall, causing the soot to run in streaks down his face and his waterproof cycling jacket.

Not wanting to hang around he made his way to the front of the house, collected his bike and set off for home. The rain was coming down in torrents now and washed the soot into his eyes. Nothing, however, was going to make him stop; he wanted to be as far away as he could get!

A voice behind him was screaming '*NO*!'

Thunder rumbled, and he cycled faster. Despite the rain and his sore eyes he was relieved to reach Dickleborough and familiar surroundings. There were people waiting at the bus stop as he cycled past; he kept his head down, hoping they wouldn't notice him. As the bus approached he recognised the driver, who waved and smiled. A little further on he stopped at the pedestrian crossing, Mrs Jones was trundling across with her trolley. She gave Timothy a *very* strange look, although this was hardly surprising as he was streaked with soot, and soaking wet.

Halfway across, she suddenly stopped and exclaimed, 'Timothy! Where *have* you been?'

'Oh just for a little bike ride,' he replied, trying to smile as the lights changed and impatient drivers began hooting behind him. The old lady stared at him for a moment, before turning abruptly and walking on causing a car to brake hard.

Timothy was more concerned about how he was going to explain his appearance to Mother. Thankfully, she was out!

10.
Missing presumed alive.

Early that evening, Timothy was relaxing in front of the television, when there came a knock at the front door. He opened it to find a neighbour standing beside a huge Irish Wolfhound. He'd only seen the chap a few times and knew him only as 'the man and the big dog.'

'Wonder if we could ask you a favour, as we're neighbours an' all?' asked the man ingratiatingly.

'What is it?' replied Timothy, eyeing the dog.

'Well, it's old Faith here, we have to go away for a few days, and we wondered if you could feed and walk him for us? It would help us out, as Faith doesn't like the kennels; he pines and won't eat.' The man looked lovingly at his dog.

Timothy felt sorry for the dog, its brown eyes gazed at him through shaggy eyebrows. ' Maybe he could stay here if you're only going for a few days. My mother loves dogs, and will enjoy his company,' he suggested, thinking it would be a great way to occupy her! The dog's shoulders came up to Timothy's hips and he hardly had to bend to look the dog in the face. Automatically he reached out to stroke his ears.

'Oh, he likes you!' exclaimed the owner. 'I'll go and fetch his food over.'

'Err yes, if you like,' replied Timothy, fussing Faith. The dog followed him into the house and immediately hitched its haunches onto the sofa, leaving its front paws on the floor. 'Well, make yourself at home, lad,' smiled Timothy. He'd always wanted a dog, but working full time, felt it unkind to leave the animal on its own. A part-time dog while Mother was staying seemed like a good idea.

There was another knock on the door. Timothy opened it to find the neighbour, and another man backing up a van to the front gate. 'Just brought a mate to give me a hand. Where would you like me to put the food?'

'Here in the hall would be okay for now,' he replied, spotting Mother walking up the path, and eyeing the van suspiciously.

'It's alright Mother,' he called, 'come and meet our new guest.'

Meanwhile sacks of dog food were being unloaded into the hall. Mother squeezed past, with a mere grunt of acknowledgement to both men, and went into the sitting room.

Faith had made himself comfortable on the sofa, and Mother just stared, glued to the spot.

'It'll be alright, he's very friendly, and only here for a few days. I thought you might enjoy an occasional walk in the park? Keep you company while I'm out too,' he said.

Mother didn't speak or move. Faith didn't move either; having claimed his place on the sofa he was planning on keeping it.

Meanwhile, Timothy realised that the hall was filling up with more sacks of dog food, and several crates of tinned meat. He coughed, both men stopped and looked at him.

'You did say it was just a few days, didn't you? Only there seems an awful lot of food here.'

'Yeah, that's right, just a few days. Big dog see, needs plenty of food,' said the neighbour.

'*How much does he eat?*' Timothy asked, picking up a huge dog bowl.

'Just fill one of those a day,' the neighbour replied.

' Just a few days?' murmured Timothy, looking at the mountain of food. Suddenly the front door slammed shut, the van roared into life, and was gone.

Back in the sitting room Mother hadn't moved and neither had the dog. ' Come along Mother, take your coat off. I'll put the kettle on. It'll be alright you know, he's a good dog,' said her son cheerfully, disguising his doubts. 'You'll enjoy walking in the park, and the company,' he tried reassuringly from the kitchen.

Faith yawned and sat up; still perched on the sofa he was now taller than Mother. Mother sighed and came alive; taking a deep breath she removed her coat, and flung it on a chair, confidently walked over to the sofa and sat beside the dog without saying a word. Timothy came in with the tea tray and stopped dead at the sight of his little, grey-haired Mum and the huge hound, side by side on the sofa. ' I knew you two would get along.'

As he poured the tea and handed her a mug, she looked up and asked, 'How often?'

'How often what?'

' *The walks*, how often will he need to go?'

'Oh, probably once or twice a day. We can do it between us, can't we?' he replied, trying to keep the atmosphere from turning frosty.

'Do you know anything about this dog?'

'Not really. I've seen the neighbours out with him, but I've never heard him barking, or anything. So I assume he must be a good dog.'

He passed a plate full of biscuits to Mother, and both beings on the sofa acted as one. Just as the dog's jaws were about to scoop up the whole plateful, Mother's hand shot out and grabbed a couple of biscuits from under the dog's slavering mouth. Neither made a sound.

'Blimey!' exclaimed Timothy, 'I'll get more biscuits in, I think! I wonder if I should buy another sofa, too?'

'That would be nice, dear,' said Mother, unusually softly. He couldn't help but wonder if she was plotting something, as she seemed to have developed a silent understanding with the dog, he suddenly felt the odd one out.

The following morning Mother seemed quite cheerful. The dog had spent the night on the sofa, and greeted them both with a furiously waving tail, knocking things off the shelves and off a table in his enthusiasm. Mother took it all very calmly, and simply picked them up again.

Faith went out into the tiny garden to relieve himself before wandering back inside, filling the kitchen with his body. He rested his head on the work surface and wouldn't be moved.

'He's asking for breakfast,' said Mother, filling the bowl. Faith ignored the food in the bowl but kept up the silent demand for food. 'Oh, he wants toast!' she said, cutting several more slices of bread. Sure enough. the dog gobbled up four thick slices of hot, buttered toast.

' I'll put extra bread on the shopping list, too,' said Timothy, thinking that this was going to be an expensive exercise.

' I think you should take him for his first walk, Timothy; I'll take him later this afternoon when I'm back from the hospital,' said Mother, clearing away the breakfast dishes.

'OK then,' he agreed, picking up the long lead, which was more a rope with a clip on the end. 'Off we go then Faith,' called Timothy enthusiastically from the hall.

Faith leapt to his feet, and with one huge bound flattened Timothy against the wall and was licking his face, tail smacking loudly against a cupboard door.

'Sit!' he cried, 'Heel!' Faith ignored him.

There was a loud whistle. The dog stopped lavishing attention on Timothy and sat obediently while Mother attached his lead.

'Just need to be firm, Timothy,' she handed him the lead. 'Have a nice walk, you two,' she chuckled.

They rushed off along the path at some speed. Faith obviously knew the way to the park, and was taking his new friend there. Timothy held on tightly calling 'Heel, Faith! Faith, heel,' as firmly as he could. The dog was intent on getting to the park and ignored him. When they reached the gate the dog calmed down and walked at a more sensible pace for a while. After about half an hour they turned to go home, although Faith was reluctant to start with, but after a few good tugs on the lead, they finally began to make their way back. Suddenly Faith's head came up, and with ears pricked he stared into the distance.

Just as Timothy was trying to focus on what the dog was staring at, the dog took off at a gallop. He'd looped the lead around his back for security, so he had no option but to gallop along, too.

It had been raining, so the grass was wet and slippery, and the paths muddy. He found himself skidding along, aqua-planing through the mud that was spraying up from Faith's motoring paws, plastering him companion from head to foot. Eventually they came to a halt by a bush near the entrance, and Timothy was able to get his breath back. The dog's expression was one of sheer joy, tongue hanging out, his eyes glazed with a look of *that was fun*! Mud-splattered, they made their way back at a more sedate pace.

As they arrived home a car pulled up and a tall blonde woman got out. 'Excuse me, do you know where I can find Mr Timothy Parkes?' she asked.

'Yes,' he said, suddenly aware of his mud-splattered, dishevelled appearance, 'I'm Timothy Parkes.'

'Oh I see,' replied the lady, 'I'm Inspector Davis, I wonder if I could have a word?'

'Certainly,' he said, thinking, *Oh no, Mother*. 'Come on in.'

'Is this your dog?'

'No, it's my neighbour's, I'm looking after him for a few days.' The front door opened, Mother took one look at her son and the dog, and laughed.

'Mother! This is Inspector Davis,' he said firmly. The dog sat obediently beside Timothy, looking meek and mild. He handed the lead over to Mother. 'Please come in, Inspector, I'll just get changed, if you don't mind.'

'Yes, do come in. He won't be a moment; I'm Timothy's mother Irma Parkes. What did you want to talk to him about?' he heard Mother ask, as he went upstairs.

'I'd really rather ask Timothy in person,' replied the inspector

When he returned to the sitting room the inspector asked, 'Do you remember a woman called Fiona Martlesham? I believe you had lunch with her a few days ago?'

How could he forget Fiona! 'Yes... is she alright?' he replied with caution, remembering the mayhem she caused in the road when they left the pub.

'We're not sure, there was some disturbance and an eyewitness said he saw you running down the street. I wonder if you could explain what happened. You see, Fiona hasn't been seen since that day,' said the inspector. 'She left her glasses in the pub, and hasn't been back for them.'

'Ooh Timothy you old devil! I didn't know you entertained ladies at lunch time!' exclaimed Mother, loudly.

Ignoring her comment he was wondering how he going to explain why he was running away. 'I had to get back,' he said, lamely, 'to work you see. Had to see my boss urgently about something.'

'I see,' said the inspector. 'So you didn't go back to see if she was alright? You just ran off down the street.'

'I was unaware she needed any help,' he replied, recalling her waving and shouting after him.

' Hmmm,' continued the inspector, 'your boss did say you popped in that afternoon. Where did you go when you left?'

He remembered flying in through the bookshop door and hiding under the counter. 'I went home,' he said, ' in fact, I went to the hospital with Mother to visit Aunt Maude and then we came home together.'

'Other people saw you both in the hospital, did they?'

' Oh yes' he replied, 'quite a few actually.'

'Yes they did!' interjected Mother, giving her son a stern look.

The inspector closed her notebook. 'Interesting. I'll leave you my number, please contact me if you hear anything from Fiona. Her family are very worried about her.'

Timothy suddenly remembered another taxi that had stopped near Fiona, besides the one that collided with the bus, outside the pub. 'There *was* another taxi, I didn't see if she got in or not,' he said.

'You wouldn't happen to remember which taxi firm?'

'No, sorry.'

'Well, thank you for your time it was interesting meeting you all,' said the inspector on her way out. 'What a lot of dog food, here for a day or two, you say? Please call if you remember anything; I may come and speak with you again if I need clarification. Good bye.' she said, making her way to her car.

'Ooh Timothy,' said Mother excitedly. 'Who is Fiona? You've never mentioned her.'

'Just a friend. I've no idea what could have happened to her. By the way, *you* didn't tell me you knew anything about dogs!' he said, rubbing Faith's ears as they all tried to squeeze along the hallway.

'No dear.'

In fact, as a child she'd spent quite a lot of time with her grandfather, who'd kept dogs, and taught her a lot about handling and training them. She felt at ease with the Wolf hound, and secretly enjoyed having him around, but she wasn't going to admit any of this to her son…just yet.

Timothy related to Derek all that had happened. His boss laughed and admitted, 'Yes, the inspector called in here. I wondered what you'd been up to this time! Did they find the vanished lady?'

'No, her family are very worried, apparently. No-one has seen her, or heard from her since the other day, but I can't think where she can have got to.'

'The plot thickens,' said Derek, rubbing his hands together, 'will you be meeting any more women through *that* agency?'

'Yes. I must make a phone call, because there is someone on the other side of town who may be suitable. I could meet her this evening.'

'I look forward to hearing all about it. I wonder if she has any animals?' said Derek, grinning.

On his way home from work Timothy saw his mother walking back towards the house, with the dog walking quietly beside her on a loose lead. He wondered if she had some magical influence over the dog; she had become quite different since its arrival. They reached the front door more or less together. Faith greeted him enthusiastically and knocked both him and his bike into the bushes.

'He's so pleased to see you,' Mother laughed, opening the front door. 'Come along Faith, tea time,' she called, leaving Timothy to climb out of the bush, and squeeze himself and his bike along the hall.

A quick phone call to Two To Tango, confirmed a meeting that evening with Miriam, on the other side of town. He decided to cycle over and after quickly changing he called out: 'I'm off now, don't know what time I'll be back, see you in the morning!'

Mother had her suspicions and believed he was leading an exciting double life. 'Do be careful; are you going to look for the Fiona woman? I hope you don't find a body? Does Inspector Davis know where you're going?' she asked.

'No, probably not; see you later,' replied Timothy, hastily closing the door.

Mother was convinced he was one of those secret undercover agents or something. Maude once said she had a friend whose son had been a 'secret policeman'. Her friend had never known this until more policemen had come to the house; they had all been in uniform and one of them had mentioned a body! Her son was now away somewhere, and it could be a few years before she would see him again!

11.
Spaghetti falls.

Timothy swung his bike into the lane and looked for number 33, which turned out to be a terraced house with a tiny front garden, surrounded by a large privet hedge. As he approached, the door opened and a tall, very slim woman with curly, dark brown hair stepped out.

'You must be Timmy!' she said, striding forward to shake his hand, 'I'm Miriam.'

'Actually, I prefer Timothy, but hello, how are you?' he said.

'Please come in. Have you got a cat or something?' she asked, looking at his trousers.

He looked down to see that Faith had deposited a good layer of hair along the side of his tidy trousers. 'No actually, it's my neighbour's dog, it's staying with me at the moment,' he replied, noticing there was no sign of any animals around.

'I'm allergic to cats and dogs, you see. Come along in, I'll make us a drink. Have you eaten, yet?' asked Miriam.

He hadn't expected to be invited for a meal, but had intended taking her out. 'Well, actually…..,' he began.

'Oh, I'm sure you can manage something. I made it specially!' interrupted Miriam.

Not wanting to hurt her feelings, he agreed.

'Great,' she said, 'come into the sitting room. I've made some Pimms for us.' Pouring some into a glass, she continued; 'Have you met many ladies through the agency?'

'One or two,' he replied, 'How about you, have you had many dates?'

'Yes lots… it's great,' she said, handing him the glass. 'Drink up, I have the meal all ready for us. Do you like spaghetti?'

' Yes,' he replied, cautiously sipping his drink. He thought it tasted very strong for Pimms and sipped slowly. While she was in the kitchen Timothy was able to look around. Rather odd, abstract paintings hung on the dark, terracotta painted walls, with abstract curtains to match, making the room feel dark and enclosed. He noticed a glass tank in one corner of the room, with a low lamp over it, and couldn't resist having a look. As he approached, he could feel the warmth from the lamp and cautiously peered into the tank. There in the corner, among the stones, foliage and several inches water, was a turtle. He had never come across a live turtle before, and knew nothing about them. It looked quiet enough so he reached into the tank and tried to touch its shell. Quick as a flash, the turtle snapped at his finger giving him a sharp bite, he hardly saw it move. 'OUCH!' he cried, leaping back. Fumbling around in his pockets, he found an old tissue, full of holes, which he used to try to stem the flow of blood from his finger.

' All ready,' said Miriam, coming into the room and noticing his finger. 'How did that happen?'

'It was that creature in there,' he said, pointing at the tank, 'it bit me!'

'Did you put your hand in?'

'Yes; it looked so quiet,' he said.

'Well, it serves you right then! I suppose you better have a plaster,' she said, heading off into the kitchen. Timothy followed. The kitchen was small with a dining area at one end; the table was tucked into a corner with room for two chairs. In the middle of the table stood a bowl of spaghetti. 'There you are,' she said, handing him a plaster. 'Please sit,' she said, pointing to the table. She sat down began to pile the plates up with spaghetti for them both.

'Oh not too much thanks.'

'Why, don't you like it?' she asked sharply.

'Well yes, but not too much,'

'Fussy are you, then?' She handed him the plate.

'Not really,' he said, quietly.

A key turned in the front door, making Miriam leap up and rush out to the hall.

'Whose is that bike?' demanded a male voice. Timothy froze.

'Oh just a friend.'

'A friend, is it?' the man flung open the kitchen door and towered above Timothy. He was obviously not going to be friendly! 'Thought you'd entertain my girlfriend while I was away, did you?' the man shouted. Timothy was standing with his back against the wall, looking for an escape. Before he could move, the man picked up the spaghetti and tipped the bowl over him. At the same time he saw an escape route under the man's raised arm, and dashed for the front door like a terrified rabbit. Covered in spaghetti he shot outside, slamming the door behind him. Looking around he couldn't see his bike at first and then noticed it had been thrown onto the hedge. While he was disentangling the bike he heard a familiar voice behind him.

'Nice evening, Timothy,' said Mrs Pugh, 'what *have* you been up to this time?'

'Oh just seen a friend for a meal,' he said, aware that he was wearing most of it. Clambering onto his bike, he muttered, 'Must be off now, bye'! Mrs Pugh grunted her disapproval as he cycled off quickly, with spaghetti hanging from him like streamers, leaving the shouting and crashing from another disastrous date behind him.

When he arrived home Mother was also surprised to see him, squeezing along the hall with his bike, and fish and chips under his arm. 'Back early dear?' she said, scrutinising his appearance, and picking a small piece of spaghetti from his hair as he manoeuvred by.

'Yes Mother, change of plan,' he said.

'Was it successful dear, the outing I mean?' she asked.

'Not especially; would you like a few chips?'

'Just a few would be nice, thank you.' She thought he sounded a little weary, and wondered what he could be up to?

'Will you take Faith for his morning walk again tomorrow?' she asked.

'Why not!' said Timothy, smiling at the dog, curled up on the sofa. At least it would give him something else to think about!

12
Body in the park.

The following morning having had breakfast and prepared for the day ahead, Timothy attached Faith's lead and they shot out of the front door and headed toward the park. A neighbour's cat ran in front of them, but somehow Timothy managed to heave Faith's head out of the hedge, minus the cat, and they went on their way.

Passing a row of small bungalows on the way to the park, they had to navigate around variously sized refuse sacks that were outside each driveway, waiting for collection. Trying to concentrate on preventing Faith lunging into the sacks, Timothy noticed a silver saloon car pull up outside the smallest, and sack-less bungalow. As he was heading toward the car he saw two smartly dressed men in dark suits get out and go inside the bungalow. They came out again a few minutes later, laden with four large refuse sacks each and left them on the pavement. Timothy couldn't help but wonder what could be in eight heavy refuse sacks from one small bungalow. And who lived there? Faith tugged on the lead so they hurried on.

He decided to risk letting the dog off the lead in the park for a good run, pretty sure that as the dog had lived with him for a few days, he would come back. This worked well and Faith happily bounded around, coming back to Timothy from time to time and then scampering off again. Suddenly the dog put his nose to the ground and began running around in circles.

'What's up?' he called. Faith, who was ignoring him, set off in a straight line across the park, nose still to the ground. No shouting or whistling from Timothy was going to stop him, as he followed the scent. He ran in pursuit calling, '*Faith! Faith, come back! Faith!*'

Two local ladies were standing together staring at him; he hoped they weren't customers of the shop!

He followed the dog down a path and through some trees, wondering if Faith would ever stop. As he approached some dense bushes, he could see leaves flying up into the air from the undergrowth, and found Faith frantically digging, sending leaves and earth shooting out behind him.

Having difficulty in getting near enough to catch him, Timothy finally hauled the dog away from his digging and noticed to his horror a dirty human hand in the earth. At first he thought it was an old discarded tailor's model of some kind, but the raised hairs on the back of his neck warned him that this was more sinister. He quickly pulled Faith over to a tree, tied him up and went back for a closer look.

Timothy froze, unable to believe what he was seeing. It *was* a human hand with painted fingernails. *Oh surely not!* he thought, going hot and cold. He groped around in his pocket for his mobile and, hoping there would be a signal, he dialled the police.

Sitting on a park bench with Faith lying on the grass beside him, Timothy was in a mild state of shock. A policewoman sat next to him, ignoring that he was covered in earth and leaves. 'I just can't believe it,' he kept saying with his head in his hands.

'Hello Timothy,' said a familiar voice. It was Inspector Davis. 'What *have* you been up to?' she asked.

'I just can't believe it,' he said again, 'I let Faith off the lead and he ran over here and began digging like mad. There it was, a human hand.' He put his head in his hands again as if that might make it all go away.

'You walk in the park often, do you, Timothy?' asked the inspector.

'Well, yes actually. Especially since I've been caring for Faith; my mother does too. Thank goodness it was me with him this time!' he exclaimed, wondering how Mother would have coped. 'Do they know who it is yet?'

'Perhaps you could take the dog home before coming down to the station to make a statement, Timothy,' said Inspector Davis.

He looked up and despite his trauma couldn't help noticing the way her golden hair shone in the sunlight.

'Good idea. I'll see you later then, at the station.' he mumbled getting to his feet. Faith stood up, wondering if they were off for another walk. 'You better stay on the lead for now old lad,' he said rubbing the dog's head and setting off across the park toward home.

'Hang on a minute sir,' called a female voice behind him. 'Inspector Davis thinks it might a good idea if I walk with you.' It was the policewoman who had kept him company on the bench, and been the first on the scene.

He liked her, she was pretty, and pleasant company. 'Sure, no problem,' he replied.

'He's a well behaved dog,' she commented.

'When he's in the mood, he is.'

As they approached home he wondered what he was going to say to Mother. The policewoman, whose name was Lizzie, suggested he be honest so there would be no nasty surprises later. Bracing himself, he opened the front door. 'Hello Mother,' he called.

'Are you alright? Mrs Fell said there were police cars in the park and she had seen you running. She asked if you were very religious.' Mother walked through from the kitchen and her manner changed when she saw Lizzie in uniform. ' Oh, is everything alright?'

'I'll explain in a minute,' he soothed.

'Yes yes, of course, would you both like some tea? I expect you would. How did Faith behave today?' She called from the kitchen.

'He was just great,' replied Timothy, with a note of pride in his voice. 'I'm sorry Lizzie,' he said more quietly, 'Mother gets a bit over-curious.'

'I understand. I'll have a cup of tea with her while you get changed, if you like?' she said.

He was still feeling a bit shaky; he could hear Mother chatting away to Lizzie as he went upstairs, and wondered how much he should tell her about all this.

By the time he'd changed his clothes, Lizzie had finished her tea and was anxious to get back to the station. Mother was taking all this very calmly, and kept smiling at both of them.

As soon as they were gone she rushed to the telephone and called her friend, Beattie Fell.

Speaking in a loud whisper she said. ' Hello. It's me, Irma. Did you see them? They were in the park and called in for a cup of tea just now. What, the body?… no they didn't say much, they probably can't, you know. They've gone back to the station together. I'll keep you updated… What gun? … No she didn't have a gun, they only have those in America!'

After Timothy had finished giving a full account of the events in the park, Inspector Davis still looked puzzled. ' It seems odd to me, how you were the last to talk to Fiona, and then it was you who found her body. We spoke to one or two customers of The Book Shop. One person did comment that they thought you behaved oddly sometimes, Timothy. I may need to speak with

74

you again, but for now you're free to go. You weren't planning on going away anywhere?' she asked with a suggestive note.

'No, no plans. And I can assure you I did not, and could not kill anyone,' he said firmly. 'My last memory of Fiona is the amount she ate, and the speed that she ate it. Not to mention the chaos that seemed to just happen around her. I only wanted to put distance between us!'

'I'll let you know if I need to ask you anything else. The forensic results should be in soon, that will tell us more,' said the inspector, her steady gaze never leaving him.

He walked out of the police station feeling sad and confused. 'Hi there,' said a cheery voice from behind. 'I'm just off duty, would you like me to walk home with you?' asked Lizzie.

'I'd love it,' he replied, as cheerful company was just what he needed.

'Inspector Davis is very good,' she told him. ' She's been working here for two years and has a reputation for being thorough, likes to cross the T's and dot the I's. Good to work with though, and usually very fair.'

'Well I hope they find out what really happened, soon,' he said thoughtfully, ' it's bad enough she's dead, without feeling like the accused!' Something nagged at the back of his mind, he couldn't quite believe Fiona had been murdered and wondered if it was all some terrible mistake. As they arrived outside his home Lizzie asked. 'Do you do a lot of cycling, Timothy?'

'Yes, I go almost everywhere on my bike, don't have to worry about parking and it keeps me fit.'

'So, do you have a driver's licence?'

'Yes, I took that years ago. I had a small car for a while but hardly used it. I've been thinking about getting another, recently, be handy for visiting friends, and not

turning up soaking wet. Or wearing waterproofs!'
Recent events flashed through his mind.

Mother's voice interrupted, ' Are you both coming in?'

'No, I have to go, thank you,' said Lizzie, 'see you again soon Timothy.' She smiled.

'Yes, soon!' he said, walking up to his front door. ' Tea would be wonderful Mother, then I *must* go to work.'

'Of course dear, Derek telephoned.' She said.

'I thought he might.' He knew if the police had been asking questions, Derek would be bursting to know what was going on.

He cycled to work, his date with Fiona playing over and over in his head. Fiona's face in his mind, always eating!

Later that day Mother mentioned she didn't want to go to the park just yet, and he decided to try different park in the area. Faith set off with his usual enthusiasm, but Timothy had to steer him in different direction. Not sure where they were going, the dog walked obediently by his side; Timothy was impressed and relieved as they had to cross a couple of quite busy roads to get to the other park.

He had a look around. There were more people in this park and a lot of mothers with pushchairs, and a children's playground. He decided not to let Faith off the lead, and that walking around together was a safer option. The dog continued to behave like an angel, and several children pointed at him as they walked by. Having walked sedately around the park they came through a wooded area on the other side of the playground. Timothy felt completely relaxed after the peaceful walk.

Suddenly a grey squirrel ran in front of them and before he could shorten the lead, they were off, flat out toward the play area. He was determined to hold on, and gripping with all his might they galloped into the play area together. Timothy was being flung around at the end of the lead, just missing the hanging tyres. He crashed into one of the seats of the merry–go–round, sending it whizzing around, much to the delight of the squealing children. They galloped under the slide, just missed the see-saw, and skidded out through the little gate, where Faith came to an abrupt halt beside a huge oak tree.

While the dog looked up into the branches of the tree, whining, Timothy leaned against the trunk to get his breath back. He was unable to speak, as a matronly woman approached them. He shortened the lead.

' Now then, young man,' she began loudly, 'can you read?' Timothy nodded still gasping.

'Well, perhaps you should get glasses! The sign says NO DOGS in the play area!' she went on, in an even louder, formidable voice.

Timothy wondered if she had been in the army; still unable to speak he simply nodded.

'*It's a disgrace!* People keep ignoring the signs! They weren't put there for fun you know. AND it doesn't set a very good example to these young children now, does it?'

Timothy shook his head. Gathering himself together, he stepped towards her and was about to explain, when Faith, who had been watching events closely, did what many dogs are known to do. By way of a greeting he lunged forward and put his cold, muddy nose under her dress, prodding firmly in the crotch area. The woman's scream could surely be heard for miles! Furiously she swung her walking stick, aiming it at Timothy, and he felt a hard thud on his back as he ducked away.

77

A quick exit at this point was best; he quickened his step when the voice behind him yelled; 'Dangerous, uncontrolled dogs should be banned! This *will* be reported!'

As they crossed the road, a familiar cheery voice said. 'In trouble again, Timothy? What a lovely dog!' It was Mrs Brown, pulling her shopping trolley behind her.

'Thanks,' he smiled, hoping it would all appear quite normal.

As they approached his home, he saw Inspector Davis' car parked outside. The previous events of the day came flooding back, along with the tense feeling in his stomach. *Now what*? he thought as he opened his front door.

13
Fiona's story.

Fiona couldn't believe her eyes, as yet another date was disappearing down the street. Oblivious of the traffic she walked into the road, calling and waving to what she guessed was Timothy's disappearing back. The man turned briefly but continued to walk on. 'He can't have heard her above the noise of the traffic', she thought.

With dreadful indigestion and a growing pain in her chest she decided to make her way home. Looking round she realised she was standing in the middle of a traffic jam. A taxi was close by and looked vacant so she opened the rear door and jumped in.

'Can you take me home?' she asked, clutching her stomach, forgetting she had left her glasses on the table in the pub.

The taxi driver looked round. 'I just came off duty and am going home myself, love,' he said, looking at her.

Fiona leaned forward, 'Please, it's not far and I don't feel all that well. I think I ate too much lunch.' she pleaded, squinting at the driver.

'Oh alright, where do you live?' the driver sighed. She gave him directions and sat back in the seat, the discomfort worsening. Finding it difficult to catch her breath, she wound down the window, wishing she could loosen her clothing. It was all a size too small, worn in an attempt to make her look slimmer and less dumpy.

'You alright, love?' asked the driver.

'I think so, it's just this pain. I'll be better in a minute,' she replied, suddenly finding it impossible to breath: Unable to speak she lay back, gasping for air, trying to focus on the ceiling of the taxi. She felt dizzy and everything began to spin before the world went black.

'You alright, love?' called the driver again.

Getting no response, he pulled off the main road, parked the taxi and got out. He could see his passenger lying on the back seat. As he opened the door he felt a thump on the back of his head, and crumpled to the floor.

'Quick, get the money off those two, I'll look in here,' said a young man in his early twenties. 'Oh my god, she's dead!'

'*What! Dead?*' exclaimed his accomplice. 'Let me see.' He leaned in and looked at Fiona's body. 'We'll get the blame for this, Brian. We better get rid of the body.'

'Shh, don't use my name! The other one might hear.'

'What are we going to do with him then?' asked the accomplice.

'Oh leave him there, he probably won't remember much. I've got an idea. The keys are still in the ignition,' said Brian.

'*What! We're going to nick a taxi now*? This will be trouble, shouldn't we just walk away with the money?'

'No dummy,' replied Brian,' finger prints, forensics? Don't you watch any telly? We'll nick this, lose the body, and then torch the taxi; but mind you keep quiet about it,' he said, quickly jumping into the driver's seat. Fiona's body had fallen lengthways across the back seat, and they had the idea of sitting her up, making it look as though she was asleep. They rummaged through her bag and found a scarf, which they tied over her head, hiding as much of her face as possible, and propped her up against the back seat of the taxi. 'Right, that looks okay, let's go.'

The taxi driver woke up lying on the pavement with a dreadful pain in the back of his head. Seeing his taxi had gone, he thought the whole thing with the woman and his attacker must have been planned. He rummaged in his pockets, and luckily they'd left his mobile phone. Feeling dazed and unable to stand he sat on the pavement and dialled 999.

'What are we going to do with this?' asked the youth, pointing to Fiona's body with his thumb.
'Dunno, I think we should hide the lot,' said Brian. 'My brother's garage is empty at the moment. We can leave it all there and get rid tonight after dark.'
As they pulled up at some traffic lights, a man opened the door of the taxi and leapt in and seeing Fiona sitting there, said, 'Oh sorry miss, I thought it was vacant,' and then to the boys, 'Did you know you've still got your vacant sign on?'
Brian began looking around for a switch to turn it off. 'No, sorry mate, I'm just going off duty, giving my friend here a lift, her in the back is the last fare today.'
Thinking as he was driving he added, 'where d'you wanna go?' with a sly wink to his mate, who rolled his eyes and pretended to pray.
'That's very kind of you,' said the man, ' I just need dropping at the end of Conningsby Street. Where are you going, miss?' he asked Fiona, 'I say, are you alright?'
'Oh, she's asleep, drunk I think. We're dropping her off on the other side of the park' said Brian quickly.

'She must be a sound sleeper. Are you sure she's alright?' asked the man, becoming more agitated and staring at Fiona. As he leaned forward to touch her shoulder, Brian spotted the movement in the rear view mirror and deliberately swerved the taxi to divert the man's attention. Fiona's body wobbled dangerously. He speeded up, thinking the sooner they get the fare and lose this guy, the better.

'Speed limits,' hissed his mate under his breath, as Brian swung around a corner, tyres squealing.

They came to an abrupt halt at the end of Conningsby Street, which made Fiona flop over onto the man, who was now aware that this was all very wrong. He flung the door open and got out the second the car came to a halt. ' Here,' he said, throwing his cash into the taxi, and as he turned to close the door, Fiona's head rolled to one side. 'Oh my God! The poor woman is dead!' he exclaimed in panic.

Brian accelerated fast, snatching the door from the man's hand and snapping it closed as he drove off, leaving the man standing open mouthed on the pavement.

His mate had his head in his hands. 'It just goes from bad to worse…now what?' he asked Brian, who was apparently enjoying the adventure.

'Oh stop fussing! It'll be okay, you'll see,' said Brian, slowing down as they met traffic. 'My brother's garage is just up here.'

They left the car with the body locked in the garage until after dark. His accomplice was more than a little reluctant, but with Brian's constant reassurances, found himself convinced that this was the best solution. Later that evening they drove the taxi with Fiona's body to the park. Brian drove over the grass to some thick bushes he had once used as cover for another, more pleasurable occupation. With the shovels they had thrown into the back of the taxi, they dug a shallow grave.

Unfortunately for them Fiona's body had flopped over and been left in a bent position, when rigor mortis had set in. This made it almost impossible to get it out through the taxi door. ' You'll have to lift her top half over the front and get her head through first,' said Brian, finding it difficult to be quiet.

'She won't fit that way!' exclaimed his mate, trying to heave the crooked body over the headrests. With a lot of heaving, pulling and pushing, and more than a little swearing, they managed to get the body at a better angle to pull it out of the taxi.

A loud, matronly voice shouted. 'What's going on in there? I know what you young people get up to.' The voice was getting closer.

In a moment of panic, though later described as ingenuity, Brian squeezed himself over Fiona's body.

His mate was shouting, 'Get off me you mad cow!' as the woman gave him a good whack with her walking stick.

'It's time someone taught you young people a lesson! Smoking your funny cigarettes! Think no one knows? This is the neighbourhood watch park patrol. *What are you doing with a taxi here in the park?*' shouted the woman.

'We don't smoke and we're just leaving.'

'What's going on in there?' demanded the woman, banging on the roof of the taxi with her stick.

'What d'you think?' called Brian, from inside the taxi. Bouncing up and down on a corpse definitely wasn't on his 'to do' list, but it seemed to do the trick.

'Well, it's a disgrace, an absolute disgrace!' barked the woman. ' You be gone from here or I'll call the police! It's all a disgrace!' She marched off, waving her stick around as she went.

'Come on, lets get the body out, now, she's gone.'

Brian had to squeeze himself free from the corpse and wriggle out of the taxi. They each grabbed hold of a bit of the body and pulled; after a lot of heaving and struggling it suddenly came free and they flew backwards with it into the leaves and soil they had piled up from the shallow grave. They laid the body on its back, but the legs stuck up in the air. They tried putting it on its front but that was worse! So they settled for laying it sideways in the grave. After quickly covering everything up, they brushed around the area with some branches to remove any footprints, and walked back to the taxi. Driving quickly out of the park, they noticed Fiona's hand bag lying in the back, so they pulled up by a refuse bin and chucked it in.   'Right lets pick up the girls and go have some fun,' said Brian callously.

They collected their two girlfriends and set off for a wild drive.   Brian was a seasoned 'joy rider' and enjoyed the fun of breaking speed limits; he knew how to handle a car and loved hearing the girls squealing and giggling in the back as they skidded around the bends.

Brian dropped his mate off to collect his own car and follow him to a disused factory site where, standing back from the battered taxi, they watched while he set it alight.

The sound of sirens sent them all scurrying to Brian's car; they piled in and drove off into the night.

14
Betty and the dead.

'The inspector and I were having a nice chat' said Mother as Timothy walked in.

'Inspector Davis? I didn't expect to see you again so soon.' He felt the familiar pit open up in his stomach, *what now?*

'I have news for you, Timothy,' she said. 'Fiona died of a natural cause: a heart attack. It seems she had a heart condition and apparently her stomach was *very* full. You said she ate a lot and quickly, didn't you?'

'Yes, and drank several pints of beer much quicker than I can!' he replied.

'So now we need to know how she came to be buried in the park. You said you saw a taxi near by. Can you tell me anything else about the vehicle?' she asked.

'Only that I *thought* she got into it ,but there was such chaos I couldn't be sure. I rushed back to the shop afterwards so didn't really see.'

'Mmm, all a bit odd, don't you think? Do you have a driving licence?' she asked.

'Yes, but I don't have a car at the moment, don't really need one that much.'

'A while since you've driven then?' she asked, her gaze never faltering.

'About a year.'

'We may be in need of some help again, Timothy, but that will do for the moment,' she said. Faith had hopped up on the sofa beside her and was watching closely. As she made to get up and leave, the dog licked her face and neck vigorously, smearing her make-up with mud and saliva. She took a tissue from

85

her bag and wiped her face, before saying, 'thank you for the tea and biscuits.'   Timothy wasn't sure if he should mention the mud smears still on her cheek.

'I'll see you out, Inspector,' he said.

As the inspector was making her way to the car, she turned and looking directly into his eyes, said pointedly, 'see you *soon,* Timothy.'

'Err…yes of course,' he replied.

Mrs Fell was walking back from the local shop lugging her trolley behind her. She stared as the inspector got into her car, and smiling at Timothy she waited for the inspector to drive away. 'This is very exciting Timothy.' Her teeth, always moving independently, were clicking away as she spoke in a loud whisper.

'Oh yes, marvellous!' he replied, not really knowing what she was talking about.   She giggled secretively and walked on.   Another batty friend of Mother's he thought, as he went back into the house.

' Timothy!'

'Yes Mother'.

'If you got another car would the police ask you for more help?'

'What!'

'If you had another car they may be interested in you helping them more,' repeated Mother.

'I don't know,' said Timothy, confused and exasperated. His mind was on getting out his list of contacts from the agency.   It was about time he had another date.   'Faith enjoyed his walk,' he said, changing the subject.

'That's nice dear,' said Mother, with a knowing look.

The following morning, Derek was beside himself with anticipation. ' Tell all, Timmy lad, tell all,' he said.

'You've had a visit from my friend Inspector Davis,' he replied, enjoying keeping his friend in suspense.

86

'Yes. Did you ask her out by the way? She's a bit tasty, isn't she?' Derek went on.

'*NO*, I haven't been dating the inspector. Look out, Mrs Jones is coming in.'

The door clanged as the elderly would-be vampire slayer, walked in with her usual pile of returns. 'Morning gentlemen!' she said brightly, winking at Timothy, which set Derek off sniggering as he went to the back of the shop. She piled the books in front of her 'conspirator'. 'What *have* you been up to? You made Mrs Battle very angry the other day. It was you she was shouting at in the park, wasn't it?'

'Perhaps she just doesn't like dogs,' he replied, wondering if there was an 'old lady network' in town, all spying on his every move!

'I'll keep your secret. We had to keep everything secret in the war, you know?' she said, with a strange gleam in her pale eyes.

He decided to play along. 'Yes Mrs Jones, mum's the word. Will you be choosing any books today, or do you want a refund?' he added patiently.

' I'll go and have a look,' she says. 'Any juicy murder or horror books come in?'

'All in that section over there, Mrs Jones,' he replied, pointing to the Horror / Thriller section of the shop. They deliberately kept this section on the ground floor, as it was so popular with the local elderly folk in the town.

She returned shortly with another stack of horror titles. 'There we are,' she said, 'wish there were a few more vampire horrors, I love those.'

He suddenly had visions of her wrinkled person lying in bed dreaming of being bitten by vampires. 'You enjoy those the best, do you?'

'Oh yes, I enjoy a good fright.' Then lowering her voice, and struggling to lean over the counter she asked in a loud whisper, 'Been working with the police long? We'd never have known, you know?'

The penny suddenly dropped and he smiled, beginning to enjoy the game. 'Not very long, it's very hush hush,' he added in a loud whisper. This confidence seemed to energise the old lady who almost skipped out of the shop. Probably to report back to the *old lady network,* thought Timothy.

'She had a spring in her step today, what did you say to her,' asked Derek.

'Nothing much,' he grinned, an idea forming in his head.

'By the way, I've got another date tonight, over at Blackwood Avenue; another animal lover!'

Derek was leaning on the counter grinning. 'Okay, come on, what have you been up to?'

Timothy related the latest developments. 'So she died of a heart attack after meeting you, then?' Derek exclaimed laughing. 'What did you do to her, Timmy boy?'

'Oh for goodness sake, nothing! Like I said, she ate huge mounds of food, and sank several pints of beer very quickly, after that I've no idea.'

'For such a quiet chap you're a bit of a one, aren't you?' Derek rolled his yes. 'I'm looking forward to the next instalment. This is better than anything on reality TV.'

Later that evening Timothy rang the bell at 13 Blackwood Avenue.

The door opened, revealing a stocky blonde girl. 'You must be from the agency. Hi, I'm Betty.' She gripped Timothy's hand and shook it firmly. 'Come on in, would you like a drink? I make all my own wine, the rhubarb is rather good this time.'

He followed her into the house and was surprised to see several chest freezers in the hall. There was another one in the small sitting room, only leaving space for a couple of chairs, a coffee table and a full-sized stuffed sheep by the fire place.

'Sit down,' said Betty, 'I'll get the wine.' She left him sitting obediently on one of the chairs, staring at the stuffed sheep and wondering how it met its demise. There were three urns on the mantle shelf, that seemed large and out of place. He was already wondering how the evening was going to go, or how it would end.

'Here we are,' said Betty, coming back into the room and handing him a full glass of pink-coloured wine.

'Thank you,' he said, taking a sip. It was nice and sweet, faintly rhubarb flavoured with a little tang to it, *very* nice in fact.

'What do you use the freezers for?' He couldn't help but ask.

'Oh I keep my old pets in them, can't bear to let them go,' she replied, sitting in the other chair, keeping the bottle in one hand and a glass in the other. He swallowed another mouthful of wine, cleared his throat and ventured, 'what sort of pets?'

'Oh, a few of my favourite sheep, a goat, and several dogs and cats. The one in the hall has a small bull calf in it and the other the best part of Lilly. All were my best friends, as was old Myrtle there,' she pointed at the sheep. ' I was wondering about dyeing her rose pink, what do you think?'

'I see, very nice,' he coughed. 'You don't eat the lamb then?'

'*Oh my God, no!* It would be like eating Uncle Roger, or Grandma!' she exclaimed, horrified.

'Will you keep them all in the freezers forever?' he wondered aloud.

'No. I intend to have them all stuffed one day. It will be like I have them back with me again. But I need to earn more money and buy a bigger place first, of course.

Pictures of a sitting room full of dead stuffed animals went through Timothy's mind. 'Dare I ask where Uncle Roger and Grandma are?' he asked, looking at the freezers.

'They're on the mantle shelf,' she nodded toward the urns, 'Mother is up there too. Sadly Dad had been scattered before I had the idea of keeping everyone together,' she informed him cheerily. Timothy cleared his throat again and finished off his wine. Betty re-filled his glass instantly. 'So will you keep the ashes, or scatter them eventually?' shades of Mrs Jones coming into his mind.

'Oh I expect I'll scatter them all together, one day. I'd like to find a house with a nice orchard. I'm sure they would love to be scattered somewhere like that, and then I'll be able to bury old Lilly,' she replied in dreamy tones.

'Who was 'old Lilly'?'

'Oh, was my cow, she had to be cut up to fit into two freezers. I won't be able to have her stuffed it would cost far too much, unless I win the lottery or something. She could go in the hall then,' she said.

He took another gulp of the wine, before asking, 'have you been doing this long?'

'Oh yes, quite a few years. That's why I've got so many,'

'Are there any *live* animals in here,' he asked, wondering if he should leave soon!

'Yes, my old collie Snap and a sick lamb I rescued from a farmer, the lamb is in the oven. Come on, I'll show you,' she said.

She was obviously delighted that someone was taking an interest, and he had stayed a lot longer than most of the others.

He stood to follow; feeling a bit giddy he steadied himself on the back of the chair. Curiosity made him follow her into the kitchen. The floor was tiled and there was an old oven at one end. The lamb was hanging out of the bottom with the door propped open. The collie, on a small chair in the corner, bared its teeth when he glanced at it. He chose to ignore it and hoped it stayed there.

'We always kept the sick lambs in the bottom of the Aga on the farm. Keeps them warm.'

The lamb looked very dead to Timothy, the pungent stench in the kitchen was unbearable. 'Well, it's been very interesting Betty,' he said, looking for an exit. 'The wine was lovely too, but I must be off now.' He wobbled back down the hall.

'Oh, don't go yet,' she cried, leaping in front of him.

Timothy wasn't sure if it was blind panic, but he suddenly pictured himself being stuffed into a freezer. He tried to manoeuvre past, but Betty was a bit on the weighty side, and stood firm. Now he panicked and gave her a firm push, which sent her falling backwards through the sitting room door; as she lay on her back, using swear words he'd only heard from workmen, he made a quick exit. Hearing the collie bark, he slammed the front door behind him; jumped on his bike and peddled away!

Still feeling a bit wobbly after several glasses of the potent home-made wine, he was cycling more slowly than usual.

As he came to the end of the road, he noticed the house on the corner; it looked empty and scruffy. The curtains were grubby and hung unevenly behind the dirty window; the paint was chipped and grey, and weeds grew in the front garden. He wondered if anyone lived there, the place always made him shiver. On this occasion the heavy, black, front door was open. An elderly man with a bald head, wearing small crooked glasses stared out. He was clearing his throat in a way that sounded more like an animal growling. He leered at Timothy, who smiled and said, 'Evening.'

'Clear off,' snarled the old man, coughing and spitting as Timothy cycled by, and when he looked back he couldn't see the old man anymore.

Unfazed by his latest experience, and as he'd previously chosen another name on the list, he arranged to meet her the following evening. He just hoped she would be a little more 'normal'. Nevertheless he felt he was getting the hang of this dating business, although he couldn't help wondering why he had never heard of anyone else having this kind of trouble.

Betty was furious at Timothy's behaviour, and the following morning she phoned the agency to complain.

'Oh I'm sure he didn't mean to be quite so rude,' said Jane, in soothing tones. She had developed a soft spot for the man and couldn't believe he had meant to upset Betty. It must have been a mistake. 'We have a farmer, called Bertrum, who has just joined, and perhaps he would suit you better. Would you like his telephone number?'

Betty brightened immediately, 'Oh yes, please. What does he look like?'

'Six foot, broad shoulders, well built, dark hair, brown eyes and ruddy complexion. He's single and says he's looking for a *'good woman,'* Jane read out. 'I think you'll like him, more your type.'

'Sounds perfect.' Betty was cheered up enormously by this news and felt the farmer could be just what she was looking for.

Jane smiled to herself. *Now that's a match, I'm sure*, she thought.

Meanwhile back at the shop; once again Derek was highly amused to hear about Timothy's latest dating expedition. ' Oh Timothy you must write a book on all this. You have more adventures than the SAS. So far, you've had women locking you in, pouncing on you, been chased by all manner of animals, and now one of these mad women might have shut you in her deep freezer, *and* you have a detective on your tail!!'

'Life used to be so quiet,' said Timothy, ruefully. He then went on to mention the house on the corner of Tumps Road.

Mrs Brown happened to be in the shop browsing and had obviously been eaves dropping.

'I know the house you mean, been empty for years, the old boy died,' she explained with relish.

'D'you mean no one lives there at all?' Timothy shivered..

'The old place still belongs to his sons who live down in London. Old boy used to be a grumpy sod. Meant no harm by it. No one has lived there since he died.' she gave him a quizzical look and went on browsing through the murder mysteries.

'It must have been that rhubarb wine!' Derek patted him on the shoulder.

As Derek went through to the back of the shop, Mrs Brown sidled up again. 'Still working with the police, Timothy?' she asked, in a loud whisper.

Convinced his suspicions were right, he asked, ' Do you happen to know Mrs Fell?'

'Why, yes,' she replied with a puzzled frown.

'And Mrs Jones?'

'Yes,'

'And a few other ladies of a similar age group?'

'Why yes dear, we have a get together quite often. Mrs Fell has asked your mother to join us this week, too,' she beamed.

Well, that's it now, he thought, the old busy-body spies would be in full swing if Mother has joined them. 'Is Mrs Battle ever there?'

' Sometimes. She's a bit busy these days, as she is a member of the neighbourhood parks watch,'

'Yes, I've seen her in the park.'

'I heard about that! I don't think Mrs Battle likes dogs very much!' said Mrs Brown sympathetically.

He was beginning to wonder if he should adopt some sort of disguise, see if he could fool them! He told Derek about the old ladies' network. 'Aha, that's it now Timothy, they'll be watching you. Spied on by the 'Old Bat' network!' chuckled his friend.

' I think they may have their uses, you know,' he replied, tapping the side of his nose with his forefinger in a joking manner.

Just then, the shop door bell jangled and a tall, slim girl with shoulder length brown hair came in. She was wearing a long knitted coat over jeans, with a horribly familiar, orange hat sticking out of one of the pockets. She walked directly to the counter; both men gazed at her for a moment in silence.

' Can we help?' said Derek finally. The girl leaned on the counter, her large brown eyes looking from one to the other, 'Would one of you be Timothy Parkes?'

'I'm Timothy, do I know you?'

'Not exactly, but you do know my friend Linda. She has a few cats.' She looked directly at Timothy. 'Oh Linda! I remember all the cats,' he replied warily.

Derek coughed loudly. 'This is my friend Derek.'

'Hello Derek, I'm Henrietta, known as Henri,' she said.

'Delighted to meet you, Henri,' smiled Derek.

'You didn't like the cats much then?' she asked, diverting her gaze briefly back toward Timothy.

'No…not for me at all, I'm afraid,' he said, aware of the looks being exchanged between Derek and Henri, 'I'll just finish up in the biography room, nice to meet you, Henri.'

Making an escape wasn't difficult. He stayed near the door of the next room to hear them chatting. Waiting until he heard Henri say goodbye, he wandered back toward the counter, just in time to see Derek grab his jacket and rush out of the shop after her.

15
The car ride & the bronco.

Several days later Timothy had a dental appointment near the hospital. He wondered if he should call in and surprise his aunt, although she had been adamant she did not wish to see him. Then he remembered the effect the hospital had had on him and changed his mind.

Mother had been chatting with his neighbour Mrs Fell, and discovered that she would be in town on the same day. Unbeknown to him she had arranged for Mrs Fell to give him a lift.

'Mrs Fell has a car?' asked Timothy.

'Oh she's had that car for years,' exclaimed Mother, 'she told me she's been driving since the war, you know'!

'That's what's worrying me,' he said. 'Should I pop in and surprise Aunt Maude?'

'Oh I shouldn't, dear, not after the last time, she couldn't stand the trauma.' That was fine by Timothy, who didn't want any more drama in his own life either. At the moment, it felt like it was following him everywhere.

On the day of his dental appointment he came home from work to find Inspector Davis waiting outside the house. 'Afternoon, Timothy,' she smiled, getting out of the car.

'Good afternoon, Inspector, I trust the day finds you well,' he replied formerly.

'Got time for a chat?' she asked.

' I wanted to have a quick chat with you too, please come in.'

Once he'd got Faith under control the inspector joined him in the sitting room. He noticed she avoided sitting next to the dog.

'I just wanted to quickly run through the events during your lunch with Fiona once more. I can't help feeling we're missing something,' she said.

He patiently went through the whole episode again, and then told her about the 'old ladies' network' and how it might be of some help regarding the taxi, and the finding of Fiona's body in the park.

'Ah, Mrs Battle! Yes, we have heard of her, but I didn't realise she patrolled the park. That could be helpful. You've met her, Timothy?' asked the inspector.

'You could say that. She doesn't like dogs much.'

'Ah I see. If you come up with anything else please let me know,' she said, walking to the front door.

'I'll keep you informed if anything comes to mind,' he replied, seeing her out.

It always made him feel uncomfortable when Inspector Davies popped round 'just for a chat.' He had nothing to feel guilty about, and she was an attractive lady; she just had that effect somehow.

He changed and was ready in good time to meet his lift.

Mrs Fell's top teeth snapped down to meet the bottom set, in a fixed smile. He followed her round to the garage and to his surprise her old, yellow Mini looked in very good condition.

She backed it out of the garage with much revving of the engine. They set off at a quick pace, and although she wasn't exactly breaking the speed limit, she didn't slow down for any corners, and was inclined to do emergency stops at traffic lights and junctions.

They zipped along, over-taking whenever possible. Mrs Fell apparently enjoyed revving the engine as often as she saw fit, and had to shout above the noise. He noticed that her teeth were moving up and down, slightly out of sync with the rest of her mouth as she chatted, and hoped she was concentrating on the road ahead.

The car suddenly screamed to a halt at a zebra crossing, letting several people cross the road. He noticed his nice policewoman, Lizzie, standing on the pavement with a colleague. He almost ducked down out of view, but smiled and waved instead, as they roared noisily off as soon as the crossing was clear.

Tyres screeching, they came to an abrupt halt at the ticket-barrier of the car park. Mrs Fell, being a small lady, was having difficulties reaching the slot on the side of the ticket machine. With a lot of grunting and puffing, she squeezed the best part of her body out of the car window, stretching up to put the money in. People in the cars behind were getting impatient and sounded their horns, some even started shouting. Timothy hoped he didn't know any of them.

Getting back into the driving seat proved even more awkward. 'Let me help,' he said, grabbing her around the middle and pulling her back into the car.

'Ooooh,' she squealed, 'thank you, dear.'

Giving the engine a few good revs and ignoring the horns and shouts behind her, she released the handbrake. They shot off around the car park like they were on a 'Go Kart' track, zooming up the ramps, engine roaring, tyres screeching. Suddenly she turned into a vacant slot and stopped dead.

Timothy breathed a sigh of relief. 'Thank you so much,' he said, not sure if he was thanking her for the lift, or the gods for sparing his life.

'A pleasure, I'll pick you up as planned, outside the flower shop. Toodle pip,' she said, slamming the boot closed, and beetling off across the car park with her shopping trolley. Essential old-lady equipment, he decided.

After his appointment, he called into the bicycle shop for a few spare parts. On his way out of the shop he bumped into Jane from Two to Tango.

'Hello Timothy,' she purred, smiling up at him. He was a little surprised by her change in manner, and even more surprised when she sidled up to him. 'Want to come for a coffee, Timmy? The shop at the end of the road does excellent cakes.'

He glanced at his watch. 'Well, maybe a quick coffee. I have to meet my lift home,' he said, half wishing he could find a polite way out of it, but Jane had linked her arm through his and was 'guiding' him towards the coffee shop. He wondered if she had been having lessons from 'The Tigress'!

As they sat with their coffee and cake, he noticed Jane was wearing more make-up than usual, and her clothes were more colourful. 'Have you had any luck with the ladies, Timmy?' she asked. He hated being called Timmy. 'It's Timothy, actually, and yes I have been meeting one or two.'

'Daphne says I have to brighten myself up a bit, and put myself out there, so to speak. I'm off to a barn dance tonight, would you like to come?'

A feeling of dread swept over him and he thought hard about how was he going to say no. 'Well, I think...' *he was still thinking.* 'I have an appointment this evening, Jane,' feeling guilty as hell. 'Nice to see you, Jane,' he said gently, as he drained his cup and prepared to leave.

She looked as if she would burst into tears any minute. Feeling more than a bit mean about leaving he put the money on the table for the cake and two coffees. 'Sorry Jane, but I'll miss my lift if I don't go now. See you soon I expect, enjoy the barn dance, bye then.' Rushing the last few words he left the shop.

What is it about saying 'goodbye' to women, he thought; they always make you feel so bad.

He waited outside the flower shop for Mrs Fell, and soon heard the little engine roaring long before the Mimi came to an abrupt halt in front of him. Mrs Fell was smiling as he got in and buckled up.

'Alright Timothy?' she asked.

'Oh marvellous,' he replied optimistically, thinking that if she'd survived this long she would probably survive a bit longer and, with luck, get them home without incident.

Her accelerator foot slammed to the floor and they shot out into the traffic, ignoring the blaring horns as usual. Timothy closed his eyes.

'Pretty lady you were with in the coffee shop, Timothy' she shouted over the engine noise. He couldn't believe it! He had deliberately faced the window to keep an eye on passers-by, and hadn't seen anyone he knew, so how did these old ladies get their information? Old bat radar, or what?

They screeched to a dead stop outside the house and he noticed with horror Lizzie approaching. There wasn't any room to hide in the old Mini and he had no intention of offering an explanation to Mrs Fell, so he thanked her and got out of the car. The Mini disappeared in a haze of fumes.

'Hi Timothy,' said Lizzie, as she reached his gate, 'was that your neighbour?' They could still hear the engine revving in the distance.

'Yes, she just gave me a lift. Would you like some tea? I'll go in first if you don't mind; when Mother isn't home Faith can be a bit boisterous. Believe me, it's safer!'

He braced himself and opened the door; the Wolfhound's big paws landed on his shoulders and pinned him up against the wall; the dog vigorously licked his face and ears. He finally managed to get the dog to sit, and keeping hold of its collar he re-opened the door.

'Quite a handful, isn't he' commented Lizzie, more as a statement than a question.

'Yes, he can be, he doesn't much like being on his own. He's better when Mother's home.'

She followed him through to the kitchen. As Timothy filled the kettle he found himself asking, 'I don't know if it's appropriate to ask you, but I was just wondering if you were doing anything this evening?' He braced himself, waiting for the reply.

'What had you in mind?' she asked.

Trying not to show his relief or surprise, he said, 'Perhaps a meal and a drink somewhere, if you won't get into trouble dating a possible 'suspect'?' He couldn't believe it…, was this going to be a normal date and maybe even pass without incident?

'That would be really nice. I'm only working here temporarily and technically I'm not connected with the case so there shouldn't be a problem; shall I come back around seven?'

'No, I'll come and pick you up in a taxi,' he said, 'where do you live?'   She wrote down her address for him. They chatted while drinking their tea, and just as Lizzie was leaving, Mother came home.

'Hello again, nice to see you,' said Mother, glancing from one to the other. 'Have you been talking business?'

'You could say that, I suppose,' Lizzie grinned, fuelling Mother's curiosity. 'See you later then Timothy,' she said, as she left.

He noticed the curtains twitching in the house opposite and smiled to himself. The old bat network is at it again, he thought.

'Aunt Maude was pleased you didn't pop in to see her I think,' said Mother, sounding disappointed.

'*You* said she didn't want me to visit her in hospital any more!' he said, thinking... *Women are confusing creatures.* 'I won't need anything to eat tonight, I'm going out for the evening.'

'Is it a very important meeting, dear?' she asked conspiratorially.

'Yes, it could be very important Mother, don't wait up.'

The taxi arrived on time and he was on his way to, what he hoped, was a normal date. He had decided to take Lizzie to a nice pub out of town, called the 'The Headless Woman'. While they were tucking into a meal of steak and chips, with a bottle of red wine, he told her all about the 'Old ladies' network'. She couldn't stop giggling at the thought of all these elderly spies armed with their shopping trolleys.

'It really is amazing, I can't move without them all knowing. Goodness knows what they think I'm up to!' he exclaimed.

'How many of them are there?' She asked, with a chuckle.

As he was totting up the numbers, a voice interrupted:

'Lizzie! we wondered where you were!' The voice belonged to a young man who had come into the pub with a group of others.

'Hi Anthony, where are you off to?' she asked, more out of politeness than interest.

'We're having a drink here first and then going to the barn dance at Wallow Farm. Might be fun. Perhaps you and your friend would join us?' Anthony was eyeing Timothy speculatively. Lizzie introduced them and somewhere along the line it was decided that they would join the party. Anthony assured them there would be spare tickets.

'Anthony is one of the police officers at the station; I don't think he knows who you are, so it should be alright, our secret.' Lizzie whispered to Timothy as they were leaving.

'Mum's the word,' he said.

The band was playing Country & Western music, and people were line dancing on the boarded floor in the huge barn. Large pieces of brightly coloured fabric had been hung up to disguise the rough walls and metal bars. The faint smell of manure suggested it normally housed cattle. The band was playing on a wooden stage, with a bar and tables to one side. At the far end of the tables there was a large black and white mechanical horse, which added to the atmosphere. Timothy was beginning to relax and enjoy himself.

The music changed to a lively tune and everyone joined in, with the lead singer calling out the moves in time to the music.

'Shall we have a go?' suggested Lizzie enthusiastically. He was not really much of a dancer, but decided to have a go anyway, and was surprised at just how much fun it was. As they danced and twirled, while listening out for the moves from the 'caller', he suddenly spotted a familiar face. The next time they swung around he was able to see that the face belonged to Jane of 'Two to Tango'.

He felt a fleeting pang of guilt. From her dour expression, Jane wasn't having such a good time and had obviously seen him dancing with Lizzie. The dancing swung him away again and he was looking into Lizzie's pretty, smiling face; he hadn't enjoyed himself like this for ages.

After three more dances they decided to take a breather and have a much-earned drink. Anthony came over and joined them. 'So, how did you two meet?'

'We met in the park where Timothy was walking his dog,' said Lizzie quickly.

'What sort of dog is that,' mocked Anthony.

'An Irish Wolfhound actually', Timothy replied defensively.

Anthony looked at him for a moment before saying. 'Going to have a go on the bucking horse, Timothy?'

'The bucking horse?'

'Yes, you sit on it, and it bucks like a real bucking bronco! The one who stays on the longest during the evening wins a free meal for two at the pub. There's a rope you hold on to. Oh, they have put some straw bales around it, to catch people when they fall off,' he explained.

Timothy wasn't too sure about this challenge, but male pride made him think he should give it a go. How difficult could it be? Plus he didn't want to lose face in front of Lizzie and the looks Anthony was directing towards her confirmed his suspicions.

On confessing that Timothy hadn't ridden before, and certainly not a bucking bronco, the man operating it gave him a quizzical look. 'You're sure you want to have a go, mate?' he asked.

'Yes, I think so,' he replied, not really sure at all, but Anthony's grin made him even more determined. He was sure he'd soon get the hang of it.

As he climbed onto the saddle the operator gave him some tips. 'Whatever you do, move with it; let your legs swing back and forth, and keeping one hand in the air helps balance. Always remember to let your body move! If you want to stop before you fall off, give me a signal. Point at something, or at me. Okay?'

He showed Timothy how to wrap his one hand with the rope, wished him luck, and stepped back to start the machine. As the bronco began to move Timothy realised the music had stopped and a voice on the loud speaker was saying, 'Ladies and Gentleman, we have our first rodeo rider of the evening. The wild rider is Timothy, give him a hand and wish him good luck, everyone!'

Timothy could hear the applause as the machine rocked back and forth like an over-active rocking horse; and then it also began to tip. The music picked up again and he could hear cheering as the front end of the bronco suddenly went down as the hindquarters flipped up. The front reared up and each time it dropped down again, the hindquarters were came up, smacking him firmly on the buttocks. He remembered what the man had said and allowed his body to rock back and forth with the movement; the machine speeded up and the flipping up and down became even more violent. Timothy thought of Lizzie, and Anthony standing beside her. He tightened his grip and hung on, swaying back and forth as the bucking bronco became more violent. To his alarm the whole machine began to spin, first one way, coming to an abrupt halt and then reversing the process, while its whole structure was violently flipping up and down.

He began to ache, his hand was numb from gripping so tightly, and with his other hand in the air he felt completely out of control. His head was spinning; it felt like his insides were coming out through his ears, and that his eyes might pop out. He couldn't hang on much longer. What had the man said about a signal to stop? Up and down, round and round, faster and faster it went. He no longer felt he had any strength left and the option to just let go became more inviting. There were straw bales to break the fall, he thought, but he couldn't really see clearly any more and felt sure his eyes were bulging now as the machine went even faster. He heard the sound of cheering and shouting somewhere in the distance. Finally he just had to let go.

This wasn't easy. He had wrapped his hand so tightly with the rope that it was now completely numb. Up and down…round and round… it just kept on going. He felt sick. He must let go! Eventually his hand came free, just at the unfortunate moment when the front of the horse vanished in front of him. The rear shot up again smacking into his bottom and sending him sailing headfirst over the bales of straw, and sprawling, belly down, along one of the trestle tables. Taking the entire contents on the table with him, he slid unceremoniously off the other end and onto the floor. With a roaring sound in his ears, he lay still, thinking, *I must not be sick*! Taking several long, deep breaths, he realised that although his body was numb, it hurt all over at the same time. He took another deep breath, *I must not be sick*!

He looked up to see Jane staring down at him. 'Oh Timothy! You said you couldn't come! Who's that woman?' she asked, her chin wobbling with emotion. When he didn't respond she threw the remains of her drink over him and ran away.

Disorientated, and confused by her behaviour, he tried to sit up. Suddenly Lizzie was stroking his hand, looking concerned, 'Are you alright, Timothy?'

He managed a weak smile, 'I think I'll live,' he said, in a hoarse whisper. Getting slowly to his feet he was surprised to find his legs still worked and nothing was broken. He was sore and bruised all over. Leaning on Lizzie he made his way back to their table. The crowd around him began to disperse; the excitement over, people went back to dancing and drinking.

'Loved the finale,' said Anthony, laughing. 'You stayed on for a full fifty six seconds apparently, not bad I suppose.'

'When is it your turn?' Timothy asked.

'Oh I'll have a go later, I think. Watch a few others first, see if I can pick up a few tips.'

'*You'd better have a go too*,' said Lizzie, glaring at him. 'Come on Timothy, let's see if we can get a taxi home,' she said, helping him to his feet.

'I'll give you a lift if you like,' said Anthony.

'*No thank you!*' they replied in unison before making their way to the door.

Arriving at Lizzie's home, the taxi waited while Timothy said good night to her. Gently she folded her arms around his neck, 'Thank you for an interesting evening. I hope you'll be okay.'

'I'll survive, I'm sure.' They stayed locked in a kiss for a few moments until the taxi sounded its horn. 'Sleep well Lizzie, see you soon, I hope,' he said.

'Next time I'm off duty I'll call you,' she said. They both said good night and Timothy got back into the waiting taxi.

Arriving at his own home he heard the familiar sound of an engine roaring. The little yellow Mini went by and a toot on the horn sounded as Mrs Fell spotted him. The 'old lady network' was at it late tonight, he thought, smiling to himself; nothing would dampen his buoyant mood.

'Are you alright in there?' called Mother the next morning.

He was so stiff and bruised that he decided to have a bath rather than a shower and lay soaking his aching body in the hot water.

He could smell bacon cooking and realised he was really very hungry. His hand that had held the rope was quite burnt, and the wrist swollen. A nasty bruise was appearing under his right eye, while his legs were stiff from gripping the bucking "horse".   The bath helped and he was able to move almost normally again; he hoped Faith wouldn't expect him to keep up their usual pace.   Mother took one look at him and shrieked. 'Whatever happened to you, was there a fight?'

'Not exactly, just a bit bruised. Nothing one of your breakfasts won't help,' he said kindly, trying to reassure her, it didn't work.

'Was the nice police lady with you? Does the inspector know about this?'   Mother went on.   'It's alright, please don't fret,' he tried to calm her. 'I'll take Faith for his walk before I go to work, and I'll be home for a meal this evening.'

'Oh, you're so brave!' she said, planting a kiss on his head as he was eating.   He wondered how she would react if she knew what had really happened!

As he left the house the curtains opposite were twitching; he wondered what story the 'old lady network' would come up with when they saw his bruised eye!

He chose to go to the smaller park, as there wouldn't be any children playing at this time of day, and hoped Mrs Battle wouldn't be on duty either.   Luckily, the park was empty. Letting Faith off the lead he walked slowly over to the swings.

The dog raced up and down quartering the ground, with his nose; he chased a squirrel, which made it to a tree and then sat on a branch chattering furiously at the dog.

Leaving the park, Timothy took evasive action when he noticed Mrs Battle walking towards him. Not wishing to meet her again, he speeded up as best he could and limped off home.

He got some very odd looks from people coming into the shop that morning, and of course Derek had to hear all about the bronco riding. During his narrative a tall elderly man, dressed in a long, dark coat and hat, and smelling strongly of tobacco, came into the shop. He enquired whether they stocked any books on poisons. Derek directed him to the right area and the man, having made his choice, came back to the counter. He stared at Timothy for a few moments, holding several books in his hand.

'Can I help you, sir?' asked Timothy, feeling a little uncomfortable.

The man didn't speak as he put the books on the counter.

'That will be fifteen pounds eighty six pence please.'

The man put the exact money on the counter and, without saying a word, took the books and left.

'That's a bit odd,' said Derek, 'I haven't seen him before.'

'Nor me,' said Timothy, picking up a card from the floor where the customer had been standing. 'Doctor Athed it says here, no address, just a mobile number and email. I wonder if we will see him again?'

'Good God! This woman must read fast, it's Mrs Brown!' exclaimed Derek.

'Only brought one back this time, Mrs Brown?' asked Timothy, as she approached the counter. 'Oh my! Have you been fighting? Did you win?' she asked eagerly, standing on tiptoe peering up over the counter, 'Ohoo, that looks nasty; have you put anything on it?'

'It's fine, thank you Mrs Brown, just a silly accident, nothing to worry about,' he said.

'I'll just have a little browse today,' she said, before turning around suddenly, 'Did your mother tell you Mrs Battle is re taking her driving test? She's just started lessons.'

' No, I don't believe she did,' he replied, hoping her driving was better than Mrs Fell's.

Later that afternoon the shop door clanged open and in walked Mrs Battle herself. 'Ah, glad I found you here, Timothy Parkes. I'd like a word,' she boomed, in her matronly way.

'Good afternoon Mrs Battle,' he replied politely.

Derek snorted and nearly choked, stifling a laugh before going into the back of the shop.

'I'm head of the neighbourhood parks patrol, you know. Now I know you have been working with the police,' she said, leaning closer to him over the counter.

'Well…a bit,' he replied, cautiously.

'I would like you and your dog to become members of the patrol as you walk in one or other of the parks anyway,' she continued, in a loud secretive whisper. 'Just a matter of keeping an eye on things and reporting anything odd. There've been some *very* odd goings on in the park lately.'

'There' have indeed,' he replied, remembering the whack she'd given him with her walking stick only a few days ago. 'Would I be reporting to you or the police?' he asked, with a straight face. 'To the police, I'll give you a number.'

'I'll certainly think about it, Mrs Battle.'

'Excellent! Have you been in a fight?'

'No, no just a silly accident.'

As soon as she'd left, Derek came back into the shop laughing. 'So you're going to join the Old Bat network now, are you? This should be good for a laugh. You really are entertaining! Chased by dogs, the police, old ladies, and flying off bucking horses. Can't wait for the next instalment.'

'You were eaves-dropping again!' Timothy exclaimed accusingly.

'Sorry, couldn't help it, old boy,' replied Derek, giving his friend pat on the back.

Knowing there was no malice intended, he said, 'You're very cheerful today, Derek, what have *you* been up to?'

'I'm always cheerful, haven't you noticed?'

'But you're extra cheerful today. Come on, what's happened? Or should I say *who's* happened?'

Derek suddenly leapt up, and swung his tall, lean body over the counter. 'I've got a date tonight, Timmy old lad,' he said. Timothy looked at him, waiting for the rest of it. 'It's with someone you've met... and she doesn't have any wild animals or bucking horses. She even appears quite normal!'

Timothy pretended to think hard. 'I know who it is!' he exclaimed convincingly, 'You're dating Henri, the cat woman's chum. I thought you said she was normal?'

'Yup, and no cats are coming on *our* date!'

'You hope!' Timothy replied as he pushed his bike out of the shop. 'See you tomorrow, have fun with the cat... sorry no, I mean Henri!' Derek threw a book at him.

Later as Timothy was leaving for his routine walk with the dog, Lizzie turned up. 'Want to come for a walk with us?' he said, really pleased to see her.

'Love to... I need to tell you my news, 'she said, as they set off down the road. He related the general gossip about the shop, just as a small blue car came up from behind them, going very slowly, only a little bit faster than walking pace. They both turned. The L-

111

plates were obviously new and Mrs Battle, her flowery hat jammed well down on her head, was in the driving seat with Mrs Fell sitting beside her, they both smiled at him as they slowly drove past. 'Friends of yours?' asked Lizzie with a grin.

'I thought Mrs Battle was having *professional* lessons! Lord help us all if Mrs Fell is teaching her,' he replied.

'Perhaps she *is* having lessons, my friend Emily is a driving instructor and mentioned she had an elderly lady just starting.'

'Oh I hope so!' They linked arms as they walked in the park, Faith off the lead scampering about near by. 'Tell me your news,' he said, enjoying the moment.

' It's good for me but not so good for us I'm afraid,' she began, 'I've been transferred to another post and I have to take it, no choice I'm afraid, but it's not here it's at Sculborough, a hundred miles away. It's for about six or eight months. I hope we can keep in touch, Timothy?'

His light mood plummeted. 'Six or eight months?'

'Yes, I'm afraid I don't have any say in the matter; we will be able to see each other when I come back' she said.

'I see,' was all he could say for a moment. 'Good for you,' he added, hugging her shoulders, his mood sinking further.

'We'll keep in touch,' said Lizzie, trying to keep cheerful.

'That would be nice,' he said, realising the relationship he'd hoped for wasn't going to happen. Not this time. Faith came bounding up, tongue hanging out, tail wagging. Timothy clipped on his lead as they made their way back to the park gates in silence.

'Your neighbours never came back for him,' she said.

'Haven't seen or heard from them since the day they left. The house is still empty, too. But I don't mind, he's a good dog.'

As they approached his house, the blue car slowly went over the cross roads in front of them with both women sitting very upright; Mrs Battle clutching the steering wheel, deep concentration etched on her face.

' I'll see you before I go,' said Lizzie.

'I hope so,' he said, giving her a hug. He kissed her on the cheek and they said their goodbyes. There was a sort of crunching sound, and revving coming from the next road, which somehow lightened the moment.

'Mrs Battle having trouble with her three-point-turns I think,' giggled Lizzie.

Inside, the smell of Mother's cooking made his mouth water. 'Had a good day?' he called.

Her head poked out of the kitchen door, 'Why yes, I've been to see Aunt Maude; she's nearly ready to go home. And the inspector called to see you again.'

'Oh really,' he said, wondering why Lizzie hadn't mentioned it. 'She didn't say what about, did she?'

'No, just said she had a few little things to clear up and you might like to help her,' said Mother. 'Oh and Mrs Fell is giving Mrs Battle a few driving tips before her lessons start,' she went on. Timothy groaned and went upstairs to soak his aching body in the bath.

The following day he decided to take his lunch break down by the river, calling at a deli on the way. He needed to get his head around Lizzie leaving, he was going to miss her. He sat on one of the benches by the river, a popular place for people to take their lunch, usually surrounded by ducks. It was the large duck and swan population that had put him off bringing Faith for a walk here. One or two people went past on roller blades; one man had a large black and white dog running alongside. A chocolate Labrador galloped passed, with a young woman on roller blades holding tight to its lead as they shot by, scattering quacking ducks in all directions. The dog wasn't taking any notice of the birds or of his owner's instructions, and seemed to be gathering speed. Timothy could see that the end of the path crossed the road by means of a bridge and wondered if they would be able to stop in time. He was too far away to help, but began to walk in that direction feeling disaster was imminent. He watched in horror as the girl, her dog and a flock of frantic ducks shot across the road. There was squealing of brakes, and as he got nearer he could see one of the stationary cars was Mrs Battle's. Mrs Fell was still in the passenger seat. He couldn't hear what was being said, but her mouth was working furiously; her arms were waving up and down but Mrs battle appeared to be frozen. Her hat was squashed down even further on her head than usual; with hands glued to the steering wheel she stared at the road in front. Eventually with other drivers impatiently sounding their horns, the little car lurched slowly on its way.

Timothy began to make his way back to the shop. A huge swan suddenly flew up from the riverbank hissing and flapping its wings angrily. 'Oh shut up, it's not my fault!' he shouted at the swan. Getting no other reaction from the human, the swan fluffed up its feathers and waddled off.

Derek had just finished serving a customer. 'You look a bit glum today,' he said, as Timothy came in. Timothy explained about Lizzie but Derek was unsympathetic. 'You'll have to get back in the saddle mate; the best way to take your mind off one woman, is to go out with another.' Timothy wasn't so sure. 'So how did the date with Henri go?' he asked.

'Looking good so far, no disasters, cats, goats or wild dogs!' Derek was in a jovial mood and gave him a friendly slap on the back.

'Yet!' said Timothy. It *had* gone through his mind to contact the agency again, and later that day he arranged to collect two more profiles. Jane was a bit short with him on the phone but he hardly noticed.

Jane was at her desk and hardly looked up as he entered. 'Hello Jane, do you have the profiles for me?' he asked politely.

She picked up an envelope and practically threw it at him without saying a word. He could hear Daphne Mortesque in the other room and it sounded like she was ending a telephone call, as the phone in the reception pinged. 'Thank you Jane,' he said, and left, thankful he didn't have to have a conversation with the Tigress or cope with Jane's strange behaviour.

After supper he opened the envelope and read through the new profiles. The first one he could meet up with at the weekend was *Melanie, 30's, divorced. 4 children, dark blond, medium build, seeks kind man as friend.* He wondered about the four children, and wasn't over-keen. But if she *was* just looking for a friend it might be okay, he would give her a call.

16
The fun fair!

Timothy walked into the fairground and aimed for the old bandstand where he knew Melanie would be waiting. An ideal way to meet her and the children, she had said. He thought it would be good to keep his mind off Lizzie, and who knows, it could be fun too. It was the first time he'd walked to the park without Faith and he missed the dog's company.

Walking towards the bandstand he noticed a large, rounded woman with children beside her. It must be Melanie. As he got nearer he realised she was of much larger proportions than described and certainly looked older; he was hoping that it wasn't her, when she noticed him. She seemed to be a friendly woman with a ready smile, a hearty laugh, and a welcoming manner. She began waving and smiling as he approached. When he told her she had guessed right, she gave him a huge bear hug! He was introduced to all four children, two girls and two boys. They all had happy smiling faces and they also hugged him as they were introduced, surprising him and making him feel very comfortable in their company.

'Have you had any ice cream, yet?' he asked.

'I like ice cream,' said Meg, the youngest.

'I think we all like ice cream, don't we?' said Melanie, beaming at Timothy.

'Right then, lets find the ice cream van,' he said, leading the way, determined to make the best of the day.

The park was full. There were different rides and stalls, people with balloons and teddies. Candy floss and

116

whirly windmills. The sound of music was everywhere and the happy shrieks of children and adults alike came from some of the bigger, scarier rides. He bought huge ice creams for them all. The children were so excited, and asked to go on the different rides. He quickly realised this was going to be an expensive outing, but he hated to refuse as they looked so happy. It was decided they would start with the scary ghost train, including little Meg who was only five years old. They piled onto the seats, as Meg sat on his lap he noticed her pale blonde hair smelled of sweets. The other children sat beside him, Meg and Howard clutching funny- face balloons. They were all wearing pirate hats, including Timothy and Melanie.

Timothy looked out at the crowd to see Mrs Brown and Mrs Fell in animated conversation with Anthony. As the train went into the tunnel Mrs Brown waved her umbrella at him.

Meg and Howard hung on to Timothy throughout the ride, their sticky faces buried in his jacket. After lots of squeals and shrieks at the scary ghosts and monsters, they went on to look at a few other rides. So far he'd managed to steer them away from the bigger more expensive ones. 'Please Timothy, just one ride on the Roller. Kids under 16 have to have an adult with them, and Mum won't go! Please!' begged Henry, the eldest at thirteen. Timothy looked over at the roller coaster and moaned to himself.

Melanies' large matronly bosom was bouncing up and down with her hearty laughter. 'Oh go on Timothy, Henry will love it,' she said.

'I'm not sure I will,' he said, looking for an excuse. Melanie and her bouncy bosom, laughed even more and all the children began to join in. 'Come on Timothy. Please. Go on.'

Feeling like he had stepped into a bad dream, he agreed to just one ride on the roller coaster with Henry, who was ecstatic!

Then he noticed Mrs Brown again, who began cheering, and waving her umbrella as he and Henry got into a car of the waiting roller coaster. He was amazed at how they had managed to erect such a monster in such a short space of time.

The car began to move, and climbed to the top of the first roll. Both Timothy and Henry were tightly strapped in and just as they were nearing the top he suddenly noticed that Meg had slipped away from Melanie and was hiding in the car in front of them. Her little face beamed a smile over the back of the seat… she wasn't strapped in. He and Henry began to shout instructions at her. 'Sit down Meg,' he shouted. 'Hold tight to the bar in front,' ordered Henry, who had gone white and was about to stand up before Timothy's hand pushed him back down into the seat. There was no way of getting to Meg from where they were all they could do was to keep shouting to her to hold tight. The other person in the same car appeared not to notice the little girl beside them. The train began its decent, slowly at first, and then whoosh, it picked up speed. Little Meg was still smiling and waving to them, and they were both frantically shouting at her. Timothy hardly noticed his stomach lurching; he was working out how he could climb over the front of his car to reach her. As they all whooshed around a sharp bend, little Meg was thrown helplessly out of the car. Timothy watched in horror as her small body fell to the ground.

When he opened his eyes, Mother was calling, 'Bacon this morning?' *He was at home in bed*!

'Thank you, yes,' he croaked, still thinking about the dream. Maybe he wouldn't arrange to meet Melanie with her children after all.

Mother produced a good old-fashioned breakfast of bacon, sausage and eggs. 'Who's Meg?' she asked. 'I don't know,' he replied honestly.

'You were shouting her name in your sleep.'

'Really? Just a dream I expect,' he answered, not wanting an in-depth discussion at this time of the morning.

There was plenty of time before setting off for work so he took Faith to the park and was relieved to see that the funfair wasn't there at all, and everything was as normal.

On the way back a car pulled up beside him, and a female voice said, 'Excuse me, I wonder if you can help me?' Faith pushed his big head through the car window, the woman stroked his ears while Timothy gave her directions to Mrs Battle's house. 'I hope you don't think I'm rude but are you Timothy?' she asked.

'Yes, do I know you?'

'Sort of. I'm a friend of Lizzie's. She told me about your dog, and you don't see many Irish Wolfhounds about.'

'And you must be Emily, the driving instructor. Yes, Lizzie has mentioned you. I couldn't do your job,' he said, remembering his ride with Mrs fell.

'Oh, it's alright really, I quite enjoy it most of the time,' she laughed, 'thanks for your help, see you around.' He said a silent prayer for her as she drove off toward Mrs Battle's house. Inspector Davis' car was outside when he arrived home. *Now what?*

'Hello Timothy, I've good news for you,' smiled the inspector.

'Oh really?' he said.

'We've found the culprits who stole the taxi and thanks to your friend Mrs Battle, we have apprehended them. I told you that Fiona died of natural causes. It was in on her way home in the taxi, and they stole the taxi with her body inside!'

'Poor Fiona.'

'Thanks for all your help, Timothy. I thought you might like to know the outcome. The dog's still here then? Looks like he may be here to stay. Funny name for a male dog, Faith, it's usually a female name,' the inspector commented, while rubbing the dog's head. Faith gave the inspector a shove in her buttocks with his nose by way of comment, as she was leaving.

'*That wasn't me it was the dog!* Faith sit!' he exclaimed, embarrassed.

'Oh, I know that Timothy! Good bye for now,' she said, defending herself from Faith's attentions. 'Bye!' he waved

as she drove off. He welcomed the feeling of relief that swept over him.

'Well dear! Fancy that poor girl being dead in a taxi!' exclaimed Mother, who'd been eaves dropping.

'Yes, awful,' he said, leaving hurriedly for work.

It was a pleasant day and he took the pretty route to work, which was a bit longer but avoided the traffic. It took him via the old part of town where the houses were larger and the tree-lined roads wider. He wound his way past the botanical gardens and on towards the lake. As he rounded a corner there was a small traffic jam. Cursing, he cycled up alongside the cars to see what the hold up was. There was a huge truck with what looked like a crane and a winch on the back, and another truck with a dinghy on board, plus a fire engine and several police cars. One of the trucks had 'Police Boat Squad' written on the side.

As Timothy got closer he could see a blue car in the lake, or at least he could see the top of a small blue car with two ladies sitting on the roof.   Mrs Battle and Emily were waiting to be rescued, perched on top of the car, facing in opposite directions. Emily's long hair hung in wet rat's tails and she sat cross-legged, hugging a clipboard. Mrs Battle was sitting with her arms folded, looking very soggy and cross. Mrs Fell's driving tips hadn't been of much help, he mused, and watched as the police set off across the lake in a small inflatable boat.   Emily hopped neatly off the car into the boat but Mrs Battle had to have help from two policemen, with one of them getting a whack for his trouble.   As the boat came to a stop near the bank, Timothy put his head down and cycled off to work.

On entering the shop he saw the tall figure of a man moving around the piles of books and shelves. Derek looked up as he came in and said in a hushed voice. 'He's here again.'

'Oh you mean Dr Athed. Yes, I noticed as I came in. Anyone else in at the moment?'

'Just one or two browsers. Anything interesting happen to you?' said Derek, with anticipation. Timothy brought him up to date on the latest events.

Derek asked, 'So, will you meet any of these new ladies on the list?'

'I might,'

'Emily sounds nice, you could ask her out,' said Derek, trying to cheer his friend up.

'She's friends with Lizzie; I'm not sure I want to do that. Definitely won't meet Melanie, but might see if I can meet Gina. She lives on a farm out of town.'

'Uh oh, *that* sounds a bit dangerous! I'll look forward to hearing about that.'

'I'm not going out with these women just for your entertainment,' said Timothy, giving Derek a friendly punch in the ribs.

'Oi, steady on, only having a joke, mate,' laughed Derek, dodging away.

'Errr hum,' said a deep, male voice at the counter.

'Good morning, Doctor Athed,' said Timothy, ' I trust you found what you needed?'

'Yes thank you,' replied the doctor, in a bland, serious voice. Timothy was always interested in the books people chose; Doctor Athed had the following titles: *The Modern Demonic, Hidden Toxins* and *The 'Friendly' Poisons.*

'Thank you, good day' he said, as the doctor left the shop: he got no response.

'He's a weird one!' said Derek.

'Yeah! We get all sorts in here.'

The rest of the day was uneventful, apart from the delivery of books. The deliveryman, Joe, was an older chap; always pleasant but chatted to himself all the time. You could never be sure if he was talking to you or not. 'We've unloaded the boxes into the usual place, haven't we? Yes, so we'll be off now then. See you soon, come on then.' he said, before getting back into his van and driving off, alone.

His regular walks in the park made Timothy feel relaxed and at peace with the world. Walking passed the 'creepy' bungalow however, he suddenly switched to neighbourhood watch alert: there was someone moving around inside. Sunlight on the window made it difficult to see much, but the person inside seemed to be wearing some kind of peculiar headgear.

As he and Faith entered the park, a young looking pointer came bounding over with no sign of its owner. The two dogs touched noses and after exchanging

122

woofs they raced off together to have fun. Timothy let the dogs play for a while and then helped the lady who owned the pointer catch her dog, and watched as the pointer pulled her out of the park. On the way back he couldn't help having another look at the bungalow. There was a dark green saloon car outside that he hadn't seen before. He must remember to walk this way again on refuse collection day, to see if the same huge refuse bags are put out again.

His thoughts kept drifting to Lizzie. He hadn't known her for very long, but knowing their chance meetings wouldn't happen anymore made him feel sad.

17
Gina and the chickens.

On his next day off Timothy had arranged to visit Gina at Plufyn Farm. This meant a seven mile cycle ride, that would probably take him just thirty minutes. Mother was home and he wanted to leave without too many questions. Pulling his waterproof cape on over his clothes, he called out a quick 'good bye.'

'Do you need water proofs today?' she fussed.

'It's only light-weight, and you never know, there could be showers,' he answered, trying to head her off.

'I wish you'd get another car, it would save you all this nonsense,' she said, pointedly. Before he got to the end of the path the barrage of questioning began. 'Aren't they your good trousers? You've just had them cleaned, haven't you?'

'Yes Mother, see you later.'

After winding his way through the traffic in the main street he was soon out in the countryside and enjoyed the ride. Two miles out of town, a deer sprang across the road in front of him before melting into the woods; always a pleasure to see. He could hear woodpeckers, buzzards and many smaller birds as he cycled along the lanes. Unsure of which turning to take he stopped by a little church just as the vicar was getting out of her car. He asked her for directions and she was happy to assist.

' Do you know Prickets wood?'

'No.'

'Oh well, it's just along there, then turn left by the 'turn pike'. Do you know where I mean?' she asked again.

'Not really.'

'Oh, I see, well just keep on up there, you'll soon find it. Dead badger on the roadside there this morning! The Lord has blessed us with a nice day today; enjoy your ride,' said the vicar in a jovial manner. Disappearing through the church gate she skipped along the path singing 'All things bright and beautiful, the Lord God made them all'.

Timothy was no wiser but carried on along the lane anyway. The sound of the vicar's exuberant singing fading as he followed the meandering lane past another wood, down a couple of one-track lanes, until he found a dead badger and the crooked sign for Plufyn Farm. He chose to walk along the dark and gloomy stone track with high hedges on both sides, and so managing to avoid the potholes and ridges.

Eventually he came to a pair of large wooden gates with a smaller one to the right. He propped his bike against the hedge and went through the smaller gate, which groaned loudly when he pushed it open. Closing the gate behind him, he looked across the moss-covered farmyard to a ramshackle old farmhouse with a blackened thatched roof. The old black well pump in the yard looked like it was still in regular use the stone trough underneath being full of clean water. Everything else was over-grown with elder, hawthorn and abundant brambles; a sweet scent wafted on the breeze from the honeysuckle growing in an old apple tree near the house.

With chickens clucking in the background, a small dog raced around the corner and barked furiously at him before retreating.

When he knocked on the front door the sound was hollow and the door looked unused. Walking around the outside of the old house calling 'hello' as he went, he found the other side was much lighter and there was a caravan parked nearby. The small paddocks that stretched out before him were full of chicken runs, with the chickens clucking contentedly as they pecked and scratched around in the sunshine. He was about to go to the back door of the house when the little dog came racing out from under the caravan barking at him. The caravan door opened and a woman with short blonde hair, rather prominent teeth and with round spectacles perched on the end of her nose, came out. She was dressed in an ankle length, floral skirt with a pretty over shirt of the same design.

'Hello, I'm looking for Gina,' he ventured.

'That's me,' she replied with a huge smile, shaking him firmly and vigorously by the hand.

'You must be of the agency? Would you like a glass of home-made lemonade?'

She disappeared inside the caravan for a few minutes before coming out with a tray. They sat at a wooden picnic table under an old pear tree enjoying her delicious home-made lemonade and ginger cake.

Gina explained that the house and land would be hers one day. 'I sleep over in the house but mainly live in the caravan with my mother. I'll show you the house if you like, it's very old.' She stood up and waited for him to follow.

'Okay then,' he answered, not really sure if he needed to see the house. *It may be interesting* he thought, following her to the back door.

'A good part of the house has been condemned, and we aren't supposed to be using it at all but we do,' she explained, as she heaved the old wooden door open. The house was indeed very old with wooden beams in the ceiling and walls, and a wooden staircase. No carpets, just stone floors with a circular worn rug in the hall; the curtains looked dusty and unused. He reflected that they would probably fall down if you tried to draw them. Lots of dust and cobwebs everywhere with the pungent smell of damp and mildew.

'This is the kitchen whichwe still use quite a lot,' said Gina, walking ahead. They stepped down onto stone tiles; it felt bitterly cold, like walking into a fridge. The grimy, white-washed walls hadn't had a wipe over for many a year and the stone sink with two ancient looking taps didn't look much better. There was an old boiler on the wall and a black range at the far end of the kitchen; they both of which looked redundant. A big wooden table stood in the centre with just a single chair, both looked rather sad he thought. He tried to imagine what it had been like when it was a working family farm.

'We still use this as it's so cool in here in the summer,' she said, waiting for his reaction.

'Doesn't it freeze up in the winter?'

'Oh yes, but we have all the water turned off in the winter, there's no heating.'

'Do you sleep in the house during winter too?'

'There's a fireplace in my bedroom, it's quite snug when the fire's lit. Come on, I'll show you the rest,' she said, leading the way back across the hall. The sitting room door was also made of heavy, dark wood and creaked loudly when she opened it. 'There's a cellar under here and this floor isn't very good, it's really damp so we don't use it. An aunt of mine had her old piano fall through the floor into the cellar once.' In the centre of the wooden floor there was a single, worn rug,. A couple of ancient chairs, and a wooden bureau, all covered in a thick layer of dust, were arranged around the outside of the room. The ruby red curtains were festooned in cobwebs.

'Come and look upstairs.'

'Well, I'm not sure I should,' began Timothy, suddenly wary.

'Oh come on, I have a bed-sitting room up there, it's quite safe,' she replied, as she started up the stairs. It wasn't just the house he was worried about, but reluctantly he followed her anyway. The stairs groaned under their combined weight, and nearly every floorboard along the dark landing creaked. Gina opened a door and walked in.

'Come and see my little home,' she said.

He walked in and couldn't believe his eyes. The room was light and recently decorated. There was a large bay window with clean, pretty curtains, and the pale carpet was thick and new. There was space for the double bed, chairs by the fireside and what looked like a built-in wardrobe along one wall. The whole room was totally different to the rest of the house. There was still the smell of damp in the air; he surmised that Gina had become used to it.

'Gosh, this is very nice,' he said, staying near the door, earlier experiences telling him that this was when things started to go wrong.

'I just wanted you to see the potential. I mean the whole house could look like this with some work.'

And a lot of money, thought Timothy. 'Well, thank you for showing me the house,' he said, walking out of the door. 'It's been interesting.'

Back in the garden Gina produced another jug of lemonade. They chatted for a while, then she asked if he would like to see the chickens.

'I don't mind.' He wondered what else there was to see as the chickens were all out in the wired- off paddocks. They walked along a path between the individual pens. 'Mum keeps them all very clean. The man from the council said he had never seen such well-kept birds.'

128

Timothy had to admit it was all very tidy. 'These are some of Mum's favourites in here,' she opened the wired paddock gate. 'Come in, I'll show you.'

He went in, knowing nothing about chickens and unable to tell one from the other. Gina explained they all had names. 'This one here is Mrs Eggletina,' she said, pointing at one of the birds. 'This is where they roost at night and lay their eggs in the morning,' Gina went on proudly. The inside was very tidy, the floor covered in a layer of straw and wood shavings. The nest boxes each had their own pile of straw for the chickens to lay their eggs on. She picked up several eggs and offered them to him. 'You can take these home with you if you like.'

'I'd love too,' he replied. As they walked out of the pen closing the wire gate a chicken made a dash for it and escaped, squawking triumphantly.

'Oh no! That's Mrs Eggfeather, she can be really naughty,' wailed Gina.

Timothy was still trying to get his head round anyone having this kind of relationship with chickens but seeing her despair said, 'I'll catch her!' running off after the escapee.

'Oh no!' he heard Gina moan behind him. He made an unsuccessful dive for the chicken, which simply flew just out of reach clucking and squawking.

'Never mind, it'll be alright,' he called, trying to sound confident. He made another dive as the chicken flew under an old wooden cart by some bushes; clucking its victory the hen walked out at the other side. To add to the mayhem the dog ran out from its hiding place under the caravan, yapping enthusiastically, ready to join in 'hunt-the- chicken.' Timothy went down on his haunches and crept carefully around the cart, stalking the chicken; the yapping of the dog meant he didn't hear the creaking of the gate. He lunged at the wayward chicken, grabbing it by the tail feathers which came away in his hand, he lunged again and managed to grab hold of the squawking bird, the dog was jumping wildly into the air still yapping. As he got to his feet the chicken pecked at his hands. 'Ouch,' he yelled and let go!! The bird flew off again, clucking and strutting - ever more triumphant. The excited dog ran after it and received a sharp peck on the nose from the disgruntled chicken, causing it to yelp and dash back under the caravan. How Timothy wanted to murder that chicken!

He began to move towards it, when an unfamiliar female voice stopped him in his tracks. 'Hey, you!'

He looked up to be confronted by a short older woman with an unruly mop of grey hair.

'Mum this is a friend,' Gina said, walking towards her, still holding the eggs.

'Eggfeather out again I see. Is that *your* bike?' the woman barked at Timothy. Not waiting for an answer she carried on, 'You townies know nothing. And you should know better my girl,' she fired at Gina, before walking into a small shed. Gina grinned behind her back and, shrugging her shoulders, handed him the eggs. 'She's very fond of her chickens,' she said.

'So it seems.' He sheepishly handed her the tail feathers off the chicken.

The woman came out of the shed carrying a small metal bucket with a little corn in it. She shook the bucket and started calling: '*cluck cluck cluck*,' in a high voice as she walked back toward the paddocks. Eggfeather put her head on one side, and clucking set off, half running half flying after her. The woman opened the wire gate, walked inside and began to throw corn into the paddock, the chicken ran in behind her and she closed the gate. Walking back she thrust the bucket at Gina. 'Put this away,' she said, giving Timothy another dark look before going into the caravan and slamming the door.

'Thanks for the cake and lemonade. Oh, and the eggs, I think I'll be off now.'

Gina just shrugged. 'Okay,' she said, walking toward the gates with him. Outside was an old-fashioned van that hadn't been there when he arrived. 'Is this your mother's?' he asked, finding safe pockets in his clothes to store the eggs for the journey home.

'Yes, the neighbours have been campaigning to have her banned from driving, apparently she's a dangerous driver.'

He wasn't surprised. 'Well, thanks, it's been interesting,' he said, pulling his cycling cape on again.

As he began pushing his bike back along the track, she called after him. 'Thanks for coming over. Perhaps you'd like to visit again sometime.'

'Maybe,' he replied, feeling guilty again!

His mind kept drifting back to Lizzie who he suddenly missed even more. As he came to the edge of town he heard the roar of a large engine behind him; keeping well into the side of the road, trying to avoid the pot-holes, he allowed the vehicle to pass. The driver obviously didn't take much notice of the back end of the van, as it scraped along Timothy's cape making him wobble dangerously. Putting his foot on the pavement to prevent himself from falling over, he tried to get off his bike but the cape had become attached to the saddle. Hopping sideways on one leg he crashed into a scruffy and unshaven man.

' Steady mate, you alright?' Large hands grabbed hold of him and his bike, pushing them both upright. A well-developed, tattooed arm was holding the handlebars; he let go as Timothy steadied himself.

'Thank you.'

'That's alright mate, I do a bit of cycling myself,' replied the man, walking away. Timothy wondered if they made bikes big enough.

As he cycled off again he was aware of the unpleasant sensation of raw egg oozing down the inside of his trousers.

Mrs Brown was standing at the pedestrian crossing as the lights changed. He stopped and waited. 'Hello Timothy, are you well?' she asked, gazing at the raw egg seeping over the side of his shoe onto the road.

The lights changed, and he cycled off before she could comment further.

He opened his front door, and made a dash for the kitchen and put the remaining eggs in a bowl before Faith could intercept. The dog's nose drew attention to the raw egg over Timothy's shoe and he happily began to lick up the mess. 'It's just an egg, it broke in my pocket. The others are in the bowl over there,' he said to Mother, as she followed the dog into the kitchen.

'Lovely fresh eggs, where did you get them?'

'From a friend,' he said, making his escape upstairs before the inevitable twenty questions.

He wondered if this dating business was ever going to work. All he *really* wanted was for Lizzie to come back, but would she want to come back to him? Hedging his bets, he should contacted Two to Tango again.

A few days later Jane was giving him customary flirty looks. 'Hello Jane, how are you?' he asked politely.

'Take a seat,' she ordered, slamming a pile files on the desk.

'He shrugged and about to enquire further when the inner office door opened and Daphne Mortesque strode into reception, wearing a red pencil skirt with matching red high heels and a white blouse, open at the top as usual. He speculated on how her bosom managed to be so pushed up that you could always see such mountains of cleavage. Her heavy scent nearly sent him running for the door, but he stood his ground and waited.

'Timmy dear ! Just the man I want!' she said, in her deep, husky voice. He was rooted to the spot. Daphne placed several files on the reception desk saying, 'Thank you Jane. ' Jane didn't speak as she picked them up.

'Come with me Timmy dear,' whispered Daphne, making him feel quite uncomfortable, as she made full body contact with him going through the door to her office.

He moved quickly to the chair by her desk and sat down before any evidence of his discomfort became obvious.

Daphne, sitting opposite, leaned forward, her bosom straining to escape. His stare was fixed on the fine gold chain with a small cross that seemed to be playing hide and seek in the folds of flesh.

Speaking in her husky whisper she asked, 'How have you been getting on Timmy, any success?'

He forced himself to look into her eyes, and clearing his throat replied, 'Not really.'

'You didn't meet Melanie did you?'

'No, I would rather not meet anyone with children... I was hoping for some of my own one day,' he said, hurriedly.

'Shame, well Timmy dear, I have another interesting lady here. In fact there are several, but this one I feel sure you will like. Jane tells me you ride horses?' She leaned forward again, the gold cross escaping and dangling free. She waited for his reply, pushing the files across the desk towards him.

He was taken aback by this comment, and not sure how to respond, said, ' I've *never* ridden a horse in my life.'

Daphne stared at him for a moment before saying, 'I'm not sure what you've said to Jane, Timmy but she seems upset with you. I thought it was good of her to mention she'd seen you riding a bronco.'

'Oh that wasn't a real horse!' he exclaimed.

'Really? Oh.well, this lady I have here, Naomi, has horses and she's very nice Timmy. I told her I thought you could ride, and she was really looking forward to meeting you.'

'I can't ride a horse, but I will meet her,' he said, hoping she didn't have too many. He suddenly visualised *himself riding through the countryside, perhaps even turning up at the bookshop on a horse, dressed as a highway-man, his faithful hound at his side.* He pushed the fantasy out of his mind, avoided looking at the gold cross, and smiled.

Daphne peered hard at him, taking a deep breath which seemed to expand her bosom, putting even more pressure on the top button of her blouse and hiding the cross completely; finally she said, 'I think there's more to you than you're telling, Timmy. Interesting, very interesting.'

He couldn't understand why people always thought this about him. He was just plain Timothy Parkes who worked in a bookshop, nothing special at all. Nevertheless feeling more in control he picked up the files she'd placed in front of him and stood up.

As usual, Daphne sat back in her chair, her sharp, hungry eyes looking him up and down.

'Thank you. I'll be in touch,' he said, leaving her office.

'Yes, soon Timmy,' crooned Daphne to his retreating back.

Jane gave him another flirty look as he walked through reception, and he thought he detected a slight smile and wondered if he would ever understand women.

Suddenly the door crashed open and a big man with long hair and a beard strode in. He reminded Timothy of a troll.

'Hello luv,' the man said to Jane, who looked like a mini-mouse by comparison. Timothy caught a glimpse of her surprised expression.

'Ooooh hello!' She replied, fluttering her eyelashes in a little-girl manner. Timothy wondered what Daphne Mortesque would make of him!

On his way back to work he noticed the local bus coming towards him, the usual faces all looking in his direction. He smiled and wondered how many would be a part of the 'old lady network'. At least this time he had no injuries or wrecked clothes for them to stare at.

Back in the shop all was quiet. Derek sidled up grinning as usual, 'Any more adventures with the ladies, Timothy?'

'Nothing too exciting,' he sighed, 'the girl was nice but the chickens and her mother would have made it very difficult.'

'Oh, do tell,' said the ever-curious Derek.

'Yes do tell, Timothy,' said a female voice from the back room.

'Oh, hello Henri.'

He was telling them what happened when the shop door opened and Mrs Battle came in. Derek and his new lady friend Henri, hurried off on the pretence of sorting some books, making quiet clucking noises at one another. Timothy ignored them. 'Good afternoon Mrs Battle.'

Mrs Battle gave the disappearing pair a dark look. 'Something wrong with them?' she demanded. Timothy spluttered. 'Something wrong with you too, Timothy?' she asked loudly.

'No. I'm just fine thank you, how can we help today?'

'I've brought the forms for you to sign with regard to the park patrol.'

He'd forgotten all about it. 'Ah yes... thank you... sorry I didn't call round... I've been quite busy.'

'Yes, yes, we're *all* busy Timothy.'

'How's the driving coming on, these days?' he asked, changing the subject.

'Not quite as straightforward as I thought, but I'll have the hang of it soon. Must be off, things to do. Toodle hoo,' she said, leaving the shop hurriedly. .

'That sent her off a bit quick.' said Derek, clucking again.

Timothy ignored him, *he was imagining riding round the park on a black horse with Faith trotting alongside, on park patrol.*

'I think Linda has found someone at last,' said Henri, leaning on the counter in a casual manner.

'Oh really, that's nice,' he replied, 'I hope he likes cats.'

'He seems to. He's doing an OU degree in ornithology,' chuckled Henri.

'Well that's an interesting combination!' he laughed, enjoying the joke.

After filling in the forms for the park patrol, he decided to drop them in at Mrs Battle's house that evening. As he was putting the envelope through the letterbox, the door swung open. '*Timothy!* Why didn't you knock? Now don't go telling me you did when you didn't!' she

136

exclaimed. 'People keep doing that it's really annoying. Now come in.'

'I'm just off to the park with Faith, he needs his walk,' he replied, hoping for a quick getaway.   'Is that Timothy?' said another voice.

'Yes, he's with his dog,' shouted Mrs Battle.

Mrs Fell came to the door and Faith lunged forward, pushing his nose firmly up her dress. 'Ooooh, get off!' she cried, sending her top set of teeth catapulting down the path.   The dog pounced after them, and so did Timothy, fearing the worst. Mrs Battle was barking instructions.

Mrs Fell had her hand over her mouth making muted moans, as he calmly extracted the false teeth from Faith's jaws and handed them back to her. She stared at her teeth covered in dirt and the dog's saliva and moaned louder.

'Give them to me! A good scrub with some kitchen bleaching cream will do the trick,' said Mrs Battle, 'don't you have any control over that dog, Timothy?' she shouted.

'Sometimes.'   Timothy and Faith made a quick exit, hoping Mrs Battle didn't poison her friend with bleach.

On his way back from the park, Emily the driving instructor drew up beside him in a new car. 'You've changed your car, since the swim in the lake, I see,' he said as Faith put his head through the open window and licked her face.

Pushing him away she laughed, 'Yes this one has, dual controls, makes me feel a lot safer.

'All in a days work for you,' he chuckled.

'The old car was written off,' she said wistfully.

' I see. How's Lizzie?' he asked, suddenly nervous.

'Lizzie is fine I think. Sounds like she's enjoying her new job.'

His heart sank. 'Oh good,' he lied, thinking, *that means she won't be coming back in a hurry.*

'I'm off home now,' said Emily, see you again Timothy.

Following the chance meeting with Emily he was feeling rather glum by the time he returned home and resolved to have a look at Naomi's file, and perhaps arrange to meet.

'You're a bit quiet this evening dear', Mother commented, as she was cooking their evening meal. 'You're not sickening for something, are you? Maude is getting better by the day; should be out of hospital soon,' she added, feeling her sons fore head with her hand.

'I'm fine,' he said, and told her all about the incident with Mrs Fell's teeth.

'A good scrub will do them no harm, they're never that clean, you know. *You* wouldn't have done any damage would you?' she said, kissing the dog on the nose and cuddling him.

Later on when Faith and Mother were settled on the sofa to watch TV, he went to his room to study Naomi's profile and make a call. He had been considering asking his mother to stay on a while longer as he couldn't leave the dog on its own all the time. It wouldn't be right. Maude didn't live that far away and she could visit easily. He decided to mention it to her later.

18
Naomi's story.

Naomi was born into a middle-class family that was 'on the up', as they say. Privately educated, she learned equestrian and other 'young ladies'' pursuits like lacrosse, tennis and music. Boarding school encouraged her independent, adventurous side. She became an accomplished horse-woman, competing regularly as a member of her local riding club, and sought- after partner at the local tennis and squash clubs. She also swam, and attended the gym regularly.

Needless to say, she was hoping to find a husband who also enjoyed some of these activities; as a club member she made a point of attending all the social activities they offered. The men she met were either married, had a partner, or were just not right for her. It seemed to Naomi that all the decent, free and single men had left the planet.

While having her horses shod she was used to chat to her farrier. An interesting chap, although quite a bit older than herself. He looked a bit rough, but was always interesting to talk to, and there was 'something' about him that she, strangely, found attractive. He took an interest in nature and the wildlife around him, and had a natural way with horses and other animals. As far as anyone knew he was single.

One dayNaomi decided to ask him in for lunch after he had finished shoeing the horses, and he had accepted the invitation. She'd prepared a simple meal of soup and bacon sandwiches, and when he came in from the stables, she directed him to the wash basin in the utility room.   There was a lot of loud sloshing of water, moaning, groaning, snorting and coughing, then more sloshing of water; he sounded like an old walrus. She handed him a large, fresh towel. He winked at her, took it and gave his whole head, neck, arms and hands a vigorous rubbing, before blowing his nose into the middle of it.

'Thanks love,' he said, handing her the towel, which she took gingerly with two fingers and dropped it straight into the washing machine.

'Sit down, the soup is ready,' she said.   Instead of sitting down he began walking around the kitchen examining everything. Looking out of the window he farted loudly, chuckled to himself and grinned at Naomi's horrified reaction. He finally sat down.

She had been embarrassed, cross and was certainly not used to such behaviour. Not sure how to react she plonked the bowl of soup on the table in front of him without saying anything. He kept grinning and winking at her, while loudly slurping and gulping his soup. He stuffed whole slices of bread into his mouth at once, before noisily slurping more soup, dribbling it down his chin. She handed him a paper napkin, which he took and blew his nose again, leaving the crumpled napkin on the table.

Having never encountered such appalling manners before, she was unsure what to do next. She removed the empty bowl, after he'd held it with both hands and slurped the last dregs, and slammed a plate full of bacon sandwiches down on the table.

She could hardly eat, his behaviour was making her nauseous; she had invited a nightmare to lunch and hoped he would eat his fill and leave soon. Surprisingly, there was still some level of attraction she couldn't understand, and it scared her. He had gone from an interesting, gentle soul to an unbelievably bad mannered ape. Sitting in the warm kitchen with him she realised he smelled like an ape too.

After eating his fill of sandwiches, he sat picking his teeth and spoke to her for the first time since entering the kitchen. ' Nice place.'

She looked at him for a long moment without speaking, then got up to make some coffee. He sat back and openly admired her behind in the tight, hugging jeans as she reached into a cupboard for the mugs. Patting his stomach he belched loudly and groaned with the pleasure of it. That was pretty much the last straw.

'Coffee is off!' she shouted, slamming the mugs down. 'I have never met anyone with such horrible manners, please leave now, I will bring your coffee down to the stables where you can slurp and dribble to your heart's content!'

He studied her for a moment and grinned as if sensing her hidden feelings. 'That will be just fine love,' he said, getting up from the table, 'I'll see you down at the stables.' Still grinning, he left the house.

Naomi breathed a sigh of relief as she leaned against the Aga. How could she feel so attracted to such a creature? The thought of him made her shiver, but at least he was out of the house. With shaking hands she picked up a horse magazine while waiting for the kettle to boil, in the personal section she saw an introduction agency called 'Two to Tango'. I'll ring them later, anything has to be better than this, she thought. The kettle boiled and she made coffee.

By the time she got down to the stables he was putting his equipment back into the van. She couldn't help admiring the strong, muscled arms as he lifted the mobile fire and heavy gas bottle. He turned, and winked when he saw her, and taking his mug of coffee he winked again.

'I'll put Soldier back in his stable,' she said, trying not to look him in the eye. She walked in front of him to untie the horse; suddenly his arms were around her, holding her close. She started to push him away, beating his rock solid muscles with her small fists. But the feel of his body close to hers awoke more animal passion than she knew she had; suddenly she found herself grabbing at him and pulling him closer, the strong scent of his sweaty body fuelling her desire. He pressed his mouth to hers, and she instinctively kissed him back.

A shrill voice interrupted the moment, waking her as if from a dream. 'Naomi! It's Mummy. Are you there darling?'

She pushed him away quickly. 'I'll call you when the horses need shoeing again. Thank you,' Not daring to look at him, she turned away and quickly lead Soldier to his stable before running to the house and the safety of her mother; brushing herself down she was deeply regretting what had just happened.

'Aye, I'll see you next time then, little darling,' the farrier chuckled quietly to himself.

'Hello darling, have you been rolling in the hay?' said her mother, picking some bits out of her daughter's hair.

'Oh don't be silly, Mother!' Naomi snapped.

Her mother watched as her daughter strode off; seeing the farrier's van leaving the drive she smiled to herself, remembering being Naomi's age once, and wondering what she had interrupted.

Naomi had rushed upstairs to take a long shower and have a complete change of clothes. Feeling clean again she greeted her mother in a more civil tone and they sat down to coffee and gossip. Later she called Two to Tango from her bedroom and made an appointment. The next man she met must surely have better manners!

Standing in the reception of Two to Tango, Naomi couldn't help wondering if she was doing the right thing - could they really find her someone nice and normal who could possibly ride a horse?

'Naomi, do come in,' said Daphne Mortesque, sounding bright and cheerful, 'Take a seat, dear.' She pointed to the chair in front of her desk. Naomi sat down and the chair made an odd rasping noise causing her to jump nervously. 'Now dear,' said Daphne, leaning across the desk, 'have you had many lovers?' She asked this in a conspiratorial whisper, smiling in anticipation. Completely thrown by the question Naomi nearly left the office, but looking directly back at Daphne, said, 'Actually that's none of your business.'

Daphne sat back in her chair, disappointed with the answer but still smiling she went on,

'Just trying to get the picture, dear. I think I have someone for you.' She got up and made her customary march across the room to her filing cabinet. She pulled out a file and closing the drawer with her usual swing of the hip she placed the file in front of her customer who opened it slowly.

'That's Alistair, nice man, he's a vet,' she said. Naomi's face lit up, a vet she thought would be ideal! 'Does he ride, do you know?'

'Not sure dear, I didn't ask. Come back if he doesn't suit and we'll find another one for you.' Naomi thought it was like buying a pair of shoes, '*if they're not right, bring them back*!' 'Thank you, is he contacting me or do I have to contact him?'

143

'If you would rather he contact you, dear, it can be arranged, no problem. I'll get Jane to call him. So there we are, you can expect a call from Alistair,' said Daphne with a somewhat fixed expression.

As a second thought when she was leaving the office, Naomi turned round and said, ' You didn't say how old he was.'

'Oh, a little older than you dear, but not ancient. I'm sure you'll get along.' It was like being dismissed by her head teacher at school. Oh well, nothing ventured nothing gained, she thought and went home to wait for a call from Alistair.

He rang that evening after supper, they chatted easily on the phone, and agreed to meet at a local pub. He suggested lunch and she agreed.

The next day she felt nervous and excited; and like before an important competition with the horses, she'd slept badly.

After mucking out the stables and exercising the horses she changed and prepared for the meeting with Alistair. Trying on various combinations of clothes, not too smart but smart enough; tidy but casual, not too casual. She settled for black slacks and a favourite black blazer with a dark cerise trim. Looking at herself in the mirror, she was still not one hundred percent sure about what she should be wearing. She sighed, *no it didn't feel right.* She changed the black trousers for best jeans and decided that would just have to do. After all, it was supposed to be a lunch date with a stranger, not an interview for a job!

They had described themselves to each other on the phone and so she had a pretty good idea what he might look like, he had been evasive regarding his age but confessed to having lots of silver hair. As she locked her car in the pub car park she noticed a tall, silver-haired man doing the same thing and wondered if this could be him. A part of her was so nervous she wanted to jump back into the car and drive away, but luckily the man turned and saw her. 'Are you Naomi?' he called.

She knew it had to be Alistair, although he wasn't anything like she had expected, but his face was warm and friendly, and she felt instantly more at ease.

'Yes! You must be Alistair?'

'That's me!' he said, with the biggest smile, 'we've found each other!' he flung his arms out wide as if meeting a friend after some epic journey. A little unsure, she giggled but kept her distance. 'Let's go and find some lunch,' he suggested, gently putting his arm around her shoulders. 'Lovely,' was all she could say, as she allowed him to guide her into the pub.

Alistair was quite a lot older than Naomi, in his mid fifties. He had a lot of unruly silver grey hair and looked like he'd been out in a gale, with mischievous blue eyes and a huge smile. A tall lean man, his trousers were a little short and he was wearing white socks. Not that there was anything wrong with white socks, but on Alistair this added to his eccentric and rather comical appearance.

She knew he wasn't her 'knight' but liked him just the same. They chatted easily, but both agreed it wasn't a budding romance. She learned that he liked horses, and that his ex-wife had kept several, but he was no rider himself. They pledged to remain good friends, and driving home she wondered if all the nice *young* men really had left the planet. Nevertheless she resolved to call Two to Tango again.

19
Oh no not horses!

Timothy arranged to go over and meet Naomi on his next afternoon off. He admitted that he couldn't ride but had thought of learning; she said she was looking forward to meeting him. She sounded nice and normal on the phone and he was looking forward to their date.

The afternoon came, and as he cycled through town he saw small red car stopping and starting and 'buck-jumping' along the road as Emily patiently tried to teach another customer to drive. The car pulled over and stopped abruptly. Emily must be a really brave woman; Timothy waved as he cycled past..

Once out of town he cycled through the peaceful countryside; this time he had a map marked with a pencil and was sure of the way. As he gazed across the fields he day- dreamed again that he was on a horse with Faith lolloping alongside. *This horse-riding thing might be okay*, he thought.

Eventually he came to large wrought-iron gates and followed a tree-lined drive before arriving at a newly renovated house and stable yard.

A young woman was in the yard grooming one of the horses; she looked up when she heard Timothy. ' Hello! Won't be a minute, I'll just put the nag back in his stable,' she called.

She was petite, with , dark hair, her small stature made the horse look huge in Timothy's eyes.

He parked his bike and removed his bicycle clips before walking into the yard. 'Lovely place you have here,' he said, as they shook hands. The strength of her grip surprised him.

'Fancy coming for a bit of a hack?' she asked.

'Well, I'd like to give it a try but I'll warn you, I can't ride.'

'Oh, you'll be alright, I'll put you on Soldier, he'll look after you. Come on, I'll get the tack,' she said, indicating that he should follow.

All the horses were looking over their stable doors and all seemed enormous. He was beginning to have serious doubts and hoped that Soldier was a smaller one.

'The girl I spoke to at the agency said she'd seen you ride a bronco, and you were an expert rider,' she said, giving him a sideways look.

'Oh no! That wasn't a *real* horse, just a silly machine and I fell off quickly enough. I've never ridden a horse in my life, honestly.'

'Oh well, don't worry you'll soon get the hang of it,' she said, handing him a saddle and bridle. Timothy looked at them as if she had handed him a bag of strangled chickens. He had no idea how or where to put them on a horse. He watched as she expertly tacked up the two horses, wondering how he was actually going to get on.

'Right, come on, up you get. Put your left foot in the stirrup, right hand on the front of the saddle and swing up,' she said, making it sound as easy as walking up the stairs.

He just about managed to put his foot in the stirrup, and with some effort grabbed the front of the saddle; he did a lot of hopping up and down on his right leg before launching himself up to the saddle and leaning half over.

'What now?' he gasped.

'Swing your right leg over, try not to kick Soldier while you're at it,' instructed Naomi crisply. He took a breath and gave his right leg a good swing over the back of the

147

horse… which resulted in him whizzing off and somehow ending up on his feet, on the ground, at the other side.

'You really *haven't* ridden before, have you?' giggled Naomi.

He was just thinking he might try a quick exit and forget the whole thing, when she said, 'Come on, try again,' grabbing him by the shoulder and pulling him over to the horse. He was again surprised by her strength.

'Left foot in the stirrup, one, two, three, up!' she shouted, giving him a smart smack on the buttocks as he struggled to get his leg over the horse without falling off. Finally he sat upright in the saddle and was aware of just how high up he was. Soldier's neck stretched out in front of him, and the two pointed ears flicking back and forth looked a long way away.

'Right, sit still and don't move, I'll be back in a tick,' she said, disappearing into the tack room. To his immense relief she was only a few seconds and reappeared with two Labradors and a riding hat. 'You better wear this,' she said, handing the hard hat to him. It was a little on the large side and came down to his eyebrows but he managed to do up the strap good and tight; he felt more like a space-man than an equestrian.

'You do look ridiculous but never mind, better than nothing!' she said, swinging easily into the saddle of her handsome bay horse; more lively than Soldier it began shaking its head and prancing on the spot. 'Ok, if you want to move forward squeeze the horse with both legs; if you want to stop or slow down pull gently on the reins; to go left pull left and right pull right,' she instructed. 'He understands the words, 'walk on,' 'steady' 'whoa lad'. Got it? Right, sit up straight, let your hips move to absorb the movement of the horse;

heels down, close your knees on the saddle and off we go!' she said, taking the lead with her prancing horse.

Luckily for Timothy, his mount knew what to do and simply moved off after them at a nice steady walk, while the two dogs raced on ahead. Timothy admired her skill and ease with the horse and wondered how long it would take to reach a similar standard. Probably longer than he had imagined, the bones in his rear grinding into the saddle might take some time to toughen up.

As they turned in to a small country lane with grass growing along the middle, Naomi's horse began to walk normally and they were able to ride side by side.

He told her of his dream, and she sounded quite interested, although she pointed out possible problems and pitfalls, like traffic and where he was going to keep a horse. She then began lecturing him on horses, types of horses, and their care, chatting away confidently. Horses were obviously her life but she didn't ask him one question about himself, or even his dog. He was learning a lot about Naomi though. A forthright lady who knew exactly what she wanted and was determined to get it. Somehow he didn't feel that he was going to figure in her plans, and while they were riding along, with Naomi chatting endlessly, his thoughts drifted off to Lizzie and her sweet smile. Perhaps he should consider moving out to one of the nearby villages, Faith would like a life in the country, and he wondered if Lizzie would too.

'Right Timothy, want to learn rising trot?' asked Naomi suddenly, interrupting his dream.

'Yes…fine,' he replied cautiously.

'Okay, shorten your reins a bit; hold on to the front of the saddle with one hand for now, that's right. Now when the horse trots you go up and down slightly, in time with the movement like this,' she demonstrated the up and down movement. 'Got that, good. Right TROT ON.'

Both horses responded to her command and began to trot along the road. This was quite different to walking, the horse seemed to be bouncing up and down completely out of sync with Timothy, who felt like his rear was coming down as the horse was coming up. He bounced uncomfortably along, hoping they would walk again soon.

A rabbit shot out of the hedge in front of the horses and both dogs went rushing after it, barking and yelping with excitement. The horses tossed their heads and Naomi's mount set off along the road at a good gallop, followed by Soldier. Timothy clinging to the saddle, was shouting 'Steady Soldier, steady! Steady lad!' Just about managing to hang on, it reminded him of the bucking bronco. This time however, he was scared. He knew he had to hold tight to the front of the saddle, and somehow haul on the reins with his other hand, it was a *long* way down!

'Sit up straight and hold tight, you'll be alright... they'll stop at the top of the lane,' shouted his companion, over her shoulder. He hoped it was a short lane and clung on as best he could. Soldier galloped steadily after Naomi, whose horse was now kicking its legs in the air and squealing as it galloped along. At least Soldier wasn't doing that! Absurdly he was thinking, *they should find better brakes for horses!*

To make matters worse a low-flying jet screamed overhead, making the horses gallop even faster. Timothy clung on with all his might.

The lead horse suddenly skidded over on its side, catapulting Naomi into the hedge. On its feet again, the frightened animal raced off, and a bit further on turned into a gateway; Soldier of course, followed.

Timothy caught a glimpse of Naomi sitting in the hedge as he went past, but he was too busy hanging on to speak. Soldier also turned into the field and came to a sudden halt by his stable mate, who was nervously eating grass.

He sat very still for a moment, getting his breath back, and hoped nothing else would happen to set the horses off again. As he felt himself calming down, he realised he was in fact okay (except for his aching legs). He decided to be brave and try to catch Naomi's mount, so he very gently squeezed Soldier with his heels, and the horse obligingly walked forward; using the reins he carefully steered alongside the other horse.

Patting Soldier on the neck he crooned, 'Now stand still, lad,' and then leaned very carefully towards the loose horse, and slowly reached for the reins which were hooked over the saddle. As his hand closed around the leather, he unhooked the reins and very slowly sat up again. As soon as the horse felt movement on the reins it threw up its head and looked around wildly. Soldier began to move too. 'Steady lads, steady,' said Timothy, trying to sound calm.

Once holding the reins of both horses, they slowly walked on. Naomi's horse, after tossing its head up and down, followed alongside.

A new challenge lay ahead in the form of a gate, and then heading back up the lane to find Naomi. At a slow walk he managed to get the horses through the gate and heading up the lane in the right direction. Quite an achievement, he thought.

A dishevelled Naomi, with bits of hedge sticking to her jumper and out of the straps of her riding hat, was walking toward them. Her clean jodhpurs covered in green stains from the grass.

Her smudged and dirty face was wearing a smile. 'Well done, Timothy, told you you'd get the hang of riding,' she said, in her usual clipped manner. 'They say every time you fall off it makes you a better rider, you know.'

Taking the reins of her horse she swung easily back into the saddle and they continued on their way at a steady walk. She was quiet for the rest of the ride, he noticed her face was a bit pale but she insisted she was okay.

Back at the stables Naomi dismounted, landing lightly on the ground. Timothy's legs ached and his rear hurt, not to mention his arms and shoulders. Getting off the horse wasn't so easy. He carefully leaned forward and after several attempts managed to swing his leg over Soldier's back and drop to the ground. His legs gave way and he fell backwards, nearly landing on one of the dogs, which yelped and ran off. 'You're supposed to land on your feet. Come on, get up,' she said, unsympathetically. He struggled to his feet; his legs were so stiff he could only just walk. He managed to lead Soldier very slowly back to his stable.

'I'll take it from here, ' Naomi said, pushing past him to remove the saddle and bridle. Timothy was surprised by her attitude.

'Well thanks lad,' he said, giving Soldier a rub on his head, 'thanks for looking after me.'

'Told you he would, didn't I?' she said crisply, closing the stable door and marching off to the tack room.

He decided she must be some sort of super woman to take a fall like that and be walking around apparently unharmed. He'd heard horsey ladies were a tough sort and could now see why. He leaned on the old pump in the centre of the yard for a moment, wondering how he was going to cycle home, he flexed his legs back and forth to try and loosen them up. Naomi was busy seeing to the horses and appeared unaware of his presence. When his legs had loosened up enough, he walked as normally as he could over to where she was hanging a net full of hay in one of the stables. 'Thanks for the ride,' he said.

After a moment she turned. 'That's alright, thanks for catching Firefly for me. That was quite brave for someone who obviously isn't used to horses. Give me a ring if you'd like to come riding again.' She held out her hand and this time he was ready for the strong grip.

'Thanks,' he replied, knowing there wouldn't be a next time.

She turned away and carried on with her stable duties; he was apparently dismissed.

He was glad to find Mother was at home, and that Faith greeted him a little less enthusiastically than usual.

'Heavens, Timothy, are you alright!' she exclaimed, watching her son move slowly toward the stairs. 'I'm just fine, Mother,' he replied, concentrating on getting his aching legs upstairs toward the bathroom. 'What have you been doing?' she demanded, standing at the bottom of the stairs watching. 'Horse riding,' he replied.

'I didn't know you could ride a horse.'

'*I can't,*' he said, closing the bathroom door. Once again he found himself lowering his sore, bruised body into a wonderful, hot bath for a good long soak.

153

20
Park patrol!

Later that evening there was a loud knock on the door. Timothy struggled to his feet and began making his way to open the front door. 'Should I go dear?' asked Mother, still sitting on the sofa.

'No I'll get it' he sighed, as Faith pushed him out of his way, determined to be there first.

Putting his hand through the dog's collar, he opened the door. There was Mrs Battle looking her usual stern self with a blue hat pulled down on her head, giving the startling appearance of a helmet. 'Are you busy this evening? We have a bit of a crisis.'

'What's the problem?' he asked, feigning interest.

'Can you do park patrol from ten o' clock this evening until one am? Only, there's a 'do' on in the hall and Mr Snitch can't make it tonight, so we won't have late cover.'

'Well actually…'

'Be a good idea to take that dog with you. Looks like it will be a fine night anyway, so you won't be out in the rain or anything. I'm sure a young, fit chap like you will cope with any problems,' she went on, deliberately ignoring any possible protest.

He sighed; she wasn't going to hear the word 'no'. He tried again. 'Well actually, I'm not…' was as far as he got.

'That's marvellous,' she went on, 'could do with a few more like you,' she hesitated, 'and that!' She pointed at Faith, who was watching her every move.

'Do I have to report to anyone?' he asked, wearily, just wishing the dreadful woman would go away.

'Here's the number to call, if there are any problems. The police know about our little neighbourhood park patrol and promise to be there if they're needed.' She turned abruptly and walked off down the path, leaving Timothy and Faith gazing after her.

'Was that Mrs Battle? What did she want at *this* time?'

'Park patrol, tonight!' he moaned, limping back into the sitting room, using Faith as a support.

'Didn't you tell her you're not well, dear?'

'She didn't want to hear that bit,' he sighed. It went through his mind that he could just wrap up warm and sit in the band stand all evening with Faith, and watch from there. 'Are there still some painkillers in the medicine cabinet?'

'Yes dear, I got you some more, you do seem to be using quite a few of them these days,' said Mother, without taking her eyes off the television.

Timothy took a couple of painkillers and started doing a few limbering up exercises in order to get his body working again. Hopefully he would be able to walk to the park without limping too much. The dog was surprised to be going for another walk and rushed up with his usual enthusiasm. 'Okay lad, were off on park patrol. See you in the morning, Mother.'

The painkillers and exercises had helped a little, it got easier the further he went. By the time they reached the park he was walking normally. He kept Faith on his lead for the first circuit of the park to check if anyone was about. Then they headed for the old bandstand, since he knew he would be able to see almost the entire park from there, except for a few wooded areas. He made himself comfortable, and listened to people coming and going from pubs and the hall nearby, while he watched the park entrance. Faith lay beside him keeping watch too, his ears up, and alert. After a little

155

while Timothy began to feel cold and thought they should go for another walk around.

As he was doing some stretching exercises to warm up, a woman's voice spoke out of the dark. 'Doing Tai Chi ?' asked the voice..

Luckily Faith was tied to a rail. 'Oh... no, just stretching,' he replied to the voice. The dog was now standing and gave a low growl.

'I mean you no harm,' said the voice.

'*Who are you*?' he was a little unnerved at not being able to see to whom the voice belonged.

'I'm Lilly, only Lilly,' said the voice sweetly, 'I really like your dog.'

'What are you doing alone in the park at this time?' he demanded, as Faith was now growling more fiercely and straining at his lead.

'Who said I'm alone?' replied the voice, a young woman now slowly coming into view.

Faith's hackles were up and he looked quite different, not his usual loveable friend. Timothy untied Faith's lead from the rail, and holding it firmly in his hand walked as normally as he could down the wooden steps and onto the grass. Just as he was about to ask where her friends were, a young male voice spoke, 'She's with us, mate.'

'Yeah,' said another voice out of the dark.

He began to feel for his mobile in his pocket: *This didn't feel right.* Faith was growling loudly. 'I thought you said the dog was alright?' said yet another male voice.

'He'll be alright, won't you, mate,' said a youth, walking out of the darkness toward them. Faith showed his teeth and growled even more loudly.

Holding tightly on to the lead, Timothy prayed he didn't have to run.   Luckily he'd been practising dialling the number with one hand, without looking.

'He's got something in his pocket,' said one of them. Another moved closer, only to jump back again as Faith lunged toward him, snarling.

Timothy managed to hang on to the dog's lead and stay upright; aware they were being surrounded, he was so glad he had Faith by his side.   Suddenly one of the youths came running out of the darkness straight toward them, he was waving a thick branch and yelling like a banshee. Faith lunged forward again, this time pulling Timothy clean off his feet. The youths began to cheer and somewhere in the background he could hear a sweet female voice chanting some strange refrain.

Realising he'd lost control Timothy was scared and decided yelling back was his only defence. Where was his back-up? Hand still wrapped around Faith's lead, he held on as the dog lunged and growled furiously, while pulling him along the ground towards the attackers.

With a quick flick of his head, Faith slipped his collar and ran at their assailants. Timothy was just getting to his feet as one of the gang sprang at him. They both fell; he was doing his best to defend himself, calling the dog at the same time, '*Faith, Faith*!'

The youth on top of him laughed. 'Have faith in this!' he said, and punched Timothy hard on the side of his head.

When Timothy next opened his eyes the youth had vanished and strong hands were helping him to his feet. 'Alright mate?' asked a vaguely familiar voice.

 'Where's my dog?' he spluttered, while nursing his bruised face.

157

The youth who had attacked him was lying on the ground, groaning.

Timothy recognised his rescuer as the man he had bumped into on the way back from visiting Gina.

The man laughed, 'Your dog's a star, he's sorted this lot out. Look, he's still running after them over there,' he pointing to where Faith was making his way at speed towards an area of bushes on the other side of the park.

'Thank you, but I must get my dog,' said Timothy, suddenly worried about where Faith was heading. Sirens signalled the arrival of several police cars, as he limped off after his dog. Reaching the bushes he could still hear Faith, but this was a different, more of a playful bark. Timothy pushed his way into the bushes only to find an embarrassed couple quickly pulling on their clothes, and brushing off leaves. He breathed a sigh of relief. If only they knew what the dog had found there last time.

'Come on Faith,' he said wearily. Faith, like many dogs who rush off without their owners, looked surprised and delighted to see him, nearly knocking him over with affection.

Timothy apologised to the couple; they were too embarrassed to reply. He quickly walked back to the bandstand where a policeman was taking notes.

'Are you alright?' said his rescuer, who was still there.

'Yes I think so, thanks to Faith here,' he replied, aware his speech was a bit odd, due to the rapid swelling of his face.

'You haven't met any of these people before, then?' said the note-taking policeman, after Timothy had given a full account of the attack.

'I've never met any of them before in my life'; he winced, as his painkillers began to wear off.

'Perhaps you should go home and take something for your injuries. sir. Could you come down to the station tomorrow, and sign the statement?'

'Yes, I can do that,' he groaned, feeling worse than ever.

'D'you need a lift, mate,' asked his new friend.

'That would be great. I don't live far away.' As they made their way over to the car park Timothy asked, 'how come *you* were in the park tonight?'

'I'm a special detective… plain clothes… to blend in with the youngsters. I get more information that way.'

'I'd never have guessed.'

'That's the idea,' he laughed as he unlocked the car, and helped Timothy and his dog get in.

'Are you sure you can't remember what any of them looked like?'

'Not much.'

'We suspect a few of that gang may be connected with another crime we're investigating. Perhaps you'll be able to recall some more after sleeping on it,' he suggested.

Getting out of the car at his home wasn't so easy. His joints were stiffening, and after a lot of groaning and a helping hand, they were finally at his front door. As the car pulled away he realised he'd forgotten to ask his rescuer's name. After taking more painkillers and giving Faith some biscuits as a reward, he crawled up the stairs and into to bed.

The following morning he could hardly move, and lay in bed slowly flexing first one leg, then the other; he felt like he had been run over by a steamroller. Trying to move his jaw was agony; he gave himself a fright when he looked in the mirror, *could that really be him*? He prodded his swollen face carefully and tried to smile…ouch, can't do that. Carefully running his tongue around his mouth, he was relieved to find that he still had all his teeth. Somehow he had to face his mother and her reaction to his injuries; and wondered if he ought to go into work; his appearance would probably frighten the customers. Better ring Derek later, he decided, as he staggered into the bathroom to run a bath.

He thought he should try speaking aloud before attempting to communicate with anyone. He lay in the bath and tried talking aloud to himself…it didn't sound very good, and moving his mouth was difficult.

'Timothy! Is that you in there? Are you alright?' called Mother from outside the bathroom door. 'Yuurrrs' he moaned.

'What?' she exclaimed, wondering if her hearing was faulty. She rubbed her ears and listened again, ear pressed against the door.

'Um fine Mudder,' he replied with difficulty.

Convinced it wasn't her son in the bathroom, she flung open the door and marched in. Taking one look at the multiple bruises and swellings she screamed, then promptly fainted.

He painfully hauled himself out of the bath to attend to his prostrate Mother. His mobile began to ring and he answered it with an unintelligible sound, '*Ullu*'

'Are *you* alright, mate?' It was a concerned voice.

'Sort uv,' he replied, recognising the detective's voice from last night.

He tried to say that his mother had fainted but wasn't sure that he'd been understood.

He quickly pulled on his dressing gown as Mother was coming around and trying to sit up, dazed and confused. He knelt down and looked at her. She stared at him for

160

a second, then fainted again. While he wondered if he should call for an ambulance, the front doorbell rang,
Faith barked loudly as Timothy tried to make his way downstairs. The front door burst open and in strode the detective; Faith stood his ground in the hall, baring his teeth at the intruder. 'Good dog, good dog,' said the detective nervously.

Timothy put his hand through Faith's collar and pointed upstairs. He pulled the dog into the kitchen and shut the door, then limped back to the hall continuing to point upstairs.

'What's upstairs?' asked the detective. Timothy muttered something in reply. The detective frowned in an effort to understand and then decided to go and see for himself. Timothy followed as quickly as he could and pointed to the bathroom.

'Oh I see, you alright, love?' said the detective, going in and rubbing Mother's hand. She began to come round, and to Timothy's surprise actually smiled when she saw the detective's face! 'Where's my son?' she asked, trying to sit up.

'He's here, love,' said the detective gently, helping her up and keeping an arm around her for support.

'Who are you?' asked Mother.

'I'm Dave Quilford, a friend of Timothy's,' he replied.

'What happened to Timothy? He looks awful!'

' He's just been involved in a little incident. He's gonna be fine,' said Dave, looking at Timothy for confirmation.

Timothy nodded and made agreeing noises. Once downstairs in the kitchen, the painkillers were kicking in and Timothy found walking a little easier. Getting a pen and paper he wrote down that he wasn't going to work and he needed to tell his employer. He wrote Derek's number and then as a last thought, wrote that

161

he needed more painkillers, and maybe a visit to the doctor.

Mother, having recovered from her shock was making breakfast. Deciding that scrambled egg would be best for Timothy, she invited Dave to join them. While they ate, Dave explained what had happened, making it sound as though Timothy and Faith were the heroes of the night. Faith earned himself some extra toast and was enjoying the attention when the doorbell rang.

The dog went into action but with a stern 'SIT!' from Mother he was quiet.

They heard Mrs Battle's voice booming along the hall. 'Heard there was a bit of trouble last night. Is Timothy alright?'

'Alright!' exclaimed Mother, 'no he's NOT! He can hardly walk, his face is black and blue, and he can't talk properly. I don't call that alright.'

'I'm sorry. I did hear that the police were able to apprehend the gang.'

Mother's tone changed as she replied. 'Oh well yes, of course. Timothy was the hero of the night, I believe.'

Huddled in the kitchen Timothy sat with his head in his hands unable to say a word.

'Looks like you're going to be Mr Popular, for a while,' commiserated Dave.

Timothy raised his eyes to the ceiling.

Dave took over operations and called the shop to explain to Derek that Timothy would need a few days to recover from his injuries. Timothy could hear Derek's voice chatting away but couldn't make out what he was saying. Dave was grinning, which was worrying, but he looked at Timothy and gave the thumbs up sign. Timothy frowned and shrugged; even that was painful. Mother came back into the kitchen, brimming with pride for her son; his injuries now battle scars.

Dave was busy making Timothy an appointment at the local surgery and promised to return later to see if he needed anything else. Timothy thanked him as best he could and limped to the door to see him on his way. Mrs Fell's curtains were twitching and he tried to smile…ouch! not yet.

The good thing about walking in the park with the dog, was that it gave him time to think things through, and Faith, sensing his human was not 'right', as dogs often do, walked less exuberantly than usual.

Timothy did a lot of thinking in the park. He was a thinker, he decided, happy among the trees. He had another date to arrange, but perhaps it would be better for him to recover from his injuries first. No one would want to meet him in his present condition. He would go back into work as soon as he could speak properly, and decided to arrange the next date in a week or two.

On their way back from the park, he heard the familiar revving of an engine, and Mrs Fell pulled up beside him. Her smile quickly faded and she was visibly shocked at seeing his face close up. ' I hear you had an exciting night in the park, but I didn't realise you'd been badly hurt.' Timothy mumbled a reply and Mrs Fell, frowning, said, 'I hope you get better soon.' She stared at him for a few moments, and with a confused smile revved the engine and shot off.

On returning home, he wrote a note for Mother, explaining he was going to the police station, as she had already left for the hospital. He knew she couldn't wait to tell Maude about his escapade in the park, even though his aunt never really believed any of her stories.

People had given him odd looks when he was out earlier, so he decided to cover up a bit; rummaging in his wardrobe he found an old bush hat with a floppy brim. This, with his sunglasses, covered most of his face. Pulling on his jacket he hitched up the collar for good measure, and hoping he looked less scary, set off. Mrs Fell's curtains moved back and forth as he walked out of his gate. People still looked at him oddly as he walked along the pavement, but perhaps it was just his imagination.

At the police station he went up to the reception desk, and the large, middle-aged duty officer glared at him. 'Inspector Clouseau, is it?' he asked impatiently.

'Uctually it's imoffy arkes, U've come to see Detective Quilford' he said, removing his sun glasses as he spoke.

' I see, wait here a minute, please,' chuckled the officer. Timothy felt like a criminal or a secret agent, as several people stared at him while he waited.

A policewoman came into reception who he recognised as one of Lizzie's friends. She recognised him too. ' Hello Timothy, I'm WPC Eve Butler. 'I've been hearing all sorts of stories about you, come this way and we'll get your statement sorted.' She lead him through the station to an interview room. The policeman behind the desk shook his head and chuckled as they went by.

'Ho..'s izzie etting on?'

'She's fine, she asked after you too. Did you know she may be coming back here in about six months time?' said Eve.

He shook his head. 'I aven't urd from her.'

 They were interrupted by the door opening and in Dave walking in. 'Alright, mate?' he asked. Timothy nodded and gave the thumbs up. 'When you've done your statement perhaps Eve can come and find me, and I'll give you a lift back if you like?'

Timothy scribbled quickly on his notepad and handed it to Dave. Reminding him that he had to visit the doctor on the way back. 'No worries I can drop you there instead.'

Even signing his statement was a slow process as his hands were bruised and swollen. Finally, Eve went off to find Dave, leaving Timothy alone. So Lizzie was coming back to the area, he thought. Probably found some dishy guy and wouldn't want to date an ordinary chap from the bookshop again. Perhaps he should just keep dating a few ladies and see what happened. The thought of Lizzie made his heart pound and his stomach churn. No one else had that kind of effect.

Dave dropped him off at the surgery, and the receptionist gave him an odd look when he walked in. He was getting used to those now. As he removed his sunglasses her expression changed to one of sympathy. ' Take a seat, you won't have to wait long,' she said kindly.

The doctor prescribed more painkillers and anti-inflammatory pills to help the healing and recommended gentle exercise and rest for a few days.

As he was leaving the surgery he collided with Mrs Pugh. Her face lit up when she recognised him. 'You look dreadful! Have you been on one of your secret adventures?' she asked in a loud whisper, giving him a sly wink.

He nodded and tried a smile, uttering a non-committal grunt.

'Ooooh you brave boy,' she exclaimed, and flung her arms around him, hugging him tightly, making him yelp. 'I'm sorry, so sorry, is it very bad?'

'A bit ore uctuawy,' he managed.

As they walked out into the car park a revving engine announced who was also in the vicinity. '*Coooo eeeeee,*' called Mrs Fell, parking the Mini and waving.

'Are you having a lift with Beattie too?' asked Mrs Pugh, linking her arm through his.

'I on't know,' he replied, wondering how he could escape without being rude, and making a run for it. 'Do you need a lift too?' asked Mrs Fell.

'He's had one of his secret adventures, you know. With the police,' Mrs Pugh said, in a loud whisper that anyone else in the car park could have heard. He looked from one to the other and decided a reply wouldn't help.

Mrs Pugh was a pear shaped lady, and insisted on travelling in the back of the two-door car, which involved squeezing past the front seat. Manoeuvring her rear half through the door and into the back was no easy feat. Grunting and puffing, she appeared to be stuck at one point, until her friend gave her a good shove. Looking a little dishevelled she straightened her hat and sat up, pulling her knees up so Mrs Fell could lower the front seat for Timothy. He climbed in carefully and fastened his seat belt.

Mrs Fell almost leapt into the driver's seat, rammed the gear stick into reverse, and after giving the engine a good revving, shot backwards, screeching to a halt just before crashing into the car behind. With a squeal of tyres they whizzed around the car park to the entrance, where they stopped abruptly before joining the flow of traffic. Timoyhy closed his eyes and even though he wasn't religious, said a quiet prayer for them all.

'Do you mind if we drop Doris off first, she's on our way?' asked Mrs Fell, looking at him and not where they were going.

'Ook out!' he cried with difficulty, as they were about
to run into the back of another car. They screeched to a
halt and then lurched on, a little more slowly.
'Honestly, fancy stopping there! People do the most
silly things today, don't they?' she said, hoping for
sympathy.

'Mmm,' was all he could manage while tightly
clutching the dashboard. Mrs Pugh was silent in the
back. They revved their way around town, with an
occasional toot on the horn. Going completely out of
their way to drop off Mrs Pugh, they eventually stopped
dead outside her house. Mrs Fell got out, swung up the
front seat, holding her hand out for her friend. There
was more grunting and wheezing as she heaved Mrs
Pugh off the back seat to the door, where once again
she became wedged.

'Give her a good shove!' called Mrs Fell. This was
awkward as the only bit of her that Timothy could
shove was her round bottom. 'Go on, just shove!' cried
Mrs Fell again.

Timothy carefully and painfully manoeuvred himself
around in his seat, put both hands on her bottom and
pushed. '*Ooohaaa*!' shrieked Mrs Pugh, as she popped
out of the door, cannoning into her friend, who lost her
footing and fell over backwards. Both women were
sprawled on the pavement, grunting and moaning.

Timothy climbed out of the car as quickly as he was
able, and limped round to see if he could help. It was
hard to know who, or which bit, to grab hold of and as
he was bending down a man came running towards
them, shouting. 'Hey you! Leave them alone!'

Mrs Fell managed to sit up, her hat askew, and teeth in
her hand. She quickly popped them back in and said,
'It's only Timothy!' Timothy stepped back as the man
approached, glaring malevolently at Timothy.

167

'You alright love?' The man asked Mrs Fell, suspicious of Timothy, who was still wearing his hat and dark glasses.

'Yes thank you. This is Timothy Parkes, he's a hero you know,' said Mrs Fell.

'What for?' replied the man, in disbelief.

'He is, really!' confirmed Mrs Pugh, straightening her hat and brushing dust and bits off her clothes, apparently none the worse from the fall.

'I'm just giving him a lift home, and had to drop my friend here off first.' explained Mrs Fell.

'Well, if you're sure?' said the man, still looking doubtfully at Timothy. The man watched from across the street as the ladies said their goodbyes. Timothy strapped himself firmly back into the passenger seat. The little car was revved up and with a squeal of tyres they were off, leaving the concerned man staring after them.

The Mini zoomed around the town until coming to an abrupt halt outside Timothy's house. 'Tank ou for the ift,' he said, as he carefully extracted himself from the car, and limped up to his gate.

'Always a pleasure, dear,' called Mrs Fell, her gleaming teeth smiling out of the car window as she roared off.

'May your gods go with you,' said Timothy, his irony wasted on Mrs Fell.

He picked up the post as he walked in, and immediately recognised Lizzie's writing on one of the envelopes. He opened it eagerly…it was a short note telling him that she would be coming back to Dickleborough in about six months time and hoped to see him. His mood lifted and he began day dreaming about a place in the country…..

21
The van !

Derek was already in the shop when Timothy walked in, still wearing dark glasses to conceal the yellow and purple bruising.

'I can't wait to hear what you've been up to this time! The policeman said there was a fight in the park at night and you were in the middle of it. Apparently you were some kind of hero.'

'Not exactly. Just happened to be there on this neighbourhood park watch thing. We were attacked by a gang and Faith frightened them off.'

The shop door clanged open and the mysterious Dr Athed walked in; he hardly looked at either of them, moving straight to the poisons, and pharmaceuticals section.

The friends exchanged a look. 'Herman Munster's here again,' whispered Derek.

'Probably poisoning his wife,' Timothy whispered back.

After a while the mysterious doctor came to the check out with several books on poisons and toxic chemicals. Timothy finally realised what was odd about him. He looked directly at you with his eyes but his head hardly moved; he appeared to move in a rather upright, mechanical way altogether. He also noticed the man didn't blink much, and found himself staring into the man's eyes a little longer than normal. He wondered if perhaps the man was ill or had suffered an injury, as he himself had recently. He took the books and tried to make conversation. 'Nice to see the sunshine today,' he said.

'Yes,' was the only reply.

Not giving up, Timothy handed the wrapped books and change to Dr Athed saying, 'Have a nice day, sir.'

'Yes,' said Dr Athed and left the shop.

Derek came back with two steaming mugs of coffee. 'Got a big delivery to shift today and thought we should have coffee first. How did you get on with the 'Munster'?'

Timothy told him his theory about the man not appearing to blink.

Derek laughed. 'You mean you stared into his eyes to see if he was blinking? You of course, were not blinking either. He probably thinks you were chatting him up.'

'Perhaps that's why he didn't say much. Oh well, lets get on with the delivery.'

Between the two of them they soon got the new books onto the right shelves and piles. Derek revealed his romance with Henri was going well, and suggested they double-date sometime. 'Perhaps, *when* I find a suitable lady,' replied Timothy.

'How long is it since you drove a car?' Derek asked as they were sorting through the second hand books.

'Just over a year, I guess.'

'Don't suppose you fancy driving the van do you?'

'Why?' he asked warily.

Derek put his arm around Timothy's shoulders, always a sign that there was a favour about to be asked that he may not be too keen on. 'Mrs Brailsford from Straw Bottom Farm is having a coffee morning and asked if I could supply any old books to sell for charity. There's a pile of books that have been hanging around in the shop for a while, they might as well be sold for charity. I've a meeting with my accountant this afternoon, and part-

time Dori is coming in to take care of the shop, which leaves you free. Just the man for the job.'

'I could,' he replied carefully.

'Ah but *will* you, Timothy, my old lad?'

'What time is Dori coming in?'

'One O'clock,' he replied, 'perhaps you can tell me more about your drama while we load up?'

'And you can tell me more about you and Henri.'

The friends chatted while they worked. Derek was laughing, then suddenly serious, he said, 'There's more to you than you let on, isn't there?'

'I don't think so.'

Timothy had driven the aged van before, but not for a while. Remembering how he had to 'double the clutch' each time he changed gear, he drove through town, stopping to get fuel. As he made his way back across the forecourt a woman's voice called out: 'Driving again, are you, Timothy?'

Surprised anyone recognised him, wearing the hat and dark glasses, he turned to see Inspector Davies. 'Just a delivery for the shop, Inspector. Nice day,' he commented, getting back into the van. He nodded and smiled as he pulled out of the garage.

She watched him drive away.

He drove along the narrow country lanes to Straw Bottom Farm, past the farm worker's cottage, over a cattle grid and a little stone bridge. Stopping at the entrance of the farm, he got out and went to open the gate. On the other side was a large pig snuffling in the grass by a farm building. He hesitated, his last encounter with animals still fresh in his mind. The pig saw him and came over, snuffling and grunting, large ears flopping around its small, steely eyes. 'Hello pig,' said Timothy, wondering how friendly it was as he walked toward the gate.

The pig grunted loudly and began to rub its large body along the gate, pushing on it. Timothy backed off, and walked around the fence looking for another way in. There was a smaller gate leading to what looked like the front porch; he carefully opened it and walked through. Half way to the house he noticed a goat, and having met a friendly goat before, he walked on. The goat bleated loudly, then with horns lowered it began to charge.

Timothy wasn't keen to acquire any more injuries, so he turned and ran as fast as he could, making it over the top of the gate as the goat's horns crashed into it.

Now he knew why Derek had asked him to do the delivery; some friend! He walked around the perimeter of the farmhouse until he found another gate, leading into a small field. Looking around, he saw no goats or pigs, so he climbed over the gate and headed heading for the farmhouse. Around the side of the house a window looked out over the field; he knocked on it loudly, hoping someone would hear.

'Hello,' someone called from outside.

'Hello,' he called back, climbing onto the fence in order to see. The first thing he saw was the goat staring back, but he could also see a middle- aged woman standing at the main gate by his van. 'Hello,' he called again, waving in her direction.

'What are you doing there?' He assumed this was Mrs Brailsford.

'The pig won't let me in.'

'Oh this old snorter won't hurt you, come on he's alright,' she said, with a jolly smile.

'NO!' said Timothy firmly.

'Well come over to the old front gate then.'

'I've already been charged by the goat,' he replied. The woman looked exasperated and finally said. 'Well, if you refuse to do that, you'll have to drive the van into the field and pass the books through the window.'

'Fine,' said Timothy.

'Mind you keep the gate closed now,' she said, walking back to the house with the snorting pig following behind.

What's in the field? Timothy thought, driving the van to the gate. After some difficulty he managed to open it wide enough for the van. He did notice dried cow-pats but no sign of cattle, so drove in and closed the gate.

Mrs Brailsford opened the window so he could pass the books through to her. 'Come and have some tea,' she invited when the last of the books had been handed over; 'you'll have to come in through the window.'

He climbed in and found the farmhouse spotless, tidy and welcoming. He followed her into the kitchen where there were piles of freshly baked buns and scones on a big central table. The kitchen walls were lined with shelves full of jars of preserves, decorative tins and crockery. Cooking pots hung from a beam and he could feel the warmth from the Aga, and delighted in the wonderful smell of newly baked cakes. The door to the pantry was open and he could see more shelves lined with even more jars, tins, and packets of all sorts. All farmhouse kitchens should be like this he thought, as he was handed a mug of tea and a warm teacake, dripping with butter. After chatting for a while, Mrs Brailsford, known as Ma Brailsford by locals, gave him two bags of buns to take home.

While he had been enjoying his tea, nosy cattle from a neighbouring field had wandered through a hidden gateway. They'd rubbed the van with wet noses, licked it all over, bent the wing mirrors and scratched their bodies along the sides, leaving the van looking as though it had been in a banger race. Having had fun with the 'new toy' they'd wandered off again. When Timothy climbed out through the window, he was struck dumb by the devastation.

'Oh those naughty cows, they're so nosy, can't leave anything alone. I expect they've got bored and gone off now,' said his jolly hostess.

'I hope so,' was all Timothy could say.

After thanking Mrs Brailsford for the buns, he drove the van out of the field, and closed the gate as the cattle were wandering back. Looking at the state of the van, Timothy grinned to himself. S*erves Derek right,* he thought.

Driving back through town he received plenty of questioning looks from pedestrians and other drivers, he could hardly stop himself from laughing aloud. *They'll all think I've been on some sort of safari;* he speculated at the old bat network reaction... *another Timothy adventure!*

Back at the shop he chatted to 'part-time Dori', as they sorted out the book shelves and tidied the second hand piles, in between serving customers.

Derek came back shortly before closing. 'Managed the delivery alright?' he asked.

'The delivery was fine. Mrs Brailsford says thank you for all the books, and I've parked the van back in the yard.'

'So it all went off okay then?'

'Yup no problem, all fine. I'll be off home now, see you tomorrow,' said Timothy, smiling innocently at Derek.

Mother was delighted when she saw Mrs Brailsford's buns. ' Mrs Weatherbutts said she thought she saw you driving a van that had been in a terrible accident. I said I didn't think it could possibly be you'

'It may have been me, the van was attacked by cattle,' he said, calmly rubbing the dog's ears. 'What! Attacked by cattle!' exclaimed Mother, 'what were you doing with cattle?' she demanded. 'Just delivering some books to a farm. It's ok the van still works and everything,' he replied. Faith was tugging on his sleeve to go for his walk, and Timothy took the opportunity to escape. 'I'll see you later.'

He left Mother curious and confused. *Who else would be attacked by cattle?* she thought, shaking her head.

Making their way to the park at a good pace, they passed the bungalow with the usual pile of refuse bags outside on the pavement. He noticed a tall figure inside. Slowing his pace to get a better look, he could see the outline of two figures: one tall and the other quite a lot smaller. Hopefully one day he would see someone going in or out, or he might be brave enough to think of a reason and knock on the door.

As he entered the park there were not many people around so he let Faith off the lead. Walking by the old bandstand a female voice spoke from behind him, making the hairs on the back of his neck prickle and stand up. He turned to see the same girl from the night of the attack and gave a low whistle to Faith.

'You're okay then?' said the girl, her large blue eyes staring at him.

'Yes,' he said shortly, as Faith came up and nudged his hand. He felt more comfortable with the dog there, plus it was daylight so he could see all around. No sign of any gang this time.

' They arrested some of the others,' she said, still staring at him.

'Yes,' was all he could say, slipping his hand through Faith's collar.

Turning to walk away he heard the welcoming voice of Mrs battle. 'Ah Timothy, out for your walk, are you,' she shouted, walking briskly along, swinging her walking stick as usual, another flowery hat jammed firmly on her head.

'Hello Mrs Battle, how are you? ' he asked, almost pleased to see her.

'Yes, it is quiet in here today. You're getting better I see, ready for another stint of park watch?'

'I think so, but I would prefer early evening if possible,' he replied.

At this point he had relaxed his grip on Faith, who took the opportunity to lunge forward towards Mrs Battle. She was ready this time, raising her stick and shouting, 'SIT!' in such a commanding way that the dog stopped in his tracks; he looked at her for a moment before wandering off to sniff something nearby. Every one in the park must have heard the 'sit' command. 'I'll be in touch. Time you got that dog trained Timothy,' she shouted over her shoulder as she marched off waving her stick, 'toodeloo!'

He carried on with the walk. It was a pleasant sunny evening and he was happy to take his time. Faith was scampering, about and Timothy was thinking about Lizzie again, wondering how soon she could be back, and hoping that she hadn't met someone else meanwhile.

Faith's nose alerted him to something interesting on the other side of the park. As he was about to take off Timothy made a grab for him but the dog was too quick and set off at a good gallop. Timothy's legs were still not a hundred percent fit; he groaned and set off after

176

the dog. They rounded a clump of trees as the girl on roller blades passed at speed, followed by a Labrador … followed by Faith in hot pursuit.

'Oh no,' he groaned, running along behind. He tried whistling and calling, which is not easy when you're running and out of breath. Faith finally caught up with the Labrador, and after a brief introduction and a bit of a growl, the two dogs ran along side by side as if having their own conversation. The girl on the roller blades was unaware of the goings on behind her.

Timothy was not quite close enough to grab Faith's tail and he was running out of steam. A short-cut was needed to head them off, so he veered off onto another path. If he could keep up the pace, this should bring him out in front of the girl and the dogs.

He passed two ladies out for a stroll and recognised one as Mrs Brown; he waved as he went past, registering her surprise as he ran on calling '*Faith*'!

There was a steep incline, which should bring him out in front of the speeding trio. His lungs were now on fire as he went over the top. He could see the three of them coming along the path, he would have to run down-hill fast to get in front of them. He began his descent, the hill was quite a bit steeper on this side and lined with trees. He skidded on the fallen loose leaves and finally tripped over a hidden root. Gravity took over and he continued the speedy descent on his bottom, finally shooting out onto the path, in front of the roller-blading girl.

She shrieked and dodged sideways. The dogs were delighted with this new game and pounced all over Timothy, making it difficult to get to his feet.

'Sam! Sam! Come here!' shouted the girl. The Labrador bounded off to his owner with a wagging tail. Then it ran back to Timothy, nearly knocking him over again, before racing back to his owner. Faith joined in, giving the girl his customary shove in the crotch by way of saying hello, sending her rolling backwards. Thinking this was a new extension of the game, the dogs continued to push the girl backwards along the path.

Timothy grabbed Faith and put on his lead; the girl called her own dog and did likewise.

'I'm sorry,' they both said in unison.

After catching his breath he explained the drama that had happened behind her. She gave a delightful giggle, and they all calmly made their way along the path to the park entrance. She introduced herself as Penny and her dog as Sam.

'Would you like to come out for a meal sometime?' he surprised himself with his boldness.

'That would be nice, thank you,' she replied, much to his relief. 'I work some evenings but would be free on Thursday.'

'Okay. I don't have a vehicle at the moment but could borrow one, unless you would like to meet at the pub?' he said, thinking on his feet.

'My own car is at the garage, so a lift would be great.'

'I'll pick you up at seven, we could go to The Pickled Cow. I need an address...' he said, rummaging in his pockets for something to write with. Between them they found an old receipt and a small pencil, and exchanged phone numbers.

'I'd love to meet up again with the dogs, look at them,' she said. Faith and Sam had become good pals; they were playing at pretend-growling and chasing, and having a great time.

'Good idea. I'll see you Thursday and we can arrange a dog walk then,' he said, not quite believing his luck.

They said their goodbyes and Timothy walked home with a spring in his step. Despite his still visible bruises and slightly swollen cheek, she had agreed to go out with him. All because his dog had chased her dog. 'Good lad!' he rubbed Faith's head.

Mother was waiting for them when they walked in. 'You were a long time today,' she said, 'is everything alright? Were you a good boy?' she said to the dog, fussing his head.

'Yes Mother. I expect Faith's hungry after his run,' he says, heading upstairs.

'Mrs Brown phoned and said she'd seen you in the park,' called Mother from the kitchen.

'Really.'

'She asked if you were training for something. Said you were running, and she didn't realise you were so religious. You're not training for anything, are you?' she asked.

He leant over the banister. 'No, I'm not training for anything, I was just keeping up with Faith.'

His mother looked at the dog with a raised eyebrow. 'Just keeping up with you, was he? That boy doesn't tell me anything,' she winked at Faith, who was patiently waiting for his meal.

Timothy lay back in the bath for a long soak and some hard thinking. He'd received a message on his mobile from the agency to say there was a new lady who he just *had* to meet. Should he cancel now that he had a date with Penny, or should he go?

If it didn't work out with Penny then he would probably go back to the agency anyway, or contact Everelda since he'd enjoyed her company, despite all the animals. *Come on Timothy just make a decision,* he said to himself. After more pondering he decided to meet the new date before his planned meeting with Penny. He wasn't committed to either, so he thought this would be okay. Then his thoughts wandered back to Lizzie's pretty, smiling face. One minute there are no women and now there are lots; but Lizzie's face stayed on his mind.

While they were eating supper, Mother mentioned that Maude was coming out of hospital later that week and asked him which taxi firm she should book to take his aunt home. 'I could borrow the van from work if you like,' he offered.

'Well, it wouldn't cost anything, would it? I'll tell her I've got a lift for her, shall I?'

'I'll talk to Derek tomorrow.'

'The van's alright, isn't it?'

'Oh fine, I'm sure we can all sit in the front comfortably,' he replied. Mother decided not to mention any of this to her sister, not who would be driving, or what sort of vehicle would be transporting her!

The following morning he called the agency from his bedroom before leaving for the bookshop. Jane answered as usual. 'Morning Jane, I believe you have someone for me to meet?' he said cheerfully. 'Oh it's you! Yes, hang on,' she replied moodily. He could hear a lot of rustling of paper while he hung on, then she giggled. ' Ooooh yes, here she is Timothy, you'll like this one.'

'She doesn't expect me to ride wild horses or bucking bulls, does she?' he asked, wondering what she found so amusing.

She giggled again and said, ' No she's not like *that*.' Still giggly, she gave him the contact details and described her to him. 'She's called *Tara, 5'8' tall, shoulder length black hair, very slim build, well*

180

dressed. Divorced with one daughter who has flown the nest. Lives alone, hobbies are the arts and reading, loves socialising, meals out etc. I've seen her Timothy, she's a bit of a stunner,' Jane whispered the last bit.

He was immediately suspicious and not sure that this was the kind of woman he wanted to meet. 'I don't know about this one, I could leave it and call again in a week or so.'

'Oh no, you must meet her! I've told her all about you and she will be looking forward to it. Timothy, please don't let us down now,' she pleaded, making him even more suspicious.

'She doesn't keep strange things in tanks, or have a house full of cats, does she?'

'I don't know what you're on about. She is a nice lady and as far as we are aware she has no pets, but a nice home. You have her contact number, you could just have a chat.' Jane persisted. Finally Timothy agreed.

'I don't know why you gave Timothy Parkes Tara Robson's details Jane,' said Daphne later, 'you know the kind of lady she is, don't you?' Jane looked blank.

'Jane dear, she is a lady who entertains businessmen at home for pocket money, she's joined the agency hoping to find a new husband. I don't think she will be right for Timothy.'

'Oh.' Jane sucked her lip with a gleam in her eyes, that belied her feigned innocence.

22
The date with Tara.

Timothy didn't have any trouble persuading Derek to lend him the van. He merely handed over the keys and said, ' All yours, mate.'

It was still in the same state as when he'd parked it there after the encounter with the cattle. He managed to bend the wing mirrors and the bumpers more or less back into place, but it was really filthy and still covered in smears where the cattle had licked it, and the dents where they had leaned on it. Fortunately it started straight away and he drove to the nearest garage to top up with fuel. A clean new van pulled in on the opposite side of the pump; the driver stared at the old battered vehicle and said, ' You driving that for a bet, mate?'

Timothy just smiled. He didn't really care; the van was a means to an end as far as he was concerned, and was free on loan.

Arriving at home all the parking spaces in the street were full and he was forced to park in the next road. At least Mother wouldn't see the state of it…yet. He lifted his bike out of the back and cycled around the corner. Mother was out, so he had the usual wild greeting from Faith, who was keen to go for his walk.

'Hang on just a minute, old lad,' he said. He rang Tara's number, hoping he could meet her tonight. A husky female voice answered the phone.

'Oh yes, I'd be delighted to meet you, would you like to come over here?' she asked. He hesitated, he would much rather meet her in a pub somewhere, feeling it would be safer.

'But I'd love you to come here Timothy, we can go out wherever you like afterwards,' purred the husky voice.

Alarm bells were ringing in his head, but as usual his curiosity and the 'well, you never know' feeling, found him saying. 'That's fine, what time?'

After completing the arrangements for that evening, he ran upstairs and changed into his dog walking gear. As he was leaving for the park, Mother came in; he kissed her on the cheek.

'I won't need anything to eat, as I'm going out. I've got the van for Aunt Maude tomorrow!' Mother watched them walk down the path; she looked around, unable to see the van; she shrugged and went inside.

Later, as he left for his date with Tara, doubts were still niggling in his mind. He parked in the driveway of a modern, semi-detached house; it all looked very neat and smart, casting even more doubts in his mind.

He rang the doorbell and Tara's husky voice called out, 'Come in Timothy, shall we have a drink before going out? '

He hesitantly pushed the door open, and looked nervously up the stairs, but couldn't see anyone. The hall had thick, new carpets, a bunch of fresh flowers on the hall table, and a thick red visitors book. He walked in a little further.

'Go into the sitting room, I won't be a tick,' called Tara from somewhere upstairs.

The sitting room was furnished with modern furniture, all immaculate, clean and tidy... not a sign of an animal or any other creature. Still he felt nervous and kept an eye on the door, in case. Soft music was playing through the speakers in the cabinet.

'Pour yourself a drink, if you like, I'll have a Scotch and soda,' called the voice.

He went over to the drinks cabinet and poured himself a neat Scotch to steady his nerves, he drank it quickly.

The door opened and Tara walked in, dressed in a long silky evening gown; she sank onto a chair and hitched her dress up to the top of her thighs, while putting on stilettos. 'Hello Timothy, have you got yourself a drink?'

He was a little taken aback by her appearance. He was dressed in the usual bright shirt and tie with checked trousers. She was a good few inches taller than him, and wearing plenty of perfume!

'Hi,' he began, ' I was planning on a meal at a nearby pub, I hope you don't mind?'

'Oh. I *suppose* that will be ok. Finished your drink already? Help yourself to another if you like;' she said, sipping her own.

'No thank you, I'm driving. Nice place you have here,' he said nervously, by way of conversation. He knew this lady wasn't for him, but unable to think of a way out he resigned himself to spending the rest of the evening with Tara. 'Perhaps we should go, I did reserve a table,' he added, trying to move things along.

'Fine.' she replied crisply, snatching up her purse. Stepping out of the front door she spotted the van in her driveway. 'Who left *that* there?'

'Actually it's mine, well…no…not actually mine. I borrowed it for this evening.'

Tara gave him a look to shrivel a slug and walked over to the van. He dashed ahead to open the passenger door for her, which creaked and groaned as bits of rust trickled onto the driveway. She climbed in and perched gingerly on the torn seat as if sitting on broken glass, holding her hand to her nose as the scent of cattle wafted around the van. Making the best of things Timothy jumped in with a forced smile and said, 'Ok let's go. Come on, old girl,' as he turned the key and the old van lurched into life. The engine was rather noisy and so any conversation had to be in a loud voice. 'It's a nice pub, the Mouldy Moggie, I hope you like it,' he shouted. Tara said nothing, perched on the edge of her seat, holding on tightly as they lurched and roared along. When they pulled into the pub car park the old van back-fired and caused other arrivals to stare at them. She pulled her shawl up over her head and waited for him to run round and open the door. Taking his hand she carefully extracted herself from the van, heels wobbling on the gravel of the car park. Keeping her head down, she clung to his arm as they walked to the entrance, pulling her shawl over her face when they went inside.

'Are you cold?' he asked politely.

'No.'

He had a quick word with one of the barmen and asked Tara if she would like another drink? 'Make it a double,' she replied. Timothy ordered the drinks and collected the menu, then led Tara over to a table near the open log fire. She carefully positioned herself with her back to the room facing the fire, which meant that he was sitting in the direct heat. 'Wouldn't you be warmer on this side?' he asked, while loosening his tie.

'No, I'm not cold,' she said, taking a good drink from her glass. As he handed her the menu, she said. 'Look, could we move over there?' pointing to a small table in the far corner, 'I'm a bit hot here.'

' I'm sure it will be okay. I'll tell them when I give them our orders.' he said, still struggling to keep the conversation going.

Tara was a lovely looking lady he thought, but not for him, and wondered why Jane had been so keen he should meet her. Still he was determined to have a pleasant evening; he liked the pub and usually enjoyed their food.

'I'll have the avocado with cream cheese and prawn salad,' she sighed.

'Oh fine, I'm having the steak. I'll go and order. Would you like another drink?' he asked, noticing she had already finished the first one.

'Make it another double.'

'Right,' he said, heading off to the bar to order.

While they were eating she asked, 'What happened to your face? Did you crash the van?'

He'd forgotten he was still a bit bruised and yellow in places. 'No…accident,' he said, going on to explain about the cattle. Tara looked at him from time to time; otherwise appearing disinterested in his reply.

As they were finishing their meal Tara began to cough violently. She took a long drink but that didn't help, in fact, it seemed to make it worse; and then she starting gagging. He realised she must be choking. Leaping to his feet, he grabbed her around the waist just below her ribs and gave a sudden squeeze inward and upward. She gave an almighty cough and gasp, as a large prawn flew out of her mouth and shot across the room. Timothy handed her another napkin. With her lipstick smeared over her red face, she took several long breaths before managing to gasp, 'thank you.'

A smartly dressed man who had been watching them from the bar walked over, 'Is that Tara?' he was smiling down at her.

She looked horrified and began to cough again, holding the napkin to her face she nodded.

'I thought it was you; are you alright?' he asked, looking at Timothy as though waiting to be introduced. Tara kept the napkin over her mouth to hide her embarrassment.

186

'I'm Timothy Parkes,' said Timothy, standing up, extending his hand. The man shook it politely.

'I see. I'm Gilbert and a friend of Tara's, too! Enjoy your evening. Nice to see you again, Tara,' he said, still smiling at the red faced woman who simply nodded.

While Tara was in the ladies' room, Timothy took the opportunity to pay the bill. He noticed Gilbert watching him from across the bar, winking and raising his glass to Timothy.

Tara clutched her escort's arm again as they crossed the car park, and in silence he drove her home. 'Thank you for the meal Timothy, it was nice to meet you,' she said. Climbing out of the van she managed to get her dress caught, and giving it a good yank she ripped the material. Her face was expressionless as she pulled the shawl over her head and walked quickly to her front door. Holding on to her torn dress, she went inside and closed the door without turning to look at him.

Timothy was not one to let things bother him too much, he gave the old engine a rev and pulled out of the drive. The van backfired noisily, puffing a cloud of black fumes from of the exhaust by way of comment. He'd enjoyed the meal, but the date with Tara made him keen to meet up with Penny, who was much more his type of girl.

23
Collecting Aunt Maude.

The van started well; it backfired heartily a few times as he drove around to his gate.

Mother was not impressed. 'We won't get Maude in this, we'll have to get a taxi,' she said, frowning.

' Oh rubbish! If I open the door and reverse up to the hospital entrance, you and the nurses can whiz her in before she sees it,' he said, in his usual cheery manner.

'It'll be hard enough to get her in when she sees *you.*' she replied, climbing in beside him. Her son leaned over and gave her a reassuring pat. 'It'll be fine Mother, you'll see.'

On the way to the hospital, they passed Mrs Battle marching towards the park. Timothy tooted and waved; Mrs Battle frowned in return, shaking her walking stick at them.

Mother had shrunk down as far as she could in the passenger seat, so that only the top of her hat would be visible to any pedestrians. 'What *are* you doing down there?' he asked.

A policeman was stopping traffic and talking to the drivers, so Timothy stopped and waited in line. Mother squeezed down in the seat even further. 'They won't be after you,' he laughed. Winding down the window, which squeaked noisily, he said. 'Good morning Officer.'

'Are you driving this for some kind of dare?' asked the young policeman.

'No, I'm borrowing it to collect my old aunt from hospital. I had to park in a field the other day, it was attacked by cows. It's got an MOT and everything.'

188

The policeman, looking puzzled, stood on tip-toe as he peered into the van at Mother, who had shrunk down into the foot-well, pulling her hat right down over her head. 'Is this your aunt?' asked the Policeman.

'No, this is my mother. She's coming along for the ride,' he leaned out of the window and whispered, ' she's very shy.' The policeman obviously decided they were harmless enough, *just barking mad like half the population in this country town*, he thought, waving them along. The van backfired as they drove off, leaving the perplexed policeman in a cloud of exhaust fumes.

'Shall I go and fetch Aunt Maude or will you?' Timothy offered, as they pulled into the hospital car park.

'I'm not sure *I* can. She'll have a fit when she sees it's you, never mind what she'll do when she sees this heap. We'll never get her in it!' Mother sounded frantic.

'Leave this to me,' he said firmly.

He went into the reception and gave his aunts details to the staff behind the desk, and a nurse immediately came down from the ward. 'We hadn't noticed any signs of dementia while she's been here, but you say she has a car phobia?' the nurse asked curiously.

'Yes, it's been difficult to get her to travel, for some time, but she won't talk about it,' he said sincerely.

'Okay, well if you want to drive right up to the doorway we'll get a couple of male nurses to help.'

'That's great, as soon as she's in I'll get Mother to sit beside her, so Maude will be between us on the journey home. I'm sure she'll be happy when we get her back in her own house,' he smiled convincingly, hoping his sneaky plan would work.

He drove the van right up to the door, so not all of it was visible from inside the hospital. He explained that the nurses were going to help Maude into the van, and Mother was to quickly get in beside her to keep her calm. His mother didn't look convinced. but agreed to give it a go. Leaving the door of the van wide open, so the marks and dents wouldn't be visible, he put on his hat and dark glasses, hoping Aunt Maude wouldn't realise it was him until it was too late.

The nurses wheeled her right up to the passenger door of the van. 'What's *that*?' exclaimed Maude loudly.

'It's a sort of mini-bus Maude, all we could get today,' said Mother, guiltily.

'Come on love, let's get you in, and on your way home,' said one of the nurses, helping her out of the chair.

'Don't call me love!' she snapped, giving the nurse a hefty whack for his trouble. While all this was going on, her nephew was skulking around the van trying to keep a low profile. Maude spotted him and shouted, 'Who's that creature?'

Timothy smiled at the nurses and whispered, 'She doesn't think much of me, I'm afraid!'

As the nurses tried to lift Maude into the van she screamed, 'Get off, I'm not going!' and gave the second male nurse a good smack.

'Alright love come on, you're going home today,' said the nurse patiently. Both nurses lifted her in through the van door.

'I'm coming too Maude, keep calm,' cried Mother.

'This is assault, GET OFF!' shouted the old lady, almost hysterical.

'Alright, I'm here,' soothed Mother. One of the nurses helped her onto the seat beside her sister. Maude turned on Mother, 'Did you arrange this? Is this some sick joke of your mad son? Who's going to drive the thing?' she demanded, waving her arms about.

190

The nurse quickly closed the door and smiled sympathetically at Mother, who mouthed 'Thank you' at them through the glass.

Timothy leapt into the driving seat and quickly started the engine, which coughed and farted into life.

'Who are you?' yelled his aunt.

'Only me, you'll soon be home,' said Timothy. As he accelerated, the van backfired loudly, and with Maude screaming abuse at him, he drove away from the hospital giving a reassuring wave to the concerned nurses.

One turned to his colleague saying, 'You know she has high blood pressure, don't you?'

'Oh dear! Feisty old stick though, she threw her breakfast at me one morning,' said the other.

As the van pulled out into the road, Mother was trying to calm Maude, who had pulled Timothy's hat off and was now beating him furiously with it. Her nephew was ducking the smacks, while trying to drive. There was a lot of noise and arm waving in the cab, as they drove back past the policeman again, but this time they didn't have to stop. Timothy smiled cheerfully and waved as they drove by.

'It takes all sorts,' muttered the policeman, shaking his head.

Getting Maude out of the van was easy, as she tried to climb out over the top of her sister. Timothy rushed round and opened the door, in time to catch her, before she fell onto the driveway. 'Get off me, you useless hooligan!' she screamed, while whacking him with her fists as he lifted her upright and tried to help her to the front door. Mother clambered out of the van and between them they got Maude safely inside. Mother had planned to stay behind and make sure her sister was settled. '*Go now,*' she hissed at her son, waving her arm at him.

'Good bye Aunt, hope you keep well,' he said, 'see you later Mother.'

When, later, he arrived back from his regular walk, in the rain today, a car pulled up outside the house. It was Dave Quilford, the detective. Hoping this visit had nothing to do with the van or Aunt Maude, Timothy smiled sheepishly as he approached, 'Hello there.'

'Hello mate, how are you keeping? Bruises nearly gone, I see?' said Dave, out of the car window. 'Your Mother alright, is she?'

'Yes fine, thanks,' he replied. Faith had moved between them to get a better look at Dave through the car window.

'Tell me, as a member of Two to Tango did you ever meet a woman called Jemima?'

Timothy flushed slightly, a little embarrassed. 'Yes, we did meet at her home. I didn't stay very long,' he remembered that dreadful day and all the soot.

'What kind of person was she?'

'A bit odd, actually. The house looked un-lived in and felt quite spooky and then, while we were having tea there was a fall of soot down the chimney. I climbed out of a window and left. Oh, and it was thundering at the time, I got soaked on the way home.'

Suddenly Faith shook himself vigorously, spraying Dave's face with water and mud from his wet fur. The detective leaned out of the car window, spat into the road and wiped the mess off his face. 'Did she mention her husband at all while you were there?'

'No. I didn't know there was a husband. I thought she was single.'

192

Dave screwed up the tissue in his hand and said, 'It's a bit odd, because her husband vanished some months ago and hasn't been seen, or heard of since. If she ever contacts you again will you let me know?'

'Sure, but I doubt she will,' he replied, as Faith got ready for another good shake. This time Dave put his window up just in time, avoiding another soaking. Letting the window down again, he thanked Timothy and wished him well, before driving off. Mrs Fell's curtains were twitching vigorously as he went inside.

While he was cleaning Faith the doorbell rang; it rang continuously for the length of time it took him to reach the door and open it.

Mrs Battle was on the doorstep, with another helmet-like flowery hat jammed down on her head. 'Now look here, you need to get this doorbell fixed. Has that dog of yours got Mrs Fell's teeth again? She asked me to come and check.' she barked loudly.

A little taken aback by the sudden verbal assault, he took a breath and replied, ' No, Faith hasn't been near Mrs Fell's teeth or her house today.'

'What! He's been to Mrs Fell's house today, did you say?' she shouted, leaning towards Timothy.

He shook his head. Then speaking as loudly as he could without yelling, '*NO*! Faith has *NOT* been to Mrs Fell's and does *NOT* have her teeth!'

'Right then. Thank you Timothy, no need to shout'; she turned abruptly. Putting her finger in her ear and giving it a good shake, she walked off swinging her stick with her other hand.

24
Don't mess with the old bats.

Eve looked at the gathering of people before her, not one of them under the age of sixty and only three men among them. She waited while they settled into their seats. Her sergeant had given her the task of talking to the neighbourhood and park watch group; with notes prepared she cleared her throat.

'Is Timothy coming?' asked Mrs Fell.

'Doesn't look like it,' Eve replied.

'He never comes to any meetings,' boomed Mrs Battle.

Eve cleared her throat again, and waited until she had their full attention. 'Welcome everyone,' she began …

She gave them strict instructions once again on the importance of watching, taking note and reporting anything suspicious to the police, and *not* getting involved. Communication and vigilance is the key, she told them; they all nodded enthusiastically; except for Dougal Broadbent at the back who had nodded off to sleep and begun to snore… until his wife Maureen gave him a kick on the shin.

'Thank you everyone, I'll be happy to answer any of your questions,' finished Eve.

'Will you be coming to the Old Dog for a drink with us?' asked Mrs Fell.

'Just a quick drink while I answer your questions.' She liked the spirit of the older folk in this town and the evening wasn't as bad as she had been warned it would be, by colleagues.

Three nights later, before retiring to bed Dougal Broadbent was walking around the neighbourhood with his wife's poodle. The little dog suddenly started to growl. A couple of men with hoods over their heads ran along an alleyway between the houses. He decided to follow; he pulled out his mobile phone and rang his wife.

'Maureen quick, call the gang. I think there's some blokes up to something around number 47, Ash Street. They're away, aren't they?' he gasped, still following the two men as discreetly as he could. He picked up the little dog and tucked it under his coat, hoping it wouldn't bark.

'Didn't the policewoman say we mustn't interfere?' whispered his wife.

'Oh never mind all that, just phone everyone. Why are you whispering?'

'I don't want them to hear me!'

'… just phone!'

Mrs Fell leapt to the challenge, and raced along in her car, collecting a few members of the group. Mrs Battle was ready for an early night and dressed in her night-dress when she got the call. She grabbed a coat and shoes before dashing out.

Mrs Weatherbutts. as a rather round lady, looked quite scary dressed for the part in running shoes, trousers and a balaclava.

Maureen Broadbent had also dressed for the part, in black, and was armed with a mobile phone, a stout cosh and a flash-light.

'I'll drive around the back way and then we can cruise silently downhill along Ash Street with the engine off,' said Mrs Fell.

'Good idea, we can creep up on them and see what they're up to. I've brought my pepper spray in case we catch them,' Mrs Weatherbutts exclaimed excitedly.

195

'I wonder if we should have called Timothy', said Mrs Battle, 'he's good in a fight.'

'So am I!' cried Mrs Weatherbutts.

They turned the corner and cruised silently down Ash Street with the lights dipped. Mrs Fell leaned forward over the steering wheel; they all stared out of the windows, on full alert.

'There's Dougal,' cried Maureen, making them jump.

Mrs Fell slammed on the brakes, skidding to a halt by a clump of trees. Dougal walked out from the shadows and bent down to the car window. ' They're in the alleyway between number 14 and 16; what are you planning to do?'

'I think we should get them,' said Mrs Weatherbutts, in a loud whisper.

'They could be going home or something, we have to be sure they're up to no good before we can act,' said Dougal.

'Okay, I'll cruise by in the car and take a look. You follow in the shadows, Dougal,' said Mrs Fell.

'Right you are,' he slunk off into the trees.

She let off the brake and steered silently down the street. Two youths ran out of a driveway and headed up the alley. In her excitement Mrs Fell braked hard and flung the car door open. 'Quick everybody out,' she cried, with one foot on the road and one in the car. She heaved herself upright holding on to the door. The car started to move forward again, she had forgotten to put on the handbrake and had no choice but to hop along with the vehicle, half in – half out. Holding tight to the door she managed to get her other foot back onto the sill as the car went faster and faster.

'Put the handbrake on,' she shouted.

'What's broken?' called Mrs Battle.

'The handbrake, put it on!'

Mrs Weatherbutts and Maureen became wedged as they both leaned forward between the front seats trying to reach the brake. Maureen grabbed Mrs Battle by her head and yelled directly into one ear, 'P*ut the handbrake on!'*

They were heading for a grass verge when Mrs Battle finally got the message and pulled on the brake. The car skidded sideways, sending Mrs Fell sprawling across the grass as it stopped. She lay there groaning; the others climbed out and went to help.

'Is she alive?' whispered Maureen.

Mrs Fell sat up and stared at them. 'I'm okay I think, give me a hand up,' she said holding her hands out. They hauled her to her feet. 'Yes I'm fine, look I can walk. Let's get after them.'

They climbed back into the car and drove along to the alleyway. Dougal came walking towards them, signalling for them to be quiet.

They stood in the shadow of the trees while Dougal explained that the youths had broken into number 47. The poodle pushed its head out from under Dougal's jacket and growled.

'Shhhhh,' they said in unison.

'Right, we need a plan,' said Mrs Weatherbutts. 'I know this house.'

The plan of action arranged, they split up to go about their various tasks. Mrs Weatherbutts switched the water sprinklers on full.

Mrs Battle and Maureen tiptoed around the back to the alley, where they quietly collected dustbins from the houses and laid them on their sides across the path.

Dougal and Mrs Fell closed the front gates to the house, wedging them with a branch. Mrs Fell also had the idea of tying some washing line across the entrance of the alley, just above ankle height.

197

They all waited while Dougal called the police station.

'Who's whistling?' whispered Maureen.

Baffled they looked at one another and then Dougal said, 'Oh no.   It's Venny coming back from the Old Dog.'

'I think he's got a woman he visits,' said Mrs Weatherbutts. 'I hope he doesn't wander down the alley.'   They all listened as the whistling got nearer.

'I'll go and head him off,' said Dougal, and ran towards the alley. Remembering the washing line across the entrance just in time, he hopped over it.

The two thieves were working their way through the house, methodically searching for money, jewellery and any other valuables. The street lamp outside gave enough light for their purpose. Hearing car tyres screeching on the road, they listened for anything further before silently continuing their search.

They looked at one another when they heard whistling. One pointed at his watch and indicated they should leave.   They made their way back to the glass garden door that they had broken in through, and stared at the water 'raining' onto the decking outside.   They shrugged at one another, pulled their hoods over their heads and, skidding on the wet decking, made their way toward the front of the house. They stopped dead when they realised someone had closed the gates and there were people walking around on the roadside. They ran to the back of the house, easily cleared the small gate leading to the alley, and ran into the dark.

They didn't see Venny in the darkness, as he'd stopped whistling when he heard the thieves running up behind him. 'Hey! What are you up to?' Venny shouted, when one of the thieves crashed right into him breaking his nose. Cursing and swearing the two youngsters tried to run on, tripping over more dustbins as they fled.

Dougal decided to wait at the end of the alley when he heard the ruckus. The ladies had flagged down the approaching police car.

More crashing and swearing came from the alley as the two thieves fell headlong over the washing line; they jumped up and raced off into the night.

Sergeant Dumple looked at the local vigilantes and sighed. This was going to take some sorting out. Dougal and Venny emerged from the alley; Venny was holding a large handkerchief over his bleeding nose. 'Come over here you two,' commanded the sergeant.

'It's alright, they're with us,' said Maureen, relieved to see her husband, with her dog peeping out from under his jacket. 'I didn't know you'd joined this mottley crew, Venny,' questioned the sergeant. Venny nodded sheepishly, keeping the handkerchief over his mouth and nose. 'Right,' the sergeant went on, 'I'll have your names, and I'll expect you all to come and make a statement at the station tomorrow.'

'But they're getting away,' cried Mrs Weatherbutts.

'Don't you worry, those two are known to us and we'll catch them soon enough,' he replied patiently.

25
Losing the van.

Timothy left for his meeting with Penny. Feeling confident he gave a toot on the horn as he pulled up outside her front door.

'Hi Timothy, how are you?' she asked smiling, pulling the door closed behind her. 'Oh grief! Did you get this from the scrap yard?'

'Attacked by cows,' he replied 'I borrowed it from a friend.' He drove to The Old Dog Inn and explained the 'cow attack', making her giggle.

The inn wasn't too full when they went up to the bar, it was the same barman who had served him when he'd been there with Fiona. He looked at them both, recognised Timothy and gave a knowing smile. 'Evening.' he said.

'Evening,' said Timothy, ignoring the knowing looks. While they were waiting for their meal a uniformed policeman came into the pub and walked up to the bar. The whole place hushed slightly in the presence of the law. The barman directed him to where Timothy and Penny were sitting. 'Timothy Parkes?' asked the policeman, recognising him from the episode in the park.

'That's me,' he replied thinking, *now what*?

'Is that battered van outside yours?'

'No, I'm borrowing it at the moment. I have the owner's details if you need them, it has an MOT.'

'Who are the two people trying to start it in the car park? Friends of yours?' the policeman waited for an answer.

'What people? Have you got the right van? I locked it!'
Timothy exclaimed, standing up and making his way to
the pub door.

As they walked outside, the van was leaving, backfiring
loudly as it went off down the road. *'Someone has
actually stolen it,'* he gasped.

The policeman was already on his radio reporting the
incident. Timothy could overhear some of the
conversation. The voice on the radio was laughing.
'You mean stolen? That old heap of junk! What nutter
would want to steal that…? Well it *is* a crime, so we
could send a car out,' said the voice, still laughing.
'Does he want it back?' The policeman looked at
Timothy for an answer. *'Of course I want it back.* It's
on loan from the shop,' he almost shouted.

'Alright, alright, keep your hair on. We'll get on to it
now;' said the voice on the radio.

'Sorry mate, you go back and enjoy your meal. Leave
it to us to find the van, there's been a break-in along
Ash Street, it's probably the same lads, ' said the
policeman, overly patient.

'How am I supposed to take my date home?' Timothy
asked gloomily.

The policeman handed him the telephone number of a
local taxi service and said, 'Give the station a ring when
you get home so we know where to contact you. I
believe you have the number.'

'And I believe you have my number. I hope you find it
soon.' He sighed, wondering how he was going to
explain this one to Derek. He went back into the pub to
find the barman chatting up Penny, but quickly
returning to his duties when he saw Timothy.
Explaining what had happened to the van, he sat down
to finish his meal, but Penny couldn't stop laughing.
'Someone really stole *that.* They must be insane.'

He was getting a bit fed up with everyone finding it so amusing. His meal was cold and he was going to have to pay for a taxi to get them both home. He just grunted at Penny in reply, ordering them both another drink as he wouldn't be driving.

His usual cheeriness was slightly dampened but Penny remained upbeat. 'Come on, cheer up. I'm sure they'll find it. I mean you can hardly miss it can you?' she said, stifling more giggles. He just looked at her. 'They'd better find it soon, I have to take it back tomorrow afternoon.'

The taxi turned up, and after dropping Penny off he explained to the taxi driver what had happened. ' You mean that old van that looks like it's been in a demolition derby? Yeah, seen it about. The police will find it, surely,' said the driver.

'I wouldn't put money on it. I can't think anyone would hang on to it for long, it's not a good drive.'

'You're not kidding,' the driver laughed.

Timothy knew that not many people would want to drive it far, the gear changes were awful and it was hard to make them work properly. It coughed out fumes and backfired, and had to have regular top ups of water as the radiator leaked. In fact he wasn't sure why Derek didn't ditch it, but by some miracle it was legal and did have a current MOT.

The following morning was his half day off work, and while he was walking the dog, his mobile rang. It was the police station informing him that they'd found the van and it had been towed to the car pound. 'Great! I'll just take the dog home and I'll be over,' he said.

He was getting quite familiar with the staff at the station, and getting to know a number of policemen and women by name. Walking up to the reception desk he found Sergeant Dumple on duty. 'Morning Sergeant,' he said cheerily. The sergeant was known for his humour, and greeted him with a grin. 'You've come to collect your junk, have you?'

'The van, yes,' replied Timothy crisply.

'We've all got bets on. Will it start and will it go? Is it legal?'

He sighed in response, 'It's got its MOT. I have the certificates all here, insurance, licence and here look - current MOT.' The sergeant looked through the papers, shaking his head and sucking his teeth, 'Seems you've got another six months legal motoring with this. I personally think it will be a bleeding miracle if you can drive it out of the pound. You should strongly recommend to the owner that he change this vehicle as soon as he can. We had a quick word with him, just to verify him as the owner, but he didn't seem that worried about us finding it. I hear scrap metal prices are quite good these days.' he said, handing Timothy all the paperwork with the keys.

He found the van among a number of other vehicles in the small pound. He thought it looked a bit sad, it's usual beaten up appearance now worsened. Reeds, bits of hedge and other plantation, were sticking out of the front grill, grass was hanging around the mud guards and the lights; a few small branches and brambles were attached to the wing mirrors.

'Where was it?' he asked a policewoman.

'It had been driven off the road, through a wood, into a bog, and abandoned,' she smiled sympathetically. 'I'm afraid you have an audience, but I hope it starts for you.'

'It *will* start and I'll drive it out of here,' he said, confidently. The old van had never let him down before and he was sure it wouldn't this time. You just had to know how to treat it.   Suddenly his mobile burst into '*The William Tell Overture*,' loudly echoing around the pound. Lots of laughter could be heard coming from the station as he answered. It was Mother.

'I'm just getting into the van now, I'll call and pick you up,' he said, opening the van door which creaked loudly, followed by the sound of bits dropping off when he slammed it shut. He gave the dashboard a little pat. 'Come on old girl, start for me; I'm taking you home,' he said, as he turned the key in the ignition. The engine turned over, coughed, spluttered and died; he gave it another pat. 'Come on,' he said more firmly.

Turning the key again there was more coughing, spluttering, and then the familiar loud bang as it backfired and roared noisily into life. He gave a few good revs and drove triumphantly out of the pound. As he looked in the mirror he could see a cloud of dark fumes, and several policemen and women clapping, coughing and cheering. He smiled to himself: there was something very satisfying about getting an old clapped-out vehicle to work. *Like the kiss of life,* he thought as he made his way through town. The old van, still recovering from its misadventure, backfired loudly each time he left a junction, making pedestrians jump with fright. There were squeals and shouts when he drove away from one crossing, leaving a cloud of dark fumes behind him.

Pulling up outside Maude's house, he tooted the horn, which struggled to work. Mother opened the door and beckoned him inside to pick up her bags. Jumping out of the van he was pleased to see his aunt on her feet again as she walked slowly toward the front door.

'Good to see you up and about Aunt Maude,' he said.

Maude looked at him for a moment, and after several gulps of air she shrieked. '*No*! You're *NOT getting me in that contraption again. Never, never again,*' she slowly walked back into the house.

'Timothy was pleased to see you, Maude. He doesn't mean you any harm,' Mother said soothingly. 'Get your lunatic son away from me,' replied Maude, slamming the door.

Timothy helped his mother into the van with her bags. 'Has it had *another* accident?' she asked.

'It was stolen and driven into a bog. I've just collected it,' he replied, jumping into the driving seat.

'D'you think you might buy your own car soon?' she asked, while strapping herself in tight.

He turned the ignition key and the van lurched back into life, backfiring as it did. They could see Maude glaring out of the sitting room window; they waved and drove off, leaving the usual cloud of fumes behind.

'I was thinking of getting a Land Rover, so I could take Faith out into the country for walks.'

'They don't look very comfy, dear,' she replied, then suddenly shouted, '*STOP!*' He slammed on the brakes, which squealed in protest as the van stopped. Mother flung the door open.

'What on earth are you doing, you can't get out here.'

'I'm letting something out,' she replied, as a toad hopped out of the van and slowly made its way to the grass verge. The cars behind were objecting to being held up, but it wasn't until the toad was safe that Mother shut the door. 'Anymore passengers in here?' she asked.

The idea of having a vehicle again appealed to Timothy more and more and he decided that later, on his way back from work, he would call at a local garage that had one for sale. Meanwhile he had to take Mother home, and go to work. He tried to think about what he was going to say about the van to Derek this afternoon.

As he drove into the parking slot at the back of the shop, Derek appeared. With arms folded and eyebrows raised, he waited in silence.

'Ah … hello. Let me explain, first there was an attack by cows and…' began Timothy.

'You better come into the office,' interrupted Derek. Timothy hadn't seen this side of his friend before. As soon the door closed he turned suddenly towards Timothy making him jump. 'Only you could borrow a vehicle, have several accidents, have it stolen, *then* be stupid enough to let the police find it again. The insurance would have paid towards another van. Lucky for you I have a scrap dealer coming to see it later today.'

'I haven't got the sack then?' said Timothy quietly.

Derek started to laugh. 'The van was a wreck before you trashed it. I wouldn't have been keen to lend it to you if it *wasn't*.'

' I'm sorry but none of it was really my doing.'

'So lets hear the next episode in the life and disasters of Timothy Parkes,' said Derek, now more like his usual self. Relieved to see Derek laughing, he explained about his adventures with the van. During their banter, mainly about vehicles, women and girl friends; Timothy noticed that Derek talked quite a lot about Henri, apparently the relationship was going well. In fact it was a bit of a record for Derek to date one lady for more than a week!

Back in the shop all was quiet. Timothy busied himself checking the shelves and making sure the books were all in the correct categories. He was wondering if he should call Penny and arrange to meet up with the dogs. He felt they could be friends, but probably no romance there, and she may not want anything more to do with him after last night.

Mrs Fell interrupted his thoughts. She smiled and he was relieved to see both sets of teeth rattling around as usual. While paying for her books she said, 'it's nearly five o'clock, would you like a lift home?'

'Oh, no thank you, I have my bike; very kind of you to ask.'

She lowered her voice, 'I heard you were working undercover. Seen driving an old van in disguise. Mrs Brown said you had been disguising it with weeds! Was it something exciting?' She peered hard at him for an answer as Derek snorted loudly from across the shop, having overheard the conversation.

'Well yes, actually I have, Mrs Fell,' he whispered, deciding to give her something to report to the 'network.' 'The van was attacked by cows in a field, then it was stolen, and found later in a bog. All very hush hush.' Mrs Fell's eyes sparkled with this snippet of information, and having paid for the books, she almost skipped out of the shop.

'Who do they think you are, Batman?' Derek laughed.

'Or similar,' he chuckled.

'Seriously, I'm thinking of getting a vehicle again and thought I might look at a Land Rover; the garage has a notice pinned up with one for sale.'

'Land Rover! Oh this should be fun!'

On his way home that evening he called at the garage and studied the notice board. There were a number of vehicles for sale and the one old, short wheelbase, soft top Land Rover with current MOT; was still available. He made a note of the telephone number.

When he arrived home Mother reported that a young lady called Penny had phoned. 'Who's Penny dear, is she coming over?' she asked, Timothy braced himself for the 'twenty questions!

'Perhaps, but not this evening; we met in the park, and Faith enjoyed playing with her dog. It's a Labrador.'

'A friend for you, too!' said Mother, rubbing Faith's ears. 'How lovely, where does she work? I like Labradors'

'I have no idea. What's for supper tonight?' he said, trying to throw her off the scent.

'Sausages tonight. Will you be in all evening?'

'Looks like it; I'll see you in a while,' he said hurriedly, collecting the dog's lead.

On his return he phoned the farmer about the Land Rover and arranged to see it later in the week. Then he phoned Penny who was curious to know if he had the van back, and what the police had said. He related the story and mentioned buying a Land Rover. She was enthusiastic about the vehicle, saying she knew several places where they could take the dogs for a good walk.

26
Meanwhile at the refuse dump.

The crows and magpies had learned that the mountains of plastic bags at the refuse site often contained food; they were well practised at pecking around, flicking anything unwanted away and flying off with edibles, such as discarded meat pies, chicken carcasses etc. Seagulls would also frequent the site, stealing booty from the opened bags.

The sun was shining and Burt Mullins was sitting in his JCB eating sandwiches for lunch. He had worked at the site for some time and enjoyed watching the birds, admiring how adept they were at accessing any food from the rubbish and squabbling among themselves. Today he noticed they were particularly interested in one area. In fact, there were many more birds than usual, all concentrating on the same place.

He wondered if he should take a look to see what was attracting them. Recently someone had thrown out a whole side of lamb in a refuse bag; and sometimes it was the entire contents of a freezer. He wandered into the hut to make himself a drink; a few of the other site-workers were sitting around having their packed lunches.

'The birds are keen today, I think we should take a look,' he said to his work mates.

'No, leave it to the boss, he'll be back on Thursday. I'm not wading up there. It took a week to get rid of the smell last time,' groaned Todd, producing a mug with a tea bag, for Burt to fill when the kettle had boiled.

'Try using soap next time, stinker!' said old Joe, sitting in the corner laughing.

'Probably just another broken down freezer anyway.'
'I'll tell the boss when he comes in,' replied Burt, going back to his sunny cab and bird watching.

27
The Land Rover.

Timothy collected cash from the bank and decided to cycle straight from work to see the Land Rover. Following the sketchy directions from the farmer along narrow lanes and tracks, he soon realised he was lost. He saw an elderly man with a sheep dog coming down the lane, so he stopped and asked for directions.

The man coughed noisily and spat, the dog ducking out of the way just in time. 'Aye what is it ye want, lad?'

Timothy explained about the Land Rover and the name of the farm he was looking for. 'Aye, yer mean old Slyes place? You go up there,' he said, pointing along the lane, 'left by the old hanging tree, yer know?'

'Not really,' said Timothy.

The man coughed and spat again. 'Aye well, you'll know it when yer sees it. You go left there and then yer come to a cattle grid. You'll not want to ride yer bike over that! Go over the cattle grid, past the sheep carcass, and take the right fork, ye'll find it up there. Not much of a road for biking.'

Timothy thanked him and rode away, hoping he would recognise the old hanging tree ... whatever it was. The lane narrowed and eventually came to a crossroads with a big, ancient oak tree in the middle. He decided to turn left and, sure enough, after a short distance he came to a cattle grid. He carried the bike over and seeing the track was very rocky and full of potholes, left it in the hedge, checking there were no cattle about. The track seemed to go on and on, up another hill and round another bend. As he was about to turn back, he smelt dead sheep! On the brow of the hill he could see there was still a long way to go, but at least it was downhill, and he could see the farm in the distance.

As he walked through the gate two farm dogs came out, barking at him. He did his best to ignore them and headed over to a Land Rover that was parked by a barn, hoping for a sneaky look before meeting the farmer. It was old and rusty; he opened the driver's door, which creaked loudly. There were weeds growing in the foot well, a thick layer of green moss growing at the base of the windows and it was full of dust. Not quite what he had hoped for.

'It'll not let yer down, lad,' said a voice behind him.

He turned to see a man of portly proportions and a big smile, revealing only two teeth and one of those was crooked. He was wearing a grey vest, shabby trousers and had slipped his boots on without tying the laces. He gave Timothy a hearty slap on the back, nearly knocking him over. 'Do you want to take her for a spin, lad?'

'Well, I had hoped to find something a bit younger and in better repair.'

'Ah, you'll not find anything as reliable as this. Goes like a good'n she does, the keys are in it, give it a go,' insisted the farmer.

Timothy had serious doubts. As the farmer had heaved himself into the passenger seat, causing the Land Rover to tilt with his weight, he felt obliged to drive it a little way, just to keep the man happy. 'Okay, but I'm pretty sure it's not what I want, I really want something a little more…'

'Start her up then, she always goes first time, you'll see. Go on lad,' interrupted the owner, flashing his two teeth and gums in a huge smile.

Timothy turned the ignition and to his surprise the engine roared into life, making the Land Rover shudder and producing a strange squealing sound from the engine. '*What's that*,' he asked, shouting above the noise.

'Oh nothing to worry about, it's just part of her character, you'll see. Go on, drive her up the track,' said the farmer enthusiastically.

'Part of her character?' exclaimed Timothy. Reversing the vehicle, he was surprised the gear change was quite smooth compared to the old van. He drove along the rough track. The noise didn't improve and the Land Rover appeared to have a mind of its own, lurching from one side of the track to the other. He had to hold tight to the steering wheel just to keep going in the right direction. He assumed this was due to the bumpy track, large stones, and potholes. Finally they reached the cattle grid, where he pulled up. With the noisy engine still running, he noticed a plume of exhaust fumes behind them.

'Thanks for letting me drive it, but I don't think it's what I'm looking for,' he shouted.

'Ah go on, make me an offer,' boomed the farmer.

'No really, I need something younger, and it's not worth the nine hundred and fifty pounds you're asking. It's hardly worth a hundred pounds, even with an MOT,' he said, still shouting.

'DONE!' replied the farmer, grabbing his hand and shaking it vigorously.

'Oh no, you misunderstand me. I wasn't making an offer,' he shouted, beginning to panic.

'Aye lad, one hundred will do nicely, only cost you a few more to do it up. I have the paperwork in my pocket,' said the farmer, producing all the documents and thrusting them at him.

Timothy raised his eyes upward and shouted. '*Oh my God, why me? I don't want it!*' He tried pushing the documents back into the farmer's hand but he was having none of it. He grabbed Timothy's hand again with his own huge ape-like grip, and gave it another good vigorous shake. 'Nice doing business with you. Hand over the hundred and I'll chuck yer bike in the back, and yer can be on yer way.' shouted the farmer, laughing at Timothy's predicament and knowing exactly what he was selling him.

As if trapped in a nightmare, Timothy was unable to see a way out. He had never really been the forceful type and with an awful feeling in his gut, he found himself reluctantly handing over one hundred pounds to the farmer. After pocketing the money the man chucked the bike into the back of the Land Rover and banged on the side shouting, 'Plenty of life in the old thing yet, she'll see yer right, lad.' he laughed and waved, no doubt feeling very pleased with himself.

The reluctant new owner slowly drove over the cattle grid wondering if the last ten minutes had really happened. Had he really bought this pile of junk for one hundred pounds? The Land Rover suddenly lurched to one side; Timothy gripped the steering wheel and hauled it back onto the road. As it lurched this way and that way along the tarmac lane, it dawned on him why the farmer had only invited him to drive it along the bumpy track. There was something seriously wrong with the steering. As he weaved into his local garage, two mechanics looked up and began to laugh. 'Oh dear, how much did you pay *for that*?' one asked.

'Only a hundred pounds.'

'It was going to cost him fifty to have it taken away. How did you find the steering?' asked the other mechanic, chuckling. 'Pretty awful. Can you give me an estimate of how much it will be to get it running safely. I'll leave my details in the office,' said Timothy, pulling his bike out of the back.

The mechanics looked as if he had asked them to produce a Porsche from scrap metal. Eventually one answered, 'Okay mate, leave the key in it for now and I'll bring it in to the workshop to have a look at it.'

Timothy cycled home, feeling that he may as well have thrown one hundred pounds down the drain. On the optimistic side, he thought, if it wasn't too expensive to fix and gave him one or two years on the road, it may not work out too badly.

He was putting the dog's lead on when the telephone rang; it was Penny who asked if he was headed for the park, and could they meet up. On his way to the park he heard the familiar sound of a revving engine, squealing of brakes and then the little Mini came into view with Mrs Fell clutching the steering wheel. The car came to an abrupt halt beside him. Mrs Fell wound the window down and Faith quickly pushed his head into the little car, licking her face and smearing her glasses with saliva before Timothy could pull him away. She beckoned Timothy to come closer and lean down to her level, she spoke in a loud whisper, teeth moving enthusiastically, 'Everything going alright, Timothy?'

He raised an eyebrow and whispered equally loudly back, 'I'm just off for a liaison with someone in the park, *shh!!!*' He put his finger to his lips and winked before walking on.

The little car got a good revving before moving off, causing yet another vehicle to come to an abrupt stop as it suddenly pulled out into the road. Timothy was amazed how she had not only managed to remain unscathed, but live to a ripe old age too.

Entering the park he unclipping Faith's lead and looked around for Penny. The dogs found each other first and raced around excitedly, as Penny came along the concrete path on her roller blades carrying another pair. 'Hi there! Thought you might want to join me, ' she said, holding out the roller blades. 'I haven't been roller blading since I was twelve. Not sure if I can anymore,' he said, looking at the size. 'They're adjustable; I hope they'll fit.'

While the dogs were playing a game of chase, Timothy adjusted them enough to fit, though it was a tight squeeze. Standing up carefully, he rolled forward, arms out to keep his balance. After some wobbling and clutching bushes (and at one point Penny), he started to get the feel of it again. Slowly they set off along the path with Penny keeping close and steadying him from time to time. The dogs were delighted with this new game and raced around them.

With some difficulty he managed to tell her all about the Land Rover. 'If you get it fixed, perhaps we could take the dogs off for a walk in the country, like you mentioned,' said Penny.

He agreed it would be fun, but in his mind he'd hoped it would be Lizzie going for walks with him in the country. His thoughts kept drifting back to her, in few months time she would be back in town. Perhaps he should have a chat with Penny and explain the situation, so no one got the wrong idea.

Eventually finding his balance, he enjoyed himself more and more. He noticed Mrs Battle hectoring several children; she stared at him in astonishment as he rolled by.

Coming to another area of the park, there were more people and it was necessary to put both dogs on leads. Faster and faster they went as the dogs began to race one another. Timothy and Penny laughed and whooped with delight as they whizzed along the path. 'This *is* fun!' he called out.

They rounded a bend before the wooded area, and without any warning Faith lunged after a squirrel, dragging Timothy with him. Luckily the grass in the park was always kept short, so he was able to stay upright. Waving one arm in the air to keep his balance, and hanging on to the lead with the other, he called, '*Faith heel!*' and '*Wait boy!*' but it made no difference. He heard similar shrieks from behind, indicating that Penny was having the same trouble.

The squirrel realised what was coming and, at what seemed like the last moment, scampered up a tree. Looking down on the drama below, it made loud chit-chit noises by way of complaint.

The dog dragged Timothy to the base of the tree, entangling him in fallen leaves and small twigs, which were too much for the roller blades, and once again gravity took over. Falling headlong onto to the grass, he lay on his back for a moment to recover; looking up at the squirrel he wondered if the noise it was making was squirrel laughter. His knees were stinging as he tried to stand up; not easy with roller blades on your feet. Faith was fussing around, licking his' face. 'Your fault again lad,' he said, finally managing to stand.

Walking along the grass he could see Penny also nursing her knees; her dog sitting patiently by her side, feigning innocence. He helped her to her feet, after which they made their way to the path. Both were covered in grass stains and leaves. Timothy found his shoes that he had hidden in the branches of a tree and was putting them on when he noticed the green car, belonging to his detective friend. He waved as Dave Quilford made his way towards them.

'Friend of yours?' asked Penny.

'Yes,' he replied, noticing that Dave's hair was uncombed and he was back in scruffy jeans.

Taking in the state of their clothes Dave grinned and commented, 'You two seem to have had an eventful walk today.'

'This isn't quite how it looks,' Timothy said, introducing them.

'Pleased to meet you Penny,' said Dave, stroking the Labrador that was happily wagging its tail. 'Any chance we could have a chat, Timothy?'

'Don't mind me,' said Penny, pulling her dog away. 'I'll be heading back, see you again soon, Timothy.'

'I'll phone you,' he called after her, as she skated off with her dog trotting beside her.

'Had a little accident did you?' said Dave with a wink.

'I haven't been on roller blades for years; it was going ok until then Faith saw a squirrel. But we all survived,'

'Yeah, yeah. I wanted to ask you a few questions.'

They walked back to the park entrance together. 'Is this a police matter?' Timothy asked.

'Yes, mate, it is.' Dave's expression was serious. 'You remember that woman from Two to Tango called Jemima. You met her once?'

'Yes, I told you I had to make a hasty escape. Strange lady, strange house.'

'Did you see anyone else at all in the house or in the grounds, while you were there? Or any sign of anyone else about?'

'I don't remember seeing anyone as I left in a hurry. There was an elderly man with a wheelbarrow in the garden who looked a bit scruffy. I only glimpsed him as I cycled up to the front door, but thought nothing of it,' said Timothy honestly.

218

'Did you see the kitchen or any other rooms in the house?'

'No, she ushered me into a sitting room; from what little I saw, the rest of the house was very dusty, and the furniture was covered with sheets…a mouse ran out of the sofa in the sitting room,' he added, suddenly remembering.

'We may have found her husband. A body has turned up at the local dump. Someone put him out with the rubbish!' said Dave, watching for any reaction.

'Seems like I had a lucky escape.'

'Could be. What troubles me, is that the last two bodies and some considerable mayhem are all in some way connected with you. Even the theft of the old van.'

'It *looks* like it's all connected with me. I just happen to be in the wrong place at the wrong time, these days. I certainly don't seek out trouble,' he answered, frowning.

'Okay mate, if you think of anything helpful, you know where to find me,' replied Dave, getting back into his car.

While walking home Timothy reflected that he had only met a friend in the park, and once again had sore knees and was covered in dirt. He glanced at the twitching curtains opposite and decided to wave this time… the shape behind the curtains quickly vanished!

Mother was in the kitchen when he walked in. 'I've bought a Land Rover and it's in the garage being done up,' he said, helping himself to one of her freshly made scones.

'I hope it's better than that old van. Mrs Battle told Beattie Fell you were roller-skating with a young woman,' she said, keen to know more.

'Yes, a friend of mine,' he replied, heading upstairs to the bathroom, still eating his scone.

'That's nice.' Fussing Faith she whispered, 'what's he been up to this time, lad?'

The following morning as they passed the 'odd' bungalow, he noticed the shapes of people moving around behind the dingy net curtains. Faith was sniffing one of the usual rubbish bags so giving him time to have a better look. As usual there was nothing suspicious, except the bungalow gave him goose bumps. As they began to walk on a light coloured four by four pulled up and two men, wearing dark suits, began unloading boxes. Timothy tried to encourage Faith to sniff a bit longer so he could get a better look, but the men looked very serious and in a hurry. They quickly unloaded all the boxes into the front door of the bungalow and, unable to hang around any longer without looking suspicious himself, Timothy walked on to the park.

He wondered if he should mention the bungalow to the police. What would they say? People coming in and out with lots of boxes and bags; putting out lots of odd shaped rubbish on collection day when there didn't seem to be anyone actually living there. Or that the place gave him goose bumps! He could imagine the expression on the desk sergeant's face, so he decided it was better to mention it to Dave when they next met.

On the way back the vehicle had gone from outside the bungalow, but there was a light on somewhere inside. Suddenly the front door opened and to Timothy's surprise Doctor Athed came out and walked along the path towards him.

Feeling guilty for 'spying' he straightened himself up and said, 'Morning Doctor Athed, nice day.'

The doctor turned abruptly towards them, his cold eyes stared for a second before he spoke. 'Mmm, morning.'

Turning away he walked swiftly along the pavement, his long dark coat billowing out behind him.

Faith growled at the man and tugged on the lead. 'Come on Faith, let's go home,' he said, the dog's reaction setting his own nerves on alert, giving him goose bumps.

'Morning, how art thee this fine day?' called Derek, from the depths of the shop, as Timothy arrived for work.   He was followed through the door by Mrs Brown, dressed in 'old lady uniform', with a blue hat that didn't match anything, pressed down on her head. Her small bespectacled face peered out from under its large brim, and the apparently bottomless shopping trolley trundled along behind her. After a lot of rummaging in the trolley she put the returned books in a pile on the counter for Timothy to check.

'Enjoyed them, have you?' he asked, out of politeness.

'Oh *yes.*   I'll just go and look for some more,' she whispered.

'You know the way, help yourself,' he replied.

'Find a decent vehicle yet?' asked Derek.   Timothy told him about the Land Rover.

'When will it be ready?'

'I'm calling in on my way home. It will be good to have a vehicle again so that I can take the dog out into the country for walks and stuff.'

'Not to mention the ladies.' replied Derek. There was a crash echoing from one of the upstairs rooms.   They looked at each other questioningly.

'There's no one up there, is there?'

Derek shook his head. 'No, it must be one of your ghosty friends. By the way, I've got a special date with Henri tonight.'

'I thought you were looking chipper recently. No wild animals, or bad tempered cats then?

'No. Henri is a *normal* lady, I can assure you of that!' grinned his friend.'

At that point Mrs Brown came back to the desk with her usual selection of gory books. Timothy totted them up for her after which she dropped them into her trolley. She stood on tiptoe leaning over the counter. Peering at him wearing an odd smile, she tapped the side of her nose with her finger. 'Your secret's safe with us, dear,' she whispered, turning to leave the shop.

He smiled politely opening the door for her. 'Good bye Mrs Brown, see you again soon.'

He had no idea what she had meant but put it down to 'the old lady network' working overtime.

He phoned Two to Tango during his lunch break and arranged for Jane to drop off two more profiles, as she would be passing the shop later that day. He still kept thinking about Lizzie, and hoped it wouldn't be too long before she came back. He wondered if he should call her? She'd included her phone number in the letter; could he pluck up the courage to call? But what would he say, and would she want to know him after having been away for so long. Such a pretty girl was bound to have met someone else by now. He thought it would be best to have a few more dates, and then decide.

Derek left the shop early this afternoon. Timothy was tidying up the paperwork on the desk prior to locking up when the doorbell jangled.

Jane came in with an unexpected smile on her face. 'Hello Timothy, I've got your profiles here. You must meet this one, you really must,' she insisted.

'Thank you Jane, it's kind of you to drop them in,' he said, puzzled by her change in attitude.

A clatter came from upstairs, which he recognised as books falling from a shelf. 'Is someone else here?' asked Jane.

'No, just some books falling over.'

'I'd like a copy of a book called *The Hidden Rose,* have you heard of it? It's a contemporary romance about a thwarted couple who go through all kinds of dramas before finally getting together,' she went on, dreamy-eyed.

'Romantic dramas are in the little room up the stairs, first on the right. If we have it, it will be there. I'll just put these papers away and come and help you look.'

Jane's face lit up. 'Oooh, will you, Timothy? I'll go and start looking; first on the right, you say?'

'Yes, I'll be along in a minute,' he said, glancing at his watch.

A few more books fell off a shelf in another room downstairs. On his way to find Jane, he went to where he'd heard the books falling, and placed them on the reading table.

'Someone's going to be doing a lot of reading,' said Jane's voice suddenly behind him, making him jump.

'Did you find your book?'

'No, but I haven't finished looking yet.'

'I'll come and help,' he led the way back to the Romance section; 'do you know the name of the author? It would really help.'

'No, sorry I don't.' There was another thump of a book falling from behind a stack on the other side of the room. He knew exactly what had happened but Jane leapt with fright. '*What's that*? I thought you said there was no one here?' she cried, clutching his arm.

'*There isn't,*' he replied, calmly extracting himself from her grip. She stood motionless as he walked around the stack of books and picked one up from the floor.

Smiling to himself, he showed her the book. '*The Hidden Rose.* Is this what you wanted?'

She stared at him for a moment and then suddenly flung her arms around him in a vice-like grip. 'Oh Timothy, I've waited so long for this moment but you never seem to notice me,' she cried, clinging on tightly and plastering his face with kisses.

He wriggled uncomfortably, then managed to extract himself and push her away. While still holding firmly on to her wrist, he spoke gently: 'You're a lovely lady, but I don't think we're suited. I'm not the right person for you, Jane.'

Her face changed. Her bottom lip wobbled and he thought she was going to cry. Instead she took a deep breath, looked him directly in the eye and snapped: 'Right then, I'll take the book, how much is it?'

He let go of her wrist and handed her the book. 'Six pounds, ninety nine pence. Bring it down and I'll wrap it for you,' he answered calmly.

She followed him down the stairs and as he rang the book up on the till, there was another loud clatter of falling books from across the room. She snatched up the book. 'I don't know who, or what you've got in there but I hope you're enjoying the joke,' she said, stomping out of the shop and slamming the door behind her.

He watched through the window as she marched off with her head held high. Her behaviour was puzzling, he could have sworn she didn't even like him. He sighed and thought he would never understand women.

He wandered around gathering up the fallen books before leaving. 'You're going to have a busy night,' he said aloud, not expecting any reply. 'Good night, and thanks for finding the book for me' He was answered by another clatter.

The young man behind the counter at the garage looked up as he walked in. 'Hello there, come about the old Land Rover, have you?'

'How is it coming along?'

'I'll fetch Arthur, our head mechanic, he can tell you himself,' said the young man.

After a few minutes he came back with Arthur, an older man with a round face and broad shoulders. His overalls, arms and hands were black with oil and grease; he leaned heavily on the polished counter.

'How soon will it be ready?' asked Timothy optimistically.

Arthur shook his head and loudly sucked air through his teeth. Always a bad sign thought Timothy. 'Well, you realise this isn't just a renovation job, don't you?' Arthur asked.

'Excuse me?'

More sucking in of air from Arthur. 'Well, it's nothing short of a resurrection, mate.' Arthur shuffled his feet, and shaking his head, blew air out of his mouth with a low whistle. 'With some of the lads off, and Jocko with a broken arm an all, we should have it ready for you tomorrow afternoon after four O'clock. We'll settle up then shall we?'

'You can't give me some idea of cost now, can you?'

A lot more sucking in of air and shaking of the head from Arthur. 'Well now, let me see, there are quite a few parts, some new, some second-hand. We managed to find some cheap for you, and the new tyres and the head-lamp,' more sucking in of air, 'hundreds, I expect,' said Arthur, looking at his feet.

'How *many* hundreds?' asked Timothy, frustrated by the mechanic's attitude.

'Oh, several I expect. We'll reckon up tomorrow, lad,' said Arthur, looking at Timothy, who decided he was as vague and unhelpful as the farmer who had sold him the Land Rover.

'Fine, I'll be here to collect it after four tomorrow.' said Timothy sternly.

While he was looking forward to owning a working vehicle again, he had this nagging feeling that maybe this wasn't the best move he'd ever made. He retrieved his bicycle and set off for home.

Mother had been baking again and the smell was mouth-watering. 'Have some scones before you take Faith out,' she suggested.

'Oh yes please,' he replied, without hesitation. Sitting at the kitchen table they talked while he was eating. 'Maude has to go back to the hospital for a check up,' she said.

Her son looked at her over his steaming mug of tea. 'Does this mean we have to get her into the van again?'

'I don't think there is a cat in hell's chance of getting her into that van again! I thought perhaps a taxi?' she replied.

'Would you like me to help?'

'Oh no, I don't think that's a good idea at all. If she sees you we'll never get her out of the front door, let alone into a taxi! I wondered if you knew of any local taxi drivers who would be accommodating?'

'Not off hand, but I'll ask around,' he replied.

As he set off Mrs Fell stopped him outside her house. 'Hello Timothy! All going well?' she asked, beaming as usual.

'Yes, all going according to plan,' he replied.

Suddenly she was in front of them blocking the path. 'I didn't know there was a plan. Is it very secret?' Her teeth gleamed, and he wondered if they'd had another scrub with kitchen cleaner.

'Yes, it's very secret, very secret indeed!' he said, in a deliberately loud whisper.

She giggled and skipped off, saying. 'Your secrets are safe with me.'

He laughed to himself; telling Mrs Fell *anything* was like sending a telegram to all the old ladies in the community. He wondered what they'd dreamed up about him this time.

28
Claire's story.

Claire had left Uni with a degree in environmental science but no idea about which career path to pursue, so she had applied for a job as and air-hostess. An attractive young woman in her late twenties, she had no trouble getting dates. However, dates that lasted more than a week or so were difficult to find. After several failed attempts a friend suggested she try Two to Tango.

Claire wasn't so sure. 'Well, they introduce you to men with similar values, so you're more likely to meet someone who won't mind your weird interests,' said her friend.

'I don't call a keen interest in the environment and the health of the planet weird.'

'*You* might not think your concern about farting cows contributing to green-house gasses weird, but most guys would.'

'Okay. I'll give this agency a try, and see if they have anyone interesting, but I can't believe they will.'

Having given her details to Jane, Claire found herself sitting in the reception area of Two to Tango. She could hear raised voices from the office next door. Suddenly a tall man, with long wild hair and beard to match, burst out of the office.

'Well, this one had better be nicer than the last one. I'm no pervert,' boomed the man at Jane, who almost hid under the desk.

'I'm sure you're not, but do try to take your time. I think you will like this lady. Her name is Jemima,' said Daphne Mortesque, following him to the door.

The man turned abruptly and stared back at Daphne. 'If I don't, I'll be back!' With that he marched out of the reception area, slamming the door behind him, making everyone jump.

Claire was sitting in a corner wondering if she should just leave, but Daphne spoke directly to her, 'Good afternoon, do you have an appointment?'

Before she could reply, Jane interrupted, 'This is Claire Watts, your next appointment.'

'Do come through, dear,' said Daphne, smiling and putting herself between the outside door and Claire, expertly blocking any escape route.

Linking her arm through Claire's she guided her swiftly into the inner office. Once inside, Claire aimed for the chair opposite the desk and sat down, while Daphne strode around to the other side of the desk, gazing at her, before sitting down herself. Leaning forward she asked, 'Have you had many lovers, dear?' Shocked by the question, Claire just stared back, unable to speak. Pulling herself upright in the chair, which made unfortunate noises, she finally spoke as confidently as she could, 'That, madam, is none of your business.'

Daphne's direct gaze didn't falter. 'Well, I'll see what we can do then, dear,' she sympathised, as if Claire had admitted to some dreadful affliction. Then she marched off to the filing cabinet. Suddenly she smiled. 'Yes, this is it!' she said, shutting the drawer with her hip as usual. Marching back to her chair, she dropped two folders in front of her new customer.

'The first one is Timothy; quite a character I must say. And an expert horseman too, I have heard… also good with dogs. Not too keen on cats though. Works in a bookshop,' Daphne leaned forward again and continued in a loud whisper. ' I think there is more to Timothy than we know,' she said, with a conspiratorial wink.

'And the other?' asked Claire, looking Daphne in the eye as she spoke.

'Ah yes, the other. He's a nice man, homely sort, and a vet . Lives out of town,' said Daphne, still wearing that fixed tiger-smile.

Claire picked up the folders and agreed to talk to Jane about arrangements to meet the two men. 'Thank you, I'll be in touch,' she said.

While Claire was putting on her coat, a flustered 'Goth' burst in and rushed up to the desk. Claire stared at the vision in black, with a black spiked dog-collar and matching nail polish. 'I must speak with Daphne Mortesque immediately! This man Jake should be struck off your agency,' she shouted.

Jane remained calm and smiled sweetly. 'Oh dear, what did he do to upset you? No one else has complained about him.'

'Well, you should have heard the suggestions he made to me on the phone, it was disgusting,' raved the woman.

Jane was unmoved. 'Well, what suits one doesn't always suit another. I'm sure he meant you no harm.'

Daphne strode into the waiting room. ' What seems to be the trouble? Would you like to step into my office?' she said, stepping aside and letting the woman pass. A knowing look passed between herself and Jane.

Claire was curious, 'Does that happen often?' she asked.

'Oh no. Just every now and then someone gets on their high horse about someone or other, there's usually nothing in it.'

Claire looked at the two folders in her hand, 'Well, I hope these two are okay.'

'I'm sure they will be fine. We wouldn't tie you up with anyone unsuitable.'

'*Tie me up*?' exclaimed Claire.

'Oh just a figure of speech, didn't mean anything by it,' said Jane, still smiling.

When Claire arrived home she called her friend, Angie, who had suggested she try the agency. 'I've joined and got two dates.'

'I'll be right over,' replied Angie, who appeared in ten minutes flat. The two girls sat with a mug of hot chocolate, and mulled over the details, 'I don't think you should bother with either, you can do much better than that, you know.'

Claire didn't agree.

'Why don't you try one of the real upmarket agencies. You might meet a millionaire with a yacht and a villa in Spain, or something.'

'I'm not sure I *need* a millionaire, *or* a villa in Spain. Maybe *you* should join one of the upmarket ones and see if you can do better,' said Claire, becoming irritated by Angie's attitude.

'Right! You're on, let's see who gets their guy first, shall we?' said Angie, rising to the bait.

'Okay, let's do that!' snapped Claire.

She'd already agreed to meet Timothy and was expecting a call from him to confirm details. Although feeling a bit apprehensive, she was also quite excited about going on a blind date.

His profile said he worked in a bookshop. So he was probably a bit too serious and studious for Angie's taste. A nice quiet man who liked books would be okay, she thought. When she spoke on the phone to him, she was surprised to find him easy-going, fun and very pleasant to talk to. They arranged for her to meet him for a meal.

Angie called later to find out what was happening. 'What vehicle does he drive?' she asked.

'I don't know, I didn't ask. He's taking me to a pub for a meal and said he might bring his dog.' '*Bring his dog*! Oh well, he won't be coming on a bike. I can't believe you didn't ask what he drives?'

'It doesn't make much difference if he's a nice guy, does it?' said Claire crisply.

'Oh you're hopeless. A car is a good indication of his financial status… he could turn up in anything.'

'Well, that's okay by me,' Claire replied. She was beginning to realise that her friend was probably jealous, but she was determined that they wouldn't fall out over it. Angie could be useful if she got into a tricky situation, especially as she had been going to martial arts classes for months, hoping to meet a Mr Right.

29
Meeting Claire.

'I'm picking up the Land Rover today. Will it be OK if I park it at the back where the old van used to be?' asked Timothy.

'I don't see why not. I'm looking forward to seeing this.' replied Derek.

When Timothy walked into the garage Arthur was behind the reception desk, 'Come for the Land Rover, have you?' he asked.

'Is it ready?' said Timothy, pulling his credit card out of his pocket.

'As ready as it'll ever be! It's all on the sheet here, including new tyres, service, parts and repairs, and a new MOT.'

Timothy studied the sheet: although he had guessed the vehicle would need a lot doing to it, the £900 charge at the bottom was still a shock. He sighed and handed over his card.

'Should be alright now, lad,' said Arthur with a smile.

'Does it still make an odd noise when you change gear?'

Arthur sucked in air through his teeth and shook his head. 'We had a look at that and can't find anything wrong. You might have to live with it, part of its character,' he said, beaming cheerfully.

Walking onto the forecourt he found the Land Rover had been cleaned and had all the dents knocked out. Its wing mirrors had been replaced and it looked quite respectable. Maybe it wasn't such a bad buy after all, he thought as he lifted his bike into the back. He jumped in and started it up; the engine roared into life. It still made the strange grinding noise when he put it into reverse. Arthur was smiling and waved as Timothy drove off. The Land Rover was much better to drive, not lurching off and changing direction on its own anymore. The engine was noisy but apart from that Timothy was happy with his new acquisition.

On the way home he passed Mrs Battle and tooted the horn that was surprisingly unimpressive for the size of the vehicle, more of a squeak than a good blast.

Mrs Battle jumped in surprise and glared fiercely, hand on her walking stick, ready to strike. 'Would you like a lift?' he shouted over the engine noise.

Mrs Battle's expression looked as though he had offered to run her over. She grabbed the handle and flung the door open, obviously ready to give him a good ticking off, before realising who it was. 'What are you doing with this?'

'I've just bought it. Would you like a lift?' he shouted, ignoring the comment.

She looked doubtful for a moment, but finally agreed.

He jumped out and ran round to give her a hand-up onto the passenger seat. It was almost as if she was mounting a horse. First she tossed her stick in, then she put her left leg up into the foot well and held on to the sides of the door with both hands. With Timothy giving her a good shove from behind, she heaved herself onto the passenger seat. After quickly rearranging her skirt, she sat bolt upright, straightened her yellow helmet-hat and said, 'Thank you Timothy, I'm alright now.'

He pulled up outside her home. 'Thank you, we must talk about more park watch duties,' she shouted over the engine noise.

'Right you are,' he shouted back.

She looked at him for a moment, then, shaking her head, slammed the Land Rover door and marched up the garden path.   He tooted the squeaky horn as he drove off.

'Got the Land Rover, Mother,' he called, on arriving home.
'That's nice dear, I'll come and have a look,' she replied.   They went out together, but she only stared glum faced at the vehicle.
'Don't be disappointed, it's ideal as I can take Faith off for walks in the country,'
His mother looked at him and at the large dog and thought that she should have stayed in her cottage in the country, where they could all have been happy. 'Very nice,' she said, 'but I hope we don't have to take Maude anywhere else in a hurry, we'll never get her into this. The taxi driver was lovely today,' she went on. 'He used to be a fireman and said he was used to difficult elderly ladies, as his own mother had been a bit troublesome.   When we arrived at her house I went in first to get Maude ready. The driver parked as close as possible, leaving a rear door open. He rang the bell but unfortunately Maude had spotted the taxi and shouted that she wasn't going anywhere. He quickly rushed in, picked her up in a fireman's lift and carried her to the taxi, where he somehow bundled her into the back.   I never realised Maude knew such filthy language. I'm afraid she probably educated her whole neighbourhood. Anyway, we got her to the hospital, and the check-up went well.   Getting her out again was quite simple. The taxi driver came into the hospital and hid. As Maude got nearer to the entrance he popped out from behind a door, scooped her up and whizzed her back into the taxi. More filthy language, I'm afraid.   Luckily the nurses and other hospital staff were very understanding. They also remembered us getting her into the van.'

'So all went well then? I hope you made a note of the taxi driver's name and number; it sounds like he could be very useful if you have to take her anywhere else.'

'Are you going out tonight?'

'Oh yes!' he said, suddenly realising he had nearly forgotten his date with Claire.

They'd arranged to meet at 'The Drowning Duck', another small pub on the edge of town.

He walked into the lounge bar and looked around. He couldn't see anyone matching her description, so he sat at a table with the menu and waited. After twenty minutes, a young woman fitting Claire's description walked in on her own. Feeling more confident at meeting a date for the first time, he walked over to her.

'Hello, are you Claire?'

'Yes, and I hope you're Timothy?' she replied nervously.

They shook hands formally and Timothy walked her to a seat at his table. 'Would you like a drink while we study the menu?'

'Yes please. Vodka and ginger ale would be lovely.'

'I used to be really nervous meeting ladies when I first joined the agency. *You do* get used to it, and get more confident each time,' he explained, trying to put her at ease, after collecting their drinks..

'Have you met many ladies?' she asked, sipping her drink.

'I've met a few; all nice enough, but not for me. I've had some funny experiences too,' he added.

'Funny experiences?' she sounded alarmed.

'I mean I've been chased by dogs, attacked by cats, bitten by a creature in a tank, and ridden a runaway horse. I put it all down to experience and I believe the right lady will turn up one day,' he went on optimistically.

'I see, sounds a bit scary to me. Don't you like animals?'

'Actually yes, I do. I have a dog at home, and I want to live in the country one day. Do *you* have any animals?' he asked, as casually as he could.

'Not at the moment, but I have a love of nature and wildlife, and I'm very interested in environmental issues. Do you think they have a vegetarian meal?' she asked, picking up a menu. The evening went well and they chatted easily. Claire had got a lift from her brother to the pub and was going to ring him to pick her up and take her home. As she felt comfortable with Timothy, even though she didn't think they would ever be more than friends, she was happy for him to give her a lift home. Calling her brother to let him know the change of plan, she discovered she had 30 missed calls and 10 text messages from Angie, but chose for the moment, to ignore them.

'What's that*?* ' she asked, when she saw the vehicle she was going home in.

'An antique Land Rover. I've just bought it and it's quite a character,' he replied, opening the passenger door for her.

She gave him a look that conveyed they probably wouldn't meet again, and a sharp smack when he tried to give her a lift onto the seat. ' I can manage, thanks,' she said sharply.

Undeterred, Timothy jumped into the driving seat and started the engine. It roared into life and began making its own customary noises as he shoved it into gear.

Claire did not look impressed. 'Are the emissions from this exhaust legal?' she asked loudly above the roar.

'Oh yes, it's been tested and has all the legal requirements, MOT and all that,' replied Timothy enthusiastically. 'Really, you'd never believe it would you?' she said, looking out of the window. Pulling up outside her home, she turned and asked. 'Would you like to come in for coffee?'

He was surprised because he had the feeling she wasn't interested in him, but accepted anyway. Her home was a mid-terrace house with no front garden, and a front door painted dark green, while all the other doors in the row were varnished wood. The house was neat, sparse and smelled of pot-pourri and he was relieved there were no animals, tanks, or cages. They sipped their coffee in the sitting room by the empty fireplace, and the conversation was mostly from Claire on environmental issues he had never heard of.

Angie was worried. She'd been calling and texting ever since Claire had left with her brother and not had one reply. What if this Timothy chap wouldn't let her reply? Or worse, what if he had her held at knifepoint? Were they even still in the pub? Angie got a taxi to the pub and went inside to look for herself; there was no sign of Claire. The barman thought he saw them leave together about twenty minutes earlier, and said that they seemed normal enough but the woman looked a bit down. Had he forced her to leave with him? Was he being really nice only to pounce when he got her alone? Perhaps she should phone the police? No. Better check if he has taken her home first. She saw the old Land Rover outside Claire's house. She paid for the taxi, and walked over to the vehicle. In the back she saw blankets, a towel, a sack and a sort of rope thing. He was going to tie her up and bury her in the woods out in the country, she was sure!

A police car cruised up the road and seeing her, stopped. 'You alright, love?' asked the officer in the passenger seat.

'I think so; I'm just going to see my friend who lives here,' she said, pointing to Claire's house. 'Best not to be out too long on your own this time of night,' he said kindly.

'I'm going in now,' replied the Angie, not sure what to say. She had no proof of anything. Making a snap decision she thought if I rush in now and he's got her, the police are nearby to help. She ran up the path to the front door. Summoning all of her inner strength she leapt into the air with a banshee scream and gave the front door a sharp kick with both feet. The door splintered and flew open.

The police officer who was driving witnessed all this in his mirror. 'I don't believe it! That woman has just run along the path and splintered the front door with both feet.' He quickly put the vehicle into reverse.

With another scream Angie charged inside and kicked open the sitting room door, standing in attack position with a frenzied expression. She stared at the two people standing by the fireplace with a mug of coffee in their hands, looking totally bemused.

'Have you gone insane?' asked Claire, who had never seen this side of her friend before. Angie remained frozen, eyes darting from one to the other.

There was a tap on what was left of the front door. 'Everything alright in here?' asked the policeman, stepping carefully over the debris.

Claire and Timothy were stunned by the sudden drama.

'I think we're okay,' Timothy managed with a half smile.

The policeman looked at him for a moment and then said, 'I know you! You're Timothy Parkes.' The other policeman tiptoed over the splintered wood and came into the room. 'Timothy! What have you been up to this time?' he said.

He recognised the policemen as the ones he'd met at the park incident. 'We've just been out for a meal in a pub and this … … just burst in on us.'

'She's my friend and I think she may have made a serious mistake.' interrupted Claire, glaring at Angie who looked at the floor and said nothing.

'There's quite a bit of damage here; do you want to press charges?' asked one of the policemen.

'Oh no, nothing like that, I'll sort it out with her myself.'

'Well, if you're sure there isn't a problem.'

'No, no problem,' said Claire, giving Angie more dark looks. 'Would you two like a cuppa?'

The policemen looked at one another, 'Why not, that's very kind of you.' They looked like nice girls, and this was a domestic that would sort its self out, they decided.

As they drank their coffee Angie confessed what she had seen in the back of the Land Rover and how she thought Timothy was going to bury Claire in the woods somewhere.

He laughed, 'those things are for my dog when I take him off walking. I wasn't planning on doing anything to Claire, or anyone else.'

The policemen gave Claire advice on fixing the damaged doors, and her brother was on his way over with hammer and nails to patch it up for now. Timothy had enjoyed a reasonable evening. He had not been bitten by anything, only almost assaulted by a mad friend; things were looking up. The two policemen were obviously enjoying the company, so Timothy said goodbye and left.

Driving home he passed the 'strange bungalow'. The lights were on and two vehicles were parked outside.

He slowed down to get a better look and noticed a tall man that looked like Dr Athed going into the front door with a briefcase. He was greeted at the door by a younger man with long hair. A short toot on a horn made Timothy look where he was going, just in time to brake before hitting another car. It was Dave. He stopped and opened the window.

'Timothy! Is this your new heap?' asked Dave, looking the Land Rover up and down.

'Yes, I'm just on my way home. There's something I've been meaning to mention,' he said, as quietly as possible over the engine noise.

Dave wrinkled his face in an amused grin. 'What's that?'

'There is something a bit fishy about that bungalow over there. I can't tell you much more, just odd things that you see there sometimes. That probably sounds silly?' he said, glad to finally have mentioned it to someone in authority.

'Not as silly as you might think. I'll call you, and see you soon' replied Dave before driving off.

30
More of Jemima.

'Morning Clive,' said Jemima, as she strode into her solicitor's office.

Clive Coombes stood up and offered her a seat. 'Good morning Jemima, you got my message I gather,' he said, sitting down again behind his desk.

'Yes, the police have been to see me again. They wouldn't say exactly *where* they found Giles, and they keep asking lots of questions. I'd like to know who bumped him off, myself. They keep on about someone else being at the house but I can't think of anyone except you, or old Seth, the gardener; he never talks to anyone. Just mutters and groans a lot'.

'You don't think Giles could have been having an affair, do you?' asked Clive carefully. Jemima stared at him for a long moment, coughing and shifting in her chair before saying, ' I doubt it. Surely *I* would know, wouldn't I? Giles, the conventional man, having an affair?' she thought aloud, 'I can't think when he would have had the time? Unless it's someone local.'

'They say the spouse is always the last to know in these matters. I had a bigamy case not long ago, where the husband had two wives, living in different parts of the country, children with both, and a job. I don't know how he managed but for six years neither wife knew about the other.'

'Well I suppose it's possible, we weren't exactly joined at the hip. We had even been taking separate holidays for the past few years, so Giles could enjoy his fishing trips.' Her expression changed to one of confused anger.

'You went through all his documents, didn't you?' Clive asked.

'Yes, and I passed them on to you, if you remember. I haven't cleared out all his stuff yet. The police told me not to, until they close the case. I'll have another look through everything and see what comes to light.' She wasn't sure how she felt: Angry and deeply sad at the same time. Maybe he really had deserved to die after all. 'I suppose there's no chance of having an advance to pay some bills, is there?'

'I can't release anything until probate is complete and I can't do that until the police close the case,' he replied, aware that this wasn't much comfort.

Later that day Jemima began going through her late husband's belongings with a fine- tooth comb. The police had taken quite a bit of stuff and she knew there was more in the attic. Mostly things from his childhood; he had even kept some of his old toys in case they decided to have children. She felt a huge pang of guilt and helped herself to a large gin before venturing up the old stairs.

The stairs were steep and narrow. She squeezed herself up and opened the dusty old door. There was only one very small window at the gable end and the dim electric light bulb still worked. Everything was covered in a thick layer of dust, with huge long dusty cobwebs hanging from the low beams. The floor was littered with leaves that had blown in where the beams ran through the outer walls; the stench of bat droppings was overpowering. Looking around there wasn't much except dusty old toys and two old trunks. The dim light made it difficult to see. Stepping on something soft, she squealed and leapt back, banging her head, causing an avalanche of dust. Lying on its back the old toy started moving and clanging. It was an old teddy with cymbals attached to its paws. *Clang clang* it went in a tired sort of way. Jemima coughed and wiped the dust from her eyes; blinking she picked the toy up and found the off-switch.

'That shut you up,' she said.

Venturing further into the attic she went to the trunks, both were covered in dust but one looked a little cleaner than the other. She was surprised the police hadn't found them, but there was no evidence of them having been opened recently. Drawn to the least dusty one she found a little padlock and gave it a good yank. It wouldn't budge. She went down-stairs to get a hammer and chisel, better to tackle the job. As she walked by the hall window the old gardener was trudging past, bent over his wheelbarrow. Flat cap pulled down over his forehead, pipe in his mouth as usual, he glanced over at her as he passed.

Back in the attic she was finally able to bash the little padlock open. With butterflies in her stomach, worried about what she was going to find, she opened the lid. It was full of what looked like memorabilia. There were old papers and letters, two photo albums and a diary. Several watches, and at the bottom the deeds to a property she'd never heard of. She sat among the dust and leaves on the floor and looked through the papers. A set of keys landed noisily on the floor; she put them in her pocket. Monkswood was, it seemed, the property of the Dunall family. It was odd Giles had never mentioned anything about it. Turning her attention to the photo albums, she discovered lots of family photos of people she didn't know. There were yellowing photos of Giles as a child, and then as a young man; another young man she assumed would have to be his brother, and there was a girl who had apparently grown up with them.   Who was she?   And to whom did Monkswood belong now?

She opened the second trunk, which was full of girls' clothing, dolls and toys. She rummaged around and found a few more photographs of the children.   She immediately recognised Giles, but he had never mentioned a sister or cousin. Who was this female with fair hair? She decided to take it all over to Clive and see if he could throw any light on the mystery.

Meanwhile she had a date with a man from the agency. She had agreed to meet him, hoping he was better than the last one they sent.   Some friendly company would be nice, and she wondered if he had a good job and any money. What was his name again? Roderick.

Jemima showered and changed, ready to meet her date. She'd chosen a long, tiered skirt with a loose comfortable top. As a lady of generous proportions this was a little more flattering then anything tight-fitting. She combed her black hair and applied plenty of make-up, choosing the diamond earrings and necklace Giles had bought her years ago. This Roderick was supposed to be taking her out for a meal; she hoped it was somewhere decent.

Dead on time there was a heavy knock at the door. She tried not to answer too quickly and when she did, she saw standing before her a great bear of a man with a bushy beard and shoulder-length hair. His bushy eyebrows framed bright blue eyes with a mischievous twinkle. She must have looked surprised as she stared and said nothing.

Roderick smiled, revealing pearly white teeth. 'Aye, you must be Jemima,' he said, looking her up and down appreciatively. His one earring caught the light as he nodded his bear-like head. Jemima cleared her throat, a little lost for words. ' Yes, I am Jemima. Are you

Roderick?' she asked, in her soft purring voice. 'Aye, that's me. Are you ready to come for a ride?' he said gruffly. 'You'll be needing a warm jacket, and I have a spare helmet on the bike.'

She suddenly realised the leather gear he was wearing were motorbike leathers; she'd never been on a motorbike in her life. ' I don't know about this. Is it safe.'

'Aye, you'll be safe with me, don't you worry,' he said, still smiling.

At least he's polite she thought, and he has nice eyes. The idea of an adventure with this interesting stranger was suddenly very appealing; she rushed off and grabbed a jacket. 'Right, I'm ready!' she said.

Roderick put his arm around her and lead her to his Ducati super bike. She knew nothing about motor bikes but a nice, big, shiny, red machine was definitely in the tick box. 'Sit up behind me, hold onto my waist, and don't forget to lean *with* me when we corner,' he said, giving her the feeling that she was in safe hands.

She nodded, too nervous and excited to speak. She put on the helmet and waited while he fastened it for her. Then hitching up her long skirt, she climbed up behind him and held on. As the bike roared into life, Jemima could feel the vibration through her body; she held on a bit tighter and closed her eyes as they set off.

Not a man to put up with any nonsense but, despite his appearance, Roderick could be quite a gentleman, and realising his passenger was feeling nervous they rode steadily. Well, steadily for him anyway. They arrived at the pub he had chosen for the evening and when the bike stopped he turned and said, 'We're here, you can get off now.'

Jemima opened one eye and looked at the twinkly blue pair looking back at her through the visor. Realising she wasn't going to get any help, she clutched her skirt and tried to lift one leg while hopping up and down on the other, trying to keep her balance. Just as she was falling over his strong arm grabbed hold of her.

'Ooooh, thank you,' she managed. He pulled her close to him while he was still sitting on the bike. She froze, but didn't object to his bold move. He undid Jemima's helmet and helped her take it off, giving her a friendly tap on the bottom before he locked up the bike and helmets. Taking hold of her arm, he lead the way into the pub. Jemima wasn't used to such bold behaviour and although a part of her wanted to object, another part of her didn't!

The landlord knew Roderick and greeted him when they walked in. 'Hello Rod, good to see you.'

'Good to be back,' he replied, turning to ask what Jemima would like to drink.

'A gin and tonic, please,' she said, already looking at the puddings on the menu board.

'Find anything you like?' he asked.

'Oh yes, I think so.' She hadn't eaten out since Giles had died and was going to make the most of it. Roderick chuckled and ordered their drinks.

People came in and out of the pub; a few of them who knew Jemima and stared in mild disbelief. She merely smiled and raised a hand in acknowledgement, enjoying the stir her companion was creating.

They found they had a surprising amount in common and enjoyed each other's company; walking arm in arm on leaving the pub. Roderick unlocked the bike and gave her the helmet, which she jammed on her head, and waited for him to fasten it. When he was astride the bike, Jemima, several large gin and tonics bolder, grabbed hold of him with one hand, hitched her skirt up with the other and swung her leg over the seat in fine style. Sitting close behind him, arms around his waist, she shut her eyes tightly when the engine roared, and kept them shut all the way home.

It was dark by the time they got back, and Jemima swung herself off the back of the bike, still hanging on to Roderick for support. Linking his arm through hers they walked up to the front door. Not a word passed between them as he closed the door. As she turned to ask if he would like a night-cap, he grabbed hold of her and kissed her hard.

Eventually, she wriggled free. 'I'm not sure if this is really what I want right now. I'll go and…'

He took hold of her again more firmly, saying, ' I know what you need, lass.' She felt her legs go weak as he firmly swept her off her feet saying, 'Bedroom is upstairs, is it?'

'I don't think we should,' she said weakly, her head telling her 'no', her body telling her quite definitely 'yes'. Her body won.

'You'll be alright with me, lass,' said Roderick, squeezing her as they made their way upstairs. '*Ooooh,*' was the only thing she could utter.

The next morning when old Seth wandered into the garden, he noticed the big, red motor bike parked outside the front door. Having a look around he couldn't see anyone and knew the 'bitch from the house' wouldn't be out of bed yet. So he wandered over to have a look at the very impressive machine. From the giggles, squeals and moans coming from the open bedroom window he knew immediately what she was doing with the owner of the bike.

The old man always kept himself to himself and said little to anyone, but not much got past him unnoticed.

He had watched her the day she picked an arm-full of fool's parsley; he had witnessed the woman who went into the house before his boss was found dead, while the bitch was away; he had watched the young man leap suddenly from a downstairs window and cycle off. It was in his interest to say nothing. He liked the easy job, despite the current lack of wages, because he was more or less his own boss, and he liked the little cottage that came rent-free. All he had to do was ignore the bitch when she came out to the garden, lording it and giving him orders. Old Seth said nothing to anyone; he shuffled off, pushing his squeaking wheelbarrow to another part of the garden.

31
Meanwhile …

Timothy lay in bed thinking about the future. He fancied life in the country; a cottage near a village, places to walk with the dog and maybe, just maybe, Lizzie along with him. She was coming back next month and he wondered if she would want to be part of his future plans. A knock on his bedroom door interrupted his reverie.

'Are you awake, Timothy? I'm starting breakfast,' called Mother.

He sat up and stretched. 'Be right there,' he replied.

Over breakfast he mentioned the possibility of a move to the country and found his mother very enthusiastic about the idea. ' If there was enough room it would be ideal, but you never know you might get married one day.'

' Well, if it wasn't big enough we could find you a cottage or a bungalow nearby. You'd still be able to visit Maude and I'd drive you if there wasn't a bus.'

'You're a very thoughtful boy. I'll get on to the estate agents and arrange to have both our places valued. We'll know then how much we have to spend.' Her eyes sparkled with the excitement of it all. 'Had you anywhere particular in mind.'

'Not too far from Dickleborough because I'll need to get to the shop… far enough to be in the country, with places to walk.'

The more he thought about it the more he liked the idea. If there was a river nearby he could even see about doing some fishing. He had a fishing rod in the wardrobe, untouched for many years. With a new

250

adventure on the horizon he walked briskly to the park with his dog, whistling as he went.

As they neared the suspicious bungalow, Faith began to growl a low warning. 'What's up, lad?' said Timothy, stroking the dogs head.

The bungalow looked closed up, no sign of people, curtains tightly drawn. It still gave him a creepy feeling; he wondered what had happened there. With a chill along his spine and Faith's hackles up, they hurried on. He could hardly contact Dave and say the bungalow was very creepy today, had something happened? Dave would think he had truly lost his marbles; and he had heard of genuine psychics being arrested when reporting evil doings, because the police refused to believe what they had to say. Their view being that a psychic having 'insider' knowledge must be somehow involved in the crime.

With Faith trotting along beside him, Timothy continued to dream of his cottage in the country. Suddenly, an energetic Labrador joined them, which he recognised as Sam, Penny's dog. Penny made her way over and they continued around the park together. He told her about the Land Rover, now safe and on the road and they arranged an afternoon trip to the country. Penny said she knew of some lovely places by the river where they could take the dogs, and he thought it would be a good opportunity to scout around for property for sale.

On his way home he found the strange bungalow had been taped off by the police, and was surrounded by squad cars with their lights still flashing. He walked around them keeping Faith close. 'Looks like our creepy feelings weren't about nothing,' he said to his dog, whose brown eyes gazed up at him through untidy eyebrows. He rubbed Faith's head reassuringly as they walked on.

Mother was in a fine mood. 'The estate agent's coming over on Tuesday to look at this house and he may have the time to look at mine on Thursday. He said there are a few properties for sale in the nearby countryside'

'Blimey, that was quick. They didn't happen to mention where, did they?'

'Oh, I didn't ask, dear. We'd better get a price first, before we start looking.'

Timothy cycled to work whistling as he went. All was well with his world. Lizzie was coming back, he wondered again if she too would enjoy a life in a country cottage.

With these positive thoughts he bounced into the shop, to be met by Derek who was quick to notice the bicycle clips around the bottom of his trousers. ' Old heap has died already has it?' he grinned.

'No, the Land Rover is fine, thank you. I cycled because it's a nice day and I felt like some exercise. I don't want to get lazy and unfit,' replied Timothy, with a jibe at Derek who was very sceptical of anything to do with exercise and fitness.

'Yeah, yeah,' Derek muttered, changing the subject. 'Any news or gossip today?'

Timothy told him about his date with Claire and about the creepy bungalow.

'Strange women attacking you and spooky bungalows. Are you ever going to live a normal life like the rest of us?'

'You're just jealous!' Timothy replied, 'dating Henri really boring, is it?'

'No, no it's just great, *we're quite normal*. Not something you would understand.'

Timothy frowned and chose to ignore the last remark. '
I'm thinking of buying a cottage in the country. Not
too far away to come and work here, but well out of
town,' he said, knowing this would wind Derek up even
further.

'Planning on keeping any goats, chickens or maybe
some horses?'

'*No.* Just a cottage with a garden, somewhere
peaceful,' he replied, as the shop door opened and Dr
Athed walked in.

'Morning,' greeted Timothy, not really sure how to
react. Dr Athed looked directly at him, sending another
cold shiver down his spine, before striding off to
another part of the shop. Timothy stared after him,
knowing that the doctor had seen him when leaving the
bungalow. He shivered again.

'You cold or something?' asked Derek.

Timothy shook his head, choosing not to mention
anything further to his friend.

Later that day Dave came into the shop. 'I wonder if we
can have a chat?'

'Sure, I finish at three today.'

They arranged to meet at Timothy's house, knowing
what it was his friend wanted to talk about, and
avoiding saying anything in front of Derek or the
customers in the shop.

'Isn't he a policeman?' asked Derek after Dave had left.
 'And a friend of mine.'

Giving him a sideways look, Derek sighed, 'Life would
be so dull without you around.'

Later when Timothy was cycling home, he heard the
familiar highly revved engine; the little Mini pulled in
suddenly, nearly knocking him off his bike. The
driver's door swung open, causing a passing car to

swerve, and Mrs Fell, apparently oblivious to the mayhem she was causing, climbed out. Her gleaming teeth moved in anticipation as she asked, 'What's happened to your new Land Rover? Did you see the police in Park Road? Do you know *anything* about it all?' She stopped for breath and before she could start again, he said quickly,

'My Land Rover is fine and I don't know anything about the police at Park Road. Sorry to disappoint you.' The old lady looked crestfallen at his reply and fell back into the Mini. As he cycled away, she called after him, 'Are you *sure* you don't know anything?'

'Nothing, nothing at all,' he called back over his shoulder, peddling faster.

He arrived at his house at the same time as Dave Quilford. 'Come on in, I'll put the kettle on,' he invited. 'Great I could do with a cuppa.' Luckily Mother and Faith were out.

While fending off Faith and waiting for the kettle to boil Timothy hunted through the various cake tins until he found a batch of freshly baked buns.

'Have you come about the bungalow?' he asked.

'We've been watching it for a while and finally have the evidence we needed to make several arrests. One of the occupants was found dead from an over-dose of drugs. Any chance you could make a statement about the odd things you've noticed and if possible, *when* you noticed them?'

'Yes of course. Are you going to tell me what was going on in there?'

'Not just yet. As soon as I'm able I will, I promise,' Dave replied, helping himself to a bun.

'You haven't interviewed Dr Athed by any chance, have you? I did see him leaving there on one occasion.'

'Dr Athed has been helping us with our enquiries. You look as if you don't like him much.'

' He gives me the creeps.'

Dave smiled. 'You're not the only one, but he really has been very helpful, and is not the criminal you might have imagined him to be. As soon as the arrests are made, I'll fill you in. Mind if I have another bun?'

' Help yourself. I'll come down to the station later this evening, if you like.'

'*Cooo eee!*' called Mother, coming in through the front door with the dog. 'Oh hello, I didn't know we had a visitor.'

'I'm just off, Mrs Parkes; your buns are delicious, by the way,' said Dave, knowing how to butter up old dears.

' Thank you. I hope we'll see you again soon,' she beamed. She liked Dave.

Timothy accompanied Dave back to his car: the detective glanced up at the house opposite.

'Is that your old lady network in action?' he was nodding towards the twitching curtains in Mrs Fell's house.

'Looks like it, bless them.'

'See you at the station later. By the way, I spoke to Lizzie today. She said she'd be calling you.' He gave a knowing wink before driving off.

Timothy all but skipped back into the house, rushed into the kitchen and grabbed hold of his mother, spinning her round. 'How did it go with the estate agent?' he asked.

'Goodness, what's got into you?' she cried breathlessly. 'He was very enthusiastic about being able to sell both properties. Someone is coming to value yours tomorrow and I've arranged for my neighbour to let another agent in to value mine.'

'That's great! We'll be off for our walk. See you later,' he said.

The crime-scene tapes were still around the bungalow, but the police cars were gone; it all looked quiet when they walked past, but it still gave him the shivers.

Timothy had arranged an afternoon out with Penny and the dogs, and intended to have a drive-by look at a couple of cottages that were for sale. With his Ordinance Survey map and a picnic they set off.

Penny was keen to show him her favourite walk by the river and directed him along a track, which opened out into fields and the riverbank. 'The footpath follows the river along the edge of fields and there's a nice spot ahead under some willow trees, where we can have the picnic.'

Penny let the dogs out of the Land Rover while Timothy stuffed everything into his backpack.

When they came to the picturesque spot under the willows they unpacked his knapsack and enjoyed a leisurely meal on the riverbank. Timothy lay back and watched the sunlight reflecting off the water into the branches of the trees, giving a strobe lighting effect on the leaves. The bird song was wonderful and when he sat up again a family of swans were gliding silently down river, like ghosts on the water. Penny was watching the swans too. 'Told you this was a lovely place,' she said. Helping her self to a home-made scone.

'It's so peaceful, I feel like I could stay and watch the river glide by for ever,' he sighed, brushing crumbs off his trousers, feeling reluctant to leave.

'You can always come back, now you know where it is,' she said. 'Come on lets go and have a look at those cottages you mentioned.'

They packed up the picnic, stuffing any rubbish into a bag to take home, leaving their picnic spot as they had found it.   Walking back along the riverbank he noticed some cattle wandering through an open gateway into the meadow.   'Better call the dogs, look,' he said to Penny.

It was as if the dogs heard him, and both noticed the cattle at the same time. A quick look passed between them before they set off toward the herd. Timothy whistled and called, to no avail. He grabbed Penny's arm. 'Let's get to the gate quick.'   From his previous experience with cattle *and* dogs, he knew exactly what could happen.

'They'll be alright, won't they?' she asked, reluctant to leave her dog.

'It's best to be out of the way, just in case.   Cattle sometimes see dogs as wolves and charge.'   Once they reached the gate, he made sure that Penny and all their belongings were safely on the other side before walking back into the field and giving his extra loud 'come back' whistle to Faith. The young cattle had seen the dogs and were curious, walking toward them, shaking their heads. The dogs, on the other hand, were up for a game and chased around, barking at these new creatures, deaf to any whistles and calls.   The cattle were also up for a game and started chasing, shaking their heads and bucking. Fortunately the dogs took fright at this new behaviour and galloped back to their owners for protection, followed by the herd of excited cattle.

'I knew this would happen,' Timothy groaned, then shouted to Penny, 'Open the gate a bit for the dogs to get through!' He whistled loudly again and ran for the gate, knowing the dogs would be likely to follow: They did … and so did the cattle.   Timothy vaulted the gate and the dogs shot through the gap. Penny heaved the gate shut just as the cattle caught up, huffing and puffing and skidding to a stop, some carried on bucking and kicking and galloping around.

'To them it's just a game,' he said calmly, 'they're very nosy creatures.'

'Some game,' she replied. 'I've never seen cattle behave like that before.'

'If we'd put the dogs on leads and walked quietly out of the field, they would probably have ignored us. Cows with calves are the most dangerous. Come on, let's load up and get going.'

Back in the Land Rover Penny spread the map out to help navigate to the first cottage.

'Someone is living in one of the them, the other one is empty. I just want to have a quick look before making any appointments to view,' he said.

As they approached the first village there was a row of dwellings, starting with a small detached cottage. 'I think this could be it,' she said. The cottage was in considerable disrepair, even the For Sale sign looked worn and leaned over the overgrown hedge.

Timothy slowed to a crawl, then pulled up saying, 'I'm just going to look over the gate, I think there is someone there…Good afternoon,' he called to a person bending down among the over-grown plants. An elderly lady stood up and glowered at him. 'Can I help you?' she said, oozing hostility.

'Would you mind if my friend and I had a little walk around your cottage? I'm in the area and noticed the for-sale sign. I'll make an appointment to look inside with the agent,' he added.

'No, you can't. Clear off! Go on, off with you!' she shouted, shaking her fist at him.

'Okay, okay. I didn't mean any harm.'

He looked back at the cottage and could see what appeared to be an elderly man watching him from an upstairs window. The angry woman made her way to the garden gate. 'Be gone! Go on, off with you!' she shouted again.

Timothy backed off. 'Good day to you, too,' he said and jumped back into the driver's seat.

'Not keen on showing you around, then,' said Penny, laughing.

'Now we know why it's been on the market for a while!'

The next place had the grand name of Monkswood , but according to the estate agent it was a cottage with three bedrooms. They were both curious. Penny consulted the map.

'It's marked with a pencilled circle, shouldn't be too hard to find,' said Timothy.

Penny was buried in the folds of the map, which nearly filled the front of the vehicle. 'Ah, I have it, I think it's left here, not far, we might be able to see it from the road.' Timothy drove slowly while Penny looked for the cottage. 'I think that could be it down there,' she said, pointing to the left. Nestled among trees was a large house with several out-buildings. The driveway was also visible. 'What's that in the drive?' said Penny.

Timothy stopped. 'Looks like a motor bike to me. I wonder who's there? It's meant to be empty,' he said, driving on again.

The narrow driveway was almost concealed with an over-grown hedge. They drove slowly towards the house until they came out of the trees to the front of the building. Penny suddenly sat bolt upright and shrieked. 'That's a Ducati Super bike!'

Timothy frowned, 'Really? I wonder who that belongs to? Perhaps it's the owner's. The estate agent said there was some legal wrangle over this one. It's a bit big; nice though, isn't it?'

Penny was staring at the bike. 'Yeah, it's gorgeous,' she sighed.

He looked at her and shook his head. 'That's some cottage. I wonder if there's a mistake, better not wander round today.' He restarted the engine. As they moved off a couple came out of the front door. He stared in disbelief. The woman was the mad date from the big house he'd visited and left via the window, covered in soot. ' *I don't believe it*,' he said. 'I'd never have guessed *she'd* go anywhere on a motorbike.'

'You know her then?' asked Penny, trying to get to grips with folding the map.

'We have met,' he replied, as they pulled out of the drive. He deliberately smiled at Jemima as he drove past. Jemima stared after them. 'Anyone you know?' asked Roderick.

'We met once,' she said.

Timothy caught the estate agents just as they were about to close. He mentioned the two cottages he'd just seen and told them about the elderly lady chasing them off. 'Oh, the old lady,' said the agent smiling. 'She sees *everyone* off. The family have to take her out so we can show people round. She's not well and they're trying to get her into a home.'

'What about her husband?' he asked.

'He died just over a year ago. She lives alone now,' replied the agent. Timothy shivered.

He dropped Penny off on his way home. He always enjoyed her company but there wasn't a glimmer of attraction between them. As a friend she was great and he hoped it would remain that way.

Mother was full of estate agent news, and keen to hear about the cottages. 'Oh, I nearly forgot dear, a nice police lady telephoned; said she'd met me before. I think she said her name was…'

'Lizzie!' Timothy finished the sentence for her.

'I'll go and call her back,' he said, taking the scribbled note with the phone number.

'She sounds very nice,' Mother called after him.

'She is!' he replied, taking the stairs two at a time..

His mother patted Faith's head. '*That* sounds promising lad, what d'you think?' she whispered to the dog.

Lizzie was pleased to hear from him and seemed quite excited about coming back to Dickleborough. Dave had told her all about Timothy's exploits in the park and the van - and that he had a new vehicle. 'Well, I wouldn't call it new, more like antique. But it does what I need it to and I can take the dog in it,' he explained.

'So you've still got Faith?'

'Yup, never seen or heard anything from his previous owners for several months, so I guess that means he's mine. I hope they don't want him back now that we've become such good friends.'

They chatted for ages, Timothy filling in the gaps from Dave's version of events. Now the first call had been made they promised to speak often and meet up as soon as she was back in town. Timothy felt like he'd won the lottery. Lizzie really was coming home.

He ran downstairs and gave his mother a hug. 'What's to eat tonight?' he said, unable to stop grinning. She looked at her son with knowing eyes. 'I've made a casserole. Have you arranged to meet Lizzie?'

'Not just yet. She's coming back to work here very soon and then we will meet up. You liked her, didn't you?' he added.

'She sounds like a nice girl.' Mother was careful not to say too much.

The doorbell rang sending Faith into guard mode. Timothy put his hand on the dog's collar as he went to the door. It was Mrs Battle. 'Hello Timothy,' she said loudly. I know it's short notice again, but could you do park patrol tonight? Just from nine to midnight?'

Not how he wanted to spend the evening, but he had nothing important planned, he agreed.

'I'll go in the Land Rover this time.'

'You're taking Rover?' replied Mrs Battle, leaning toward him.

'*I said, I'll take the Land Rover*!' he repeated loudly.

'There's no need to shout,' she answered, just as loudly. He suppressed a grin and managed a nod as she turned on her heel and marched off down the path. 'Thank you, Timothy. Toodle-oo', she called over her shoulder, waving her stick.

'As you probably guessed, I'm on park duty tonight. I'll take Faith in the Land Rover.'

'Yes, I heard. Are you sure about this? I mean after what happened to you last time, I can't believe you would want to do this again?' Seeing her son's expression, she knew he would go anyway. ' I'll make up a flask and some sandwiches. It'll be cold later,' she said, putting the casserole on the table.

He gave his mother an appreciative wink. 'I'll be fine Mother,' he reassured her.

After supper he put on some warm clothes and loaded Faith into the Land Rover. Watched as usual by Mrs Fell, he was tempted to wave, but decided it was more fun to pretend he hadn't noticed.

After parking the Land Rover where he could see a good deal of the park, and the main entrance, he walked the perimeter, with Faith, then settled back in the vehicle. Not much was happening. A few people wandered in, walking through the park to another destination. Suddenly there was a tap on the side of the Land Rover, which made him jump and Faith bark.

'Alright lad, let's see who it is,' he said, sliding open the window.

Penny was standing outside with a female friend. 'Didn't expect to see you so soon. What are you doing here?' she asked.

'I'm on park watch tonight, a last minute thing,' he replied.

'This is my friend, Angel,' said Penny, introducing Timothy and his dog.

'Hi Timothy, I've been hearing lots about you,' said Angel.

'Really?' he was surprised.

'We're going to pick up some chips from 'Fat Chips' over there,' said Penny, pointing across the park. 'Do you want some?'

'Why not. I'll walk over with you, if you like?' he suggested, glad of the company to pass the time. Timothy and Faith waited inside the park gates under some trees, while the two girls went over to the chip shop. People walking past stared at the man and the huge dog lurking in the shadows; he was glad when the girls came back. Walking across the park together they saw a police car parked beside his Land Rover.

A policewoman got out as they approached. 'Hello Timothy, is this your vehicle? Another antique, I see', she smiled.

'Yes, this is mine. I'm on park watch tonight till midnight,' he replied, recognising her as Eve from the police station.

'I thought it was probably you, we had some calls about someone lurking in the trees with a big dog!' said Eve, looking over at Penny and Angel. 'Enjoy your chips, we won't be far away if there's any trouble,' she said, getting back into the police car.

'Thanks,' he said turning back to the girls.

They all squeezed into the front of the Land Rover to eat their chips, except Faith who sat in his place in the back, head hung over the seats, ever hopeful when food was about. When they'd finished Timothy thought he'd better do another walk around. The girls gathered up the chip papers to put in the nearby bin and they said their goodbyes. He watched them go and noticed how close they were, as they walked away linking arms. So maybe there was the reason there was never any spark between himself and Penny, he chuckled to himself.

His thoughts turned back to Lizzie and her home-coming. He was looking forward to taking her out for a meal to celebrate their reunion. Not long to wait now.

Suddenly Faith, who was on his long lead, launched himself into the bushes, causing a girly squeal and some unrepeatable language from a man. He reeled the dog, in only to discover it was the same couple he had disturbed on the night of fight.

'Not you again!' exclaimed the young man, grabbing at his trousers. The girl was busy re-arranging her clothes and too embarrassed to say anything.

'I'm really sorry we disturbed you,' said Timothy.

'Are you some kind of perv, or what?' the man shouted at him. He took a step forward threateningly, but stopped dead as Faith uttered a low growl. Taking hold of his girl friend's arm they stomped off across the grass.

Timothy rubbed Faith's head. 'Never mind, we weren't to know. They should be thankful it wasn't Mrs Battle who found them.'

32
And then….

Jemima sat in the chair opposite Clive Coombes, her legs crossed, swinging one leg and tapping the arm of the chair with her hand. 'I know it's mine, I just feel it,' she said.

Clive looked at her over the top of his glasses, 'I think you mean you *hope* it's yours?'

Jemima just grunted a reply. 'Look, according to this it belongs to the siblings. Rogue lions in Africa ate Giles's brother, and now Giles is dead. Is there another sibling?' he asked pointedly.

'I don't think so,' snapped Jemima.

Clive looked at her again and coughed. 'Well?' he said.

'Oh alright! There might be, but I've never met her or heard of her,' she muttered reluctantly.

'I need all the information you can find, including any photos.'

'I could bring in what I've found, but why can't you just get on with the will without all this nonsense? I'm sure no one else knows about Monkswood,' she moaned.

'Only the estate agents. I'll write to them and ask if they can confirm who owns Monkswood,' he said sternly. 'Look Jemima, Giles died in suspicious circumstances and there is a police investigation in progress. The coroner will not issue a death certificate until after the inquest into his death. We cannot obtain probate without a death certificate. Now there is this other property that will have to be looked into carefully.

I know patience doesn't come easily, but in this case it's essential. You'll just have to wait.'

She wasn't happy but thanked him anyway, and accepted his promise to let her know of any developments. In the meantime she promised to deliver any evidence that she found of Giles's possible relative ASAP.

She left the office and headed up town to meet Roderick, who was giving her a lift home. She still hadn't got the hang of getting onto the back of the Ducati in anything resembling a lady-like manner. She grabbed hold of Roderick with both hands, and gave her right leg an almighty swing over the back of the bike; hitching herself upright by using him as a hand-rail was the best she could manage. Straightening her clothes and gripping him firmly around the waist she shut her eyes tight. 'Okay, I'm on!' The engine gave a throaty roar and they set off for home.

The old gardener was just clearing up some leaves as the bike rumbled down the driveway. He watched as 'the bitch' climbed off the bike, in reverse fashion to getting on. Roderick was locking the Ducati as Seth wandered over, pushing the squeaky wheelbarrow. He stopped to admire the machine.

'Alright?' nodded Roderick.

Seth nodded, then actually spoke, 'Aye, I used to race bikes.'

Roderick studied the old man for a moment, the most unlikely-looking ex-biker he had ever seen. 'Really, what did you race?'

The two men talked about bikes for nearly fifteen minutes before Jemima came out to see where Roderick had got to, at the same time as a green saloon car came down the drive.

Dave Quilford got out and, seeing the Ducati, more or less ignored her. 'Nice bike, mate,' he said to Roderick. Seth shuffled off squeaking his way to the compost heap. Jemima stood on the doorstep, while the two men, as if bewitched by the Ducati, became involved in bike-talk. 'Excuse me!' she said, 'I assume you would both like a drink?' She'd recognised Dave as one of the policeman she had talked to after Giles first disappeared.

Both men looked up. 'Yes,' they said in unison.

'Can you tear yourselves away from that bike and come in?'

'Yes,' they said in unison again, as if waking from a dream.

'What is it about men and machines?' she thought, going back inside.

Seth listened to all of this from the depths of a nearby Rhododendron bush. When he realised they were going inside he moved off to another part of the garden where he could observe through the windows without being noticed, taking his gardening tools and wheelbarrow with him.

Hearing the wheelbarrow move off Dave asked Roderick, 'Does he ever talk to anyone? All I got out of him was a grunt.'

'Just try mentioning motor bike racing. Apparently he used to race in his youth,' he replied, as both men went inside.

'I'll give that a try,' said Dave.

'Tea or gin?' asked Jemima, as they walked in. Both men asked for tea, while Jemima helped herself to a large gin.

Dave decided to hang around a while, because by the time Jemima was on her third large gin, she was chatting freely, giggling and enjoying the company.

'So, Jemima, can you think of anyone else who may have been connected to Giles? Any long lost relatives?' asked Dave.

'There must be a relative somewhere, how else would the estate agent know about the house?' said Roderick, trying to be helpful.

Jemima was enjoying the chat with the boys and the gin, but she shot a glance at Roderick that meant *shut up*. 'My solicitor is looking into all that. He'll let you know when he knows,' she giggled.

'So you know there *is* someone, any idea who it could be?' Dave persisted, keeping the friendly chat going.

Jemima was now on her fourth gin. 'Well, there is this woman. I suppose she could be a relative, but I don't see how she could own the house. I was married to Giles long enough... surely I would have met her or something?' she said, now eyeing Roderick seductively. Dave took the hint, ' I'll leave you two in peace for now, but might call for a chat again sometime.'

The squeaking wheelbarrow made them all look towards the window. Seth was trudging past with his cap wedged down over his forehead, and his pipe in his mouth as usual, the wheelbarrow as always no more than half full. He glanced up as he went by, obviously bored with spying for now. The detective nipped out quickly and caught up with him. They walked together for a few yards, with Seth not even acknowledging his presence. There were squeals and shrieks of laughter from inside the house. Seth trudged on, puffing on his pipe.

'Nice bike over there, isn't it,' Dave tried. A grunt and a snort was his only reply. Sooner or later he was going to have to get tough with this old man; he felt sure there was more to him; the old gardener probably knew a lot more than he was telling.

33
Thermal knickers.

Timothy had just finished serving Mrs Brown with her usual selection of gory thrillers when Inspector Davis came in. The old lady tried hard to linger but Derek very politely showed her out.

'Any chance I can have a chat with you two?' asked the inspector. There was no one else in the shop so they both agreed and Derek made them all a mug of tea. 'I could do with a list of people who buy books from here, especially anything to do with pharmacology or any medical science.'

'That would be virtually impossible except for a few with an account, or cheque payments,' explained Derek.

'The only one very recently has been Dr Athed,' added Timothy.

Derek nodded and then remembered someone else, 'She came in and purchased a few books on modern and natural medicines. Blond, slight woman I think, and paid by cheque, so I will have her name. Hold on, I'll see if I can find it for you.'

While Derek was rummaging through the paperwork Timothy asked. 'This is about the bungalow, isn't it?'

'I read your statement,' said the inspector.

'But you haven't arrested Dr Athed?'

'We won't be arresting Dr Athed, despite your feelings about him. He's been very helpful and supplied us with information leading to the arrests we have made so far.'

Seeing his quizzical expression she went on to say. 'We found the body of a young man in one of the back rooms; the place was being used to manufacture medicines, which were sold on the internet as miracle

269

cures for certain types of cancer. Sadly it didn't work and several people died as a result. The families of the victims alerted us to the case. It's thought the young man died from taking the same drugs, but we're not sure if he took them willingly or not.'

'That was all going on in that bungalow,' exclaimed Timothy.

The door bell jangled and Mrs Jones came in. Seeing him and the inspector standing together she winked at Timothy, then peered hard at the inspector, hoping for an introduction. When one didn't come, she tugged at her shopping trolley and made her way into the rear of the shop.

'I think I've got what you need Inspector,' said Derek. Timothy gave him a nod to indicate someone else was in the shop. Derek handed the piece of paper to Inspector Davis. 'I'll let you know if I find anything else,' he said quietly. The name on the cheque was H. Dunall-Smith.

'Thank you Derek, you've both been very helpful.'. As Timothy walked her to the door, she nodded in the direction of Mrs Jones. 'A fan of yours, is she? I've heard all about your old ladies.'

'I suppose so, bless them.'

'She's a bit of alright,' whispered Derek, when Timothy came back to the desk.

'Nice lady, but before you go thinking anything, she's not my type,' he said, giving Derek a sideways look and a friendly shove. 'How's Henri?'

'*Henri is*,' Derek sighed. 'Henri is lovely. How's the house search coming along?' he asked, coming back to earth and changing the subject.

'From the sale of our two properties we should be able to find something quite decent and big enough,' he replied, suddenly thinking of Lizzie.

'Could be a while before you move then?'

'Months probably.'

By the time he arrived home Mother was buzzing. 'The estate agent has someone interested in my house already. And did you know about the dead body, and what was going on in that bungalow near the park?' she asked, handing him a plate of teacakes dripping with butter..

'What have you found out? Who did you talk to?'

He was curious, how had Mother got to know about it in such a short time?

'I went to one of the ladies' meetings. Beattie Fell had been chatting to one of the young police officers outside. He told her. At the meeting Maureen Broadbent said she knew someone, who knew someone, who lived next door, and they told *her* about it. Apparently the police managed to track down and catch the criminals, who were also making fake cancer cures and selling them on the internet. The owner of the bungalow is living abroad under a palm tree somewhere, and had believed a friend was staying there. He has since put it up for sale,' she said, pausing for breath.

Timothy laughed. 'Well, God bless the ladies' network.'

'Mrs Jones said she thought *you* knew all about it?'

'I did notice some odd goings-on there when walking past with Faith, so I mentioned it to Dave.'

'He knows all about it then?'

'So, how are all the ladies? Any more gossip?' he asked, in the mood to be amused.

'Mrs Battle has a new hearing aid and isn't shouting as loudly. Mrs Fell is planning on visiting the dentist to see about some more teeth. Mrs Jones and Mrs Brown are still wittering on about their horrible books...

271

another teacake before you walk the dog, dear?' she said, taking a breath.

' No thanks, we'll go now. One or two things to do this evening,' he replied. Phoning Lizzie was high on his list.

As he set off , closing the front door behind him, Mrs Fell almost galloped down her path to 'accidentally' bump into him. 'Hello Timothy, fancy seeing you. Have you heard about the bungalow?' she gasped, leaning on the gatepost to catch her breath.

He smiled patiently. 'Yes, Mother has just told me.'

'Mrs Battle said *you* would know all about it, and that you helped the police with their enquiries. Who was the poor young man?' she asked, teeth clattering in overdrive to keep up.

'What I discuss with the police,' he said, in a loud whisper, 'is really confidential. I can't tell you anything.'   She studied him for a moment, having recovered from her dash along the path, and putting her finger to her lips, said, 'I understand Timothy.' then off she went.

He was whistling a happy tune as he walked along, when he noticed a bicycle leaning on a gatepost outside one of the more modern houses in the area. On hearing familiar voices he glanced up the drive into the front garden. Mrs Battle, Mrs Jones and MrsWetherbutts were struggling with a ladder. They'd leaned it towards an upstairs window and Mrs Wetherbutts was already half way up when he walked into the garden.

'Need a hand, ladies?'

'Timothy! Just the man we need,' said Mrs Battle. 'Mrs Wetherbutts is going to climb in through that window.'

He knew the ladies were an active, feisty lot, but a 70 + pensioner climbing up a ladder into an upstairs window, probably wasn't such a good idea.

'If you come down I'll climb up there for you,' he called.

'Very kind of you. *I'll* be alright, used to be a Girl Guide you know,' she answered.

'I really think it might be better if you let me, that window won't be easy to get through,' he tried again, remembering getting her out of Mrs Fells' Mini.

Mrs Battle gave him a hefty shove, and said, 'Yes, you tell her. She won't take any notice of us.'

Mrs Wetherbutts looked down for a moment. 'Oh rubbish,' she barked, continuing her slow climb.

'You can't tell her, she just won't listen!' insisted Mrs Battle.

Timothy wondered if he should call the fire brigade or an ambulance in advance. He tied Faith to the garden fence and held on to the bottom of the ladder. Mrs Wetherbutts finally reached the window. Not quite sure how to tackle climbing in, she first tried to lift one leg but couldn't reach, so she tried lifting the other, which couldn't reach either. Wavering slightly, she studied the window for a moment then looked down at Timothy and said, 'I think I'll go in head first.'

Groans from the ladies below.

Timothy tried again, 'I think you should come down and let me try.'

She grunted and went back to her task. Tiptoeing on the very top rung she poked her head through the small window, followed by a good part of her body... another heave and she was half way through. By this time her front half was hanging down inside, with her bottom half hanging outside. Waving her legs around she tried to wriggle through but nothing happened, except to reveal her copious, knee-length thermals.

'I'm stuck,' she wailed upside down through the bottom half of the window.

'I knew it, the silly woman. We'll have to call the fire brigade to get her out,' Mrs Battle cried.

'Maybe not,' said Timothy, on his way up the ladder. Reaching the top, and avoiding the flailing legs, he grabbed hold of her by the ankles, making her squeal.

'Stop wriggling a minute,' he shouted. Closer inspection revealed her bottom was only a bit larger than the window opening where she had become wedged. 'I'm going to have to give you a good push. Have you got something to hold on to?' he asked.

'Only the windowsill. Don't you be looking at my unmentionables!' cried the elderly woman in panic.

'No never,' he replied, unable to see anything else at that moment.

'The police are here,' announced Mrs Jones from the gateway.

Timothy closed his eyes for a minute, muttering, '*Oh great, just what we need.*'

He looked down and saw Eve walking up the drive.

'Well Timothy, what *are* you doing now?' she asked, barely suppressing a giggle.

'Helping Mrs Wetherbutts through a window.'

'Right,' chuckled Eve, 'is it her house?'

'Is this your house?' he called to Mrs Wetherbutts.

She stopped wriggling for a second, and shouted back , 'No, of course it isn't. I'd have a key if it was.'

Timothy looked down at Eve. 'No, it's not.'

'Do you know the owner of the house?' asked Eve, tears prickling in the corners of her eyes.

'No, I don't,' he replied, suddenly realising his position. 'Do you know *why* you're aiding and abetting Mrs Wetherbutts to break into someone's house?'

'Actually, no.'

'I don't feel very well,' called Mrs Wetherbutts, still hanging upside down.

274

Timothy braced himself, 'Hold on, I'll give you a good push.' Climbing further up the ladder, while her legs waved dangerously around on either side of his head, he grabbed hold of both buttocks and gave an almighty shove. There was a loud scream as the rest of Mrs Wetherbutts fell in to the bedroom.

He climbed up and poked his head through the window. She was lying in a crumpled heap on the floor. 'Are you alright?'

'No, I'm not. You idiot, you could have broken my neck,' shouted the affronted old lady, suddenly coming to life and struggling to her feet.

'Just wanted to make sure. The police are down here asking whose house you're breaking into?' he said.

'I'm not breaking in. I'm trying to feed their cat.'

'Didn't they give you a key?'

This comment infuriated Mrs Wetherbutts and she swung round and gave him a good slap on the face, shouting, 'Of course they gave me a key, but the stupid thing doesn't work.'

Timothy began to extract himself out of the window, his face red and stinging. A male voice spoke from behind him. 'Everything alright in there?'

'Yes, she seems fine. I'll come down now,' he said to Tom the policeman, who had climbed up the ladder behind him.

Mr Smith had been looking forward to a quiet evening after work as he drove home. When he turned into his road, he saw a police vehicle and a number of people in his garden. ' I don't need this,' he groaned to himself. Unable to pull into his own drive, he parked the car and walked. In his garden he found two elderly ladies standing on the lawn, a large dog tied to his fence, a policewoman at the bottom of a ladder, and two other people, one a policeman, climbing down from his bedroom window.

'What's going on?'

'Is this your house, sir?' asked Eve.

'Yes. Has there been a burglary?' he replied, feeling guilty for leaving the bedroom window open. 'Not really. An elderly lady climbed in through your open window to feed your cat. We were just wondering how she was going to get out.'

'*But I don't have a cat.* How did *that* get here?' he exclaimed pointing at the huge dog tied to his fence. 'It belongs to the gentleman up the ladder, sir,' said Eve.

'What was *he* doing? Helping someone to break in?' said the house owner, beginning to go red in the face.

'Sort of. The lady was stuck in your window and he came to help,' replied Eve, soothingly.

Mr Smith opened the front door with his key and called, 'You can come out now, and I haven't got a cat!' Shaking his head, he said to Eve, ' I don't know what to do, should I press charges or something?'

'That would be up to you sir, but perhaps we should hear an explanations first. I have a feeling this is a mistake.'

'Oh, it's a mistake alright!' said Mr Smith, his face colouring even more.

Mrs Wetherbutts came out of the front door looking dishevelled. She staggered down the step, pulling herself together as she joined the others on the lawn.

'The man just said he hasn't got a cat!' said Mrs Jones.

'And who are you?' demanded Mrs Wetherbutts.

'I'm Mr Smith and this is my house.'

'What have you done with Elspeth Williams? And this stupid key doesn't work!'

'Who the hell is Elspeth Williams, and *what* key?' shouted Mr Smith.

Mrs Battle and Mrs Jones looked at each other and said, 'It's the wrong house!'

'Mrs Williams lives down there on the corner,' remembered Mrs Jones.

Eve put her hand over her mouth finding it even harder not to laugh.

'Well, someone should have told me. This is your fault!' Mrs Wetherbutts shouted at Timothy, who shook his head and began to walk backwards towards Faith.

'I didn't know you were breaking into the wrong house,' he said.

'I wasn't breaking in, I was trying to feed the cat.'

'The cat doesn't live here!' yelled Mr Smith.

'That's ENOUGH!' shouted Mrs Battle, in her sergeant major voice, making everyone jump and step back a little. 'Right,' she went on, ' we will escort Mrs Wetherbutts to the *right* house and help her feed the cat. Thank you Timothy for helping, you can take yourself and dog off now. Mr Smith, we apologise to you. Good day! Officer thank you, we will be on our way.' With that she grabbed Mrs Wetherbutts by the arm, signalled to Mrs Jones to do the same and they marched out of the garden. Mrs Jones grabbed her bicycle with her free hand and Mrs Wetherbutts, who was limping slightly, with the other.

Mr Smith slumped down on his front step holding his head in his hands. 'Are you alright, sir?' asked Eve.

'Oh yes,' he muttered, ' I think I'll get over it. After all it's not every day you have a bunch of mad old ladies trying to break into your house to feed a cat you haven't got. Is it, Officer?'

'No indeed it isn't, sir. You won't be pressing charges then?' asked Eve.

'No. I like a peaceful life, there's no damage done, so I'll let it go. Thank you Officer, good evening,' he said, walking slowly into his house, rubbing his head.

'Well, that's that sorted,' said Eve to her colleague Tom, who was leaning on the police car shaking with laughter. 'The folks in this town are all barking mad!' he said, getting into the driving seat.

'I think they're wonderful. Such colourful characters. I love working here.'

'Oh yes, lovely characters. I've heard they murder one another occasionally, too.' Tom replied.

'Only *very* occasionally,' smiled Eve.

34
At the end of the day.

Daphne went back to her laptop; the first file was that of Tara Robson. It had been fortunate the press had not included any reference to Two to Tango in the articles concerning Tara's dubious professional activities. The alleged misdemeanours involving a local MP, inadvertently linked with her own agency could make or break the business.

Then there was Betty Mills and her strange collection of dead animals. She'd hit it off with farmer Bertrum Muddlestone and although they were an unlikely couple, they were now planning a life together on his farm, along with Betty's macabre collection.

The eco-lady Everelda had been introduced to Julian, a seismologist of biblical appearance. After a rocky start due to her goat eating a hole in the soft-top of his treasured MGB, the two were already living in her cottage along with the rest of the menagerie. The goat often accompanied them on car rides.

An older couple had sent a huge bunch of flowers to say 'thank you' for introducing them. Michael Collinson was sixty eight years old and Lorna Daily was sixty two. They were both keen on caravanning and after their initial meeting, pitched side by side at a mutually chosen caravan site for one weekend, there was no stopping them. The romance had further cemented while they were camped in the hills, not on an official site. Lorna had been nervous about camping wild, but was comforted in the knowledge that Michael and his caravan were only a few yards away. One day just before dawn, her caravan had begun to rock backwards and forwards. She had been terrified and had hardly dared to breathe. Eventually she had plucked up the courage and decided to make a run for it to Michael. She had banged on the side of his caravan with her fists, calling for help. After calming her, he had started to laugh. The 'culprit' rocking her caravan was an old ram scratching his scabby coat on the wheel arch. For the next outing Lorna and Michael had taken one caravan, and there was talk of marriage.

It had been Jane's idea to introduce Jemima Dunall to the hairy biker Roderick Mackenzie and to Daphne's dismay, it had worked extremely well. There was, however, something strange about the woman as she'd told the Detectives Quilford and Davis. Despite the soft round face, brown cow eyes and sweet voice, Daphne felt the woman was quite sinister, and wasn't entirely surprised when she'd heard of her husband's murder. Could Jemima really be the murderer? The police seemed to think so, and the rather gorgeous Detective Quilford seemed certain she was involved in some way. Timothy Parkes, who is apparently worshipped by the crazy elderly vigilantes of the town, had not had the most successful time while being a member of her agency. She wondered how much longer Timothy would be on the register; not very long if he continues his relationship with the policewoman. Daphne sighed and poured another Scotch, before turning to the page of the latest new customers. One of whom looked rather interesting; she sipped her drink and read on.....

35
A date for Daphne!

Daphne ended the call, leaned back in her chair and smiled. Could this be the one she'd been waiting for? An interview was arranged and he would be coming into the office the following day. All she had to do now was decide on strategy and what to wear. Duncan Dainty had no idea what he was in for.

Years ago Daphne realised she was a natural at introducing her friends to potential partners, and many were now happily married. One friend suggested she run a marriage bureau, so after her divorce from Wayne, when Uncle Miles had given her a sum of money to help her 'get on her feet' she had developed the idea of starting her own business, and so Two to Tango Dating Agency was born. Many had walked in through the doors, some more interesting than others, many were now matched with their perfect partner.

Married at the age of twenty, divorced at twenty-two she had yet to find a suitable match of her own. She would of course never tell anyone she was looking, but always hoped that one day he would walk in through her door.

'Jane, we need to clean up the office while it's quiet, and can you order some fresh flowers for the morning too, dear,' she said, as Jane was pulling the vacuum around the reception area.

'Yes I'll get on to that in a minute, any particular sort or just a cheap bouquet?'

'I think we'll have some roses this time Jane; I feel like roses.'

In contrast to Daphne's tall attractive, voluptuous stature, Jane's more petite, plain appearance and softly spoken character belied the passion and mischief within. So far there had been several male customers she really liked the look of, but they apparently didn't feel the same about her. Jane had mentioned her desire to her boss, who had simply said, 'Patience Jane, patience.'

Daphne always wanted the offices cleaned up, and fresh flowers, when someone of interest to her was due for an appointment but never mentioned her reasons to Jane, who pretended not to notice! She looked on the appointment list and found a Duncan Dainty from Many Wollops Hall booked in for 11 am. No description or further details, which meant Daphne is interested.

Duncan and his brother Dermot were born into the Dainty family, who had owned Many Wollops Hall and its large estate for over a hundred years. The estate had originally been won in a duel, fought by the great Arthur Timsonby de Dainty, it had been swords at dawn and many said he'd cheated. Duncan and his brother Dermot were packed off to boarding school as soon as they were out of nappies, and privately educated at a well-known 'College for boys'. They learnt useful skills, including horse riding, cricket and rugby. Also going to the races, drinking alcohol, and as tall dark-haired good looking young men, everything you could wish to know about women, for all of which Duncan and Dermot had a keen appetite.

Duncan walked into the office of Two to Tango without ringing the doorbell and made straight for Jane behind reception, saying ' Good morning, I have an appointment with Daphne Mortesque for eleven sharp.'

'Good morning, I'll just buzz Ms Mortesque,' said Jane.

Before she could press the buzzer the office door swung open. 'You must be Duncan, how lovely to meet you, please come into my office,' crooned Daphne.

Duncan could hardly take his eyes off her. Sitting opposite her at the desk he leaned comfortably back in the chair that made peculiar noises. His mischievous eyes travelled over her, coming to rest on the little gold cross playing hide and seek among her cleavage. What an interesting and exciting woman he mused.

'Now then Duncan, I need a little more information about you,' purred Daphne, her sharp blue eyes meeting his gaze.

'I'm sure you do,' he smiled.

'How long did you say you'd been divorced?'

'I didn't.'

Daphne studied him for a moment and guessed he was playing with her, returning his smile she leaned toward him, 'how long have you been divorced?'

'Two years.'

'Have you had many lovers since your divorce?'

Duncan chuckled, 'Mmmm.'

Daphne studied the computer screen, giving herself time to think. 'What kind of lady were you hoping to meet? Duncan stood and leaned over the desk toward her. Meeting her gaze he said, 'Come to supper with me tonight, I'll give you all the details you need.'

'Really?'

'Yes, really.' Duncan's dark steel eyes worked their way from the illusive little gold cross to meet Daphne's steady gaze.

'Pick me up at seven,' said Daphne, handing him her card.

'Seven sharp, I look forward to it,' Duncan turned to leave her office.

'Could be an interesting evening,' purred Daphne.

'Oh yes,' he replied.

Daphne stared at the closed door; she heard him say goodbye to Jane, and wondered what the evening's meeting would bring. What an interesting man! She got straight on-line to see if she could find out more about Duncan Dainty from Many Wollops Hall.

' Mrs Battle says there's been a murder! D'you know anything about it, Timothy?' cried Beattie Fell excitedly, moving her new top set of teeth around in her mouth as usual. Timothy smiled, what was Mrs Fell going to talk about when the new owners moved into his house later that day? He had no doubt that via Mrs Fell, Mother would hear all about the new people and be very keen to pass all the information on to him and Lizzie at the first opportunity. 'Yes I believe someone may have been murdered and I know the police will be asking you all lots of questions at the neighbourhood and parks watch meeting tonight,' he replied patiently. 'Are you going along?'

Mrs Fell thought for a moment. 'Yes!' she announced, 'I'll be there. Will you and Lizzie be going? What about your mother? I'll miss Irma being just next door.'

'No, not tonight, we have a lot to do with the move and everything, and Mother is still unpacking and settling into her cottage.'

It would be strange not having Mrs Fell watching him from her house opposite, and her regular updates of the goings-on in the town and with the 'old bat network.' He was really looking forward to settling into his own new cottage with Lizzie and his dog. The alleged murder at Monkswood did sound interesting.

Apparently it was somehow connected to Jemima Dunall, but it would have to wait for now. He would talk to Lizzie about it later.

Timothy watched the removal men close up the lorry containing the entire contents of his house. He waved them goodbye and locked the front door. Stepping back for one last look at the place, he sighed. No regrets', he thought, and the next one will be even better. Especially as Lizzie was moving in too, he turned back to the Land Rover. Faith whined noisily from the back as he got into the driver's seat. 'Not long now, lad. We're going to have a new life in a cottage; you'll love it, I'm sure. Don't worry, Mother is just down the road, so you'll still have plenty of spoiling'. He smiled as he drove away from his old home for the last time.

Lizzie was waiting for him when he pulled up beside their cottage. He couldn't stop grinning; at last they would be together in their own place. They fumbled with the keys and finally got the front door open. Keeping with tradition he scooped Lizzie up in his arms and carried her inside. Faith dashed in ahead of them and began sniffing around excitedly. They wouldn't be going to the meeting tonight.

36
Monkswood.

Jemima tucked the knife into the back of her rather tight-fitting jeans and quickly made her way to the open front door of Monkswood . She hadn't really noticed the black Panamera pulling out of the driveway but focused instead on who could be the owner of the small blue car parked in the drive; she was sure they were not there for any good reason.

She crept inside and listened. There was someone moving around upstairs. She carefully made her way up the old staircase and headed towards the sounds.

There was a shadow of someone moving around, visible through a partly-opened door. Trying to get the knife out of her jeans, she tugged at the handle but the tight waistband gripped it fast. She stepped forward and flung the door wide open, standing across the door way, still trying to pull the knife free with one hand.

'*Who the hell are you*', shouted the fair haired, rather skinny woman. She had obviously been sorting through the cupboards and drawers in the room.

'Who the hell are *you*!' shouted Jemima, 'this is *my* house!'

'I'm sorry, this is *my* property. I'm Harriet Dunall-Smith and *I* have inherited this property. It's been confirmed as mine from this morning. What the hell makes you think it's yours!' she barked.

'I was married to Giles Dunall, now deceased. I've never heard of you,' raged Jemima. Both women were convinced they were right, and that the property belonged to them; both were furious, and not for backing down. As Harriet picked up a large soft toy and took aim, the knife that was stuck in Jemima's waistband suddenly came free and shot across the room at the same time as the large teddy hurtled toward her. The knife caught the toy and pinned it to the wall! Harriet had more ammunition than Jemima, who was forced to retreat back towards the stairs as she ducked out of the way of a pair of flying roller-skates. Luckily they missed. Quickly grabbing them, Jemima hurled them right back at Harriet. One caught her on the side of her head, which made her even more wild and angry. As she stormed toward Jemima she stepped on one of the skates. Momentum and gravity sent her almost flying in the direction of Jemima and the stairs. Jemima jumped out of the way, crashing into the wall behind her, and knocking herself out as Harriet tumbled head first down the stairs. Deathly silence followed.

Verity Ainswick cycled down the lane to Monkswood. She was surprised to see a couple of cars in the drive and find the front door open. She had been asked to give the old place a clean, and to take as long as she needed, as the owner was planning on living in it. She had seen the place and knew it was going to take about a week to clean it up. This would, she hoped, pay for her old boiler to be serviced. The strong feeling that something was very wrong here gave her goose-bumps. She parked her bike and cautiously walked in. She knew the woman lying on the floor at the bottom of the stairs was Harriet Dunall-Smith, as it was her that had given her the job. But who was that at the top? She felt for a pulse in Harriet's neck, there was nothing; the poor woman was definitely dead. She started to make her way upstairs when the other woman groaned and slowly sat up. She blinked and stared at Verity, who smiled and asked quietly 'Are you alright, love?'

'Ohoo, I think so.' Jemima sat up, rubbing her head and wincing. Glancing around and seeing Harriet sprawled on the floor below she quickly realised the situation. 'I'm not sure what happened,' she almost whispered. 'We were attacked.' She managed to get to her feet but felt quite dizzy, and clung to the banister for support. 'Who are you?'

'I came to clean the place, I expected it to be empty.' Verity pulled her mobile phone out of her pocket. 'I better call someone about this lady here,' she nodded toward Harriet.

'Yes, good idea.' Jemima began to walk carefully down the stairs. 'I need some fresh air,' she muttered, still holding her head. Once outside she got straight into her car and left at speed, driving for home.

Verity had a quick look around, careful not to disturb anything. Once she realised there had obviously been a serious quarrel between the two women, she sat beside the dead woman and waited for the police to turn up. She had a genuine reason to be there and would be happy to talk to the police when they arrived. Sitting on the bottom step of the staircase she could feel the energies in the house were disturbed and she felt the house was calling to her. Or was it Harriet? The blue lights of a police car appeared in the drive. Verity wondered if she should bother cleaning; she'd been paid half of the money up front but the police may want to close the house for a while. She sighed and whispered, 'won't be getting the boiler serviced soon then.'

Dave Quilford, quite a hulk of a guy, walked over to the stairs and explaining who he was he sat down beside Verity. She told him what she had found and why she was there. She also told him about the other lady's swift exit. He nodded and was not altogether surprised by the information. 'The other lady I'm sure is Jemima Dunall. Did she mention why she was here in the first place?'

'No she hardly spoke, really. It looks like there was some sort of fight going on upstairs from the mess up there. Plus there is a teddy bear stuck to the wall with a knife. Not good energy.' Verity stretched her legs and stood up. 'I'd like to go now, if that's alright?'

'No problem. Could you make sure the officer over there has your contact details in case we need to chat some more? Oh and before you go, who was it booked you to clean here?'

'It was Harriet, Mrs Harriet Dunall-Smith. She found my number on the notice board in the village shop and booked me a few weeks ago. She has already paid half the money up front. I hope I don't have to give it back,' she added sulkily.

'I think that's unlikely,' smiled Dave. He watched as she went over to talk to the officer.

Upstairs he carefully picked his way through the mess and instructed the forensic team to check out the area on the stairs where Jemima had fallen over, and supposedly hit her head. He also asked them to confirm as soon as possible if there was any DNA belonging to anyone else other than that of Harriet or Jemima. Why had Jemima been there? The house belonged to Harriet, who was a relative of Jemima's dead husband Giles. Did Harriet have anything to do with the murder of Giles? Could she have helped Jemima in some way? Or was there someone else? Many questions and he was going to find the answers.

The following day Jemima fidgeted in her chair as she stared at her solicitor, Clive Coombes. ' So Monkswood will now be part of Giles's estate, will it?'

'Hold on, don't leap to conclusions. We have yet to sort out Giles's affairs and then we can try and find out who now owns Monkswood. As both Giles and Harriet were possibly murdered this could take a long time to sort out.' Clive shuffled the papers in front of him before looking up and meeting Jemima's gaze. He felt suspicious of Jemima, and Giles *had* been his friend. 'Right, that's all I can do for you at the moment.'

'But what am I supposed to be living on now?' cried Jemima, 'I can't live on fresh air!'

Clive leaned back in his chair and shrugged, his patience running out.

He watched as Jemima stormed out into the street and headed for the café, he assumed to meet her new boyfriend. He knew Giles had been involved in something dodgy in Africa, or with some very dodgy people anyway. The so-called S.A.A. Company was on the surface meant to be Save Africa's Animals but was in fact the exact opposite, paying local poachers a pittance, and very dangerous to anyone who got in their way. There was more to all of this and he needed to find out who exactly was involved.

Roderick had got in a bit deeper than he had originally intended with Jemima, and needed a way to back up a little while still keeping an eye on her. He had told her to stay well away from Monkswood after she'd told him about Harriet suddenly falling down the stairs. Jemima, ignoring any advice, really wanted to get back into the house and see if she could find a safe or desk where any old documents could be. Giles's old mother had talked about it years ago, so she thought that Monkswood would belong to Giles after his brother had died. Clive Coombes was taking too long, she needed to know now. She had no idea what her husband and his

290

brother had been involved in while in Africa. It was a part of his life that had always been a mystery to her. Roderick had refused to give her a lift to Monkswood on his bike, so after dark, ignoring the threat of trouble with the police and possible storms, she drove her car to a nearby lane and decided to walk across the fields. She was afraid to use a torch in case she was spotted, so she decided to manage without one. Dark clouds raced across the night sky, obscuring any moonlight. A silhouet of the old place was just visible on the skyline. Jemima shuddered as she made her way through the spooky woods. She fell over once or twice, and walked into low branches. She tried hard to be quiet but as more twigs snapped underfoot, plus the noise she made when walking into another log, her passing was anything but quiet. Low rumbles of thunder accompanied her grunts and squeals. Someone fired a shotgun not too far away. She screamed and threw herself down onto the wet grass. She kept still and listened, there were no further shots or any voices, just thunder and the wind whining in the trees. She continued.

There was a light on inside the house and police tape around the outside. She couldn't see any people or a police car. She squinted her eyes to get a better look just before stepping into a soggy ditch. Swearing she scrambled out and peered at the house again. Two dark hooded figures were running across the lawn heading toward the house. She froze and watched.

'What was that?'

'Oh just wildlife and thunder, keep your voice down.'

'There's a light on inside, I thought you said it would be empty.'

'I think it is. Let's get closer and find a way in'.

The two would-be thieves crept around the outside of the house, concealing themselves as best they could from anyone looking out of the house, blissfully unaware of the woman disguised in leaves and mud, who was watching them from the rhododendrons. .

Thunder and lightning crashed overhead as they found a loose window and climbed in. 'God this is a creepy place, I don't want to be in here long.'

'Shush, will you,' and then grinning, 'did I tell you about the monks that have been seen wandering on the ground floor and in the grounds?' the braver thief whispered.

'No. For God's sake, it's creepy around here without your weird tales. And a woman's been murdered,' he glanced around nervously.

'Hooo! It could be her ghost waiting inside,' joked his friend.

They quietly made their way through the house. It was a little easier as the landing light had been left on, so they could see enough to move around carefully while keeping to the shadows. All they could find were a few trinkets in the sitting room, which they pocketed. The old oil paintings were portraits of ancestors; their eyes following you from wherever you looked at them, creating the feeling of being watched.

In the study they found a safe in one corner. 'I'll have a go at the combination, keep still and be quiet.' He knelt down and pressed his ear to the safe as he turned the tumbler. The thunder rumbled and lightning flashed as the rain beat down on the windows. The thief sighed, 'this is so noisy!' he rolled his eyes skyward.

'I can't stay in this house much longer. Can't we just go? Hurry up,' his mate whispered. He shivered and looked around as lightning flashed and crackled. In the doorway stood a silhouette of a human-like figure, the face and eyes just shadows. He screamed, grabbing his accomplice by the collar, who yelled. 'What the hell is the matter with you!' Looking around he too saw the figure, which also screamed.

Terrified, the thieves ran for the door, knocking a very soggy Jemima over and running for a way out, any way out would do. The lights came on and they ran straight into the arms of several waiting police officers.

The officers had been in the house all the time. They'd had a reliable tip off that the two local thieves would be breaking into this house tonight. The house was under police surveillance anyway since the death of a woman. No one had expected to find Jemima breaking in too. Dave Quilford walked in, 'Hello Jemima, perhaps you can explain what you're doing here?' He stood in front of Jemima who had collapsed onto a chair.

Soaking wet, filthy and exhausted she sighed. 'I was just going for a walk when I saw the light and two people,' she started to explain.

Dave laughed. 'Don't give me that, Jemima. You are going to come with me to the station and I am going to get to the truth about what you're really up to, and how two people in connection with you have died.' Dave spoke firmly and taking Jemima by the arm lead her to a waiting police car.

'Good night's work, sir', said Sergeant Dumple

'Yes it is,' Dave replied, getting into his car.

37
Many Wollops.

Duncan's solicitors Hitchin & Hatch contacted him regarding information on the ownership of a nearby property called Monkswood. They believed that there could be documents somewhere, stored away in Many Wollops Hall, as there had been family connections years ago. Could Duncan help?

There were some documents tucked away in the fire-roof safe. Something Duncan had hardly ever looked at. He found the combination of the lock glued behind a painting and opened the aged safe, pulled out a bundle of old, very dusty documents and placed them on his desk in the study to look through later.

Many Wollops Hall is a large rambling Victorian house. The curtains and décor hadn't been changed in years but they were in good repair, though faded in places. Duncan employed minimal staff to run the house, and gardens, and the stables where he kept several horses. Many Wollops estate included a number of surrounding tenanted farms and cottages. His secretary and accountant mostly looked after the business side of things; his secretary had been muttering something about retiring.

His ex-wife had long gone, she ran off with the man who used to deliver the groceries. Although Duncan was always attracted to women, he had never found the right woman to have a family with. The thought of his own children running around the hall was something he rather liked; his ex had shuddered at the idea. He was a fit man, and the ladies in his life told him he was good looking.

He passed his part-time cleaner, Lena, at the bottom of the stairs.

'Good morning', she said breathlessly, clutching dusters and cleaning paraphernalia. 'Good morning Lena, what hot gossip have you got today?' Duncan knew Lena would be bursting with gossip of any exciting happenings in the village.

Eyes gleaming, she took a breath, 'There's been a death at Monkswood, they say it could be murder, and there was a break-in there last night, the police have arrested some people.'

'Well, I knew I could rely on you to keep me up to date, Lena! Keep up the good work.' He carried on upstairs toward his dressing room to change into riding gear, before heading down to the stables. He was looking forward to a hack across his land.

Jim, the groom, was waiting for him. 'He's all tacked up and ready for you.'

'Thank you. I'll be about an hour.' Duncan hopped easily up onto his mount, Busby. The 16.3 hh chestnut gelding was his favourite. He found riding a good way to relax and think things through. He wanted to think about his date with Daphne later, something to look forward to. And he must force himself to start reading through a load of old documents he hadn't ever given a thought to before now.

He decided to hack over in the direction of Monkswood and have a look around. He was sure the property didn't belong to him, and thought it was something to do with the Dunall family, who had gone to Africa years ago. After a good canter up a hill he rode through a small wood from where he could look down at Monkswood. There were several cars in the drive and two police cars. He sat and watched for a while but nothing seemed to be happening so he turned his horse around and rode on. The path took him along the bottom end of Monkswood land and passed the gardens of Prickets End. He waved to the gardener as he rode by.

Looking through the dusty papers later, he was surprised to find the old deeds to Monkswood but with other, conflicting and confusing documents and letters. From what he could gather, Arthur Timsonby de Dainty had married three times and had four children. His one and only daughter Tatiana had married Miles Dunall, whose family had owned two large houses in the area. One was Dark Wood House, currently owned by the deceased Giles Dunall, and the other was Monkswood, allegedly owned by his also deceased brother Herbert. The brother had gone off to Africa with the rest of the Dunall family and not returned. Something to do with encountering nasty lions. Or so the story went.

Dark Wood House was built 200 years ago on a woodland area where it is alleged witches had gathered for their dark ceremonies. In contrast, Monkswood was built on ancient heath land where, it's told, monks from a nearby priory used to roam in search of enlightenment or similar. Both were of Tudor style and near to the younger, Victorian Many Wollops Hall. Duncan sighed and decided to take the whole lot to his solicitor to sort out. Plus it looked as if there was some trouble going on there and he didn't really want to be involved; he had more interesting things to think about.

She hadn't felt this nervous about a date since she was a teenager. 'Steady girl', she told herself. Daphne had one last check in the mirror. Do I look smart but not over-dressed? Do I look interested but not too keen? Should I change these earrings, or leave them? Too late, the doorbell rang. 'He's here!' She jumped at the sound and tried not to race to the front door. Duncan Dainty

296

stood on her doorstep clutching a red rose. 'For you, my lady,' he grinned, handing her the flower

'Why thank you kind sir,' laughed Daphne, admiring this handsome dark-haired man on her doorstep. He took her hand and led her to his BMW Z4 Roadster. It was a warm evening so the top was down. A gentleman through and through he opened the door for her to slide in. 'Where are we going?' purred Daphne.

'To a nice little restaurant on the edge of Dickleborough. The food is always good and it's a nice, cosy, little family- run place. I hope you like it?'

'Sounds lovely,' she smiled; butterflies were doing aerobatics in her tummy.

As they approached the restaurant they saw a small open-top red MG going in the opposite direction. A goat was sitting in the back, looking quite content and it appeared to be enjoying the ride. Daphne laughed and managed to stop herself from waving at the couple in the car. 'Anyone you know?' Duncan noted her reaction.

'Well yes, I introduced them earlier in the year.'

'The goat?' he glanced at Daphne.

'She was living with the goat when they met. So I guess they are a happy threesome now,' chuckled Daphne, showing her lighter side.

The evening went smoothly as they both chatted easily whilst enjoying their meal. On the way back to Daphne's Duncan asked, 'Do you ride at all?'

'I used to, but haven't for quite a few years.' Daphne was curious.

'I have a few horses at home. Would you like to come over for a hack and some lunch?'

'I'd love to,' she said, a bit too quickly.

'Great,' he grinned, ' come over tomorrow at eleven and we'll sort a horse out for you.'

Daphne gulped. It was a long time since she'd sat on a horse and they were nice steady ones. 'I hope you have a nice quiet one, that isn't too tall.'

Duncan laughed. 'Don't worry. Jim will sort you out with one, and none of my horses are wild anyway.'

Daphne couldn't believe her luck. The evening with Duncan had gone really well. She poured her morning coffee and picked up the phone. 'Jane dear, d'you think you could manage this morning? Only something's come up that I really have to attend.'

'I expect I can, is it anything exciting?'

'I'm out for lunch too, so you may have to be a darling and cover for me this afternoon. I hope you don't mind?' Daphne didn't want to tell Jane anything at this early stage.

'Oh no, I don't mind at all.' Jane always enjoyed being left in charge, as she had ambitions of running her own agency one day; plus there was a rather nice-sounding man coming for an interview that day, so she would have him all to herself.

Daphne drove down the sweeping drive, through neatly mown lawns that surrounded large well-established Rhododendrons. Eventually the large Victorian house came into view. She pulled up beside Duncan's car and wondered if she should go to the front door or the side door. She opted for the front and walked into the large stone porch. After noticing the huge doorknocker she was pleased to also find a doorbell. After a little while a woman wearing a brightly coloured flowery pinny opened the door, 'Hello, can I help?' she asked brightly. 'I have an appointment to meet Duncan Dainty here at eleven.'

'Oh yes, yes, do come in. I'm sure he won't be a minute'. Lena showed Daphne into the main hall. While she was waiting she took the opportunity to have a look around. The polished wooden staircase swept upward to her left and she could see it lead to a galleried landing with a crystal chandelier hanging from the centre of the ceiling. A further four doors lead from the hall, the walls were decorated with old oil paintings, mostly of horses.

'Daphne! Good morning,' Duncan kissed her on the cheek. 'Are you ready?'

'Yes, I managed to find some old riding gear. I hope it will be alright?' She thought Duncan looked dashing in his jodhpurs, riding boots and thick fleece.

Jim had sorted her out with a smaller, pretty bay mare called Flicka. Duncan sprang up on-to Busby and they set off at a comfortable walk.

Daphne found she was able to relax and let her eyes wander over the house and the estate; her gentle steed seemed to know where she was going. They rode down through some trees before coming to what looked like an old orchard. They both pulled up and stared. There was a cow in the orchard that was absolutely still, not a flick of a tail or an ear.

'That's odd,' muttered Duncan, leaning forward in his saddle to get a better look. 'It appears to be stuffed, or a model of a cow.'

'Look over there,' cried Daphne, 'it's a sheep that's not moving either. And there's another,' she pointed across the orchard. They both sat dumb-struck for a minute; even the horses were looking over the hedge with their ears pricked forward as if trying to understand what they were seeing.

'This is part of Bertrum Muddlestone's farm; he is one of my tenants. It used to be known as Many Wallops

Hall Farm. The Muddlestone family has lived there for generations, hence the unofficial name change. I have no idea why he would put models or stuffed animals into his orchard. I wonder if Jim knows anything about it?' They rode on at a leisurely pace, Duncan understanding that Daphne hadn't ridden for a few years and was a little nervous. Back at the stables he asked Jim what was happening at Muddlestone's farm.

'Ah well,' he began, 'he went and met a woman, she didn't want to part with the animals after they died and old Bertrum went and paid for her to have them stuffed. Proper nonsense if you ask me'. Jim led the horses back to their stables.

'Oh goodness, I know who she is!' exclaimed Daphne.

'Would she be another one of your customers?'

'Yes she would, I think. What's her name?'

Jim came out of Busby's stable. 'He calls her Betty, I think. Nice woman, just a bit daft.'

'Yes, I did introduce them. I'm glad they're making a go of things; it's always nice to find out. Not everyone tells us; they just tend to vanish.' Daphne was happy; it gave her a warm glow whenever customers 'found each other'.

Duncan looked at Daphne as they walked back to the house. 'You haven't got any cats, goats or goldfish you want stuffing, have you?' he grinned.

'NO!' she exclaimed. He put his arm around her as they both dissolved into laughter. In that moment Daphne knew she wouldn't be going back into work that day.

38
The neighbourhood watch.

Eve smiled as she looked at the small group of people settling themselves into the chairs in front of her. Not one would be aged under 60 and a good proportion of them were aged over 70. A feisty bunch nonetheless.

'Good evening everyone', she said, 'thank you for coming. Welcome to the new members who are joining us tonight for the first time. I'm sure we can all become acquainted later over at the pub. As you know we're expanding the area for 'neighbourhood and parks watch' out of Dickleborough to include several villages and the surrounding countryside.' Nods and grunts of approval all round. 'There is one area in particular we, the police, are keeping an eye on.' Eve continued, ' between Dickleborough and Many Wollops, just on the edge of the Many Wollops Hall estate is a property called Monkswood, some of you may know of it. We have been getting reports of prowlers around the property and around that side of the estate. As usual I will ask you to be cautious and call us if you see anything suspicious, but do not get involved. We don't know what the prowlers may be capable of. So no heroics!'

'Will Timothy know? He lives over that way now.' asked Mrs Battle, in her usual forthright manner.

'Yes, I'm sure Timothy will be kept informed.'

'I heard someone was murdered there? Is this true? Who was it? Will we need to get some younger blood on the team here in Dickleborough?' asked Maureen Broadbent, remembering several incidents last year where Timothy had saved the day.

'All are welcome to join and I'm sure we will be recruiting more new members soon.' Eve smiled. ' I would also ask those of you on parks watch to look out for any groups of young people acting suspiciously.   I can't tell you any more about the incident at Monkswood but as I have said, we would appreciate you keeping a look out for anything suspicious or any unknown vehicles in the area.

Eve didn't talk about the murder enquiry as the local neighbourhood watch could get a bit over-enthusiastic and she didn't want any of them interfering with the case. She felt sure that somehow this was all connected with the death of Giles Dunall, but unproven as yet.

To her surprise one of the new people sitting near the back at the meeting was Seth, the gardener from Dark Wood Manor. Dave Quilford had claimed there was more to the old guy than was apparent. He had been interested in chatting more with Seth, with regard to the Giles Dunall murder. She sent Dave a text message and hoped Seth would join them all in the pub.

The meeting came to a close and as they all filed out of the hall Eve sidled up to Seth. 'Are you joining us in the pub? It's Seth, isn't it?' she asked.

'Aye, that's me. I was wanting a bit of a talk with one of you lot.' His voice was gruff and husky. 'Come and have a drink with us; perhaps we can have a chat,' smiled Eve. She hoped Dave would be able to turn up. In the pub Seth sat at a table with his unlit pipe in his mouth. Eve went up to the bar with the others. She bought herself a drink and one for Seth. 'You're not buying him a drink, are you?' snapped the disapproving Mrs Battle.

'Yes I am, I just want a little chat with him,' Eve replied firmly.

'Hmmm, that looks dodgy,' Mrs Battle muttered to anyone who was listening.

Eve was relieved when at last Dave walked in. He got himself a drink at the bar and came to sit with them.

'Hello Seth, I hear you want a chat with us?'

'It were two women I see coming out of the house before the bitch came home,' he coughed.

'Can you describe them?'

'Aye, well, they were separate really. The one was quite small and had short dark hair and was wearing some sort of camouflage gear; she was only in the house a few minutes and I didn't see any vehicles in the drive. Then the other one turns up; she were a blond skinny woman. Looked like she bin' abroad, all brown like. She drove a small blue Fiat. Came out of the house like a scalded cat; ran to her car and drove off at some speed. I liked to think it was the 'bitch' that killed him, but now I don't know. I didn't see her with him that day. The bitch appeared to be doin' a lot of running around the house, and looked real shifty when she got back, but that's all I can tell yer, really. I haven't seen the other two again.'

' I better go and join the others. I'm sure they will have lots of questions'.   Eve left the table, thinking Seth may open up a bit more man to man.

' Thanks Seth,' said Dave, 'so you hoped it was Jemima that killed him. Why?'

'Nasty piece of work, I never liked her. She only married him to get her hands on his money. The family and Giles had always been good to me; always made sure I was alright.' Seth finished his drink and got up to leave.

'Seth, are you absolutely sure that no one else went into the house that day? Any deliveries?'

'Seth wrinkled his face. Well, I'm just thinking, it may have been that day,' he sat down again. 'There was a smart looking well built bloke in a grey suit. He was selling some insurance or somet. I told him he was wasting his time, and left him to knock on the door. I didn't see what happened but when I came back around to the front of the house later, his car had gone. I remember thinking it was odd that someone who drives a black Panamera Porsche would be selling insurance.

'That's really interesting, can you remember anything else about him? '

'Na, I only remembered him a minute ago, and yes, thinkin' on it, it was on the same day, and before them other women turned up. And then the bitch came back later that same day. I think I should tell you that Giles may have been dealing with some dangerous people back in Africa. The kind that wouldn't think twice about arranging a nice little accident if you upset 'em.' He touched the side of his nose.

'That's really helpful Seth, thank you. You know where to call if you remember anything else?'

'Aye, a do.' Seth patted down the bonfire in his pipe and was feeling around in his pocket for some matches as he left the pub.

Dave took a sip of his beer. 'Interesting information from the old boy', he thought, hoping the DNA samples from Monkswood came in soon. He would have to re-evaluate the information and DNA from Dark Wood House now, too. He had a feeling Jemima was capable of murder, but not sure if she would actually be guilty. This time anyway. It takes some guts to stab someone once through the heart and then leave without being seen by anyone. Except the gardener of course. So often the most obvious suspects are the least likely to be guilty. He just had a feeling this was going to be one of those cases where all the main suspects are innocent and someone else turns out to be the culprit. The whole thing was a tangled mess of family, inheritance and death. He smiled, thinking that Jemima may not be the beneficiary in this case; it was so obvious she was convinced that she was. He did wonder what had happened to make old Seth come forward with this latest information. He'd leave him to stew for a while and then go and have a another chat.

39
The village.

'How are you settling in at the cottage, Timothy? Like village life, do you?' asked Mrs Brown.

'Yes, thanks,' replied Timothy, totting up the prices of her new selection of books.

'How does your mother like village life? She told Beattie Fell she was enjoying it. Did you know they have a witch living in the village?' She leaned toward him hoping for further information.

He smiled patiently, 'that will be £11.50, Mrs Brown. Mother said she'd met some of the locals. It's not far from where she lived before so she knows most of the villagers already. I don't know anything about a local witch though.'

Mrs Brown stuffed her new purchases into her shopping trolley and trundled out of the shop. 'Thank you Timothy, toodeloo!' she called over her shoulder as usual.

'What was that about?' chuckled Derek. 'Your mother is fraternising with a witch now? Mmm that could be interesting'.

'Oh, don't take too much notice, Mother lives in her own little world half the time'.

On his way home that evening Timothy noticed what looked like a very tall black and white cow, sort of gliding along on the other side of the hedge. He slowed down for a better look. That must be the lane to Muddlestone's farm, he thought. The cow just stared over the hedge as it was travelling along. Timothy scratched his head as the cow disappeared behind trees and around the corner. No, that can't be real he thought.

The cow couldn't be gliding. But why would a farmer be taking a life-size model of a cow to his farm when he had a field full of real ones?

Irma Parkes quickly found her way around the small village. She had friends there already, but had never been inside the village shop. Today she decided to venture into what was now her local grocery shop. 'Florry's Greens & Groceries' the sign read across the small shop front; the window was full to overflowing. Pretty flower baskets hung either side of the white door and a neatly planted flowerbed ran along the path from the road. The stone building probably used to be a dwelling before becoming a shop. Inside it resembled a mini-supermarket. Florry, the middle-aged shop owner greeted Irma in a friendly, helpful manner. Irma marvelled at all the shelves stuffed with goods literally right up to the high ceiling, with just about everything from fresh bread and cakes, local vegetables, toilet rolls and washing powder, to small well-stocked freezers along the back wall. Handy lightweight steps were left out for customers who wanted to help themselves to anything from the top shelves.

In the middle of the shop there were shelves forming an island leaving a narrow corridor for browsing either side. The counter and till were at the end, by the door. This way no one could enter the shop without being spotted by the shopkeeper's beady eyes.

'Settling in, are you, dear?' asked Florry, her glasses perched on the end of her nose.

'Yes, thank you. What a wonderful shop.'

'Thank you. We can also supply coal and kindling if you need any. Did you move here with your husband?' she asked.

'My husband passed away a few years ago, but my son Timothy and his partner Lizzie have moved into the village too; they live along Mucks lane.'

'Ah, Mrs Parkes, is it?' she exclaimed, pleased with herself for guessing right.

'Yes, that's right.' Irma wondered how much Florry knew about them already!

As Irma was filling her basket with groceries a small, younger lady with dark bobbed hair came into the shop. " Good afternoon Florry, not a bad day after the heavy mist last night,' she smiled.

'That mist wasn't anything to do with you, was it? I could hardly see one foot in front of me when I was walking home.' Florry pushed her glasses further up her nose and took a breath. ' The vicar says it's your doing that his fish have gone again, too! This is Mrs Parkes, just moved into Myra's old cottage. This is Verity Ainswic our local herbalist.'

Verity laughed. 'Nothing to do with me, the heron's been visiting the vicar's pond again, I'm sure of it.'

After the initial introductions Irma arranged to visit Verity on her way home with a view to buying some herbs for the garden. She knew that word would spread quickly in the village and everyone who didn't know already would know she had moved into 'Myra's old cottage' by tonight!

'This is lovely,' exclaimed Irma as she wandered around Verity's very tidy and organised garden.

'Glad you like it. Have you got time for a cuppa?' This was Verity's way of finding out more about the newcomer. A large black cat wandered out of the garden shed. With a raised tail it walked over to Irma, winding itself around her legs, purring and mewing. 'Hello, who are you?' Irma asked, not really expecting an answer.

308

'That's Georgina, she likes to introduce herself and inspect any new visitors,' explained Verity.

'I like cats. I don't have one as I often look after my son's Wolfhound. I don't know if it would get on with a cat.'

'Georgina is good at sorting dogs out. Any trouble and they get a swift scratch on the nose,' chuckled Verity, handing Irma a mug of odd smelling green tea. 'It's herbal and very good for you,' she said.

Irma sniffed and took a careful sip, it was very hot but didn't taste too bad.

' I'm having a few friends over for a get-together and a drink next week. Perhaps you would like to come?' Verity invited while bending to stroke her cat, which leapt straight up onto her shoulder. The cat turned and as it stared directly into Irma's face, she thought its eyes had become large like saucers, but at a second glance they looked normal again. She looked at the tea she was drinking and wondered what the herbs were. 'That would be very nice, I look forward to meeting everyone.'

While they were chatting, Verity had gathered some herbs for Irma's garden. Bay, thyme, rosemary, feverfew and lavender. 'Just a few to get you started. Don't worry about carrying them all, I'll bring them round in a wheel barrow for you,' she said kindly.

Walking home to her cottage Irma enjoyed the view and the peace: cows were grazing in the fields, and birds were singing. She noticed a rather odd cow moving along the top of the hedge, or that was how it looked. As she stared she realised the cow was moving along the lane on the other side of the hedge but it appeared much taller than normal. I must find out what those herbs were in the tea, she thought.

309

As she arrived at her gate, Timothy pulled up in his Land Rover. 'Hi Mother, are you well?' he asked giving her a hug.

'Yes dear, but I've just seen something rather odd.' She explained about the cow.

Timothy smiled, 'Yes, I've just seen it, too. It was standing on top of a trailer and heading off to the farm.'

Irma told her son all about the herbal lady and the get-together. Timothy was pleased to hear his Mother was settling in and mixing with the locals. Irma was relieved that Timothy had seen the strange cow too and that it hadn't been anything to do with the strange tea.

Irma's semi-detached old estate-workers cottage was called No 2, Lavender and nestled into a hillside facing east. It was a timber framed building made with local stone and a slate roof. There was a small garden that had become overgrown with nettles and other invasive wild plants; in places various herbs had taken advantage of being allowed to grow unchecked. The cottage walls were about three feet thick, ideal to keep her warm in the winter and cool in summer. She had been assured the fire was good for burning wood and that she could buy logs locally. Although the cottage was smaller than she was used to, there would be plenty of room for her sister Maude if she could convince her to come and stay and that her son really wasn't a wicked mad man!

Verity turned up with a barrow full of herbs as promised, and managed to negotiate Irma's narrow path to the garden. ' I've brought a selection, but I'd better have a look around, you may already have some of these.'

'What's this one here?' asked Irma pointing to a large leafy green plant with pretty small blue-ish flowers.

'That's comfrey, it's sometimes known as 'knitbone'. It has good healing properties and tea can be made from its leaves and roots. It makes an excellent poultice too, years ago they believed it helped with healing broken bones. The roots are alleged to have magical properties. If you were to take a large root of comfrey with you on a journey, no harm will come to you. Also gamblers would wrap some of their money in comfrey leaves, as they were believed to protect it from loss. Others believe it brings wealth and good fortune.'

'I'll keep that!' exclaimed Irma.

Verity laughed, 'it's very invasive and you'll never get rid of it, even if you wanted to. The leaves are sometimes mistaken for the leaves of foxgloves. Comfrey leaves are hairy, not smooth like foxglove leaves. People have poisoned themselves by making tea from the wrong leaves.' Verity turned and looked directly at Irma as she said this, making sure she understood.

As Verity was leaving Irma's garden, one of the local dog-walking ladies called over the gate, 'Have you seen what Muddlestone has put in his orchard? He's lost his marbles this time.' She strode off before either of them could react. Verity shrugged, manoeuvring her barrow onto the road.

Later that evening, having read from one of the books, Herbs and Spells, that Verity had brought for her, Irma decided to have a go at making a spell. She glanced over in the direction of Timothy's cottage and hoped they didn't decide to call in tonight. Walking around the garden with the book in hand she gathered what she hoped were the right herbs. She also found a green candle among her unpacked boxes. She put an old roasting tin on the kitchen table, placed the green candle in the middle, and the herbs, mostly lavender,

311

around the candle. She quickly wrote a few words, asking for good fortune for her son and his new lady. She lit the candle and waited, and waited. The spell said she had to burn the candle right down to nothing, then bury the remains in the garden. As it was taking some time to burn down she decided to make something to eat. She ate her small meal of locally bought cheese and crusty bread, and still the candle burned. She had just started to nod off in the chair when there was a sizzle and crackle from the roasting tin as the herbs caught fire. Vast amounts of smoke quickly filled the kitchen, setting the fire alarm off. Hardly able to see or breathe, she pushed open the door into the garden and with her oven gloves picked up the tin with the burning, smouldering mass. Coughing and gasping she carried it into the garden. Grabbing the watering can she sloshed water over the flames, which had flared up further in the fresh air. This was now a black smouldering mass once more. She refilled the watering can and sloshed more water over the whole thing. It sizzled and steamed, then eventually calmed enough for her to rush into the house and deal with the fire alarm that had been screaming the entire time. She caught a glimpse of her reflection in the window. Black smudges, soot and smuts were all over her hair and face. 'So much for my first attempt at spell casting', she thought. 'Oh no, who's that now?' The persistent hammering on her door wasn't stopping. As she made her way through the house to answer it, a voice shouted from behind her. 'Irma are you alright, what's happened?' Irma turned to meet Lizzie, who had come in through the back door. 'Oh Irma! I thought something dreadful had happened. Your fire alarm was going for ages,' gasped a worried Lizzie, suddenly clutching Irma in a tight hug. 'Thank goodness you're safe. What have you been doing?'

Before she could answer, Timothy raced into the house, 'Mother, what's happened?' he stopped dead in the kitchen and looked around. 'It stinks in here! What on earth where you cooking?'

Someone else started rapping on the front door, they also became impatient and appeared at the open back door. It was Verity. 'Oh thank goodness you're all right! I could hear the alarm from my cottage. What's that smell?' She hesitated for a minute and raised an eyebrow at the suddenly sheepish Irma.

'No harm done everyone,' said Irma quickly, 'shall I put the kettle on as you have all come to save me? The scones are in the tin on the side, Timothy. Hopefully they won't taste of soot.'

'Are you going to tell us what happened?' Lizzie was concerned.

'Oh, nothing major, I was just experimenting with some cooking. At least I know the fire alarm works; it's very loud,' she said with a sooty grin.

After scones and tea, and the kitchen cleaned up, Lizzie and Timothy left.

Verity leaned on the doorjamb, as she was about to go home, 'So what spell were you trying out?'

Irma explained, and added 'I think I'll read a bit more before I try again.'

Verity laughed, she gave Irma a kiss on the cheek and was still laughing as she left.

40
Prowlers and poachers.

Dougal and Maureen Broadbent were both tall and very slim. Dougal had slightly long dark hair and even today as an older man he looked like a well-worn hippy. Maureen always tried to dress smartly, her deep auburn hair made her look quite striking, and even her brightly coloured wellingtons were trendy. They had met and married while still at Uni. Both having a slightly bizarre sense of humour and an overly enthusiastic sense of adventure. Their two children are now away at college; both studying forensic pathology, partly influenced by their parents who have always had a keen interest in crime drama and thrillers, on the screen and in literature.

'Will they let me come on any investigations with you, d'you think?' Maureen had asked her eldest child and son.

'No Mother, I don't think they will let you anywhere near,' was his patient reply.

Dougal's eccentric parents Nigel and Philamina, lived nearby on the edge of Many Wollops village. Maureen's parents were Scottish and still lived up in the highlands, refusing to venture down to any sort of comfortable civilisation.

Maureen had been disappointed to learn she wouldn't be welcomed by either of her children or their bosses/lecturers in any investigations of any sort. However she had been delighted to learn about the local neighbourhood watch and parks watch teams, and had signed herself and Dougal up immediately.

Nigel Broadbent, Dougal's father, had lived on the outskirts of Many Wallops since he'd retired. He had bought the house called Prickets End from the Many Wallops estate. (Pricket is an old name for yearling male deer). He had sold his small chain of teashops that produced beverages and a wide selection of meals, which for the most part hardly ever tasted as they were described on the menu.

The family had had a reputation for being a little potty. Nigel had confirmed these rumours when he would appear randomly at any one of his teashops to loudly serenade the confused customers. Nigel was of medium height, and a rather portly, balding fellow these days. He loved to show off his garden and employed a regular gardener by the name of Jasper.

Jasper enjoyed working for the Broadbents; he didn't mind their eccentricities and could do more or less as he liked with the two-acres of garden that backed on to the ground belonging to Monkswood. As far as anyone knew there had never been any animosity between the two houses, non that anyone could remember anyway.

As hardly anyone had been living at Monkswood over the years, Nigel had been able to practice his 'going back to nature' moments, which involved him removing all of his clothes and wandering around the garden totally naked, without complaint, from any neighbours. His long-suffering wife Philamina ignored her husband's bizarre behaviour as best she could. She was a tall, slim, elegant, well-spoken lady, who liked to dress smartly and enjoyed entertaining the members of her ladies book club for Wednesday lunch or afternoon tea. Years ago she had found Nigel amusing and good fun. While she accepted his antics as being a part of him, she struggled to keep another, more normal and ordered side to her life. She did manage to maintain a fairly normal relationship with their son Dougal and his wife Maureen.

In one part of the garden there was a small lake, some may describe it as a large pond, which was surrounded by plants and grasses, with two mature weeping willows whose branches reached down kissing the surface of the water. This was ideal for the resident ducks to take shelter and hide. Grass snakes and other wildlife had also made this area their home. The grasses had been allowed to grow and mingle with the water-loving plants growing around the pond, it would be hard for a stranger to see where the ground and the water met.

Nigel was convinced poachers were trying to steal his fish. Jasper had explained to him many times that no one would be interested in stealing a few old carp, but Nigel wasn't convinced and was always on the look-out. He had persuaded Jasper to build him a small hut by the pond under one of the willows so that he could hide inside and wait for his imaginary poachers without being seen. Jasper had obliged; he had included a tiny spy hole or two and had even painted it green so that it would blend in and become almost invisible among the slender long branches of the willow.

Late one Wednesday morning Nigel had gone down to the pond and noticed human footprints along the edge, and convinced it must be a poacher he quickly shut himself inside the hut and waited…

'Why are we doing this again?' asked Dougal.

Maureen walked on ahead, tugging their little dog along on its lead. ' For the tenth time Dougal, we're taking our dog for a walk around the back of Monkswood near to your parents' house, so it doesn't look suspicious.

Then if we find or see anything 'iffy' we can report back to Eve, the police lady,' snorted Maureen.

'Why can't we just go into Dad's garden and look from there? You've become obsessed with this neighbourhood watch business. I'm sure the police didn't mean for you to actually go out looking for evidence. I'm not sure what evidence you expect to find down here, anyway. Plus if Dad sees us, you'd better get ready to duck,' grumbled Dougal.

'Your father is potty. I don't think we have to worry about him.'

'Don't bet on it.'

'Get down, I see something!' Maureen ducked down behind a shrub.

Dougal looked around; unable to see anything he crouched down beside her. 'There's nothing there, woman,' he whispered. As they watched they could just about see a couple of policemen doing the rounds at Monkswood house. Their little dog started to growl and wag its tail at the same time, looking towards Nigel's pond. 'Is there someone in your parents' garden?' asked Maureen.

'Only Jasper probably. It could be Dad patrolling his patch. We better keep well out of sight.'

Suddenly a Muntjac deer shot out of the undergrowth and raced off across the over-grown gardens, making the two spies jump. They shrank down as low as they could and watched.

Unbeknown to Dougal and Maureen, Nigel had taken his old shotgun to the hut with him. Was that movement in his neighbours' field? Aware that there were police present next door, he surmised there was something amiss. He grabbed his gun and moved around the pond to get a better look. He hadn't fired this particular old gun for a long while. With his back to the edge of the pond he loaded a cartridge, took aim at somewhere he thought he saw something and, forgetting about the powerful recoil of a shotgun, he fired. With his ears ringing from the loud bang, he went flying backwards into the pond, dropping the gun as he went.

Dougal and Maureen jumped up and ran away, back to their car. The little dog broke loose and streaked ahead of them. Jasper ran toward the noise, wondering what his boss had done now.

The book-club ladies all looked up and around at the bang from the gun, but thought it was probably someone shooting rabbits. Philamina anxiously glanced into the gardens, hoping that her husband hadn't shot anyone important.

Nigel managed to struggle out of the pond, despite the sticky muddy bottom; Jasper appeared and gave him a hand. 'Missed the bastards!' grizzled Nigel, accepting help out of the mud. He grimaced in the direction of Monkswood. 'I'll get them next time, you wait and see.' He started to remove his clothes as he made his way towards his house.

Police officers Tom and Ben had heard the gunshot and decided to investigate. They rang the doorbell at Prickets End.

Philamina opened the door and gasped;' Is someone dead?' she cried.

'Hope not, did that shot come from here? We wondered if we could see your gun licence. Can we come in?'

The two policemen walked directly into the living room, only to be faced with the book-club ladies.

'Has someone been shot?' two of them asked at the same time.

'We hope not, we just need to have a chat with the owner of the gun, if they're around.'

'I think we should all leave,' said one of the ladies.

'No, we don't! I want to stay and find out what's going on,' said another.

Poor Philamina started to gather up the cups and saucers and really wished the book group would just leave, she was far too polite to say it, though. Instead she offered the two policemen a cup of tea. They both accepted. The ladies from the book group settled themselves back in their chairs, ready to listen.

Jasper followed his boss back up the garden towards the house, picking up the discarded clothes as he went. Remembering that Philamina was entertaining her ladies in the house today, he tried to call Nigel back. Nigel's ears were still ringing from the loud bang; he was stark naked and temporarily totally deaf. The shortest way into the house was through the large, partially open sitting room windows. Jasper took his arm and tried to indicate that he should go in around the side. Nigel shook him off. As he was going in through the windows when he finally looked up and stopped dead. His sitting room was full of people, six mature ladies and two policemen. The ladies all gasped and one or two covered their eyes.

'Is there a problem, Officer?' Nigel asked loudly and unashamedly. Philamina rushed out of the room.

'Errm, we'd like to have a look at your gun licence please, sir,' said Tom the older of the two officers, while the other got out his notebook. 'Perhaps you would like to get dressed, sir?' he continued.

'Oh right. Yes, I suppose I'd better, good afternoon, ladies. I'll be right back, officer, I want to tell you about the poachers.' Nigel chuckled.

As he left the room he walked head on into his wife. '*How could you, Nigel*? Put these on,' she thrust a bundle of clothes at him. 'I'll *never* be able to entertain the ladies here again. How *could you!*' she cried, rushing back upstairs sobbing.

'It wasn't difficult darling, I nearly shot a poacher. Please don't be upset, Philly.' He dressed and went to find is shotgun licence. He kept a surprisingly organised study and found the licence quickly.

On returning to the sitting room he saw that the two policemen had encouraged the book club ladies to leave. Disappointed and grumbling about missing out on any action, they were gathering themselves and their belongings as Nigel walked in. 'Sorry to have disrupted the gathering, ladies. Feel free to come again, won't you,' he invited.

'Your wife has a lot to put up with,' complained one of the ladies, who considered herself a friend to Philamina. The police officers looked at each other, making a mental note of Nigel's reaction. He was ultra polite and smiling as he saw them all out to their cars.

'He reminds me of Toad of Toad hall, he even looks a bit like him,' giggled Ben, the younger of the policemen, while making notes. He looked up and smiled as Nigel came back into the room.

'Ah officers, now let me tell you about the poachers. I'm sure they're trying to steal my carp, you know. Several have definitely gone missing. I always had two mirror carp in there and now I can only find one. Plus some of the common carp, there were fifteen of those, and I can only count eight. I can show you the pond and the strange footprints that were there this morning. Come and see,' he went on while heading out of the open garden windows.

The policemen followed. Speaking quietly, knowing Nigel wouldn't hear them, Ben said, 'The vicar said some of his fish had gone missing recently, he was blaming a local lass called Verity Ainswic.'

'My money's on a local heron feasting on these fish, not poachers or Verity,' Tom muttered quietly.

'Aren't witches supposed to be able to turn themselves into birds?'

'Absolute rubbish, don't start believing everything you hear from the old locals, they'll tell you any nonsense. This is down to nature. The bottom of this land joins up with the land of Monkswood and there's a bridle-way that runs between the two so it's worth having a look. The old boy's pond is a good place to hide out.'

'As long as he isn't out with his gun!'

'Quite. You'll soon learn it's better to be fairly laid-back and tolerant of the folks around here, they're all a bit… different, odd if you like.'

'Right here!' shouted Nigel, pointing at the ground beside the pond where a single footprint had dried in the mud. 'Jasper says it wasn't him, and it definitely wasn't me!'

The policemen made a note of the angle of the print and decided it could have been someone watching Monkswood, you could just make out part of the house from there.

'There was definitely someone over there earlier, I saw them moving in the shrubs,' said Nigel.

'This is of interest sir but please leave the detective work to us. We have several officers keeping a watch on Monkswood since the death of a woman there. Please don't go using your shotgun. It's illegal to shoot at people, even if they are trespassing. We wouldn't want to have to arrest you sir. Call us straightaway if you or your wife or gardener see or hear anything suspicious; the police are not far away. We will solve the mystery of your disappearing fish as soon as we can sir,' explained Tom, trying to appease the agitated Nigel.

'So it's definitely illegal to shoot at people even if they're trespassing on your own land?'

'Yes sir', they said in unison.

'What, even if I just wing 'em a bit?' Nigel's eyes gleamed at the thought as he shuffled from one foot to another.

'Still illegal'.

'Couldn't I say self-defence, or that I'm defending my property? Surely that would be alright?'

'No, not really sir. Please call us if you see anyone suspicious,' Tom persisted.

Nigel shuffled his feet again, with his hands in his pockets like a naughty schoolboy. 'Do you want a drink? I've got plenty of gin at the house, I've even got some in my shed,' he invited.

'No, thank you sir. We don't drink on duty. Isn't it a bit early for a drink?'

Nigel laughed, 'no, no it's never too early. Come round when you're off duty, you can drink as much as you like.'

The policemen declined the offer and after persuading the reluctant Nigel to promise not to use his shotgun for a while, and getting him to promise never to shoot it at poachers, they made their way back to the squad car. As Nigel hadn't actually shot anyone or as far as they knew pointed it at a real person, they decided not to confiscate his gun and licence and save themselves a vast amount of paperwork.

Nigel watched the policemen drive away. 'Right,' he chuckled and with a little skip he went into the house and retrieved his gun. It would need cleaning after the soaking in the pond, he could get Jasper to do that later. Meanwhile he went into his study and got his archery equipment out of the cupboard. No one said he couldn't fire arrows at the poachers, and the policemen over at

Monkswood wouldn't be able to hear it if he did. He chuckled to himself as he counted his arrows. He would take his second best bow down to the hut and keep the best one to hand in the house. If he put a target up in the garden he could practice and that would also explain to any busybodies why he had a bow and arrow around in the house. Plus Jasper was brilliant at finding any lost arrows that had missed the target.

The study door opened, ' There's salmon for supper. Oh no, what are you going to do with those?' cried his exasperated wife.

'Don't worry Philly, the policemen said I mustn't use the shotgun. They didn't say anything about these!' he giggled.

She sighed helplessly. 'At eight o' clock, supper will be ready,' she walked off to the kitchen. Knowing he wasn't a good shot with the gun and especially with the bow and arrows, she assumed he wasn't going to do too much damage. She went to her phone to call Jasper and warn him. He was a brilliant gardener and so tolerant of her husband's idiosyncrasy, she would hate anything to happen to him. She also made a call to her son, warning them not to walk into the garden unannounced as Dad had got his bow and arrows out.

Dougal put the phone down and immediately told his wife, 'Dad *will* shoot at anything, you should avoid being anywhere near Prickets End at the moment. He's not a good shot but you don't want to get in the way of one of those arrows, honey; they can do some serious damage.'

'The shotgun was bad enough,' grumbled Maureen, ' I'm not surprised the policemen told him he's not to use it. I am surprised they let him keep the gun and his license. Suddenly Maureen started to smile. 'It would be quite funny if the mad woman from Darkwood went creeping around there again… wouldn't she get a surprise. Shame she's locked up at the moment.'

'I don't suppose I can dissuade you from tonight's escapade to Darkwood then?' Dougal asked.

'No, we should go and check it out; you never know, Giles's killer might come back for a look around the house.'

'That's what worries me,' groaned Dougal.

As old Seth called his cat in later that evening he noticed shadows moving in the grounds of the main house. Darkwood had a reputation of being haunted, like many old houses but Seth was a born sceptic. When he was a young man he had spent ten years in the army and a number of those had been attached to Special Forces. Old as he was he still knew how to move around the gardens silently and unseen. With his aged cat safely in the house, he put on his boots, a dark coat and went to see who was wandering in the grounds.

It didn't matter to him if the place was burgled, serve the 'bitch' right. Since Giles had been stabbed to death he had been wondering, what *was really* going on? Anyway, it made a change from his usual routine, and a bit of sleuthing would make life more interesting.

He had been surprised to see Roderick Mackenzie arrive at the house a few weeks earlier; he remembered meeting Mackenzie when he was in Africa with the Dunalls. Even though he had chatted with him about his bike, Mackenzie hadn't recognised him. Both had been younger men back then, when Mackenzie had been working for a security firm involved in guarding a diamond mine, partly owned by a few members of the Dunall family. Seth had already been a middle-aged man; they had both looked quite different in those days.

Seth moved out into the garden to the old oak tree. He climbed with ease and settled himself down to watch from its branches. When he recognised the people wandering clumsily around the garden he smiled, this was going to be entertaining. He also noted the black Porsche coming down the drive with its lights off. It stopped half way, he assumed it had seen the Mini and the small group of locals around it. The Porsche reversed unseen by the old bats, and almost silently moved back along the drive and out into the lane; its lights came on as it drove off.

'There's someone moving inside, I'm sure,' whispered Dougal. He crept as best he could closer to the hall window, a rose bed being in his path. He leaned forward and squinted his eyes, trying to see inside. 'No, I think it's just a picture, or a mirror maybe.' He looked at his mobile to check he still had a signal. Maureen was on the other side of the house with Mrs Weatherbutts and Mrs Fell. 'What's he saying? Has he seen someone?' he could hear loud whispers through Maureen's phone.

'Shh. No it's just a mirror,' hissed Maureen.

There was a loud crack as Mrs Fell who was creeping up behind Maureen and Mrs Weatherbutts, stepped on some twigs. They span around. 'Oh it's you, shhh,' they whispered loudly.

'I don't know why we're here. Is there someone in there or something? Are you sure she hasn't been let out and has come home?' Mrs Fell's teeth rattled loudly by way of emphasising her concern.

'No, we're here 'cos the police lady asked us to keep an eye on things.'

'I'm not sure she expected us to go creeping about in gardens,' Mrs Fell whispered as she grabbed hold of Maureen for support on the uneven ground.

'Ow', they heard more muttering from Dougal through Maureen's mobile.

'What's happened'? They all whispered so loudly that Seth could hear them easily.

'I'm trying to get a closer look, these roses are very prickly. O*uch!*'

They crowded around Maureen's phone. 'Can you see anyone inside?'

'No, but I'm nearly at the window,' he leaned forward and managed to peer right into the room. A dark shadow suddenly moved across the room, Dougal froze and watched intently. He couldn't make out the dark shapes in the room, then another shadow moved. Could there be more than one person lurking in there?

'Dougal what's happening? said the loud whisper of his wife through the speaker-phone. '*Ssh*', he whispered, mesmerised by the moving shadows. The shadows grew strangely as he watched. Suddenly he saw a reflection in the window loom large behind him. He shivered with fright and turned around, only to see his wife standing behind him. 'Oh blimy, it's you!' he gasped, catching his breath. 'You silly woman. If there is someone inside they'll see us all here. O*uch*!'

'D'you think we should get inside and have a look? *Ouch, I'm stuc!*'

'NO, but we need to get out of this rose bed, I'm prickled all over,' grumbled Duncan, disentangling his jacket and his wife from a particularly clingy thorn. 'There's nothing in there but shadows.'

'Come on, let's go, this place gives me the creeps,' Mrs Fell croaked hoarsely. She clung to Maureen's arm as they started to make their way back to the driveway.

Seth decided to have a bit of fun as he watched the inept vigilantes make their way back through the garden. He had always been quite good at imitating birds, so cupping his hands together, he hooted loudly. The intruders started to run and scrambled over the lawn and along the drive. He could hear their loud panicky whispering as they went. Leaning back on his branch he chuckled. What did they think they would find? The house was empty, the bitch was locked up, and the owner Giles was dead. He heard the Mini's revving engine as they drove off.

It was a still, warm evening and he wasn't in a hurry to get down from his perch. His owl call had brought a tawny owl into the garden. He decided to watch a while and anyway the Porsche may come back. He lit his pipe.

One of Dave Quilford's colleagues had come up with some very interesting information about the Dunall family and their exploits in Africa. It turned out that Mackenzie and the old gardener had both been in Africa at the same time. He decided to set up a meeting with them both and felt he may get more out of them if they met in a local pub. He also wanted a chat with Clive Coombes, Giles' solicitor, who was sure to know more about Giles, his African past and contacts. Another chat with Timothy might be interesting too, only because he had met Jemima and may have forgotten something that could be helpful.

41
Smoke and arrows.

It was late afternoon and Timothy was enjoying a wander along a nearby lane with his dog. The chocolate-box countryside was gorgeous, with hedgerows full of honeysuckle and dog roses, birds flitting in and out; the scent and sound of nature filling the warm air. He watched a herd of cattle in the field to his left steadily munching as they grazed peacefully, flicking their tails and occasionally shaking their heads against the flies and other buzzing insects. He looked back towards the village. The track across the field between him and the lane leading directly into the village and passed Mother's cottage was just ahead. There were animals in the next field. Faith started to growl suspiciously. Timothy leaned over a gate to get a better look. The animals were totally motionless. The memory of another stuffed animal, and his disastrous experience with a lady he had met through the agency came back to him and a cold shiver crept along his spine. He walked on quickly, not wishing to encounter the same lady again. Glancing over towards Mother's cottage he could see smoke pouring from the back Was it coming from her cottage or the garden? *Oh no, what was Mother doing now?* He whistled Faith and began to run. As he rounded the corner he almost ran headlong into an approaching police car. It stopped abruptly, just missing him. 'Are you alright?' asked the diver through the window.

'Sorry Officer, I was running to that cottage just there,' he said, pointing back up the lane. 'My mother lives there and I can't tell where all that smoke is coming from'.

'Hop in mate we'll give you a lift,' the Policeman offered. Timothy jumped into the back even though the cottage was only a short distance away.

Irma had had a busy afternoon in the garden, clearing out loads of rubbish and dead plants. She had made a huge pile in a clearing and had set fire to it. Filled watering cans stood by just in case a spark caught on anything else. She was surprised how much the fire was smoking; great plumes of grey smoke and sparks roared up to the sky. She hurled another armful on top making it sizzle and crackle, and even thicker smoke bellowed from the mass. She was coughing and could hardly see from one end of the garden to the other. Suddenly she could see shapes of people coming through the smoke and heard them all coughing.

'Mother where are you?' cried her worried son.

'I'm over here by the fire', Irma coughed. The three shapes turned out to be two policemen, her son and then a fourth person came running through the smoke. It was Verity. Mother chuckled. 'Well, if ever I want some company I'll just light a fire.' She blinked through the smoke at them all.

'Oh Mother!' moaned Timothy, he sat down and rubbed his face and hair with his hands.

'What's that?' exclaimed Verity, pointing to the huge hound, the size of a donkey, looming out of the smoke.

'That's my favourite dog Faith.' Mother fussed the dog and smiled at everyone. 'Well, you better have some tea as you're all here. Sorry, I don't need saving. Don't do that', she snapped at one of the policemen who was about to pour water from a can over her fire. 'It'll burn down in a little while.'

'You won't leave this fire unattended, will you?' said the policeman patiently. Mother shook her head like a naughty little girl. 'We'll be on our way now. Thank you for the offer of tea and please make sure that fire is out properly before you all go to bed tonight.'

'Thank you for the lift,' called Timothy as the two officers started to leave.

As the officers were getting into the police car two people on horseback appeared out of the smoke. The horses were snorting and shaking their heads.

'Is everything alright?' asked Duncan from his horse.

'Yes sir, it all seems to be under control. Are you going to ride along the bridleway passed Prickets cottage?' asked the older of the policemen.

Duncan pulled up, his horse still snorting from the smoke. 'Yes I was planning on doing the circuit, is there a problem?'

'There could be. Broadbent has been shooting at imaginary poachers again, you'd better get a move on if you're riding passed.'

'I'll keep an eye out and canter on a bit. Broadbent is a useless shot; he can't see properly for one thing. Thank you for the warning,' laughed Duncan as they moved off.

'We're not going to get shot at, are we?' exclaimed Daphne, riding alongside Duncan. 'Don't worry, Broadbent couldn't hit the broadside of a barn if he tried. We'll canter passed just to be on the safe side. He reached over and squeezed her arm by way of reassurance.

Daphne had become more confident since they'd been riding out together on most days and was happy to have a good canter. 'Okay, no problem,' she smiled at Duncan.

Nigel was stowing a set of arrows and a bow in his secret hut. He looked through one of the spy-holes and saw movement through the trees along the perimeter fence. With a chuckle and a skip he gathered a couple of arrows, picked up his bow and crept out of the hut. He took aim across the lake and waited. Yes there was movement; they were running or travelling fast, anyway. He loaded, lifted the bow and took aim. When he thought the moment was right he released and peered into the distance as the arrow flew across the lake. 'That'll teach 'em,' Nigel did a little dance and giggled. He always believed that he got his quarry, as whatever he aimed at vanished after he had fired either with his gun or with the arrows. He skipped and danced back into his hut, chanting, ' I got em, I got em, I got em.'

The arrow flew between Duncan and Daphne and landed in the trunk of a tree with a loud thwack. Both horses shied sideways, but luckily the riders were competent enough not to fall off.

'Ride on!' cried Duncan with a hint of excitement in his voice. Daphne urged her horse on after Duncan and they both escaped unscathed. At the edge of Monkswood land Duncan pulled up. 'Are you alright?' he asked.

'Yes, what the hell was that?' cried Daphne, breathlessly.

'I think old Broadbent has got his bow and arrows out again. I can't understand how he always gets away with it. He *is* madly eccentric'.

'I'm very pleased he missed!' exclaimed Daphne. They rode on for another good canter.

At the office of Two to Tango Jane was finishing writing up the reports on the day's customers when the door burst open. She leapt up, startled.

'Can I help you?' she asked. She was cross because they hadn't even rung the bell, and they didn't have an appointment. The tall man was wearing a hat and a long dark coat; various tattoos ran up his neck, and he had a gold stud in one ear. His sinister looking grey eyes stared directly at Jane, making her take a step back.

'Have you got anyone called Dunall registered here?' the man asked in a hoarse voice.

Jane shook her head.

'You better not be lying to me,' the man growled and leaning down, putting his face closer to Jane's, he said, 'I've been informed that a Jemima Dunall, registered with you and her husband Giles Dunall has disappeared.'

Jane shuddered, the man's breath stank; she leaned away from him. 'The papers said that Jemima Dunall has been arrested and that Giles Dunall is dead.' She looked across at the newspapers on the table in the waiting room. 'I don't know anything more than that.' She pointed towards papers.

The man grunted and walked over to the pile of newspapers and magazines. After looking through them he found the one with the headlines regarding Giles Dunall and marched out of the office, letting the door slam shut behind him. Jane gulped and sat down. Once she had sufficiently recovered she phoned Daphne. This was something her boss could deal with. Jane was normally quite good at dealing with difficult people but this man had really spooked her.

'Oh Jane, I'm so sorry!' exclaimed Daphne, 'could you look up the number of that nice detective, Dave Quilford? He's the one to contact. Would you mind?'

Daphne was enjoying herself and only felt a tiny bit guilty about off loading everything on to Jane.

'Fine. Will you be coming back to the office soon?' grumbled Jane.

'Soon Jane, soon. Keep up the good work. You're a star Jane, you really are.' Daphne hung up.

For a moment Jane was furious, then she looked around the office and wondered; she could just take over, move into Daphne's office and run the whole thing, with a wage increase for herself. As Daphne had gone ga-ga over her new man it would be the perfect time. She would call the nice detective and deal with this later and then put a few of her plans into action.

'Dougal said he saw a black car pulling out of Monkswood, a stranger was driving. I thought I should report it?' Maureen told Eve excitedly on the phone.

'Thank you yes. Do you know what sort of car it was? Eve could hear all sorts of whisperings in the background. 'He says it was a posh black one. Sorry, he didn't get the number.'

Eve smiled as she made a note. 'It's not a good idea to go anywhere near Monkswood at the moment. We are keeping a close eye on the place, but thank you for the information.'

Maureen was disappointed, she had hoped it would be a good excuse to go there and watch. 'No, definitely NO.' Dougal was adamant. 'The police obviously want us out of the way at the moment, AND Father has his bow and arrows out. It's positively dangerous.' Maureen slumped into a chair and sighed in defeat.

42
Out and gone!

'A simple 'thank you' would be nice, Jemima'. Clive Coombes had gone to some trouble to extract sufficient money out of his friend Giles' estate to get Jemima out on bail. Mainly because he wanted to have a talk with her when she was relaxed and more likely to come up with some evidence. Clive knew there was a risk, as Giles had mentioned the ruthless people he had had the misfortune to deal with in Africa and even though Giles hadn't told him everything by far, Clive sensed it could be dangerous for Jemima.

'Well, it's about time, it's hell in here,' Jemima snapped while pushing past her rescuer and heading for the doors to the outside world. She had no idea about her husbands' earlier activities in Africa. She had interpreted the bits and pieces she'd gleaned from Giles' Mother purely in her own favour.

The police had handed her mobile back with a warning to behave herself and stay in the area, no matter what. Clive agreed to give her a lift back to Darkwood house and gave her some cash to live on.

'Keep all the household utility bills and bring them in to me,' he said, walking up to the front door of Darkwood with her.

'Okay, what's brought this on? You're being very generous suddenly.' She was suspicious of this sudden change of heart.

'As a friend of Giles' I'm sure he wouldn't want to see you stuck in jail, or starving. I'll come in with you and make sure everything is as it should be,' he offered.

Jemima glanced at the new Clive. 'Fine, come on in.' She was actually quite grateful as the house had an empty, cold feel to it. 'I'll see if I can find the coffee but there won't be any milk, unless you prefer gin?'

'No thank you, I'll be going when I've had a quick look around. Just in case you've had a visitor.' He set off around the spacious house. It all looked ok with no evidence of intruders. Jemima had scrubbed part of the house from top to bottom after Giles' death and when she believed that Roderick could be more than a casual friend. There was still evidence of this and a strong aroma of soot and vermin in the drawing room where the mice living in the sofa had had several families since Timothy's visit. He could smell the mice amongst the smells of cleaning fluids and soot. Oddly when he had visited Jemima before she was arrested he didn't remember it being so clinically clean, and the mice appeared to have had free reign. Jemima had always been odd; very entertaining at times, but definitely odd.

He popped back into the kitchen on his way out where Jemima was sitting hunched over her black coffee. She was waiting for the water to heat up and Clive to leave, so that she could have a shower and a change of clothes and rid herself of the prison smell.

'Find anything interesting?' she muttered into her mug.

'No, everything looks fine. Jemima, I have to tell you to be careful. Giles was mixed up with some dangerous people in Africa; promise you'll call the police straightaway if you see anyone or anything suspicious, won't you?'

Jemima groaned, she was tired, hungry and desperate for some peace. 'I promise,' she half smiled.

Clive saw himself out, watched by Seth from the laurel bushes,

'Hmm, so the bitch is out,' Seth sighed.

Jemima removed all her clothes and threw them in the bin; she showered, chose a change of clothes and rummaged in the freezer for something to eat. She found a frozen lasagne that could be cooked immediately without defrosting. Anything would be better than that prison food. She didn't feel like her normal feisty self and was in need of some comfort, nice food and a large gin. She looked at her phone. It was nearly charged up enough to use. After she'd eaten she gave Roderick a call; some nice male company would be very comforting. 'Hello Jemima, they've let you out, have they? Or did you escape?' he chuckled.

'No, I'm out on bail. Coombes finally came up with the money,' she explained. She went on to tell him how dreadful it had been in prison and how the other women had been really mean.

Roderick chuckled. 'Met your match then, did you Jemima?'

'Oh please come round and see me. I missed you so much; I need you now', she moaned. 'Hold on Jemima, I will come and see you but I need to talk seriously with you. There are one or two things you need to be aware of.'

She ended the call and smiled. A night with Roderick was just what a girl needed right now. Despite him going on about talking to her seriously, she knew she could persuade him to stay. She poured another gin and tonic and swallowed it quickly. As she was checking her hair in the mirror she saw the reflection of car lights swing into the drive. Blimey he's keen, she thought, looks like he's got a car now, too.

She opened the front door, there was no one, no car either. He's playing games, she thought, walking into the drive to look for the car. 'Roderick, stop mucking about, I know you're here!' she called. She sensed a movement behind her and turned, ready to receive a Roderick-style bear hug, only to see a stranger grinning at her. As she opened her mouth to scream the stranger grabbed hold of her and quickly put his hand with a strange smelling cloth over her mouth and nose. She struggled for a moment before slipping into unconsciousness.

Roderick swung his motorbike into the drive. He'd been working out how he was going to remain friends with Jemima without her believing they were more involved than he would like, and warn her that she could be in danger. The lights were on in the house and the front door was open. He parked the bike and walked up to the door. The old familiar prickle in the back of his neck warned him all was not well. He walked into the hall which always felt a bit creepy. He called for Jemima. No reply. He called again even louder, still nothing. He went into the kitchen and found evidence of her meal and coffee, and grinned when he saw the empty glass; she'd had a gin already. After looking all over the house and unable to find Jemima, alarm bells were ringing in his head. He decided to go to the old gardener's cottage and see if Seth could shed any light on her whereabouts.

The old-fashioned cottage was more or less hidden among the trees and shrubs. He made his way to the faded, chipped wooden front door. There was a faint light in one of the small Georgian style, dirty windows. After knocking on the door he could hear movement inside, and eventually the shabby door creaked open.

'Alright mate, could I have a word?' Roderick asked.

Seth opened the door wider and invited him in quickly, noting the concern in his voice and the worried expression. 'What's she done now then?' growled the older man.

'She's disappeared and I don't think it was her idea'.

Seth indicated that he should sit in one of the tatty old chairs and, turning, he picked up the whiskey bottle and two glasses.

'Do you remember me from your time in Africa? We both helped out the Dunalls. You were working in security for one of the mining companies. We met quite a few times,' he poured them both a whiskey, ' I was working for Giles and his brother back then.' Roderick looked at Seth as he took the whiskey glass; the expression on his face suddenly changed as recognition dawned. 'We were both quite a bit younger, but now you've said it I can see it. Yes I remember you.'

'Jemima has no idea what she could be mixed up with. I don't think Giles ever told her or his Mother what really happened to his brother. I've been watching the place and there have been a couple of suspicious visitors. You know they're from 'The Company' by the posh cars they drive. You'd think they'd have more sense than to show off their wealth over here.'

'When you've got that much wealth I don't suppose you care. They believe they can buy themselves out of anything and unfortunately they usually do. I wonder what they think they'll find at the house, or at the other place, Monkswood.'

'Well, I'll tell you what I know, but right now I think we better give that Dave Quilford a call. God knows what these people will do to the bitch. We need to get the police on side and the quicker the better.' Old Seth had suddenly come to life and it was clear to Roderick there was a lot more to the old boy than he had first thought. Seth pulled out his mobile and brought up the number.

Dave Quilford had finished his evening meal and was preparing for an early night when his phone rang. ' Hold on, what d'you mean gone? Are you sure she hasn't just gone off for a walk?'

Seth took a breath, 'No, Roderick has been all over the house and the gardens. She had arranged to meet him here at the house only minutes before he turned up.'

'Shit! Okay, I'll come over now and meet you both at your cottage. Give me fifteen minutes or so.' Dave put the phone down and called the station straightaway. She's on bail and missing, that usually ranks as a priority. He hoped so for Jemima's sake.

Jemima's head felt fuzzy, she was vaguely aware that she was moving, as lights flashed past her eyes occasionally. There was a smell she almost recognised, pipe smoke or a cigar she thought. When she tried to move she found she couldn't. She was feeling so weak and tired and very confused. Was she in her parents' car travelling home from somewhere? She was drifting and faintly nauseous as she tried to sit up. She managed a quick glance out of the back window of the car and noticed a Mini with its lights on travelling behind. She collapsed back onto the seat. Perhaps they would be home soon. Why couldn't she move her arms? She blacked out.

A few members of the old-bat vigilantes, were out on patrol that evening.

'What's that car? I don't think I've seen that one before!' cried Mrs Battle, leaning forward in the passenger seat to get a better look.

'Get the number! Here I have a pen, is there anything to write on in here?' Mrs Weaterbutts leaned between the two front seats, choosing to disregard the rear seat belts.

339

Beattie Fell pointed to the glove compartment. Paper found, pen in hand, Mrs battle leaned as far forward as the windscreen would let her. 'You'll have to get a bit closer Beattie, and hurry up we'll be out of town in a minute and I'll never see the number.' She peered out.

'Go on, put your foot down Beattie,' encouraged Mrs Weatherbutts.

The three elderly neighbourhood watch vigilantes stared at the back of the car in front of them, all trying to read the number plate. They all saw the sudden appearance of a face in the car's rear window; it was only a glimpse. 'There's someone in the back,' they shouted together.

'Keep with it, they might be in trouble!' Mrs Weatherbutts was always fearless and enthusiastic despite her age of seventy-nine.

Both cars sped along the narrow country lanes. The tall hedges either side made it seem darker and the high grassy banks made it almost impossible to pass any car coming from the opposite direction. The few passing places often lead into a ditch.

The driver of the black car didn't realise the small car behind was actually following him. The woman on the back seat seemed quiet enough, he hadn't bothered to gag her, as the chloroform mixture he'd used was pretty strong. He hoped he hadn't overdone it. Jemima was sleepily muttering nonsense. As he drove out of town towards the farmhouse where they had planned to hold and interrogate her, he noticed the little car was still behind him and wondered briefly why they were driving so closely. He put his foot down and sped away, smiling to himself as he knew there was no chance of the small car keeping up with this vehicle. There was a groan from the back as he swung around a sharp bend and vanished into the night.

Beattie pressed her accelerator foot to the floor when the black car took off. 'Go Beattie, go!' Mrs Battle and Mrs Weatherbutts cheered her on.

The bigger car may be more powerful but not so nippy around the sharp bends in a narrow country lane. The Mini on the other hand is not very powerful, some would be relieved to learn, but it is very nippy around sharp bends, and Beattie loved driving fast. Her two passengers hung on tightly as they raced along. The headlights on the small car were not very good, so vision was limited. To add to their problems it had begun to rain; the window wipers were working at top speed with a regular thump, thump. The little car clung to the road as Beattie swung it around the corners. She leaned forward over the steering wheel, trying to see into the blackness. She drove on over a steep hill, the bottom of which looked like a dark abyss where water had gathered. The vigilantes squealed as they sped through the water. Mrs Battle had her hand over her eyes shouting, 'May the angels be with us!' At the top of the next hill, around another sharp bend they screamed as the headlights of an on-coming pickup truck suddenly blinded them. Beattie swung the Mini sharp left, out of the trucks way and drove it into a shallow ditch where they came to an abrupt stop.

Mrs Weatherbutts found herself jammed between the two front seats. The air bags-went off in the front, nearly suffocating Beattie and smacking Mrs Battle in the face. They were all moaning and groaning while taking in what had happened. The driver's door opened and a large farmer smiled in at them. 'Anyone hurt?'

He had had two near misses, one with what looked like a black BMW and now with these ladies in a Mini. All driving like hell in the night. What *was* going on? 'Can

I help you out so we can get this out of the ditch?' he offered kindly.

'Thank you, I hope my car is alright!' moaned Beattie.

'What about your passengers?' the concerned farmer asked.

'We're alive, but I'm completely stuck,' gasped Mrs Weatherbutts, hardly able to breathe as the seats compressed her rib cage.

'Hmmm, I think I'll pull this out of the ditch and then see if we can get you both out. Stay there a minute.' The farmer chuckled as he headed back to his truck.

'Stay there, he says. Ha! As if we have any choice!' coughed Mrs Battle, her face still full of air bag.

' I can easily pull the car out of the ditch, but I have no idea how you'll get the one old dear out of the car. She's jammed tightly between the two front seats and her fat arse will never squeeze through.' the farmer explained to the fire brigade officer from his mobile phone.

'I suppose we better have an ambulance as well, but I think they're okay..ish'. He ended the call and turned to see Beattie Fell standing beside the truck glaring at him.

'Alright love, I'll get your car out now, the fire brigade and ambulance are on their way.' Beattie leaned back and took an almighty swing at the farmer. She missed and fell over. Struggling to her feet she shouted 'It's your damn bright lights! They nearly blinded me.' She gathered herself to have another swing at him.

'Whoa! I'm trying to help you here, love. You were going much too fast for these lanes at night. Calm down and let me help you,' he soothed kindly, catching her before she fell over again. 'Sit in my truck while I get the ropes and pull your car out'. He took her arm and guided her to the passenger side, and careful that she

342

didn't have another swing at him, he helped her onto the seat.

The Mini was now safely back on the road, and Mrs Battle was sitting in the ambulance while being checked over. Both doors of the Mini were open and the rear end of a fireman was sticking out of each door. 'Try lifting yourself up a bit now', said one of them.

'If I can just get this seat forward a bit more we can get her through,' said the other.

Mrs Weatherbutts could be heard moaning and grunting as the firemen tried to free her.

Another fireman turned up carrying a huge metal cutter. 'We could try this, lads,' he said.

Mrs Weatherbutts looked up and panicked at the thought of a metal cutter was going to cut. She gave a strangled scream...'You're not cutting me up with *that*!' she cried.

'You're alright love, he's not cutting anything yet,' soothed one of the firemen.

'What d'you mean, yet?' she gasped.

Eventually the passenger seat was moved forwards, freeing her enough to be lifted up and pushed back onto the rear seat. Then after manoeuvring both the front seats forward she was able to squeeze out with a helping hand and a good tug from the two firemen.

Beattie and Mrs Battle practically pounced on the two policemen when they arrived. 'You've got to get that car! There was someone in the back, and we think they were in trouble. It went that way, and you're losing it!' they both cried.

'Both cars were going like a bat out of hell along these lanes! I don't know how I managed to miss them. The first car was a black BMW. It was too dark to see who was inside. It was in a big hurry, though. Then this Mini came flying around the bend, missed me and ended up in the ditch here. Apparently they were following the first car,' the farmer shrugged. 'Okay. I think we should all discuss this in more detail at the station. Ladies, please get into the car over there, and Jim here will tow the Mini back, won't you Jim?' the policeman looked at the farmer who shrugged again. 'I suppose so,' he muttered reluctantly.

'Well that's it, they're getting away and you've lost them,' groaned Beattie.

'You let us worry about that, love.' The officer said. He was used to dealing with the local elderly vigilantes.

Eve smiled when she saw the ladies waiting for her. 'Okay ladies, what have you been up to this time?' She caught the eye of Lizzie who came to join her. They were both quite fond of the 'old bat network'. They often came up with helpful information even if they were a bit over-enthusiastic.

They all tried to talk at once.

'The car has got away. It was a big black car. Someone was in the back.'

'I think it would be better if you all sat in a separate room and talked to us individually. If you can remember any of the registration number it would be helpful.' Eve and Lizzie herded them off into an interview room each.

43
That car... what car?

'I see in the local rag there've been some disappearances and deaths in the area. It wouldn't have anything to do with you and the 'mad bats' would it, Timothy old lad?' said his boss and friend, Derek. Timothy shuffled the books he was sorting and looked up at his friend. 'Mad bats could be right, but according to Lizzie they *can* be useful. I wouldn't want to get on the wrong side of any of them. I don't know any more about the two deaths than you do. I do know the woman who's been reported missing, she is one of the women I met through 'Two to Tango' and she was a *real* oddball. Rumour has it that she may have bumped off her husband.' They were both sorting out the books Derek donated to Mrs Brailsford's annual charity sale. Timothy would deliver them to Strawbottom Farm. He had agreed to take them in his Land Rover as the old shop van had long been sent to the breakers yard. Oddly Timothy did have a pang of regret, even though the van had caused him some grief; it had always started and run in the end. He had an illogical soft spot for vehicles that somehow kept going despite the odds. They loaded the books and as Timothy jumped into the driving seat Derek stuck his head through the window, grinning. 'Watch out for any mad farm animals, won't you?' He tapped the roof of the Land Rover as Timothy set off.

The drive to Brailsford's farm was always an enjoyable one, out of the town and into the surrounding countryside, with winding narrow lanes for most of the way. A few miles from the farm he noticed a vehicle

345

close behind him. Another glance in the mirror and he could see it was black and looked like a BMW. He remembered Lizzie saying something about looking out for a black BMW. He couldn't see the number plate in his mirror. He thought of pulling over and letting it pass but the track to Strawbottom Farm was ahead with no passing places on his side of the road. He came to a turning to his right leading to another farmhouse, but he couldn't read the name on the sign as it was too old and faded. He had slowed down without realising and the black car was very close behind him now. Suddenly it turned off and went down the lane to the other farm. It was quickly out of sight and he had only been able to get the make and colour of the car and he thought just the driver, no passengers. He would tell Lizzie tonight .

The track to the farm was ahead, and the gate was shut. He looked down the track and even stood on top of the gate to get a better look. His experiences with loose animals at this farm had left him wary, to say the least. He opened the gate and drove through, then closed it behind him while continuously looking around for nosy cattle or mad goats. When he pulled up at the farmhouse he realised that, unlike the last time, the gate into the front garden was open. Encouraged, he cautiously got out. Still feeling suspicious he went to the front door and rapped loudly. There were often animals grazing where a lawn normally might have been. He had left the driver's door open in case he had to make a quick getaway. Eventually the front door creaked open and Mrs (also known as Ma) Brailsford's round, beaming face was smiling at him.

'Ah Timothy, please bring in the books. My goat has gone AWOL so you're quite safe today.'

'I'll bring them in quickly then, in case it decides to come home.' Timothy ran back to the Land Rover closed the driver side door. Then he opened the back and quickly carried the two boxes of books into the house. As usual Mrs Brailsford invited him into her fabulous kitchen with multiple shelves stocked up with all manner of home-made goodies. He always loved the smell of this kitchen, he breathed in the aromas of home made bread, cakes, buns and sweet spices. As he sighed with delight a plate of buns and a steaming mug of tea were pressed into his hands. 'Oh, thank you,' he said with genuine delight. 'I always love your kitchen, it smells divine.'

'You enjoy your buns and I'll put a few in a bag for you to take home. I can't think where the old goat has gone; he can jump over the gate but usually never bothers much. I let him live in the garden as a sort of guard dog. I expect he'll find his way home soon.'

She was obviously worried and before he could stop himself Timothy found himself offering to have a look for the goat.

'Oh, don't worry dear, he'll probably only attack you if you find him, he can be a bit like that. Mind you, he has taken to some folk and even let them fuss him.' She beamed at Timothy.

His mouth full of the last piece of bun he managed to smile back, with both relief and delight at the taste. He inhaled deeply before leaving the kitchen and wondered if he should take up baking bread. With the bag of buns in his hand he left the house. Approaching the Land Rover he realised with horror that he had left the back door open. He had a good look around him, no animals, no grunts from pigs or snorts from cattle could be heard. He slammed the back door shut and jumped into the front. As he drove along the track to the gate he heard the terrifyingly loud sound of a bleating goat in his left ear. He stopped and steeled himself to look around; there was the goat looking right at him from the back seat. It appeared calm and bleated again when he looked at it. He sat frozen for moment. Well, it wasn't attacking him; he briefly wondered if it enjoyed the ride. Slowly he put the Land Rover into reverse and drove carefully back to the farmhouse. How was he going to let the goat out and keep out of its way? He went back up to the front door and rapped loudly.

'I've got something of yours in the back of my Land Rover,' he said when it finally opened. The old lady looked puzzled.

'Come and see', Timothy lead her to the back of the vehicle making sure of an escape route, and the driver's door was also open. He carefully opened the back. The goat looked at them both and bleated its hello.

'Oh, where have you been? I've been so worried for you. I hope you haven't been chasing those nasty men from Moors End, have you?' she chastised.

The goat simply walked forward and hopped out of the back as if it was an every day occurrence. Timothy had flattened himself against the side of the Land Rover and was ready to make a dash, but the goat simply glanced at him, bleated and walked into the garden. It headed straight for the food that had been put out for it to try and tempt it to come home.

Ma Brailsford hugged Timothy and thanked him profusely for bringing her goat home.

He told her about the black car, and she said that the people who were currently renting Moors End had been to see her, and the goat had chased them out of the garden and away. She said they weren't very nice and had threatened to shoot the goat if it came anywhere near them. She didn't know their names but thought they had rented the place for a few months. They kept themselves to themselves after the incident with the goat.

After more hugs and profuse thanks Timothy managed to leave. On his own this time. He did have a quick check before closing the gate and was relieved that nothing else had hitched a ride. Feeling quite pleased with himself he was looking forward to telling Lizzie all he had found out about Moors End and about the black BMW. His hand suddenly shot to the bag of buns on the passenger seat. Phew, the goat hadn't found them!

'So you survived!' Derek jibed as Timothy walked back into the shop. 'Is the beloved Land Rover in one piece too?'

'Yes all in one piece, it just smells of goat. I had to give one a lift, you see,' grinned Timothy, knowing how his friend would react. Derek feigned complete astonishment.

'That's it, he's finally lost it.'

'Nope, it was the goat who had got lost. I just gave it a lift home. I *think* it was grateful'.

'You're actually serious, aren't you?' said his friend.

With a huge grin on his face, he turned to Derek. ' Of course I'm serious, go and sniff the back of the Land Rover if you don't believe me. It stinks.' As he said it he hoped the lovely buns on the front seat wouldn't take on the aroma. 'Mrs Brailsford was absolutely delighted when I took the goat home to her, ring her and ask if you don't believe me. Are you closing up the shop or am I?

'I'm taking Henri to hear a local choir at the town hall later, but you go, it won't take long for me to close up.' As he said it there was a loud thump upstairs. 'Uh oh, one of your ghosty friends is sulking.' He patted Timothy on the shoulder as he said this.

'Good night!' called Timothy, laughing. He was always quite chuffed that who or whatever it was in the shop seemed to like him….maybe?

Timothy's dog Faith shot out of the door to greet him and then straight to the Land Rover to check out any new smells around the doors.

'I think I'll miss out the bits about the goat when I report all this to Dave Quilford,' laughed Lizzie in the kitchen later. 'He probably wouldn't believe it anyway'.

'Sergeant Dumple might, he knows the folks around here well. He grew up here, so he's one of them really.'

Lizzie nodded. Lizzie was a comparative newcomer but like her friend Eve she enjoyed working in the area, the local folks were a bit off the wall but as long as you accepted this they were fine. She didn't have big ambitions to further her career and quite liked the idea of becoming one of the locals. She knew this could take years and that to the real locals she would always be a newcomer. Timothy spotted her sudden melancholy expression and gave her a big hug. ' You're one of us now Lizzie, like it or not.'

The following day at the station Lizzie reported to Dave Quilford, explaining everything that Timothy had told her.

'I'd better go and check this out then. Where did you say the house was?'

Lizzie gave him directions, ' Mind you take the turning on the right, apparently the sign for Moors End is worn and unreadable. If you go straight on you'll come to a five bar gate. Open that at your peril. That's the track down to Mr and Ma Brailsford's farm, the lady who had a confrontation with the men from Moors End.'

'I could take you with me and then you could have a chat with her about the incident while I have a poke around,' says Dave.

'Errm, I'm not sure.'

'Why the hesitation', Dave was puzzled, Lizzie was always up for anything.

'Well, it's the goat that worries me, to be honest sir.'

'Goat?'

Eve who was in the same room joined in, ' Yes, rumour has it that old Ma Brailsford bewitches her animals to attack people if they think they're intruders. Many people have left there in a big hurry, including Timothy.'

Dave scratched his head and looked from Lizzie to Eve. 'Well, I guess you'll both have to come with me and protect me from these bewitched farm animals then.' Dave wasn't sure if they were winding him up. There were times when he wondered if he'd blundered into a surreal pantomime.

They decided to visit Moors End first. The old farmhouse had received little cosmetic attention over the years and looked almost derelict on the outside; paths were overgrown with weeds and the dishevelled outbuildings were empty. Two BMW cars were parked outside, one black and one red, looking out of place in the scene around them.

As Dave knocked on the front door old peeling grey paint sprinkled his shoes. They all waited and listened for any sign or sound to indicate that someone was being held against their will on the property. Before the door opened Lizzie and Eve nipped off for a look around the outbuildings.

Dave was surprised when a pleasant, well-mannered African man opened the door and invited him in. His English was excellent and as he shook hands with Dave he said his name was Ori Robinson. He told Dave that they had come over from Africa and were renting the farmhouse. They were over here on business, working for an African diamond company that wanted to buy land for property development in the UK. His colleague, Sebastian Sears was out at the moment he said, and if there was anything he could do to help he'd be happy to oblige. Very nice and polite; too polite thought Dave. The atmosphere changed when Dave mentioned the Brailsfords and the complaint Ma Brailsford had made. The shift in attitude was brief but significant. 'Oh, we wouldn't hurt her animals, we like animals,' the man explained. Dave didn't believe him.

There was no sign of anyone else in the house or anything he could use to obtain a warrant to gain entry later and search the place. 'Do either of you have any firearms on the premises?' he asked. The fleeting guilty shift of the man told Dave that there could be, but he could find no reason to insist on searching the house further…yet.

The man didn't invite Dave into any of the rooms, the entire conversation took place in the hall. He decided to leave it for now but keep a close eye on the house and the two men. 'Your colleague is out, you say? How did he leave? Do you have another vehicle?' Ori seemed briefly uncomfortable but quickly regained his composure.

'The black car is mine, we've only just purchased the red one. My colleague left with a friend.' Another lie thought Dave.

'How long are you planning on staying here?'

352

'About 6 months.' The man showed Dave to the front door. Eve and Lizzie were sitting in the car waiting for him.

'I'll need to come back here sometime soon,' said Dave strapping himself into the driver seat. 'There's more going on than he's telling me. Did any of your mad bats mention the driver of the car being black African?'

'No, I don't think they got a good look at the driver. Pull up by this gate here,' Lizzie directed. 'Just wait by the gate and see what happens,' she advised.

They all got out of the car, walked over to the five bar gate and waited. ' How long is this track to the farm?' asked Dave.

'Not long, it dips after you go around the bend there, explained Lizzie, 'oh look, there are some pigs coming up the track.' They all waited by the gate hoping Ma Brailsford would follow, but a tall, rather thin looking man wearing old blue overalls and a worn, scruffy hat came into view behind the huge pigs. 'I think that's Mr Brailsford,' commented Eve.

Dave put his hand up and waved to the man, who waved back while he and the pigs continued towards the gate. The pigs were grunting and snuffling but began to speed up when they noticed the visitors.

'They can't jump out, can they?' asked Dave, taking a step back.

'No, they'll be pretty tame. I heard that the Brailsfords love their animals,' Lizzie said, leaning over the gate and rubbing one of the pigs on the head. The pig grunted its approval. 'Here's Ma Brailsford,' said Eve, giving her a wave. She waved back with a loud hearty laugh as she waddled up the track towards them. Eve introduced them all and Ma Brailsford introduced them to her husband, who she called Pa, and Priscilla and Sophie, the two pigs.

She was happy to tell them about the men at Moors End threatening to shoot her goat and how she was worried they would come and steal her animals. 'They eat monkeys and things in Africa, don't they?' she said. 'Pa here says he heard some singing coming from the house up there; said it sounded like a woman, and a bit opera like.'

Pa nodded in agreement but didn't speak.

Eve smiled, 'We'll come out if there's any trouble, you just have to phone the station. Try not to let any of your animals wander off.'

After further reassurances they said their goodbyes. As Dave looked back at the couple waving to them from behind the gate he was reminded of the ornamental couple that pop out of a cuckoo clock. The woman singing; jangled in his head.....it could be a radio or TV...maybe.

44
Mystery steps.

It was the break of dawn when Verity was having her usual commune with nature. She leaned over the gate by the old orchard where Muddlestone had planted the stuffed animals. Verity knew this was an ancient magical place that had once been used for rituals, and possibly burials. She shivered as mist rose from the ground surrounding the shrubs and old fruit trees, making the stuffed animals look even more surreal. Betty, Muddlestone's new woman had told her that she had sprinkled her relatives' ashes in the same orchard as she felt it was the perfect place for them. She may be right, Verity mused; she wasn't so sure about the stuffed animals though, that was just plain odd.

Two figures appeared at the far end of the field, striding purposefully back and forth. One appeared to have some sort of clip-board and the other a shovel. As they moved nearer, Verity did her disappearing trick of blending in and watched. It looked to her like they were marking out the orchard and writing something down on the clipboard. They were both looking around and nodding in agreement. Were they looking for something or looking for somewhere to bury something?

She was able to see that they were both dressed quite smartly. One was a tall black guy and the other white and smaller. Engrossed in conversation they didn't notice the mist from the ground growing higher and getting thicker. Verity could hardly see them now, so she crept along the hedge to get a better view. The two men left the orchard via the bottom gate where she could just make out a black car parked in the lane. She was sure Muddlestone had no idea these men were tramping all over the orchard, she was also sure the men had no idea that they had left their footprints all over the ground in the heavy dew. While walking back to her cottage she decided to go directly to Duncan and report the intruders, as it was his land.

Later that morning Betty went down to the orchard to pay her respects to the numerous deceased. The mist had cleared but there was still a chill in the air. She was shocked to see all the footprints in the dew all over the orchard. In one or two places deep marks had been made in the grass. She crept onto the grass to get a better look. As she put her own foot, adorned with a wellington, into one of the footprints she gasped. They must be giants she thought, as her own feet appeared small inside the prints, and the strides across the orchard seemed pretty big too. She wondered if the ghosts of her relatives had risen up and had been checking around. But she didn't remember them all having such large feet. She decided to go back to the farm and talk to Bertrum; he was always so kind and understanding with her, she was sure he would have an explanation.

Bertrum was used to Betty's fanciful ideas. This morning he could see she was quite disturbed and gave her a big hug. He was simply delighted to have female company again after four years on his own. It didn't matter to him that she was definitely quirky. He thought she was lovely and found her oddities quite amusing, though he would never tell her so. Plus she could cook.

They went back to the orchard together. Meanwhile the sun had risen and warmed the dew in the grass, making the footprints disappear. 'Oh, they've taken them away!' cried Betty, 'they were all over the place, like someone had been pacing up and down,' she went on.

'Never mind dear, we can come and look again tomorrow morning, the sun has probably dried them all up,' Bertrum was being as sympathetic as he could, but he couldn't help wondering if the footprints had been there at all. He decided to give Duncan Dainty a call to see if he knew anything about it.

Verity walked up to Many Wollops Hall. She guessed all was not quite as it should be at Muddlestones farm and felt almost possessive about the old orchard; someone had to keep it safe, she thought.

Lena opened the front door. ' Hi Lena, is Duncan at home?' Verity asked. Lena opened the door and let her in, 'I'll go and find him, I think he's in the study,' she said.

'Hello Verity, come in and have a seat,' Said Duncan, always polite. The study contained several easy chairs by an open fire as well as his desk and some office type chairs. A thick neutral carpet covered the floor and long Laura Ashley style curtains were hung at the sash windows. He moved to sit in an easy chair and gestured to Verity to do the same.

Verity explained what she had witnessed that morning and expressed her concerns for the orchard.

'That old orchard wasn't part of the farm until a few years ago. I let Muddlestone have it for grazing as we didn't really need it anymore. It hasn't been very productive for years; the trees are too old. I told Muddlestone he could plant new fruit trees in amongst the old ones if he wished. He hasn't, but I notice he is using it as somewhere to keep his woman's stuffed animals. Very odd.' Duncan smiled and shook his head.

357

'There were a few live sheep in there the other day,' Verity commented.

'So you think the orchard has some history? That's interesting, I may have some old documents with regard to that tucked away in an old safe. I was looking in there the other day and found lots of old papers I've never looked at,' Duncan explained. 'I'll have a look later and let you know if I come up with anything.'

'I'd be happy to give you a hand with that if you're busy,' suggested Verity. She used to work in an office before moving to Many Wollops. 'I used to be a secretary.'

She smiled at Duncan. ' Ah, I might take you up on that, I'm not keen on any form of paperwork.'

They agreed that Duncan would contact her if he needed some help and he promised to let her know what those men were up to when he found out himself. He made a mental note that Verity might be interested in being his new secretary when his current one left at the end of the month.

Shortly after Verity left the phone rang, it was Muddlestone. He explained about the alleged footprints and intruders in the old orchard that morning. Duncan agreed to visit him later.

He decided to ride over to Muddlestone's farm on his horse Busby, that way he could have a look around at the same time. Also it meant he wouldn't have to spend too long talking with Bertrum and his potty woman. He wanted to do some serious thinking and preferred to do this on horseback, riding around his estate. He needed to think more seriously about his relationship with Daphne.

Bertrum was waiting for him. He was sitting on an old milk stand, where years ago they used to leave milk churns full of fresh milk to be collected by the local dairy every morning. Duncan pulled up beside him. 'So you think who ever it was may have been looking around my land? I can't believe the cheek of it. You didn't see the men at all?' Bertrum shook his head.

Betty came over to join them with several dogs at her heels. 'Have you told him about the big footprints?'

'Yes love, I've told him.' Bertrum put a reassuring arm around her.

'They may turn up and make you an offer for the orchard or something, send them along to me if they do. In fact, send them to me or call me if they turn up at all. Did you see the footprints too?'

'No, I didn't see the footprints they left all over the orchard, Betty saw those.'

'Yes, and they were huge and all over the orchard in lines'. She was nodding enthusiastically to emphasise her point.

'Right. Just to put your mind at rest, I have no intention of selling the orchard or any of my land at the moment.' Duncan went on to thank them both for their help. He had to admit that he hadn't seen Bertrum look so happy for years. He left them sitting on the milk stand together with their small pack of dogs; and rode off to have a good look over his small estate, in case the intruders had been seen looking and measuring up anywhere else. He decided to give a friend of his at the police station a call later and see if they'd heard anything about these people.

Luckily Dave was at his desk when Duncan called. He was sitting in his usual, casual pose, feet up on the desk and leaning only so far back to enable him to still reach the phone and computer. Even though he'd been promoted to inspector he didn't feel it really necessary to change his personal habits. 'Hello Duncan, what can I do for you?'

Duncan explained about the two mystery men and the footprints Betty had seen, plus Verity's version of events.

'Don't do anything for the moment, the two men fit the description of two that are known to me. I'll look further into this. I need to get hold of Clive Coombes, Giles Dunall's solicitor. I have a feeling this is somehow all connected with the Dunalls,' Dave explained.

'They've not been having much luck lately,' said Duncan. 'Are there any Dunalls left?'

'I don't know, Jemima has disappeared too. I'll get more information from Coombes, I hope. How's it going with your new lady?'

'Very well, I'm considering asking her to marry me. Please don't rain on my parade and tell me you've heard some dreadful things about her,' Duncan sighed.

'No, nothing nasty. You know about her divorce and Two to Tango, of course?'

'Yes, yes that's all fine. Jane is running the dating agency at the moment. In fact Jane had a visit from an unpleasant character asking about the Dunalls a few weeks ago. I told Daphne she should report it but I don't think she did in the end.'

'That's interesting, we'll go and have a chat with Jane, thanks.'

They ended the call and Dave leaned back in his chair, tapping a pen against his teeth while he was thinking. He had to have a chat with Timothy, the old regular customers of the bookshop often confided in Timothy. They were a good source of information, and he knew Timothy wouldn't be fazed by a visit from him. He called Lizzie and Eve into his office and told them of his plan to visit Timothy.

'Oh Timothy won't mind; the old vigilantes are always chatting to him. The Brailsfords think he's great at the moment since he saved their goat,' Lizzie explained.

'More about goats,' Dave rubbed his head and gazed patiently at Lizzie.

'Yes, well there's only one goat. It had got out and then hopped into Timothy's Land Rover, so he drove it home. They were delighted.' Lizzie was grinning at the thought of Timothy finding the goat in his vehicle. 'The same goat chased Timothy out of the front garden the previous time he visited.' She noted Dave's puzzled look, 'oh, he takes old books from the shop there each year for a charity sale Mrs Brailsford runs; she always thanks him with a big bag of freshly made buns,' she explained.

'Okay, I'll go and chat with Timothy, and I need to pay a visit to Muddlestone's farm. You two go and have a chat with Jane at Two to Tango. She'll be in the office, I don't think the proprietor is there at the moment.'

'Got better things on her mind I've heard,' Eve commented.

Dave smiled. 'Is there anything I should watch out for at Muddlestone's farm?'

'Only the stuffed dead things in the orchard, sir,' Lizzie was grinning.

Dave rubbed his head again, 'Right, I'll look out for those,' he sighed.

Timothy was sorting books in the window of the shop when Dave walked in.

'Hello, how goes you?' asked Timothy, leaving his task. They shook hands. Dave had been very helpful and kind to Timothy after he'd been beaten up and his mother had totally panicked. They exchanged pleasantries and wandered over to the counter where they could both lean and have a chat.

'I heard about your experience at Brailsfords' farm,' said Dave, 'Lizzie said that you saved their goat or some such'

'Ah, I thought she wasn't going to mention that. Yes, the goat had jumped into the back of my Land Rover so I simply drove it home. They were *so* glad. I think the people living at the other place along the lane had threatened to shoot it and they told Mrs Brailsford that they eat goats where they come from. It upset her terribly. The animals on that farm are all loved and a number of them are kept as pets.'

'You didn't see anything of the people at the other farm, Moors End, or any vehicles?'

'There was a black BMW behind me when I drove up to the Brailsfords. I couldn't see who was driving and it sped off the road and up the drive before I could catch its number. Apparently they're renting the place for a while and keep themselves to themselves. Apart from threatening to kill Ma Brailsfords' goat that is. It *can* be quite a nasty thing mind you.'

'So I've heard.' Dave looked up suddenly as there was a loud thump from one of the rooms upstairs. 'I thought we were alone in here? Is there someone upstairs?'

'No, there's only Mrs Jones in the Horror/Thriller section, just through that door,' he pointed to the other side of the shop. 'She's a bit deaf so won't have heard much of our conversation and as far as I'm aware there's no one upstairs.' Dave looked alarmed and rushed off up the stairs to find the intruder that Timothy knew wasn't there.

Upstairs Dave looked in all the rooms and found them empty. In one of the rooms a few books were on the floor and one on the reading table in the middle. It looked as though someone had been reading there and had left, leaving all the books where they were. He shivered, there was an odd atmosphere in the room. He looked around for any clue of who may have been there and shivered again when a page of the book on the table flipped over on its own. Get a grip, he told himself, that *must* be a draft from somewhere. He went back downstairs to find Timothy with Mrs Jones. 'Thank you. I'll be alright, it was the ghosts knocking me over', she whispered, still holding on tightly to Timothy's arm.

'I'll get you a glass of water Mrs Jones, rest there for a minute.' Timothy gave Dave a conspiring look and went into the kitchen at the back to fetch the water.

'Are you the detective sergeant that helped Irma Parkes?' whispered Mrs Jones.

Dave was quite patient with older folks, he crouched down to her level and said, 'I'm a detective inspector now. Are you going to be able to get home alright?'

'Oh yes', she seemed to rally. She suddenly clutched Dave's arm, and surprised him as she asked 'Have you found out who killed that woman yet? Was there a lot of blood?' her eyes gleamed. Dave cleared his throat while he wondered how to respond.

'Don't mind Mrs Jones, she loves a good murder story,' said Timothy, handing her the glass of water. 'I've put the books in your trolley', he pulled the trolley over to her.

She drank the whole glass of water, rummaged in her handbag and handed Timothy the money and the empty glass. 'I'll be fine now, just a funny moment,' she whispered. 'Tell your ghosts to behave themselves, Timothy.' She left the shop tugging her trolley behind her.

Timothy chuckled at the expression on Dave's face, 'Would you like a mug of tea?'

'I think I need one. What's all this nonsense about ghosts, and why does she whisper all the time?'

'She had an operation on her throat years ago and has whispered ever since, according to Mother. Oh, and a few of the older ladies love gory horror stories. We keep a selection of second-hand horror and vampire books on the ground floor in the old part of the shop, especially for them. They're very regular customers. So don't be too alarmed by their blood thirsty comments.' He handed Dave his cup of tea.

'You know, when I told my old colleagues I was going to work here in Dickleborough just over a year ago now, they all looked at me with raised eyebrows and said they thought the folks around here were very different. Apparently people are not the same once they've been here, and so on. It feels a bit like walking in on a drama or a farce. I don't mean I'm not enjoying working here, but... shall we say I'm still getting used to it. How's your mother settling into her new cottage?'

'She's fine, she's only nearly set her cottage on fire twice so far,' Timothy laughed, 'but yes she's fine, thank you for asking.'

'Can you tell me any more about Jemima, and your visit to the house, anything at all? Did you see anyone else there, or anything that didn't quite fit?'

'Jemima was a bit scary for me, she was odd and the house was old and shabby, it smelled of mice. There were several living in the sofa in the sitting room. I had the scary feeling she wanted to lock me in. I escaped by jumping out of the sitting room window. There was someone in the garden but I didn't get a good look at him or her. I did see Jemima again with a guy on a motorbike, at Monkswood. They appeared to have been looking around, it was on the market at the time. That's all I can tell you. I've been a bit preoccupied with moving house and everything.'

Dave nodded and sipped his tea. ' So who left the books on the floor upstairs?'

Timothy feigned looking puzzled. 'Ah, yes … books fall off the shelves from time to time; it must be that.' He watched Dave's reaction and waited, he needed to be careful. Not everyone understood. He decided to divert him with a question. ' Was there a book on the reading table?'

Dave stared at him for a minute before saying, 'Yes, actually there was a book on the table, it was open like someone had been reading it. Was it you who forgot to tidy up?'

'Yes. I guess I must have forgotten. I was looking something up.' He'd just lied to Dave and Dave knew it.

'Ok, let me know if you hear anything from the oldies. Jemima is still missing, so any information no matter how trivial could be helpful.' They shook hands and Dave thanked him for the tea.

Timothy hated that he'd lied to Dave but couldn't think of a credible explanation that Dave would believe. After Dave had left the shop, Timothy raced upstairs to the reading room. The book on the table was from the mythology section and was open at a page describing Sea Sirens, mythical creatures that live in the ocean. Some believe them to be mermaids. It's alleged that they sing the most beautiful song to lure hapless sailors to their watery death. How could this be helpful? Jemima definitely wasn't a Siren, was she? She definitely wasn't at sea… was she? He felt it could be a sign, as whoever or whatever was in this building had helped him before. Even one or two customers had remarked, 'I had been looking for this book for ages and then there it was on the floor, right in front of me'. He tidied the books away and decided to keep it in mind.

'Thank you', he found himself saying as he left the room.

Lizzie and Eve went to speak to Jane at Two to Tango. Jane looked quite different to the mousy, shy girl she had been when she had first started working at the agency. Her clothes were up to date, her hair was styled and coloured mauve and pink, she had applied more make-up, and altogether looked more the part for her new role as manager. She explained now that she was the manager of the agency she was hoping to recruit another person to help in the office. She described the man who had scared her as tall, well-built, and white. He had kept his hat on so she didn't know the colour of his hair but he had looked to be in his fifties.

'He was really scary, and looking for Jemima or any of the Dunalls. They owed him, he had said, and he *would* find her'. She also remembered his teeth had been chipped and his breath had smelled. As the man had loomed over her she had been too scared to ask him anything.

The three of them then had a chat about Daphne and Duncan; it seemed everything was rosy there. Jane was unable to convince Eve to join the agency. 'I'm a career girl, I don't want to get hitched at the moment. This job takes up such a lot of my time, I'd rather concentrate on that.'

'How do you manage now you're living with Timothy, then?' Jane asked Lizzie.

Lizzie was aware that Jane had had a soft spot for Timothy and had been quite miffed when she had learned that they were together. 'Timothy understands,' she replied simply.

Jane promised to call them if the man came back.

45
Message or not?

Duncan sat at his desk that was now piled high with old documents, with both Verity and Daphne helping him to go through them. The two ladies had become friends, putting aside any social differences. Duncan had suggested that Verity became his part time secretary, relieving him of the tedious paper-work involved in the running of Many Wollops estate. Verity had happily accepted.

Duncan didn't want to load the paper-work on to Daphne, since the two had become engaged, and there was the wedding to organise. Daphne had insisted on keeping her family out of the planning of the wedding, and had warned Duncan that it really would be for the best if they were invited but not involved. She also had declined a horse-drawn carriage, remembering the fiasco at her previous wedding.

'Here's something,' said Verity, waving a document at them. She continued to read through it while the others waited. 'It looks like I was right, that old orchard had been an ancient burial ground long before the estate had planted fruit trees there'.

'There's never been any sign of graves or anything,' said Duncan.

'They wouldn't have been Christian burials, so there wouldn't be gravestones as we know them. Would you mind if I kept these papers, so I can read through them properly?' Verity was always interested in history.

'Sure, let me know if you find anything interesting.'

'It's odd that those men should choose the orchard to measure and look at. I wonder what they were really doing?' mused Daphne.

'Dave Quilford's looking into it. He seems to know who they were, but not what they were doing,' said Duncan, folding away another document. 'I should go and have a chat with Clive Coombes, the Dunall's solicitor, he may have some idea what this is all about. Truth is I've got more important things to concern myself with at the moment,' he smiled at Daphne.

'We should photo copy this one,' said Verity standing up. 'Can I use the copier?'

Duncan nodded and pointed to the machine, 'Good idea, make a few copies would you.'

Lizzie was packing up her stuff and getting ready to go home when Dave signalled her to come into his room at the station. 'I talked to Timothy today, Lizzie. One of his 'oldies' was in the shop; odd lady. As far as I could tell there was no one else there. Then there were bumps and crashes coming from a room upstairs, but when I went up to see who it was, whoever they were had done a vanishing act. I mentioned this to Timothy who was convinced there was no one there, or he was lying and hiding someone. Please could you put my mind at rest and tell me whom or what Timothy is protecting?'

Lizzie looked at Dave's puzzled face and started to smile, stifling a giggle. 'Trouble is sir, I don't know if you're going to believe it, which is definitely why Timothy didn't tell you what it was.' She could tell by his expression that this wasn't going to be easy. 'The shop is an old Victorian building and it has been a book shop since Victorian times. An old man used to live and work in the shop, and some say he's still there. Timothy's boss Derek has the documents and evidence

369

to verify the age of the shop.' She watched as Dave's expression started to change. He rubbed his head, something he always did when he did not altogether believe what he was hearing.

Lizzie went on, 'Do you believe in ghosts sir?' she held her breath.

'Oh god, in this town anything's possible! Do you believe in them Lizzie?'

'Well, I have been in the shop when books just appear to come off the shelves on their own. Timothy always says that it's a shame the ghost doesn't put them back,' she smiled at Dave.

Eve knocked on the door and said, 'Duncan Dainty's here and would like to see you, sir.'

'Thanks, bring him in, will you? Okay Lizzie, I'll believe this ghost story for now, but
I warn you, I'm very sceptical'.

Duncan came striding into the room carrying a large brown envelope.

'I don't know if this would be helpful but I have found this document about the old orchard. It seems it once was an ancient burial ground. It's alleged that the druids buried their dead there; it's supposed to be a sacred place. I can't imagine why anyone would be interested in this, unless they're archaeologists.'

'Or maybe they think something else is buried there?' replied Dave with a sigh. 'I'm meeting a couple of guys for a chat and a drink in a minute,' he looked at his watch, 'they may have some useful information about all this. Do you want to come?'

Duncan agreed and the two of them left together.

'D'you think he believes you, about the book shop I mean?' asked Eve as they were both getting ready to go home.

Lizzie took a breath, 'I'm not sure, I only barely believe it myself. I haven't been able to come up with any other explanation, so who knows? Timothy believes it helps him sometimes. Anyway I'll worry about all this tomorrow, right now I'm going home. I'm doing the cooking tonight.'

46
Clouds and arrows.

It was late summer and dusk was around nine thirty, it would not be dark for another half an hour or so. Nigel dressed in his camouflage gear as quietly as he could. He'd convinced his wife Philly he was having a really early night. She'd retired to her own room but as he crept across the landing to the stairs he could see a light under her door. He hesitated, she would be furious if she knew what he was up to. He continued to creep down the stairs, watched by their cat that was sitting on the sideboard. He put his finger to his lips, 'shh', he whispered. The cat squinted its eyes in reply. He made his way across the oak floor of the hall to the kitchen. Earlier, with his plan in mind he'd stashed a packet of chocolate biscuits, and now he quickly slipped these into his pocket; that would keep him going for a few hours. After gathering up two longbows and a good selection of arrows he crept out of the back door, closing it as quietly as he could. He stopped and listened, no movement from the house. She hadn't heard him; with a snigger and a skip he set off to look for his boots that he had hidden under a shrub… but which shrub? His wife had been known to hide his boots and shoes to ensure he couldn't sneak off and get into any trouble…. It never worked.

Philamina heard the floor creak and guessed her husband was on the prowl. She'd had a really busy day organising and helping the WI with a charity tea-dance. Most of her book club ladies had been involved. It had been well attended, mostly by women. There were always a few of the older men at these venues but usually the same ones. The ones who enjoyed being in the company of lots of ladies and being fussed over after they'd helped move tables and carry boxes. The cakes were usually very good and this was more than enough reward. Her husband had turned up but hadn't been particularly helpful, preferring to eat cake and dance over-enthusiastically with other ladies. It had been a huge relief when he had left without incident. She sighed as she heard him creep out of the back door and wondered briefly if he would fall into the pond again. Smiling she went back to her book.

Nigel, unaware that his wife had any idea what he was up to, was creeping around outside in his stocking feet looking for his boots. Aha, there they were! He pulled them on and made his way down to the hut. It was a warm evening, the moon was playing hide and seek behind the drifting clouds. A gusty breeze wafted through the garden lifting the perfume off different plants and roses, filling his nostrils with their scent. The garden rustled and whispered around him, the shrubs and trees casting occasional moving shadows in the moonlight. Once inside his hut he arranged, by torch light, all his arrows and his two best bows. The hut was quite small with just enough room for a small bed that also served as a couch, and a cupboard along one wall, just right for hiding his weapons and a bit of booze; well, actually a case of gin and a box full of tonic. He placed his packet of biscuits in there for later. Once settled with everything in order he took his binoculars, switched off his torch and crept outside for a look around. He squeezed under the willow branches next to the pond where he could look up the hill towards Monkswood unseen. It wasn't easy to see with everything waving in the breeze, but he could make out the house each time the moving clouds cleared the moon. He was about to give up and go back to the hut for a drink when an unfamiliar shadow moved between the foliage nearer to Monkswood house. He managed to stop himself squeaking with excitement; he grabbed hold of one of the willow branches instead and watched, holding his breath. He was right, there were poachers on the land next door… and he was going to get 'em!

He raced back to the hut to quickly gather his weaponry before running to the far side of his pond where there is a good view of Monkswood and the overgrown gardens. Big old rhododendron bushes growing around the grounds, sadly taken over by brambles these days, made a good hiding place for any poachers. Anyone could be hiding behind or even in one of those, he thought and quickly let off an arrow towards the nearest one. He loved the whoosh sound as arrows sped through the air towards their target, sometimes he could hear the thwack they made when they hit a tree or a post. He heard the sound of a cry somewhere in the dark. Dancing around from foot to foot he quickly reloaded the bow and fired off another one towards where he thought he'd seen intruders. He listened… nothing. The arrows that didn't meet their intended target, or otherwise, usually hit the ground at such a speed that they instantly buried themselves under any grass or foliage, travelling a little way under the surface before stopping, therefore impossible to find.

He reached for another arrow; this was the best fun he'd had in ages. As the clouds moved away from the moon again he could just make out two more dark figures near the house. He took aim and released the arrow...*whoosh*. The figures ran back into the shadows and out of sight. Nigel didn't hear a cry or shout and realised that he'd missed. Not deterred, he quickly loaded another arrow and moved as close as he could to the perimeter fence. It was hard to see anything as the breeze was moving everything and then the clouds covered the moon once more. He peered into the darkness and let the arrow fly, *whoosh.*

After a few more tries he shouldered the bow and walked along the fence staring across the bridleway into the old gardens. He must have scared them all away he thought, while wandering back to the hut for a drink and a biscuit.

The men had managed to gain entry to both Monkswood and Darkwood house; they'd searched both and found nothing. They had found maps that turned out to be useless. Their search of the grounds surrounding Monkswood and Darkwood were the only places left to search.

The woman they'd kidnapped was no help, as she obviously knew nothing of the crate of ivory that had been smuggled into the UK.

She was talking utter gibberish and was humming and dancing around her rooms in the attic. They decided to release her when they were ready to leave the UK. Keeping her permanently intoxicated with alcohol wasn't difficult as she certainly had a taste for gin.

In her drunken state she believed she was staying with a friend of her husband's who was holding a week long party. She no longer had any sense of time or place and as long as the food and alcohol kept arriving and the music playing she was fairly happy to stay there. After all it was a lot better than prison.

The men moved quietly around the grounds of Monkswood looking for any likely places or evidence of a buried or hidden crate. It wasn't easy moving around in the unkempt, over-grown garden, especially as they had no idea what it all looked like in daylight. They found one or two areas where the ground was softer but further investigation and digging revealed nothing. Suddenly startled, they stopped dead. 'What was that!' they looked around, unable to see any sign of anyone or any animal. *Whoosh*, another arrow whizzed passed, missing them by mere inches.

'AAAAH what the hell is this?' cried one of the men nursing his shoulder that had just been winged by one of Nigel's arrows. 'I think we should get out of here, these English folk are really weird. Who knows what they could be up to.' They quickly gathered up their spades and torches. Whoosh…thwack… 'Someone's firing arrows at us, where the hell are they?'

The men ran back to their hidden car. 'I didn't know they had someone guarding the place. Let's get out of here,' the man gasped.

The police had eased off their presence at Monkswood. The local patrol cars had been instructed to keep an eye on the place and drive up to the house from time to time during their routine patrols of the area.

A police car swung into the drive of Monkswood. The two policemen, Ben and Tom had decided to have a break while parked up at the house. They got out of the vehicle to stretch their muscles they set off for a walk around. As they approached the back of the house they both spotted the men running through the overgrown shrubs. 'Stop, police!' they both shouted together.

Whoosh….thwack, a stray arrow flew between the two policemen and embedded itself into the wooden beam on the outside of the house.

'Oh my god, what's going on here? Call for back up'.

They both ran back to the patrol car. Ben rammed the car into reverse. Scattering gravel it raced back up the drive in an attempt to cut off the intruders, Tom called for back up. 'Trespassers running from the grounds at Monkswood and someone's firing arrows at them, and us!'

'Oh that'll be 'nearly normal Nigel' firing the arrows,' Sergeant Dumple chuckled in reply.

'What, that nutcase from Prickets End? Why doesn't that surprise me? What the hell is he doing firing arrows at everyone?' moaned Tom.

'Those trespassers won't come back in a hurry. Did you get a look at them?'

'No. Whoa! Hang on!' cried Tom as Ben slammed on the brakes, narrowly missing the speeding yellow Mini coming towards them.

The clouds cleared the moon once more, Nigel thought he saw movement, much closer this time. Were they in his garden? He grabbed another arrow and took aim …whoosh. There was no other sound in the breeze. Unable to see anything, he crept forward. He thought he heard a groan. This unnerved him and while he was quite excited at the thought of actually getting one of 'them,' he decided to get back to his hut for an extra large gin.

Mrs Battle and Mrs Weatherbutts were both squeezed into the back of the Mini, with Maureen Broadbent in the front next to keen driver Beattie Fell. The eager vigilantes had their eyes on the road ahead. Beattie was driving a *little* more slowly that usual; her nasty experience with the farmer's truck had unnerved her slightly. 'I'll drive if you like?' offered Maureen.

'No, you'll have to bring your own car if you want to drive,' retorted Beattie.

Maureen sighed. As she looked out of the passenger side window she spotted a black car inside an open field gate. 'Stop! There's that black car!' she shrieked.

Beattie swerved sharply left and slammed the brakes on at the same time, causing the little car to skid into the hedge at the side of the lane. The police car they had narrowly missed stopped behind them. Beattie sighed, 'Oh well, that's it now, the police have got in the way, we'll never catch sight of that black car again tonight.'

She looked in her rear view mirror and to her surprise the police car had turned around and set off along the lane again at speed. She managed to reverse the Mini out of the hedge, and with lots of verbal encouragement from her passengers, and accelerated after the police car.

'If they're not chasing that black car we're going to look very silly,' commented Mrs Battle. Suddenly Beattie slammed on the brakes again, narrowly missing a man running across the road with what looked like an arrow in his head.

'Must be a fancy dress party somewhere,' said Mrs battle. Beattie accelerated and resumed the chase.

All three cars raced along the dark, narrow lane passing the entrance to Prickets End drive. The police car was a bit too far behind the black car to see which way it turned at the junction. They stopped and Tom, who was still on the radio, asked,' which way will they have gone? Where is it from, does anyone know?' He could hear Sergeant Dumple talking to colleagues at the station. The radio crackled and then the sergeant said, 'Try turning right, we think they could be from the other side of Dickleborough near Strawbottom farm, Ma Brailsford's place.'

'We won't catch up with them now, that's for sure,' groaned Tom.

'It's alright, another car has gone out to try and find them.' Dumple said.

'STOP!' cried the passengers in the Mini as it rounded the corner before the junction. Beattie braked causing the little car to skid to a halt, just missing the back of the police car. 'That was close. Is everyone alright,' Beattie asked, 'shall I try and get around it?'

'I think we should back up and leave the area. That's two near-misses with the same police car, and anyway we don't know which way the black car went.'

'Yes, I suppose you're right. Don't worry about the police car, my cousin's' son and I think old Dumple are on duty tonight, so we'll be alright.' Beattie reversed the Mini back along the lane until she was able to turn around and drive away.

'It's those mad old bats, they only just missed us again. Should we go after them?'

'No, they don't mean any harm and I don't need all the paperwork. Aren't you related to one of them?'

'My mother's cousin is Beattie Fell, the Mini driver,' said Tom, 'lets go back to Monkswood and have a proper look around. We might be able to work out what they were up to.'

'Oh, and risk the arrows of the madman next door? Let's leave that until tomorrow so we can have a chat with him in safety.' Ben smiled suddenly imagining them both turning up to interview the would-be William Tell and finding him dressed in chain mail.

47
Dead man running.

He was well known by all the locals, both in Many Wollops and Dickleborough. The running man could be seen regularly. He wore tracksuit bottoms in the winter and shorts in the summer and always a sky-blue top. He ran for miles, in all weathers and at all times of the day and night. He had a rather odd style, slightly pitched forward looking like he was running on eggs. He'd been keen on running since he was a young boy and was determined not to let anything put him off. Regularly he had to run for his life out of fields, chased by playful cattle that thought it was all a great game. Horses nearly always galloped after him trying to bite a lump out of his shoulder. Even an old donkey would lurch into a canter and chase after him, racing across the field braying loudly like a fog horn. A flock of noisy geese flew at him once when he was following a footpath through a farmyard, and gave his legs his legs a good pecking.

Dogs really hated him, even the most docile pooch would do its best to take a piece out of the running man. Any dog, even from half a mile away, would react when it saw him or picked up his scent on the wind. Despite the frantic owners shouts and calls the dogs would race after the running man, barking and yelping, before attacking his legs and ankles or leaping up and biting his waving arms.

The running man never understood why animals hated him so much; he quite liked them really and wondered what it was about him that sent them into an unexplained rage. Even the nesting birds in the woods would attack him. Bombing him with poop and pecking his head, he protected himself by carrying a branch, holding it over his head as he ran. This helped to keep the buzzards and other woodland birds off but nothing protected him from the swans along the riverbank. They would spread their wings, and half running half flying, go after him, hissing loudly and giving him a nasty peck on the back of his leg if they could. Despite all of this and regular visits to the hospital to have various infected bites and pecks treated, the man kept running. For pleasure he said.

One fateful night he ran along the narrow bridleway between Monkswood and Prickets End. The tall trees and shrubs on either side of the path made it feel safe and secluded. At first he wondered what the sudden whooshing passed his head was; a bird or an early bat perhaps? He wondered no more when one of Nigel's arrows made contact. He had no conscious knowledge of running back along the bridleway, forcing his way through branches and brambles and across a lane into a field. He thought he was heading for home, the childhood home where he was brought up. He leapt over the garden fence, and not recognising the glass door, he smashed through it finding himself in a kitchen that was only vaguely familiar. In the hall he pushed open the sitting room door, expecting to see his parents there. They had both died a few years ago. He finally collapsed into an armchair where he died.

Irma had agreed to help out with looking after a few holiday cottages in the village, so early that morning she went along to cottage number one. She followed what looked alarmingly like a trail of blood; it couldn't be, could it? A feeling of dread surrounded her like a dark cloud. She held the key in her hand and as agreed with Verity she was to take a look inside the cottage and carry out any vacuuming and a general cleaning up. A friend who had been coming to stay with her had cancelled at the last minute on account of having all her teeth removed and a new boiler fitted, which left Irma plenty of time to help Verity who was busy up at the hall. The new guests for this particular cottage weren't due to arrive until later in the week but she had decided to make a start.

As she put the key in the door she felt a cold shiver run down her spine, something was very wrong here. She pushed open the door and with her other hand felt for her mobile phone. The cottage was very still and cold, she went into the kitchen and was pleased to find that it had been left clean and tidy by the last occupants. The sun shone in through the small window over the sink making that part of the cottage feel warm. A few specks of dust danced in the sunlight but the atmosphere still felt wrong. The unexpected cold draught lead her to the utility room where she found the glass door had been shattered and someone had obviously broken in. She followed the blood trail back into the hall and dared herself to open the sitting room door, then froze at the sight of the dead man who had collapsed in an armchair with an arrow stuck in his head. The trail of blood across the floor had become more visible in the light coming through the open door. His hands and legs were badly cut and he had slices of glass in his ankle. Irma remained frozen to the spot, she suddenly felt hot and slightly dizzy. *Come on get a grip and phone someone,* she thought. Police or Timothy or Lizzie? Finally she dialled the police. 'Is that Dumple?' she asked, her voice quavering.

'No, this is Constable Noah Troon here' said a friendly, young male voice.

'Oh right, errm well, I'm Irma and I'm in a cottage with a dead body that has an arrow stuck in its head,' she spluttered, still swaying slightly from the shock.

'One moment', said the voice.

'Irma, this is Sergeant Dumple, where exactly are you?' Irma swayed dangerously before collapsing in the opposite chair to the body. She gulped and wondered if she might be sick. 'Take a deep breath and tell me where you are,' said the Sergeant gently. Finally she was able to explain the situation and tell the sergeant which cottage she was in.

Lizzie was at the station but was needed on an urgent call regarding a stolen bus full of pensioners. She called Timothy and explained the situation. 'Oh blimy, trust Mother to find a body! I'll get over there as soon as I can.' He looked at his boss Derek as he spoke. Derek indicated via hand signals that he should go to his mother.

Timothy arrived at the cottage at the same time as the police and raced up to the door. Sergeant Dumple put a hand on his shoulder. 'Hang on son, I'll go in and get your mother, there will be enough people going in and out to upset the 'frensics' folk without you adding to them,' said the sergeant.

Timothy was shocked to see his mum, she was very pale and obviously upset by what she had found inside. They sat on the garden wall outside the cottage, Timothy had his arm around Irma as she managed to give Eve a statement and then allowed Timothy to take her home. He collected Faith from his own cottage on the way and left him with Mother for company while he went back to the bookshop; the dog and Irma were very close. Verity had been contacted and was going to call in and sit with her after she'd finished at the hall.

A large police dog called Arni tracked the blood trail from the cottage all the way to the footpath between Prickets End and Monkswood, where they assumed the running man had been shot with the arrow and somehow staggered off for help and found himself at the cottage. How he'd had the strength to break in was yet to be discovered.

Ben and Tom had been despatched to visit and pick up 'nearly normal Nigel' and take him back to the station. They'd decided to play along with Nigel's eccentricities as this was going to be the best and simplest way to deal with him.

'Hello officers, you're here bright and early today, would you like a drink?' Nigel was feeling quite pleased with himself for seeing off all the poachers the night before.

'We'd like to see your arrows sir.' Tom said firmly.

'Why would you like some?' Nigel replied still smiling.

'In a manor of speaking yes. We are going to take you and your arrows for a trip back to the station with us. We need to ask you all about the poachers,' Tom continued, hoping to persuade Nigel to go with them without any drama. If the arrows matched they would arrest him at the station.

'Oh right, come on then, I'll fetch the arrows.'

They followed Nigel closely as he went down to his hut. They were surprised to see his arsenal of shotguns, longbows and many arrows stashed away in there. Arrows collected they made their way back through the garden.

Philamina watched from the house. Nigel must have hurt someone important this time, she thought before going back to her breakfast.

Jasper the gardener arrived at Prickets End as Nigel was getting into the police car. He stared at his boss, not knowing what to say. Nigel grinned at him and appeared quite cheerful. 'Just taking some arrows to the police station, they want to ask me about all the poachers I shot last night.'

'Okay,' was all Jasper could bring himself to say.

'Can you leave any arrows you find around the garden where they are, please. There will be more officers coming to search the grounds later,' said Tom.

'Okay', Jasper muttered again, wondering whom his boss must have shot during his nightly escapade.

As the police car disappeared along the drive the front door opened and Philamina called, 'I think Nigel will be gone for a while, would you like to come in for coffee and some breakfast?'

Jasper grinned, 'I'd love to.' There would be no gardening for him today.

At the station Nigel was arrested. He was completely mystified, believing that he had done the police job for them by shooting a poacher. People are so ungrateful, he'd gone to a lot of trouble to get a poacher and they had thrown him in jail for his trouble. They didn't even have any gin. All he'd had was a nasty tasting cup of warm tea; he was properly miserable and decided to sulk. Sitting on the small uncomfortable bed, he stared at the floor. Why *were* they all being so mean and unreasonable?

48
Finding Jemima.

At work Timothy was busy sorting out the thriller section when Henri came rushing in, looking bemused and concerned. 'There's a Ma Brailsford on the phone, she sounds very upset. Her goat has gone missing and apparently you helped find it last time. She said something about her neighbours eating it?'

'Oh blimey, not again!' Timothy sighed, I suppose I should speak with her, is she still on the line?'

'Yes, Derek's in the office talking to her now. How many goats has she got?'

'Just the one.'

Timothy walked into the office to hear Derek trying to console the distraught woman. 'Here's Timothy now, I'll put him on.' Derek handed Timothy the phone saying quietly, 'I think you'd better go and help.'

Both Henri and Derek watched as Timothy listened to the distressed Mrs Brailsford.

'His name's Moses? Ok, but I'm not sure he'll come to me. I could leave the Land Rover open up there I suppose, he might jump in like last time,' soothed Timothy.

'Oh Timothy you're an angel, I knew you'd help', cried Ma Brailsford. 'Hubby says he heard a woman singing up there, sort of singing and wailing he said. You don't think it's some horrid ritual and they're killing Moses, do you?' she wept down the phone.

' No, I think that's unlikely. I'll come now and go straight up to Moors End. Don't worry.' Timothy put down the phone. Derek and Henri were both grinning at him. 'To the rescue Timmy, old lad', laughed Derek, pointing to the door.

'Yes' he said, pulling out his mobile on the way to the Land Rover. He remembered that the police had been watching Moors End and decided to try calling Lizzie. There was no reply; she couldn't always answer the phone at work so he decided to try the station. The woman wailing and singing had set alarm bells ringing in his head, he just had that 'feeling'. 'Hi. this is Timothy, is Dave Quilford available please?' He started the Land Rover and began backing out with the phone in one hand. Finally Dave came on the line. Timothy explained about the call and told Dave he was on his way over to Moors End. 'There isn't much of a phone signal up there, so I thought I'd better tell you.'

'A woman wailing and singing you say. Well, there was no sign of anyone else being present when we were there last. Hmmm, it could be something. Ok Timothy, I'll meet you up there. Oh, and see if you can get the goat *before* we arrive.'

Timothy chuckled at a vision of Dave and a police squad being chased around the countryside by Moses the goat.

He decided to park the Land Rover at the edge of the drive near the old farm buildings. He got out and looked around. Unable see the goat or hear any singing, he left all the doors of the vehicle open, both for the goat and a quick getaway for himself in case the goat was in a feisty mood. He wandered warily around the disused farmyard. It was a sunny day, a light breeze moaned through the holes in the roof's of the old buildings, causing loose boards to sway and creak. It was almost spooky but the warm sun countered this. Then he heard the voice. It was the voice of a woman singing. He listened and walked slowly towards the sound. The voice was singing an old folk song, slightly out of tune. '*I heard a maiden sing in the valley below. Oh never leave me .....*' He made his way around to the back of the farmhouse where he saw Jemima sitting on an old milk-stand. She appeared to be serenading the goat and was totally lost in her own world. The goat was standing in front of her with its head on one side, looking as though it was listening. Timothy approached with caution, hoping that Dave would turn up soon.

When Jemima saw Timothy she glared at him.

'Who the hell are you,' she growled, squinting like an angry cat. The goat bleated its hello. Timothy decided to ignore the goat for a moment. 'Hello Jemima, I've come to give you a lift home,' he tried the softly softly approach. She stared at him for a few minutes, he wasn't sure if he should stand his ground or just run for it. Jemima turned away suddenly and when she turned back she was a different person.

She smiled at Timothy with eyes that seemed bright and clear, she held her hand out to him and said, 'Come on, lets dance. I've been waiting for you.' He approached with caution and really wished Dave would turn up now!

Not sure if this was a good idea he went along with her and they began to waltz, sort of, all around the garden at the back of the house. Jemima laughed and started to sing. 'Shall we dance, tra la la.'

Timothy thought that if they made enough noise Dave and the others would hear them and come and rescue him, so he joined in. 'Shall we dance, tra la la.' The goat got bored and wandered off.

What had they given this woman? he wondered. Breathing a huge sigh of relief, he noticed Lizzie and Eve walk around the corner of the house and then Dave and two others around the other side. He sang louder to keep Jemima's attention. When they had more or less surrounded them he stopped dancing and exclaimed, 'Look Jemima, friends have come to join in!' He let go of her and she carried on twirling around the garden and into the arms of Tom and Noah.

'Hello Jemima, come and dance this way', said Tom, realising the situation. Timothy quickly went to Lizzie, and giving her a kiss on the cheek said, 'watch her, she can suddenly change into a very different person.'

Tom and Noah linked arms with Jemima and firmly steered her towards the police car. When she saw the cars she appeared to wake up and stopped dead.

'Get off me, you filthy bastards!' she screamed. They handcuffed her quickly and put her in the car, for her own well-being.

'Have you found the missing goat yet?' asked Dave, looking around.

'It was here a minute ago, I'll see if I can find it now,' said Timothy, feeling braver.

'You haven't seen anyone else here?'

'No, I thought I was on my own until I found Jemima. The place feels empty. I wonder what they've given her, she's behaving very oddly.'

'We'll find out in due course I expect, poor woman,' commented Eve.

Timothy said his goodbyes to Lizzie and the others and watched as they drove off.

Now where's that goat? he thought, walking back around the farm buildings. He searched in most of them, daring himself to call the goat by name, 'Moses! Where are you, Moses?' There was no sign of it anywhere. After about fifteen minutes he decided he would drive down to Strawbottom farm and tell them that Moors End is empty and it's safe for them to come and look for the goat themselves. At least he could tell them it was alive and well.

He began to shut the doors of the Land Rover and to his surprise there was the goat in the back. It had chosen to lie down in there and simply looked at Timothy while chewing. He shut the door quickly and jumped into the driver's seat. 'I'm taking you home, Moses,' he said, starting the engine. Moses bleated his response.

He sounded his horn as he drove up to the front of Strawbottom farmhouse. Opening the back door he motioned to the goat that it could come out. 'Come on Moses, you're home,'

he said, keeping a wary eye on the animal, just in case.

'Oh, you've found him! Darling Moses, I thought you were dead for sure!' cried Ma Brailsford, flinging her arms around the goat. The goat responded by bleating, then raced off to the front garden where some food had been left for it. Having hugged the goat Ma Brailsford turned to Timothy and gave him a hearty hug too. 'Thank you Timothy, I knew you would be able to help!' she exclaimed with tears of joy in her eyes. Timothy didn't like to say too much about the incident at Moors End, or complain about the stink of goat in his Land Rover. He did tell her that there was no one at Moors End anymore and it would be safe to go and get Moses if he went walkabout again.

Henri and Derek were keen to hear all about the goat's capture when he arrived back at the shop.

'Yup, I found the goat and Jemima, who is now safely with the police, and the goat is back at Strawbottom farm,' he said, grinning at his two friends.

'Ta da! Timothy saves the day yet again!' exclaimed Derek, 'they haven't got the men that kidnapped Jemima then?'

'No, I think that will be down to CID; they're watching the airports, but no one knows when they left so they may be out of the country already. I've no idea why they kidnapped her in the first place, as far as I know they didn't demand a ransom. I don't know what they gave her either, she was behaving very oddly.' The shop door jangled. 'Back to work then,' he said, making his way through to the front of the shop.

Mrs Jones trundled in with her trolley and came straight up to Timothy. 'Are you and Lizzie going?' she whispered loudly.

'Going where,' he replied.

'The wedding, you know the one at the hall?'

'No, not to the wedding, but we have been invited to the summer party afterwards with the rest of the villagers. Lizzie read the invitation to me this morning. They've sent personal invitations to all the residents in Many Wollops. Yes, we will probably be going, and so will Mother.' He tried to pre-empt her next question.

'Ooh how exciting', she said wandering off toward the horror section.

Roderick Mackenzie was born in Scotland and despite having lived in many places during his life he still had the accent. He'd lived a varied life from being a keen sportsman and adventurer to a trained detective and security guard, mostly employed in security work for various large companies. As a younger man he'd spent time working for diamond mining companies in Africa.

He rode his bike up onto the heath to enjoy the fresh air, the view and solitude, he needed to think. His present employers, he knew, were about to take over JJ Mining, and they were paying him a load of money to check out any of the Dunalls left in the UK, and report back. They knew that Harriet had returned to England, but they didn't know what interest, if any, either Jemima or Harriet had in the business in Africa. The recent demise of Giles and his sister Harriet had made everyone suspicious of Jemima. And they had recently learned about the vanished crate of ivory illegally shipped into the UK.

Perhaps now was the time to arrange to meet up again with Dave Quilford and Seth.

Once Seth had recognised him he was happy to open up and talk about the Dunalls. Seth had been concerned for Jemima, even though he didn't have anything good to say about her.

They were both sure Jemima was completely oblivious to any danger she may be in and she certainly knew nothing of the missing ivory, or the business in Africa. He decided to have a chat with Clive Coombes too, as the family solicitor and also as a friend of Giles' he would surely know more than he had so far admitted.

When he walked into the police station there was a flurry of activity and in the midst of this chaos was the rather drunk and delirious Jemima. She was swiftly lead off to see the police doctor. Still singing at the top of her voice, making everyone cringe. Eventually Roderick was able to see Dave Quilford. They both agreed to call a meeting with Clive Coombes and Seth. At last this could be the breakthrough Dave was hoping for.

The four men sat around a table in a quiet corner of the Drowning Duck, each with a drink of their choice supplied by Dave.

Roderick spoke first,' I'll fill you in on what I know and then you can fill in any blanks'. Dave was the one with the least knowledge at this stage so Roderick tried to start at the beginning. 'The Dunalls had been shareholders of one of the diamond mines in Africa. The majority of the holdings are owned by another limited company called Jones and Jones Mining, known as 'JJ Mining'. As I'm employed in security I have done some digging of my own into JJ Mining and the other shareholders. I discovered the dubious and fraudulent goings on, including the demise of Herbert Dunall, allegedly killed by lions'.

He looked at Seth for confirmation of this. Seth just nodded and took a sip of his whiskey.

Roderick went on, 'I discovered that the current directors of JJ Mining had convinced Herbert, via unscrupulous methods involving alcohol and women, to leave the Dunalls share in the mine to them in his will. They then paid thugs to murder Herbert and leave his body where the lions and other wildlife could feast on it, which they did leaving just enough remains for Herbert to be identified.

It was several years before this that Giles and his mother had returned to England and Giles had married Jemima. Giles' father, his daughter Harriet and son Herbert, had stayed in Africa. Giles's Father passed away through natural causes. They were all involved in JJ Mining and also in the fight against the poachers, or so it was believed. Unfortunately not all of the other shareholders were against poaching. Giles and Herbert had not made themselves popular, as they were actively against any poaching, and were trying to protect the local wildlife'.

Seth nodded, coughed and took a sip of whiskey, 'I don't think the two bumbling idiots that kidnapped the bitch really knew what they were doing,' he said. 'They were probably sent to check out Jemima's and Harriet's interests in the mining company and, if possible, recover the lost crate of ivory. I bet you won't find

393

them in this country now, I reckon they'll be on their way back to Africa. The one you need to watch out for is Igor, I saw him at Darkwood just before Giles was found dead. I tried to follow him but he's a slippery character. I feel that I failed Giles as he employed me to keep an eye on the place and on Jemima, in the guise of gardener. I should have known an insurance salesman with a posh car was iffy, and should have alerted Giles. I just let him walk into the house believing he had an appointment. How was I to know that Giles hadn't been feeling too well and had gone for a lie down.'

'Hold on a minute,' interrupted Dave. Seth looked up as both Dave and Clive asked in unison,

'Who's Igor?'

'Not someone you'd want to meet anytime soon. Though he would appear educated, smart and pleasant enough…he's deadly.'

'He would be the driver of the black Porsche?' said Dave.

'He would indeed.' Roderick continued, 'I'm relieved that he didn't get his hands on Jemima; the other two actually did her a favour by locking her up in the house for a while. What will happen to her now?'

'She'll be in hospital for a few days and then be transferred to a clinic, where she'll get some help to recover fully,' Dave said. 'Pity you couldn't have told me all this earlier.'

Clive said, 'It's not all bad for her, if she recovers she'll discover that she has inherited Darkwood and money from the company in Africa. It should be enough to keep her going for a while. Seth, you will be pleased to know Giles left you the cottage in his will.'

'God bless Giles,' Seth smiled and raised his glass, 'not a bad chap, really.'

'Who found out that Jemima had been hidden at Moores End farm?' asked Roderick.

'A goat,' smiled Dave. The others looked up from their drinks. He explained what had happened.

'Jemima will never know how lucky she was,' Clive commented.

'Ah, so that Timothy lad found her, did he? Seth smiled, ' I saw him leap out of a window at Darkwood after meeting Jemima. There was a lot of screaming and shouting coming from the house and there'd been quite a substantial fall of soot. He cycled away from her a bit quick that day,' he chuckled. 'So does anyone know who owns Monkswood?'

'I know who owns that,' said Clive, 'both Harriet and Jemima believed it had been left to them, and it has but not yet. There is someone else and I have only just discovered who she is. She was the…..'

'Nanny!', said Seth suddenly, 'of course she is older than Harriet, nearly my age, I think. She was very friendly with Giles' father and partly the reason why Mother came back to the UK, bringing Giles with her.'

Clive continued, 'the nanny, Dorothea, is here in the UK and has been informed of her good fortune. She can't sell the property as it goes to Jemima and Harriet on her demise, and of course Jemima will eventually inherit the lot now. Dorothea was talking about possibly running the house as a B&B, or a guesthouse.'

'So Dorothea is here in the UK, that's interesting,' smiled Seth. The others all looked at him hoping for a bit more information but the old man simply sucked on his unlit pipe and smiled.

'So what happened to this crate of ivory you mentioned?' asked Dave.

Seth took the pipe out of his mouth, lay it on the table and took a sip of whiskey before speaking, ' It's with

Customs now and hopefully it will be destroyed. Giles arranged for it to be 'disappeared', as far as the shareholders back in Africa, who sent it over here, were concerned. They obviously believed that Giles had profited from it himself, or had it hidden somewhere, hence the idiots they sent to try and locate it. Igor probably had words with Giles and on discovering he didn't have the ivory, he killed him. What is odd is why Jemima felt the need to get rid of his body. I'm not sure about that one, I don't think she thought it through.'

'She probably thought that she would get the blame for killing him,' replied Dave, 'but actually she made things worse for herself. She may not have actually set out to kill either Giles or Harriet but she is involved in both deaths. I'm afraid she probably will be spending some time in prison. Possibly a good proportion of this time will be spent in a medical unit drying out.

Catching these men from Africa will be down to CID.' concluded Dave, 'more drinks anyone?'

49
Lady of the manor.

Duncan decided to have a peaceful morning ride before the start of the general chaos of his brother arriving as well as the people with the marquee. Daphne and Verity appeared to enjoy organising everything. His home help Lena also proved to be really helpful and was happily putting in extra hours. They'd organised the wedding between them, all he had had to do was provide addresses and information of any family and friends he wanted to invite, and stay around to do whatever was asked of him.

'Leave us to it', they had said. This suited him very well.

He urged Busby forward and headed up the hill that overlooked most of his estate. He cantered the last bit and pulled up facing towards Monkswood. His solicitor had made contact with Clive Coombes, and the question of ownership had been resolved. A lady was moving in today, so nothing for him to worry about. He could see cars and removal vans in the driveway, and a small lady with dark hair appeared to be directing proceedings.

The potty man from Prickets End was now locked up. Duncan wouldn't have to watch out for flying arrows anymore. He'd always quite liked the man, and had found him very welcoming and amusing. He would miss him, but not his crazy and hazardous obsession for shooting at imaginary poachers. He gathered that Nigel's wife Philamina and their gardener were hugely relieved that he was now safely out of the way. 'Out of harm's way, you understand,' Philamina had said to Duncan.

In a few days time he would be married to Daphne and for the first time in his life he felt that he had a purpose and a future. He planned on spending more time on running the estate, which would be easier since he'd discovered Verity. His last secretary had shocked everyone when on one dark, snowy, night in winter, she had absconded with a deliveryman. Neither had been seen or heard from since.

His brother Dermot had been enthusiastic about coming to his wedding and was due to turn up sometime today. His brother lived on and managed a small farm and estate near Sennybridge in Wales. This had been left to both brothers, as had Many Wollops Hall and estate. It had been easy to decide who would live where as Dermot had spent quite a lot of time in Wales when he was in the armed forces and had fallen in love with the area. He'd always been the more rugged and outward bound sort. He had said that he had a surprise wedding gift for Duncan. This was a little worrying, as last time he had said that he'd bought him an elephant, leaving Duncan with the task of finding a suitable home for it in a safari park. He smiled at the memory; it would be good to see his brother again. He decided to take his time riding back and reflect on events leading up to this point in time. The next chapter in his life looked promising.

Jane was beside herself when she received the wedding invitation from Daphne.

She thought she'd found herself a partner at last, so the words, ' and partner' on the invitation hadn't freaked her out. He'd agreed to come along, which was all the more wonderful. Mervyn, a tall, willowy, quietly-spoken man with longish dark hair, wore old-fashioned glasses and a permanently bewildered thoughtful expression. He'd been 'taken' with Jane at first sight. She was very different to the women his friends and peers seemed to like. Jane had warmed to him straightaway and had been delighted when he'd nervously asked her on a date. The two were made for each other. Jane was now manager of Two to Tango and had employed another girl to work in reception. All she had to do now was buy something wonderful to wear at the wedding and reception. Mervyn had promised to iron his trousers for the occasion.

Daphne had been quite firm about the people she wanted to ask to her wedding. Her mother and father had met Duncan. Her mother had nearly fainted twice with the excitement when on a visit to the hall for afternoon tea Daphne and Duncan had announced their engagement and told them of their wedding plans. Daphne had had to insist that she would plan and organise the wedding herself this time. No, she wouldn't be using the same horse-drawn carriage, or any doves, and the ceremony would be at the hall. Depending on the weather there would be a marquee so the ceremony could be held under cover if necessary. Yes, of course Uncle Miles would be invited along with other aunts and uncles. Duncan had his own guest list and between them they discovered they would be inviting around fifty people. Duncan's own parents had both passed on, but his brother and various uncles and aunts had been invited along with a few cousins. They'd also decided to hold an after-wedding party the day after the wedding and reception. Residents of Many Wollops village would be invited to join in the merriment. It would be held in the style of a barn dance.

Verity knew of a local band that she was going to book for the occasion. There was a buzz in the air and the whole village was looking forward to joining in with the celebrations.

When Verity gave up her well-paid job in London for a quiet country life she hadn't realised how quickly old cottages eat money. Her living on the whole was costing her more than she'd planned for. Growing and selling her herbs didn't bring in sufficient cash. She'd taken a few jobs locally, looking after holiday cottages, and a couple of extra cleaning jobs. These paid cash and she was managing. She really liked that there was no pressure involved. She had been hesitant when Duncan offered her the job as his full-time secretary at the hall. It wasn't what she'd planned, but she loved the hall and the estate. Duncan was nice to work for, pleasant and easy-going. She had been surprised that she got on so well with Daphne, whose reputation as a bit of a tigress had made Verity wary to begin with.

Planning the wedding between them had been fun and had given them both the idea of organising a few select events at the hall in the future. She'd been assured that she would have a job there for as long as she needed one, primarily as estate secretary, but also occasional events organiser.

Her own interests would fit in around the hours she would be working at the hall. Her ex- husband was leaving her alone since he had found a new love, and she was rather enjoying her independent lifestyle and had no plans to change. Most of the villagers had made her welcome, even the local vicar. She'd managed to wriggle out of being enlisted as a bell-ringer and was politely avoiding the choirmaster. While she appreciated the church building, hearing the bells, and the community spirit of the worshipers, church was not really her scene. On the whole her new life couldn't be better.

As Duncan rode towards the hall he could see two cars turning into the driveway, one large SUV, and what looked like a classic Morgan. It was his brother Dermot. He rode on taking a short cut directly to the front of the house arriving as his brother and current girlfriend Miara were getting out of the cars. Duncan dismounted allowing Busby to calmly make his own way back to the stables where Jim was waiting for him.

'Hey brother mine, how are you?' The two brothers exchanged a brotherly embrace.

Miara smiled and went to the back of the SUV. She opened the door and a young black Labrador leapt out and treated them all to an exuberant greeting. 'This is one of our wedding presents! His name is Poacher, he's four months old and house-trained. He's very playful,' said Miara smiling, 'I hope you both like him.' She gave Duncan a hug.

'Wow, thank you, I love him. It's great to see you again, Miara.' Duncan fussed the dog and was quite relieved that it was an animal he could easily accommodate this time. The dog raced in through the front door. Shrieks of delight could be heard inside as the dog greeted everyone enthusiastically. He quickly made friends with the two resident dogs, who lead him off to explore the gardens.

'Why two cars?' asked Duncan.

'The Morgan is yours, it has been reconditioned. I hope you like it.' Dermot patted the car. 'It runs well.'

'Wow, thank you!' He called to Daphne to come and have a look.

She immediately jumped into the driver's seat. 'Oh yes, I'll enjoy this, it's fabulous! Dermot you've spoiled us!'

she exclaimed. Duncan jumped in beside her and indicated that she should carry on. She did and they drove off along the drive, thinking it would be great fun to take the car on their honeymoon to Scotland.

The following day was the wedding day. Everything went as smoothly as could be expected with so many guests from both families arriving at the hall. They all relaxed after the first few beverages. The short ceremony was held outside, and lunch was served in the marquee.

A stiff breeze had got up by then but no one appeared to notice the marquee moving ever more precariously in the wind, like a giant jellyfish devouring its prey. It takes more than a stiff breeze to drive people away from good food and celebrations, which went on well into the evening before the guests began to retreat to their nearby accommodation.

The following day the catering staff were back and after the clean up another buffet was laid out and a floor put down in the marquee for dancing. The party started early evening and most of the invited villagers turned up with their spouses, partners and friends. A few were there to get a good look at Duncan and his new wife, and of course a closer look at the hall itself. Most however were there to have a good time and enjoy the food and dancing. Towards the end of the evening Duncan and Daphne were standing on the veranda, enjoying a glass of champagne while watching the merry-making. 'A toast to us,' said Duncan 'to our future'.

Daphne was happier than she ever remembered being, finally her life was on track, she had found the man of her dreams, a home she knew she would love, and her business that she had worked so hard to establish would continue with Jane as manager. She smiled as she watched couples that had found each other, with or without her help, dancing at the party. Jane was dancing with her new man. There was Betty and Bertrum, an odd couple but well matched she thought. She noticed Timothy Parkes, who was laughing and dancing with his police lady.

All in all this had been a very good few days and a most excellent year.

The end.